THE ALBERT N'YANZA, GREAT BASIN OF THE NILE

AND EXPLORATIONS OF THE NILE SOURCES

by Sir Samuel W. Baker, M.A., F.R.G.S.

Gold Medallist of the
Royal Geographical Society.

THE NARRATIVE PRESS
TRUE FIRST PERSON ACCOUNTS OF HIGH ADVENTURE

To Her Most Gracious Majesty
THE QUEEN
I dedicate, with Her permission,
THIS BOOK,
Containing the Story of the Discovery of the Great Lake
From which the Nile ultimately flows,
And which,
As connected so intimately,
As a NILE SOURCE, with the VICTORIA LAKE,
I have ventured to name
"THE ALBERT N'YANZA,"
In Memory of the Late Illustrious and Lamented
PRINCE CONSORT.

The Narrative Press
P.O. Box 2487, Santa Barbara, California 93120 U.S.A.
Telephone: (800) 315-9005 Web: www.narrativepress.com

ISBN 1-58976-195-2 (Paperback)
ISBN 1-58976-210-X (eBook)

Produced in the United States of America

CONTENTS

*Programme – Start from Cairo – Arrive at Berber –
Plan of Exploration – The River Atbara – Abyssinian
Affluents – Character of Rivers – Causes of Nile In-
undations – Violence of the Rains – Arrival at Khar-
toum – Description of Khartoum – Egyptian
Authorities – Taxes – The Soudan – Slave-Trade of
the Soudan – Slave-Trade of the White Nile – System
of Operations – Inhuman Proceedings – Negro Allies
– Revelations of Slave-Trade – Distant Slave Markets
– Prospects of the Expedition – Difficulties at the
Outset – Opposition of the Egyptian Authorities –
Preparations for Sailing – Johann Schmidt – De-
mand for Poll-Tax – Collision before starting – Ami-
able Boy! – The Departure – The Boy Osman –
Banks of White Nile – Change in Disposition of Men
– Character of the River – Misery of Scene – River
Vegetation – Ambatch Wood – Johann's Sickness –
Uses of Fish-skin – Johann Dying – Johann's Death
– New Year – Shillook Villages – The Sobat River –
Its Character – Bahr Giraffe – Bahr el Gazal – Ob-
servations – Corporal Richarn – Character of Bahr
el Gazal – Peculiarity of River Sobat – Tediousness
of Voyage – Bull Buffalo – Sali Achmet killed – His
Burial – Ferocity of the Buffalo – The Clumsy on the
Styx – Current of White Nile – First View of Natives
– Joctian and his Wife – Charming Husband – Na-
tron – Catch a Hippopotamus – "Perhaps it was His
Uncle" – Real Turtle is Mock Hippopotamus – Rich-
arn reduced to the Ranks – Arrival at the Zareeba –
Fish Spearing – The Kytch Tribe – White Ant Towers*

Her's People – Death of my Deserters – My Prophecy
Realized – Apprehensive of an Attack – The Turks in-
sult the Women – Ill Conduct of the Turks – Well
Done, Bokke! – Results of the Turks' Misconduct –
Interview with Commoro – Awkward Position – The
Latooka War Signal – Preparations for Defence –
We Await the Attack – Parley – Too Wide Awake –
Camp at Tarrangolle – Scarcity in View of Plenty –
Wild Duck Shooting – The Crested Crane, etc. – Ad-
da's Proposal – Obtuseness of Natives – Degraded
State of Natives

Thieves – Ibrahimawa's Reminiscences of England – Party Recalled to Obbo – White Ants – Destructiveness of Birds – Cattle Stealers at Night – A Thief Shot – My Wife Ill with Fever – March to Obbo – Great Puff Adder – Poison-Fangs of Snakes – Violent Storm – Arrive Again at Obbo – Hostility Caused by the Turks – The M.D. Attends Us – Death of Mouse – Marauding Expedition – Saat Becomes Scientific – Saat and Gaddum Her – Will England Suppress the Slave Trade? – Filthy Customs of the Natives – The Egyptian Scarabaeus – Bacheeta, the Unyoro Slave – Intelligence of the Lake – Its Probable Commercial Advantages – Commerce with the Interior – Obbo the Clothing Frontier – Death of My Last Camel – Excellent Species of Gourd – A Morning Call in Obbo – Katchiba's Musical Accomplishments – Loss of Remaining Donkey – Deceived by the Turks – Fever – Symptoms – Dismal Prospect, "Coming Events," etc.

Physician in General – Influence Gained oOer the People – Katchiba is Applied to for Rain – "Are You a Rainmaker?" – Katchiba Takes Counsel's Opinion – Successful Case – Night-Watch for Elephants – Elephant Killed – Dimensions of the Elephant – Wild Boars – Start for the South – Mrs. Baker Thrown From Her Ox – The Asua River – Stalking Mehedehet Antelope – A Prairie Fire – Tracking an Antelope – Turks' Standard-Bearer Killed – Arrival at Shooa – The Neighbourhood of Shooa – Fruitfulness of Shooa – Cultivation and Granaries – Absconding of Obbo Porters – "Wheels within Wheels" – Difficulty in Starting South – Departure from Shooa – Fatiko Levee – Boundless Prairies – Fire the Prairies – Deceit of the Guide – Arrive at the Victoria Nile – Arrive at Rionga's Country – Start for Karuma – The Karuma Falls – Welcome by Kamrasi's People – Passage of the River Forbidden – To Await Reply of Kamrasi

PREFACE

In the history of the Nile there was a void: its sources were a mystery. The ancients devoted much attention to this problem; but in vain. The Emperor Nero sent an expedition under the command of two centurions, as described by Seneca. Even Roman energy failed to break the spell that guarded these secret fountains. The expedition sent by Mehemet Ali Pasha, the celebrated Viceroy of Egypt, closed a long term of unsuccessful search.

The work has now been accomplished. Three English parties, and only three, have at various periods started upon this obscure mission: each has gained its end.

Bruce won the source of the Blue Nile; Speke and Grant won the Victoria source of the great White Nile; and I have been permitted to succeed in completing the Nile Sources by the discovery of the great reservoir of the equatorial waters, the Albert N'Yanza, from which the river issues as the entire White Nile.

Having thus completed the work after nearly five years passed in Africa, there still remains a task before me. I must take the reader of this volume by the hand, and lead him step by step along my rough path from the beginning to the end; through scorching deserts and thirsty sands; through swamp, and jungle, and interminable morass; through difficulties, fatigues, and sickness, until I bring him, faint with the wearying journey, to that high cliff where the great prize shall burst upon his view – from which he shall look down upon the vast Albert Lake, and drink with me from the Sources of the Nile!

I have written "he." How can I lead the more tender sex through dangers and fatigues, and passages of savage life? A veil shall be thrown over many scenes of brutality that I was forced to witness, but which I will not force upon the reader; neither will I intrude anything that is not actually necessary in the description of scenes that unfortunately must be passed through in the journey now before us. Should anything offend the sensitive mind, and suggest the unfitness of the situation for a woman's presence, I must beseech my fair readers to reflect, that the pilgrim's wife followed him, weary and footsore, through all his difficulties, led, not by choice, but by devotion; and that in times of misery and sickness her tender care saved his life and prospered the expedition.

> *"O woman, in our hours of ease*
> *Uncertain, coy, and hard to please,*
> *And variable as the shade*
> *By the light quivering aspen made;*
> *When pain and anguish wring the brow,*
> *A ministering angel thou!"*

In the journey now before us I must request some exercise of patience during geographical details that may be wearisome; at all events, I will adhere to facts, and avoid theory as much as possible.

The botanist will have ample opportunities of straying from our path to examine plants with which I confess a limited acquaintance. The ethnologist shall have precisely the same experience that I enjoyed, and he may either be enlightened or confounded. The geologist will find himself throughout the journey in Central Africa among primitive rocks. The naturalist will travel through a grass jungle that conceals much that is difficult to obtain: both he and the sportsman will, I trust, accompany me on a future occasion through the Nile tributaries from Abyssinia, which country is prolific in all that is interesting. The philanthropist – what shall I promise to induce him to accompany me? I will exhibit a picture of savage man precisely as he is; as I saw him; and as I judged him, free from prejudice: painting also, in true colours, a picture of the abomination that has been the curse of the African race, the slave trade; trusting that not only the philanthropist, but every civilized being, will join in the endeavour to erase that stain from disfigured human nature, and thus open the path now closed to civilization and missionary enterprise. To the missionary – that noble, self-exiled labourer toiling too often in a barren field – I must add the word of caution, "Wait"! There can be no hope of success until the slave trade shall have ceased to exist.

The journey is long, the countries savage; there are no ancient histories to charm the present with memories of the past; all is wild and brutal, hard and unfeeling, devoid of that holy instinct instilled by nature into the heart of man – the belief in a Supreme Being. In that remote wilderness in central equatorial Africa are the sources of the Nile.

Frequently Used Local Words

angarep – traveling bedstead
coorbatch – whip (made from hippopotamus tail)
choush – sargeant
hawaga – master, sir
merissa – native beer
kisra – pancake
nogara – drum
razzia – raid
reis – ship
vakeel – headman, leader

French, Latin, and other foreign words and expressions appear in italic the first time they are used.

INTRODUCTION

The primary object of geographical exploration is the opening to general intercourse such portions of the earth as may become serviceable to the human race. The explorer is the precursor of the colonist; and the colonist is the human instrument by which the great work must be constructed – that greatest and most difficult of all undertakings – the civilization of the world.

The progress of civilization depends upon geographical position. The surface of the earth presents certain facilities and obstacles to general access; those points that are easily attainable must always enjoy a superior civilization to those that are remote from association with the world.

We may thus assume that the advance of civilization is dependent upon facility of transport. Countries naturally excluded from communication may, through the ingenuity of man, be rendered accessible; the natural productions of those lands may be transported to the seacoast in exchange for foreign commodities; and commerce, thus instituted, becomes the pioneer of civilization.

England, the great chief of the commercial world, possesses a power that enforces a grave responsibility. She has the force to civilize. She is the natural colonizer of the world. In the short space of three centuries, America, sprung from her loins, has become a giant offspring, a new era in the history of the human race, a new birth whose future must be overwhelming. Of later date, and still more rapid in development, Australia rises, a triumphant proof of England's power to rescue wild lands from barrenness; to wrest from utter savagedom those mighty tracts of the earth's surface wasted from the creation of the world, – a darkness to be enlightened by English colonization. Before the advancing steps of civilization the savage inhabitants of dreary wastes retreated: regions hitherto lain hidden, and counting as nothing in the world's great total, have risen to take the lead in the world's great future.

Thus England's seed cast upon the earth's surface germinates upon soils destined to reproduce her race. The energy and industry of the mother country become the natural instincts of her descendants in localities adapted for their development; and wherever Nature has endowed a land with agricultural capabilities, and favourable geographical position, slowly but surely that land will become a centre of civilization.

True Christianity cannot exist apart from civilization; thus, the spread of Christianity must depend upon the extension of civilization; and that extension depends upon commerce.

The philanthropist and the missionary will expend their noble energies in vain in struggling against the obtuseness of savage hordes, until the first steps towards their gradual enlightenment shall have been made by commerce. The savage must learn to want; he must learn to be ambitious; and to covet more than the mere animal necessities of food and drink. This can alone be taught by a communication with civilized beings: the sight of men well clothed will induce the naked savage to covet clothing, and will create a want; the supply of this demand will be the first step towards commerce. To obtain the supply, the savage must produce some article in return as a medium of barter, some natural production of his country adapted to the trader's wants. His wants will increase as his ideas expand by communication with Europeans: thus, his productions must increase in due proportion, and he must become industrious; industry being the first grand stride towards civilization.

The natural energy of all countries is influenced by climate; and civilization being dependent upon industry, or energy, must accordingly vary in its degrees according to geographical position. The natives of tropical countries do not progress: enervated by intense heat, they incline rather to repose and amusement than to labour. Free from the rigour of winters, and the excitement of changes in the seasons, the native character assumes the monotony of their country's temperature. They have no natural difficulties to contend with, – no struggle with adverse storms and icy winds and frost-bound soil; but an everlasting summer, and fertile ground producing with little tillage, excite no enterprise; and the human mind, unexercised by difficulties, sinks into languor and decay. There are a lack of industry, a want of intensity of character, a love of ease and luxury, which leads to a devotion to sensuality, – to a plurality of wives, which lowers the character and position of woman. Woman, reduced to that false position, ceases to exercise her proper influence upon man; she becomes the mere slave of passion, and, instead of holding her sphere as the emblem of civilization she becomes its barrier. The absence of real love engendered by a plurality of wives, is an absolute bar to progress; and so long as polygamy exists, an extension of civilization is impossible. In all tropical countries polygamy is the prevailing evil: this is the greatest obstacle to Christianity. The Mahommedan religion, planned carefully for Eastern habits, allowed a plurality of wives, and prospered. The savage can be taught the existence of a Deity, and become a Mussulman; but to him the hateful law of fidelity to one wife is a bar to Christianity. Thus, in tropical climates there will always be a slower advance of civilization than in more temperate zones.

The highest civilization was originally confined to the small portion of the globe comprised between Persia, Egypt, Greece, and Italy. In those countries was concentrated the world's earliest history; and although changed in special importance, they preserve their geographical significance to the present day.

The power and intelligence of man will have their highest development within certain latitudes, and the natural passions and characters of races will be governed by locality and the temperature of climate.

There are certain attractions in localities that induce first settlements of man; even as peculiar conditions of country attract both birds and animals. The first want of man and beast is food: thus fertile soil and abundant pasture, combined with good climate and water communication, always ensure the settlement of man; while natural seed-bearing grasses, forests, and prairies attract both birds and beasts. The earth offers special advantages in various positions to both man and beast; and such localities are, with few exceptions, naturally inhabited. From the earliest creation there have been spots so peculiarly favoured by nature, by geographical position, climate, and fertility, that man has striven for their occupation, and they have become scenes of contention for possession. Such countries have had a powerful influence in the world's history, and such will be the great pulses of civilization, – the sources from which in a future, however distant, will flow the civilization of the world. Egypt is the land whose peculiar capabilities have thus attracted the desires of conquest, and with whom the world's earliest history is intimately connected.

Egypt has been an extraordinary instance of the actual formation of a country by alluvial deposit; it has been created by a single river. The great Sahara, that frightful desert of interminable scorching sand, stretching from the Red Sea to the Atlantic, is cleft by one solitary thread of water. Ages before man could have existed in that inhospitable land, that thread of water was at its silent work: through countless years it flooded and fell, depositing a rich legacy of soil upon the barren sand until the delta was created; and man, at so remote a period that we have no clue to an approximate date, occupied the fertile soil thus born of the river Nile, and that corner of savage Africa, rescued from its barrenness, became Egypt, and took the first rank in the earth's history.

For that extraordinary land the world has ever contended, and will yet contend.

From the Persian conquest to the present day, although the scene of continual strife, Egypt has been an example of almost uninterrupted productiveness. Its geographical position afforded peculiar advantages for commercial enterprise. Bounded on the east by the Red Sea, on the north by the Mediterranean, while the fertilizing Nile afforded inland communication, Egypt became the most prosperous and civilized country of the earth. Egypt was not only created by the Nile, but the very existence of its inhabitants depended upon the annual inundation of that river: thus all that related to the Nile was of vital importance to the people; it was the hand that fed them.

Egypt depending so entirely upon the river, it was natural that the origin of those mysterious waters should have absorbed the attention of thinking men. It was unlike all other rivers. In July and August, when European streams were at their lowest in the summer heat, the Nile was at the flood! In Egypt there was no rainfall – not even a drop of dew in those parched deserts through which, for 860 miles of latitude, the glorious river flowed without a tributary. Licked up by the burning sun, and gulped by the exhausting sand of Nubian deserts, supporting all losses by evaporation and absorption, the noble flood shed its annual blessings upon Egypt. An anomaly among rivers; flooding in the driest season; everlasting in sandy deserts; where was its hidden origin? Where were the sources of the Nile?

This was from the earliest period the great geographical question to be solved.

In the advanced stage of civilization of the present era, we look with regret at the possession by the Moslem of the fairest portions of the world, – of countries so favoured by climate and by geographical position, that, in the early days of the earth's history, they were the spots most coveted; and that such favoured places should, through the Moslem rule, be barred from the advancement that has attended lands less adapted by nature for development. There are no countries of the earth so valuable, or that would occupy so important a position in the family of nations, as Turkey in Europe, Asia Minor, and Egypt, under a civilized and Christian government.

As the great highway to India, Egypt is the most interesting country to the English. The extraordinary fertility being due entirely to the Nile, I trust that I may have added my mite to the treasury of scientific knowledge by completing the discovery of the sources of that wonderful river, and thereby to have opened a way to the heart of Africa, which, though dark in our limited perspective, may, at some future period, be the path to civilization.

I offer to the world my narrative of many years of hardships and difficulties, happily not vainly spent in this great enterprise: should some un-ambitious spirits reflect, that the results are hardly worth the sacrifice of the best years of life thus devoted to exile and suffering, let them remember that "we are placed on earth for a certain period, to fulfil, according to our several conditions and degrees of mind, those duties by which the earth's history is carried on." (E. L. Bulwer's *Life, Literature, and Manners.*)

Chapter I

THE EXPEDITION

In March, 1861, I commenced an expedition to discover the sources of the Nile, with the hope of meeting the East African expedition of Captains Speke and Grant, that had been sent by the English government from the South via Zanzibar, for that object. I had not the presumption to publish my intention, as the sources of the Nile had hitherto defied all explorers, but I had inwardly determined to accomplish this difficult task or to die in the attempt. From my youth I had been inured to hardships and endurance in wild sports in tropical climates, and when I gazed upon the map of Africa I had a wild hope, mingled with humility, that, even as the insignificant worm bores through the hardest oak, I might by perseverance reach the heart of Africa.

I could not conceive that anything in this world had power to resist a determined will, so long as health and life remained. The failure of every former attempt to reach the Nile source did not astonish me, as the expeditions had consisted of parties, which, when difficulties occur, generally end in difference of opinion and retreat: I therefore determined to proceed alone, trusting in the guidance of a Divine Providence and the good fortune that sometimes attends a tenacity of purpose. I weighed carefully the chances of the undertaking. Before me – untrodden Africa; against me – the obstacles that had defeated the world since its creation; on my side – a somewhat tough constitution, perfect independence, a long experience in savage life, and both time and means which I intended to devote to the object without limit. England had never sent an expedition to the Nile sources previous to that under the command of Speke and Grant. Bruce, ninety years ago, had succeeded in tracing the source of the Blue or Lesser Nile: thus the honour of that discovery belonged to Great Britain; Speke was on his road from the South; and I felt confident that my gallant friend would leave his bones upon the path rather than submit to failure. I trusted that England would not be beaten; and although I hardly dared to hope that I could succeed where others greater than I had failed, I determined to sacrifice all in the attempt. Had I been alone it would have been no hard lot to die upon the untrodden path before me, but there was one who, although my greatest comfort, was also my greatest care; one whose life yet dawned at so early an age that womanhood was still a future. I shuddered at the prospect for her, should she be left alone in savage lands at my death; and gladly would I have left her in the luxuries of home instead of exposing her to the miseries of Africa.

It was in vain that I implored her to remain, and that I painted the difficulties and perils still blacker than I supposed they really would be: she was resolved, with woman's constancy and devotion, to share all dangers and to follow me through each rough footstep of the wild life before me. "And Ruth said, 'Entreat me not to leave thee, or to return from following after thee: for whither thou goest I will go, and where thou lodgest I will lodge; thy people shall be my people, and thy God my God: where thou diest will I die; and there will I be buried: the Lord do so to me, and more also, if aught but death part thee and me.'"

Thus accompanied by my wife, on the 15th April 1861, I sailed up the Nile from Cairo. The wind blew fair and strong from the north, and we flew towards the south against the stream, watching those mysterious waters with a firm resolve to track them to their distant fountain.

On arrival at Korosko, in Lat. 22 degrees 44 minutes, in twenty-six days from Cairo, we started across the Nubian Desert, thus cutting off the western bend of the Nile, and in seven days' forced camel march we again reached the river Abou Hamed. The journey through that desert is most fatiguing, as the march averages fifteen hours a day through a wilderness of scorching sand and glowing basalt rocks. The simoom was in full force at that season (May), and the thermometer, placed in the shade by the water skins, stood at 114 degrees Fahrenheit.

No drinkable water was procurable on the route; thus our supply was nearly expended upon reaching the welcome Nile. After eight days' march on the margin of the river from Abou Hamed through desert, but in view of the palm trees that bordered the river, we arrived at Berber, a considerable town in lat. 17 degrees 58 minutes on the banks of the Nile.

Berber is eight days' camel march from Khartoum (at the junction of the White and Blue Niles, in lat. 15 degrees 30 minutes), and is the regular caravan route between that town and Cairo.

From the slight experience I had gained in the journey to Berber, I felt convinced that success in my Nile expedition would be impossible without a knowledge of Arabic. My dragoman had me completely in his power, and I resolved to become independent of all interpreters as soon as possible. I therefore arranged a plan of exploration for the first year, to embrace the affluents to the Nile from the Abyssinian range of mountains, intending to follow up the Atbara river from its junction with the Nile in lat. 17 degrees 37 minutes (twenty miles south of Berber), and to examine all the Nile tributaries from the southeast as far as the Blue Nile, which river I hoped ultimately to descend to Khartoum. I imagined that twelve months would be sufficient to complete such an exploration, by which time I should have gained a sufficient knowledge of Arabic to enable me to start from Khartoum for my White Nile expedition. Accordingly I left Berber on the 11th June, 1861, and arrived at the Atbara junction with the Nile on the 13th.

There is no portion of the Nile so great in its volume as that part situated at the Atbara junction. The river Atbara is about 450 yards in average width, and from twenty-five to thirty feet deep during the rainy season. It brings down the entire drainage of Eastern Abyssinia, receiving as affluents into its main stream the great rivers Taccazy (or Settite), in addition to the Salaam and Angrab. The junction of the Atbara in lat. 17 degrees 37 minutes N. is thus, in a direct line from Alexandria, about 840 geographical miles of latitude, and, including the westerly bend of the Nile, its bed will be about eleven hundred miles in length from the mouth of its last tributary, the Atbara, until it meets the sea. Thus, eleven hundred miles of absorption and evaporation through sandy deserts and the delta must be sustained by the river between the Atbara junction and the

Mediterranean: accordingly there is an immense loss of water; and the grandest volume of the Nile must be just below the Atbara junction.

It is not my intention in the present work to enter into the details of my first year's exploration on the Abyssinian frontier; that being so extensive and so completely isolated from the grand White Nile expedition, that an amalgamation of the two would create confusion. I shall therefore reserve the exploration of the Abyssinian tributaries for a future publication, and confine my present description of the Abyssinian rivers to a general outline of the Atbara and Blue Nile, showing the origin of their floods and their effect upon the inundations in Lower Egypt.

I followed the banks of the Atbara to the junction of the Settite or Taccazy River; I then followed the latter grand stream into the Abyssinian mountains in the Base country. From thence I crossed over to the Rivers Salaam and Angrab, at the foot of the magnificent range of mountains from which they flow direct into the Atbara. Having explored those Rivers, I passed through an extensive and beautiful tract of country forming a portion of Abyssinia on the south bank of the River Salaam; and again crossing the Atbara, I arrived at the frontier town of Gellabat, known by Bruce as Ras el Feel. Marching due west from that point I arrived at the River Rahad, in about lat. 12 degrees 30 minutes; descending its banks I crossed over a narrow strip of country to the west, arriving at the River Dinder, and following these streams to their junction with the Blue Nile, I descended that grand River to Khartoum, having been exactly twelve months from the day I had left Berber.

The whole of the above-mentioned Rivers – i.e. the Atbara, Settite, Salaam, Angrab, Rahad, Dinder, and Blue Nile – are the great drains of Abyssinia, all having a uniform course from southeast to northwest, and meeting the main Nile in two mouths; by the Blue Nile at Khartoum, 15 degrees 30 minutes, and by the Atbara, in lat. 17 degrees 37 minutes. The Blue Nile during the dry season is so reduced that there is not sufficient water for the small vessels engaged in transporting produce from Sennaar to Khartoum; at that time the water is beautifully clear, and, reflecting the cloudless sky, its colour has given it the well-known name of Bahr el Azrak, or Blue River. No water is more delicious than that of the Blue Nile;

in great contrast to that of the White River, which is never clear, and has a disagreeable taste of vegetation. This difference in the quality of the waters is a distinguishing characteristic of the two Rivers: the one, the Blue Nile, is a rapid mountain stream, rising and falling with great rapidity; the other is of lake origin, flowing through vast marshes. The course of the Blue Nile is through fertile soil; thus there is a trifling loss by absorption, and during the heavy rains a vast amount of earthy matter of a red colour is contributed by its waters to the general fertilizing deposit of the Nile in Lower Egypt.

The Atbara, although so important a River in the rainy season of Abyssinia, is perfectly dry for several months during the year, and at the time I first saw it, June 13, 1861, it was a mere sheet of glaring sand; in fact a portion of the desert through which it flowed. For upwards of one hundred and fifty miles from its junction with the Nile, it is perfectly dry from the beginning of March to June. At intervals of a few miles there are pools or ponds of water left in the deep holes below the general average of the River's bed. In these pools, some of which may be a mile in length, are congregated all the inhabitants of the River, who as the stream disappears are forced to close quarters in these narrow asylums; thus, crocodiles, hippopotami, fish, and large turtle are crowded in extraordinary numbers, until the commencement of the rains in Abyssinia once more sets them at liberty by sending down a fresh volume to the River. The rainy season commences in Abyssinia in the middle of May, but the country being parched by the summer heat, the first rains are absorbed by the soil, and the torrents do not fill until the middle of June.

From June to the middle of September the storms are terrific; every ravine becomes a raging torrent; trees are rooted up by the mountain streams swollen above their banks, and the Atbara becomes a vast River, bringing down with an overwhelming current the total drainage of four large Rivers – the Settite, Royan, Salaam, and Angrab – in addition to its own original volume. Its waters are dense with soil washed from most fertile lands far from its point of junction with the Nile; masses of bamboo and driftwood, together with large trees, and frequently the dead bodies of elephants and buffaloes, are hurled along its muddy waters in wild confusion, bringing a rich harvest to the Arabs on its banks, who are ever on the look-out for the River's treasures of fuel and timber.

The Blue Nile and the Atbara receiving the entire drainage of Abyssinia, at the same time pour their floods into the main Nile in the middle of June. At that season the White Nile is at a considerable level, although not at its highest; and the sudden rush of water descending from Abyssinia into the main channel, already at a fair level from the White Nile, causes the annual inundation in Lower Egypt.

During the year that I passed in the northern portion of Abyssinia and its frontiers, the rains continued with great violence for three months, the last shower falling on the 16th September, from which date there was neither dew nor rain until the following May. The great Rivers expended, and the mountain torrents dried up; the Atbara disappeared, and once more became a sheet of glaring sand. The rivers Settite, Salaam, and Angrab, although much reduced, are nevertheless perennial streams, flowing into the Atbara from the lofty Abyssinian mountains; but the parched, sandy bed of the latter river absorbs the entire supply, nor does one drop of water reach the Nile from the Atbara during the dry season. The wonderful absorption by the sand of that River is an illustration of the impotence of the Blue Nile to contend unaided with the Nubian deserts, which, were it not for the steady volume of the White Nile, would drink every drop of water before the River could pass the twenty-fifth degree of latitude.

The principal affluents of the Blue Nile are the Rahad and Dinder, flowing, like all others, from Abyssinia. The Rahad is entirely dry during the dry season, and the Dinder is reduced to a succession of deep pools, divided by sandbanks, the bed of the River being exposed. These pools are the resort of numerous hippopotami and the natural inhabitants of the River.

Having completed the exploration of the various affluents to the Nile from Abyssinia, passing through the Base country and the portion of Abyssinia occupied by Mek Nimmur, I arrived at Khartoum, the capital of the Soudan provinces, on the 11th June, 1862.

Khartoum is situated in lat. 15 degrees 29 minutes, on a point of land forming the angle between the White and Blue Niles at their junction. A more miserable, filthy, and unhealthy spot can hardly be imagined. Far as the eye can reach, upon all sides, is a sandy desert. The town, chiefly composed of huts of unburnt brick, extends over a flat hardly above the level of the River at high water, and is occasionally flooded. Although containing about 30,000 inhabitants, and densely crowded, there are neither drains nor cesspools: the streets are redolent with inconceivable nuisances; should animals die, they remain where they fall, to create pestilence and disgust. There are, nevertheless, a few respectable houses, occupied by the traders of the country, a small proportion of whom are Italians, French, and Germans, the European population numbering about thirty. Greeks, Syrians, Copts, Armenians, Turks, Arabs, and Egyptians, form the motley inhabitants of Khartoum.

There are consuls for France, Austria, and America, and with much pleasure I acknowledge many kind attentions, and assistance received from the two former, M. Thibaut and Herr Hansall.

Khartoum is the seat of government, the Soudan provinces being under the control of a Governor-general, with despotic power. In 1861, there were about six thousand troops quartered in the town; a portion of these were Egyptians; other regiments were composed of blacks from Kordofan, and from the White and Blue Niles, with one regiment of Arnouts, and a battery of artillery. These troops are the curse of the country: as in the case of most Turkish and Egyptian officials, the receipt of pay is most irregular, and accordingly the soldiers are under loose discipline. Foraging and plunder is the business of the Egyptian soldier, and the miserable natives must submit to insult and ill treatment at the will of the brutes who pillage them ad libitum.

In 1862, Moosa Pasha was the Governor-general of the Soudan. This man was a rather exaggerated specimen of Turkish authorities in general, combining the worst of Oriental failings with the brutality of a wild animal. During his administration the Soudan became utterly ruined; governed by military force, the revenue was unequal to the expenditure, and fresh taxes were levied upon the inhabitants to an extent that paralyzed the entire country. The Turk never improves. There is an Arab proverb that "the grass never grows in the footprint of a Turk," and nothing can be more aptly expressive of the character of the nation than this simple adage. Misgovernment, monopoly, extortion, and oppression, are the certain accompaniments of Turkish administration. At a great distance from all civilization, and separated from Lower Egypt by the Nubian deserts, Khartoum affords a wide field for the development of Egyptian official character. Every official plunders; the Governor-general extorts from all sides; he fills his private pockets by throwing every conceivable obstacle in the way of progress, and embarrasses every commercial movement in order to extort bribes from individuals. Following the general rule of his predecessors, a new governor upon arrival exhibits a spasmodic energy. Attended by cavasses and soldiers, he rides through every street of Khartoum, abusing the underlings for past neglect, ordering the streets to be swept, and the town to be thoroughly cleansed; he visits the marketplace, examines the quality of the bread at the bakers' stalls, and the meat at the butchers'. He tests the accuracy of the weights and scales; fines and imprisons the impostors, and institutes a complete reform, concluding his sanitary and philanthropic arrangements by the imposition of some local taxes.

The town is comparatively sweet; the bread is of fair weight and size, and the new governor, like a new broom, has swept all clean. A few weeks glide away, and the nose again recalls the savory old times when streets were never swept, and filth once more reigns paramount. The town relapses into its former state, again the false weights usurp the place of honest measures, and the only permanent and visible sign of the new administration is the local tax.

From the highest to the lowest official, dishonesty and deceit are the rule – and each robs in proportion to his grade in the government employ – the onus of extortion falling upon the natives; thus, exorbitant taxes are levied upon the agriculturists, and the industry of the inhabitants is disheartened by oppression. The taxes are collected by the soldiery, who naturally extort by violence an excess of the actual impost; accordingly the Arabs limit their cultivation to their bare necessities, fearing that a productive farm would entail an extortionate demand. The heaviest and most unjust tax is that upon the *sageer*, or water wheel, by which the farmer irrigates his otherwise barren soil.

The erection of the *sageer* is the first step necessary to cultivation. On the borders of the River there is much land available for agriculture; but from an almost total want of rain the ground must be constantly irrigated by artificial means. No sooner does an enterprising fellow erect a water wheel, than he is taxed, not only for his wheel, but he brings upon himself a perfect curse, as the soldiers employed for the collection of taxes fasten upon his garden, and insist upon a variety of extras in the shape of butter, corn, vegetables, sheep, etc. for themselves, which almost ruin the proprietor. Any government but that of Egypt and Turkey would offer a bonus for the erection of irrigating machinery that would give a stimulus to cultivation, and multiply the produce of the country; but the only rule without an exception is that of Turkish extortion. I have never met with any Turkish official who would take the slightest interest in plans for the improvement of the country, unless he discovered a means of filling his private purse. Thus in a country where Nature has been hard in her measure dealt to the inhabitants, they are still more reduced by oppression. The Arabs fly from their villages on the approach of the brutal tax-gatherers, driving their flocks and herds with them to distant countries, and leaving their standing crops to the mercy of the soldiery. No one can conceive the suffering of the country.

The general aspect of the Soudan is that of misery; nor is there a single feature of attraction to recompense a European for the drawbacks of pestilential climate and brutal associations. To a stranger it appears a superlative folly that the Egyptian government should have retained a possession, the occupation of which is wholly unprofitable; the receipts being far below the expenditure, *malgre* (in spite of) the increased taxation. At so great a distance from the seacoast and hemmed in by immense deserts, there is a difficulty of transport that must nullify all commercial transactions on an extended scale.

The great and most important article of commerce as an export from the Soudan, is gum arabic: this is produced by several species of mimosa, the finest quality being a product of Kordofan; the other natural productions exported are senna, hides, and ivory. All merchandise both to and from the Soudan must be transported upon camels, no other animals being adapted to the deserts. The cataracts of the Nile between Assouan and Khartoum rendering the navigation next to impossible, the camel is the only medium of transport, and the uncertainty of procuring them without great delay is the trader's greatest difficulty. The entire country is subject to droughts that occasion a total desolation, and the want of pasture entails starvation upon both cattle and camels, rendering it at certain seasons impossible to transport the productions of the country, and thus stagnating all enterprise. Upon existing conditions the Soudan is worthless, having neither natural capabilities nor political importance; but there is, nevertheless, a reason that first prompted its occupation by the Egyptians, and that is in force to the present day. THE SOUDAN SUPPLIES SLAVES. Without the White Nile trade Khartoum would almost cease to exist; and that trade is kidnapping and murder. The character of the Khartoumers needs no further comment. The amount of ivory brought down from the White Nile is a mere bagatelle as an export, the annual value being about 40,000 pounds.

The people for the most part engaged in the nefarious traffic of the White Nile are Syrians, Copts, Turks, Circassians, and some few Europeans. So closely connected with the difficulties of my expedition is that accursed slave trade, that the so-called ivory trade of the White Nile requires an explanation.

Throughout the Soudan money is exceedingly scarce and the rate of interest exorbitant, varying, according to the securities, from thirty-six to eighty percent; this fact proves general poverty and dishonesty, and acts as a preventive to all improvement. So high and fatal a rate deters all honest enterprise, and the country must lie in ruin under such a system. The wild speculator borrows upon such terms, to rise suddenly like a rocket, or to fall like its exhausted stick. Thus, honest enterprise being impossible, dishonesty takes the lead, and a successful expedition to the White Nile is supposed to overcome all charges. There are two classes of White Nile traders, the one possessing capital, the other being penniless adventurers; the same system of operations is pursued by both, but that of the former will be evident from the description of the latter.

A man without means forms an expedition, and borrows money for this purpose at 100 percent after this fashion. He agrees to repay the lender in ivory at one-half its market value. Having obtained the required sum, he hires several vessels and engages from 100 to 300 men, composed of Arabs and runaway villains from distant countries, who have found an asylum from justice in the obscurity of Khartoum. He purchases guns and large quantities of ammunition for his men, together with a few hundred pounds of glass beads. The piratical expedition being complete, he pays his men five months' wages in advance, at the rate of forty-five piastres (nine shillings) per month, and he agrees to give them eighty piastres per month for any period exceeding the five months advanced. His men receive their advance partly in cash and partly in cotton stuffs for clothes at an exorbitant price. Every man has a strip of paper, upon which is written by the clerk of the expedition the amount he has received both in goods and money, and this paper he must produce at the final settlement.

The vessels sail about December, and on arrival at the desired locality, the party disembark and proceed into the interior, until they arrive at the village of some negro chief, with whom they establish an intimacy. Charmed with his new friends, the power of whose weapons he acknowledges, the negro chief does not neglect the opportunity of seeking their alliance to attack a hostile neighbour. Marching throughout the night, guided by their negro hosts, they bivouac within an hour's march of the unsuspecting village doomed to an attack about half an hour before break of day. The time arrives, and, quietly surrounding the village while its occupants are still sleeping, they fire the grass huts in all directions, and pour volleys of musketry through the flaming thatch. Panic-stricken, the unfortunate victims rush from their burning dwellings, and the men are shot down like pheasants in a battue, while the women and children, bewildered in the danger and confusion, are kidnapped and secured. The herds of cattle, still within their *kraal,* or *zareeba,* are easily disposed of, and are driven off with great rejoicing, as the prize of victory. The women and children are then fastened together, the former secured in an instrument called a *sheba,* made of a forked pole, the neck of the prisoner fitting into the fork, secured by a cross piece lashed behind; while the wrists, brought together in advance of the body, are tied to the pole. The children are then fastened by their necks with a rope attached to the women, and thus form a living chain, in which order they are marched to the headquarters in company with the captured herds.

This is the commencement of business: should there be ivory in any of the huts not destroyed by the fire, it is appropriated; a general plunder takes place. The trader's party dig up the floors of the huts to search for iron hoes, which are generally thus concealed, as the greatest treasure of the negroes; the granaries are overturned and wantonly destroyed, and the hands are cut off the bodies of the slain, the more easily to detach the copper or iron bracelets that are usually worn. With this booty the traders return to their negro ally: they have thrashed and discomfited his enemy, which delights him; they present him with thirty or forty head of cattle, which intoxicates him with joy, and a present of a pretty little captive girl of about fourteen completes his happiness.

But business only commenced. The negro covets cattle, and the trader has now captured perhaps 2,000 head. They are to be had for ivory, and shortly the tusks appear. Ivory is daily brought into camp in exchange for cattle, a tusk for a cow, according to size – a profitable business, as the cows have cost nothing. The trade proves brisk; but still there remain some little customs to be observed – some slight formalities, well understood by the White Nile trade. The slaves and two-thirds of the captured cattle belong to the trader, but his men claim as their perquisite one-third of the stolen animals. These having been divided, the slaves are put up to public auction among the men, who purchase such as they require; the amount being entered on the papers (serki) of the purchasers, to be reckoned against their wages. To avoid the exposure, should the document fall into the hands of the government or European consuls, the amount is not entered as for the purchase of a slave, but is divided for fictitious supplies – thus, should a slave be purchased for 1,000 piastres, that amount would appear on the document somewhat as follows:

Soap	50
Tarboash (cap)	100
Araki	500
Shoes	200
Cotton Cloth	150
Total	1,000

The slaves sold to the men are constantly being changed and resold among themselves; but should the relatives of the kidnapped women and children wish to ransom them, the trader takes them from his men, cancels the amount of purchase, and restores them to their relations for a certain number of elephants' tusks, as may be agreed upon. Should any slave attempt to escape, she is punished either by brutal flogging, or shot or hanged, as a warning to others.

An attack or *razzia*, such as described, generally leads to a quarrel with the negro ally, who in his turn is murdered and plundered by the trader – his women and children naturally becoming slaves.

A good season for a party of a hundred and fifty men should produce about two hundred cantars (20,000 lbs.) of ivory, valued at Khartoum at 4,000 pounds. The men being paid in slaves, the wages should be nil, and there should be a surplus of four or five hundred slaves for the trader's own profit – worth on an average five to six pounds each.

The boats are accordingly packed with a human cargo, and a portion of the trader's men accompany them to the Soudan, while the remainder of the party form a camp or settlement in the country they have adopted, and industriously plunder, massacre, and enslave, until their master's return with the boats from Khartoum in the following season, by which time they are supposed to have a cargo of slaves and ivory ready for shipment. The business thus thoroughly established, the slaves are landed at various points within a few days' journey of Khartoum, at which places are agents, or purchasers; waiting to receive them with dollars prepared for cash payments. The purchasers and dealers are, for the most part, Arabs. The slaves are then marched across the country to different places; many to Sennaar, where they are sold to other dealers, who sell them to the Arabs and to the Turks. Others are taken immense distances to ports on the Red Sea, Souakim, and Masowa, there to be shipped for Arabia and Persia. Many are sent to Cairo, and in fact they are disseminated throughout the slave-dealing East, the White Nile being the great nursery for the supply.

The amiable trader returns from the White Nile to Khartoum; hands over to his creditor sufficient ivory to liquidate the original loan of 1,000 pounds, and, already a man of capital, he commences as an independent trader.

Such was the White Nile trade when I prepared to start from Khartoum on my expedition to the Nile sources. Every one in Khartoum, with the exception of a few Europeans, was in favor of the slave trade, and looked with jealous eyes upon a stranger venturing within the precincts of their holy land; a land sacred to slavery and to every abomination and villany that man can commit.

The Turkish officials pretended to discountenance slavery: at the same time every house in Khartoum was full of slaves, and the Egyptian officers had been in the habit of receiving a portion of their pay in slaves, precisely as the men employed on the White Nile were paid by their employers. The Egyptian authorities looked upon the exploration of the White Nile by a European traveller as an infringement of their slave territory that resulted from espionage, and every obstacle was thrown in my way.

Foreseeing many difficulties, I had been supplied, before leaving Egypt, with a firman [sic] from H. E. Said Pasha the Viceroy, by the request of H. B. M. agent, Sir R. Colquhoun; but this document was ignored by the Governor-general of the Soudan, Moosa Pasha, under the miserable prevarication that the firman was for the Pasha's dominions and for the Nile; whereas the White Nile was not accepted as the Nile, but was known as the White River. I was thus refused boats, and in fact all assistance.

To organize an enterprise so difficult that it had hitherto defeated the whole world required a careful selection of attendants, and I looked with despair at the prospect before me. The only men procurable for escort were the miserable cutthroats of Khartoum, accustomed to murder and pillage. in the White Nile trade, and excited not by the love of adventure but by the desire for plunder: to start with such men appeared mere insanity. There was a still greater difficulty in connection with the White Nile. For years the infernal traffic in slaves and its attendant horrors had existed like a pestilence in the negro countries, and had so exasperated the tribes, that people who in former times were friendly had become hostile to all comers. An exploration to the Nile sources was thus a march through an enemy's country, and required a powerful force of well-armed men. For the traders there was no great difficulty, as they took the initiative in hostilities, and had fixed camps as *points d'appui*, but for an explorer there was no alternative but a direct forward march without any communications with the rear. I had but slight hope of success without assistance from the authorities in the shape of men accustomed to discipline; I accordingly wrote to the British consul at Alexandria, and requested him to apply for a few soldiers and boats to aid me in so difficult an enterprise. After some months' delay, owing to the great distance from Khartoum, I received a reply enclosing a letter from Ishmael Pasha (the present Viceroy), the regent during the absence of Said Pasha, refusing the application.

I confess to the enjoyment of a real difficulty. From the first I had observed that the Egyptian authorities did not wish to encourage English explorations of the slave-producing districts, as such examinations would be detrimental to the traffic, and would lead to reports to the European governments that would ultimately prohibit the trade; it was perfectly clear that the utmost would be done to prevent my expedition from starting. This opposition gave a piquancy to the undertaking, and I resolved that nothing should thwart my plans. Accordingly I set to work in earnest. I had taken the precaution to obtain an order upon the Treasury at Khartoum for what money I required, and as ready cash performs wonders in that country of credit and delay, I was within a few weeks ready to start. I engaged three vessels, including two large *noggurs* or sailing barges, and a good decked vessel with comfortable cabins, known by all Nile tourists as a *diahbiah*.

The preparations for such a voyage are no trifles. I required forty-five armed men as escort, forty men as sailors, which, with servants, etc., raised my party to ninety-six. The voyage to Gondokoro, the navigable limit of the Nile, was reported to be from forty-five to fifty days from Khartoum, but provisions were necessary for four months, as the boatmen would return to Khartoum with the vessels, after landing me and my party. In the hope of meeting Speke and Grant's party, I loaded the boats with an extra quantity of corn, making a total of a hundred urdeps (rather exceeding 400 bushels). I had arranged the boats to carry twenty-one donkeys, four camels, and four horses; which I hoped would render me independent of porters, the want of transport being the great difficulty. The saddles, packs, and pads were all made under my own superintendence; nor was the slightest trifle neglected in the necessary arrangements for success. In all the detail, I was much assisted by a most excellent man whom I had engaged to accompany me as my head man, a German carpenter, Johann Schmidt. I had formerly met him hunting on the banks of the Settite River, in the Base country, where he was purchasing living animals from the Arabs, for a contractor to a menagerie in Europe; he was an excellent sportsman, and an energetic and courageous fellow; perfectly sober and honest. Alas! "The spirit was willing, but the flesh was weak," and a hollow cough, and emaciation, attended with hurried respiration, suggested disease of the lungs. Day after day he faded gradually, and I endeavoured to persuade him not to venture upon such a perilous journey as that before me: nothing would persuade him that he was in danger, and he had an idea that the climate of Khartoum was more injurious than the White Nile, and that the voyage would improve his health. Full of good feeling, and a wish to please, he persisted in working and perfecting the various arrangements, when he should have been saving his strength for a severer trial.

Meanwhile, my preparations progressed. I had clothed my men all in uniform, and had armed them with double-barrelled guns and rifles. I had explained to them thoroughly the object of my journey, and that implicit obedience would be enforced, so long as they were in my service; that no plunder would be permitted, and that their names were to be registered at the public Divan before they started. They promised fidelity and devotion, but a greater set of scoundrels in physiognomy I never encountered. Each man received five months' wages in advance, and I gave them an entertainment, with abundance to eat and drink, to enable them to start in good humor.

We were just ready to start; the supplies were all on board, the donkeys and horses were shipped, when an officer arrived from the Divan, to demand from me the poll tax that Moosa Pasha, the Governor-general, had recently levied upon the inhabitants; and to inform me, that in the event of my refusing to pay the said tax for each of my men, amounting to one month's wages per head, he should detain my boats. I ordered my captain to hoist the British flag upon each of the three boats, and sent my compliments to the government official, telling him that I was neither a Turkish subject nor a trader, but an English explorer; that I was not responsible for the tax, and that if any Turkish official should board my boat, under the British flag, I should take the liberty of throwing him overboard. This announcement appeared so practical, that the official hurriedly departed, while I marched my men on board, and ordered the boatmen to get ready to start. Just at that moment, a government vessel, by the merest chance, came swiftly down the River under sail, and in the clumsiest manner crashed right into us. The oars being lashed in their places on my boat, ready to start, were broken to pieces by the other vessel, which, fouling another of my boats just below, became fixed. The *reis*, or captain of the government boat that had caused the mischief, far from apologizing, commenced the foulest abuse; and refused to give oars in exchange for those he had destroyed. To start was impossible without oars, and an angry altercation being carried on between my men and the government boat, it was necessary to come to closer quarters. The *reis* of the government boat was a gigantic black, a Tokrouri (native of Darfur), who, confident in his strength, challenged any one to come on board, nor did any of my fellows respond to the invitation. The insolence of Turkish government officials is beyond description. My oars were smashed, and this insult was the reparation; so, stepping quickly on board, and brushing a few fellows on one side, I was obliged to come to a physical explanation with the captain, which terminated in a delivery of the oars. The bank of the river was thronged with people, many were mere idlers attracted by the bustle of the start, and others, the friends and relatives of my people, who had come to say a last good-bye, with many women, to raise the Arab cry of parting. Among others was a tall, debauched-looking fellow, excessively drunk and noisy, who, quarrelling with a woman who attempted to restrain him, insisted upon addressing a little boy named Osman, declaring that he should not accompany me unless he gave him a dollar to get some drink. Osman was a sharp Arab boy of twelve years old, whom I had engaged as one of the tent servants, and the drunken Arab was his father, who wished to extort some cash from his son before he parted; but the boy Osman showed his filial affection in a most touching manner, by running into the cabin, and fetching a powerful hippopotamus whip, with which he requested me to have his father thrashed, or "he would never be gone." Without indulging this amiable boy's desire, we shoved off; the three vessels rowed into the middle of the River, and hoisted sail; a fair wind, and strong current, moved us rapidly down the stream; the English flags fluttered gaily on the masts, and amidst the shouting of farewells, and the rattling of musketry, we started for the sources of the Nile. On passing the steamer belonging to the Dutch ladies, Madame van Capellan, and her charming daughter, Mademoiselle Tinne, we saluted them with a volley, and kept up a mutual waving of handkerchiefs until out of view; little did we think that we should never meet those kind faces again, and that so dreadful a fate would envelope almost the entire party. (The entire party died of fever on the White Nile, excepting Mademoiselle Tinne. The victims to the fatal climate of Central Africa were Madame la Baronne van Capellan, her sister, two Dutch maidservants, Dr. Steudner, and Signor Contarini.)

It was the 18th December, 1862, Thursday, one of the most lucky days for a start, according to Arab superstition. In a few minutes we reached the acute angle round which we had to turn sharply into the White Nile at its junction with the Blue. It was blowing hard, and in tacking round the point one of the noggurs carried away her yard, which fell upon deck and snapped in half, fortunately without injuring either men or donkeys. The yard, being about a hundred feet in length, was a complicated affair to splice; thus a delay took place in the act of starting which was looked upon as a bad omen by my superstitious followers. The voyage up the White Nile I now extract verbatim from my journal:

"Friday, 19th Dec. – At daybreak took down the mast and unshipped all the rigging; hard at work splicing the yard. The men of course wished to visit their friends at Khartoum. Gave strict orders that no man should leave the boats. One of the horsekeepers absconded before daybreak; sent after him. The junction of the two Niles is a vast flat as far as the eye can reach, the White Nile being about two miles broad some distance above the point. Saat, my *vakeel* (headman), is on board one noggur as chief; Johann on board the other, while I being on the diahbiah I trust all the animals will be well cared for. I am very fearful of Johann's state of health: the poor fellow is mere skin and bone, and I am afraid his lungs are affected; he has fever again today; I have sent him quinine and wine, etc.

"20th Dec. – The whole of yesterday employed in splicing yard, repairing mast, and re-rigging. At 8:30 a.m. we got away with a spanking breeze. The diahbiah horridly leaky. The 'tree,' or rendezvous for all boats when leaving for the White Nile voyage, consists of three large mimosas about four miles from the point of junction. The Nile at this spot about two miles wide – dead flat banks – mimosas on west bank. My two cabin boys are very useful, and Osman's ringing laugh and constant impertinence to the crew and soldiers keep the boat alive; he is a capital boy, a perfect gamin, and being a tailor by trade he is very useful: this accounts for his father wishing to detain him. The horses and donkeys very snug on board. At 1 p.m. passed Gebel Ouli, a small hill on south bank – course S.W. 1/2 S. At 8.30 p.m. reached Cetene, a village of mixed Arabs on the east bank – anchored.

"21st Dec. – All day busy clearing decks, caulking ship, and making room for the camels on the noggurs, as this is the village to which I had previously sent two men to select camels and to have them in readiness for my arrival. The men have been selecting sweethearts instead; thus I must wait here tomorrow, that being the *Soog*, or market day, when I shall purchase my camels and milch goats. The banks of the River very uninteresting – flat, desert, and mimosa bush. The soil is not so rich as on the banks of the Blue Nile – the *dhurra* (grain) is small. The Nile is quite two miles wide up to this point, and the high-water mark is not more than five feet above the present level. The banks shelve gradually like the sands at low tide in England, and quite unlike the perpendicular banks of the Blue Nile. Busy at gunsmith's work. The nights and mornings are now cold, from 60 degrees to 62 degrees F. Johann makes me very anxious: I much fear he cannot last long, unless some sudden change for the better takes place.

"22d Dec. – Selected two fine camels and shipped them in slings with some difficulty. Bought four oxen at nine *herias* each (15 s.); the men delighted at the work of slaughtering, and jerking the meat for the voyage. Bought four milch goats at 9 ps. each, and laid in a large stock of dhurra straw for the animals. Got all my men on board and sailed at 4:30 p.m., course due west; variation allowed for. I have already reduced my men from wolves to lambs, and I should like to see the outrageous acts of mutiny which are the scapegoats of the traders for laying their atrocities upon the men's shoulders. I cannot agree with some writers in believing that personal strength is unnecessary to a traveller. In these savage countries it adds materially to the success of an expedition, provided that it be combined with kindness of manner, justice, and unflinching determination. Nothing impresses savages so forcibly as the power to punish and reward. I am not sure that this theory is applicable to savages exclusively. Arrived at Wat Shely at 9 p.m.

"23d Dec. – Poor Johann very ill. Bought two camels, and shipped them all right: the market at this miserable village is as poor as that at Getene. The River is about a mile and a half wide, fringed with mimosas; country dead flat; soil very sandy; much cultivation near the village, but the dhurra of poor quality. Saw many hippopotami in the River. I much regret that I allowed Johann to accompany me from Khartoum; I feel convinced he can never rally from his present condition.

"24th Dec. – Sailed yesterday at 4:5 p.m., course south. This morning we are off the Bagara country on the west bank. Dead flats of mimosas, many of the trees growing in the water; the river generally shallow, and many snags or dead stumps of trees. I have been fortunate with my men, only one being drunk on leaving Wat Shely; him we carried forcibly on board. Passed the island of Hassaniah at 2.20 p.m.; the usual flats covered with mimosas. The high-water mark upon the stems of these trees is three feet above the present level of the River; thus an immense extent of country must be flooded during the wet season, as there are no banks to the River. The water will retire in about two months, when the neighbourhood of the River will be thronged with natives and their flocks. All the natives of these parts are Arabs; the Bagara tribe on the west bank. At Wat Shely some of the latter came on board to offer their services as slave-hunters, this open offer confirming the general custom of all vessels trading upon the White Nile.

"25th Dec. – The Tokroori boy, Saat, is very amiable in calling all the servants daily to eat together the residue from our table; but he being so far civilized, is armed with a huge spoon, and having a mouth like a crocodile, he obtains a fearful advantage over the rest of the party, who eat the soup by dipping *kisras* (pancakes) into it with their fingers. Meanwhile Saat sits among his invited guests, and works away with his spoon like a *sageer* (water-wheel), and gets an unwarrantable start, the soup disappearing like water in the desert. A dead calm the greater portion of the day; the River fringed with mimosa forest. These trees are the Soont (Acacia Arabica), which produce an excellent tannin; the fruit, *garra*, is used for that purpose, and produces a rich brown dye: all my clothes and the uniforms of my men I dyed at Khartoum with this garra. The trees are about eighteen inches in diameter and thirty-five feet high; being in full foliage, their appearance from a distance is good, but on a closer approach the forest proves to be a desolate swamp, completely overflowed; a mass of fallen dead trees protruding from the stagnant waters, a solitary crane perched here and there upon the rotten boughs; floating water-plants massed together, and forming green swimming islands, hitched generally among the sunken trunks and branches; sometimes slowly descending with the sluggish stream, bearing, spectre-like, storks thus voyaging on nature's rafts from lands unknown. It is a fever-stricken wilderness – the current not exceeding a quarter of a mile per hour – the water coloured like an English horse-pond; a heaven for mosquitoes and a damp hell for man. Fortunately, this being the cold season, the winged plagues are absent. The country beyond the inundated mimosa woods is of the usual sandy character, with thorny Kittur bush. Saw a few antelopes. Stopped at a horrible swamp to collect firewood. Anchored at night in a dead calm, well out in the River to escape malaria from the swamped forest. This is a precaution that the men would neglect, and my expedition might suffer in consequence. Christmas Day!

"6th Dec. – Good breeze at about 3 a.m.; made sail. I have never seen a fog in this part of Africa; although the neighbourhood of the River is swampy, the air is clear both in the morning and evening. Floating islands of water-plants are now very numerous. There is a plant something like a small cabbage (*Pistia Stratiotes*, L.), which floats alone until it meets a comrade; these unite, and recruiting as they float onward, they eventually form masses of many thousands, entangling with other species of water-plants and floating wood, until they at length form floating islands. Saw many hippopotami; the small hill in the Dinka country seen from the masthead at 9:15 a.m.; breeze light, but steady; the banks of the River, high grass and mimosas, but not forest as formerly. Water lilies in full bloom, white, but larger than the European variety. In the evening the crew and soldiers singing and drumming.

"27th Dec. – Blowing hard all night. Passed the Dinka hill at 3:30 a.m. Obliged to take in sail, as it buried the head of the vessel and we shipped much water. Staggering along under bare poles at about five miles an hour. The true banks of the River are about five hundred yards distant from the actual stream, this space being a mass of floating water-plants, decayed vegetable matter, and a high reedy grass much resembling sugarcanes; the latter excellent food for my animals. Many very interesting water-plants and large quantities of Ambatch wood (*Anemone mirabilis*) – this wood, of less specific gravity than cork, is generally used for rafts; at this season it is in full bloom, its bright yellow blossoms enlivening the dismal swamps. Secured very fine specimens of a variety of helix from the floating islands. In this spot the River is from 1500 yards to a mile wide; the country, flat and uninteresting, being the usual scattered thorn bushes and arid plains, the only actual timber being confined to the borders of the River. Course, always south with few turns. My sponging-bath makes a good pinnace for going ashore from the vessel. At 4:20 p.m. one of the noggurs carried away her yard – the same boat that met with the accident at our departure; hove to, and closed with the bank for repairs. Here is an affair of delay; worked with my own hands until 9 p.m.; spliced the yard, bound it with rhinoceros thongs, and secured the whole splice with raw bull's hide. Posted sentries – two on each boat, and two on shore.

"28th Dec. – At work at break of day. Completed the repair of yard, which is disgracefully faulty. Re-rigged the mast. Poor Johann will die, I much fear. His constitution appears to be quite broken up; he has become deaf, and there is every symptom of decay. I have done all I can for him, but his voyage in this life is nearly over. Ship in order, and all sailed together at 2:15 p.m. Strong north wind. Two vessels from Khartoum passed us while repairing damages. I rearranged the donkeys, dividing them into stalls containing three each, as they were such donkeys that they crowded each other unnecessarily. Caught a curious fish (*Tetrodon physa* of Geof.), that distends itself with air like a bladder; colour black, and yellow stripes; lungs; apertures under the fins, which open and shut by their movement, their motion being a semi-revolution. This fish is a close link between fish and turtle; the head is precisely that of the latter, having no teeth, but cutting jaws of hard bone of immense power. Many minutes after the head had been severed from the body, the jaws nipped with fury anything that was inserted in the mouth, ripping through thin twigs and thick straw like a pair of shears. The skin of the belly is white, and is armed with prickles. The skin is wonderfully tough. I accordingly cut it into a long thong, and bound up the stock of a rifle that had been split from the recoil of heavy charges of powder. The flesh was strong of musk, and uneatable. There is nothing so good as fish skin – or that of the iguana, or of the crocodile – for lashing broken gunstocks. Isinglass, when taken fresh from the fish and bound round a broken stock like a plaster, will become as strong as metal when dry. Country as usual – flat and thorny bush. A heavy swell creates a curious effect in the undulations of the green rafts upon the water. Dinka country on east bank; Shillook on the west; course south; all Arab tribes are left behind, and we are now thoroughly among the negroes.

"29th Dec. – At midnight the river made a bend westward, which continued for about fifteen miles. The wind being adverse, at 5 a.m. we found ourselves fast in the grass and floating vegetation on the lee side. Two hours' hard work at two ropes, alternately, fastened to the high grass ahead of the boat and hauled upon from the deck, warped us round the bend of the River, which turning due south, we again ran before a favourable gale for two hours; all the boats well together. The east bank of the River is not discernible – a vast expanse of high reeds stretching as far as the eye can reach; course p.m. W.S.W. At 4 p.m. the *Clumsy*, as I have named one of our noggurs, suddenly carried away her mast close by the board, the huge yard and rigging falling overboard with the wreck, severely hurting two men and breaking one of their guns. Hove to by an island on the Shillook side, towed the wreck ashore, and assembled all the boats. Fortunately there is timber at hand; thus I cut down a tree for a mast and got all ready for commencing repairs tomorrow. Poor Johann is, as I had feared, dying; he bleeds from the lungs, and is in the last stage of exhaustion. Posted six sentries.

"30th Dec. – Johann is in a flying state, but sensible; all his hopes, poor fellow, of saving money in my service and returning to Bavaria are past. I sat by his bed for some hours; there was not a ray of hope; he could speak with difficulty, and the flies walked across his glazed eyeballs without his knowledge. Gently bathing his face and hands, I asked him if I could deliver any message to his relatives. He faintly uttered, "I am prepared to die; I have neither parents nor relations; but there is one – she – " he faltered. He could not finish his sentence, but his dying thoughts were with one he loved; far, far away from this wild and miserable land, his spirit was transported to his native village, and to the object that made life dear to him. Did not a shudder pass over her, a chill warning at that sad moment when all was passing away? I pressed his cold hand, and asked her name. Gathering his remaining strength he murmured, "Krombach." (Krombach was merely the name of his native village in Bavaria.) *Es bleibt nur zu sterben. Ich bin sehr dankbar.*" These were the last words he spoke ("I am very grateful"). I gazed sorrowfully at his attenuated figure, and at the now powerless hand that had laid low many an elephant and lion, in its day of strength; and the cold sweat of death lay thick upon his forehead. Although the pulse was not yet still, Johann was gone.

"31st Dec. – Johann died. I made a huge cross with my own hands from the trunk of a tamarind tree, and by moonlight we laid him in his grave in this lonely spot.

'No useless coffin inclosed his breast,
Nor in sheet nor in shroud we wound him;
But he lay like a pilgrim taking his rest,
With his mantle drawn around him.'

"This is a mournful commencement of the voyage. Poor fellow, I did all I could for him although that was but little; and hands far more tender than mine ministered to his last necessities. This sad event closes the year 1862. Made sail at 8.30 p.m., the repairs of ship being completed.

"1863, Jan. 1st, 2 o'clock a.m. – Melancholy thoughts preventing sleep, I have watched the arrival of the new year. Thank God for His blessings during the past, and may He guide us through the untrodden path before us! We arrived at the village of Mahomed Her in the Shillook country. This man is a native of Dongola, who, having become a White Nile adventurer, established himself among the Shillook tribe with a band of ruffians, and is the arch-slaver of the Nile. The country, as usual, a dead flat: many Shillook villages on west bank all deserted, owing to Mahomed Her's plundering. This fellow now assumes a right of territory, and offers to pay tribute to the Egyptian government, thus throwing a sop to Cerberus to prevent intervention. Course S.W. The River in clear water about seven hundred yards wide, but sedge on the east bank for a couple of miles in width.

"2d Jan. – The *Clumsy* lagging, come to grief again, having once more sprung her rotten yard. Fine breeze, but obliged to wait upon this wretched boat – the usual flat uninteresting marshes: Shillook villages in great numbers on the terra firma to the west. Verily it is a pleasant voyage; disgusting naked savages, everlasting marshes teeming with mosquitoes, and the entire country devoid of anything of either common interest or beauty. Course west the whole day; saw giraffes and one ostrich on the east bank. On the west bank there is a regular line of villages throughout the day's voyage within half a mile of each other; the country very thickly populated. The huts are of mud, thatched, having a very small entrance – they resemble button mushrooms. The Shillooks are wealthy, immense herds of cattle swarm throughout their country. The natives navigate the River in two kinds of canoes-one of which is a curious combination of raft and canoe formed of the Ambatch wood, which is so light, that the whole affair is portable. The ambatch (*Anemone mirabilis*) is seldom larger than a man's waist, and as it tapers naturally to a point, the canoe rafts are quickly formed by lashing the branches parallel to each other, and tying the narrow ends together.

"3d Jan. – The *Clumsy*'s yard having been lashed with rhinoceros' hide, fortunately holds together, although sprung. Stopped this morning on the east bank, and gathered a supply of wood. On the west bank Shillook villages as yesterday during the day's voyage, all within half a mile of each other; one village situated among a thick grove of the dolape palms close to the River. The natives, afraid of our boats, decamped, likewise the fishermen, who were harpooning fish from small fishing stations among the reeds.

"The country, as usual, dead flat, and very marshy on the east bank, upon which side I see no signs of habitations. Course this morning south. Arrived at the River Sobat junction at 12:40 p.m., and anchored about half a mile within that River at a spot where the Turks had formerly constructed a camp. Not a tree to be seen; but dead flats of prairie and marsh as far as the eye can reach. The Sobat is not more than a hundred and twenty yards in breadth.

"I measured the stream by a floating gourd, which travelled 130 yards in 112 seconds, equal to about two miles and a half an hour. The quality of the water is very superior to that of the White Nile – this would suggest that it is of mountain origin. Upward course of Sobat south, 25 degrees east. Upward course of the White Nile west, 2 degrees north from the Sobat junction.

"4th Jan. – By observation of sun's meridian altitude, I make the latitude of the Sobat junction 9 degrees 21 minutes 14 seconds. Busy fishing the yard of the *Clumsy*, and mending sails. The camels and donkeys all well – plenty of fine grass – made a good stock of hay. My *reis* and boatmen tell me that the Sobat, within a few days' sail of the junction, divides into seven branches, all shallow and with a rapid current. The banks are flat, and the river is now bank-full. Although the water is perfectly clear, and there is no appearance of flood, yet masses of weeds, as though torn from their beds by torrents, are constantly floating down the stream. One of my men has been up the river to the farthest navigable point; he declares that it is fed by many mountain torrents, and that it runs out very rapidly at the cessation of the rains. I sounded the river in many places, the depth varying very slightly, from twenty-seven to twenty-eight feet. At 5 p.m. set sail with a light breeze, and glided along the dead water of the White Nile. Full moon – the water like a mirror; the country one vast and apparently interminable marsh – the river about a mile wide, and more or less covered with floating plants. The night still as death; dogs barking in the distant villages, and herds of hippopotami snorting in all directions, being disturbed by the boats. Course west.

"5th Jan. – Fine breeze, as much as we can carry; boats running at eight or nine miles an hour – no stream perceptible; vast marshes; the clear water of the river not more than 150 yards wide, forming a channel through the great extent of water grass resembling high sugarcanes, which conceal the true extent of the river. About six miles west from the Sobat junction on the north side of the river, is a kind of backwater, extending north like a lake for a distance of several days' boat journey: this is eventually lost in regions of high grass and marshes; in the wet season this forms a large lake. A hill bearing north 20 degrees west so distant as to be hardly discernible.

"The Bahr Giraffe is a small river entering the Nile on the south bank between the Sobat and Bahr el Gazal – my reis (Diabb) tells me it is merely a branch from the White Nile from the Aliab country, and not an independent river. Course west, 10 degrees north, the current about one mile per hour. Marshes and ambatch, far as the eye can reach.

"At 6:40 p.m. reached the Bahr el Gazal; the junction has the appearance of a lake about three miles in length, by one in width, varying according to seasons. Although bank-full, there is no stream whatever from the Bahr el Gazal, and it has the appearance of a backwater formed by the Nile. The water being clear and perfectly dead, a stranger would imagine it to be an overflow of the Nile, were the existence of the Bahr el Gazal unknown. The Bahr el Gazal extends due west from this point for a great distance, the entire river being a system of marshes, stagnant water overgrown by rushes, and ambatch wood, through which a channel has to be cleared to permit the passage of a boat. Little or no water can descend to the Nile from this river, otherwise there would be some trifling current at the embouchure. The Nile has a stream of about a mile and a half per hour, as it sweeps suddenly round the angle, changing its downward course from north to east. The breadth in this spot does not exceed 130 yards; but it is impossible to determine the actual width of the river, as its extent is concealed by reeds with which the country is entirely covered to the horizon.

"The White Nile having an upward course of west 10 degrees north, variation of compass 10 degrees west, from the Sobat to the Bahr el Gazal junction, now turns abruptly to south 10 degrees east. From native accounts there is a great extent of lake country at this point. The general appearance of the country denotes a vast flat, with slight depressions; these form extensive lakes during the wet season, and sodden marshes during the dry weather; thus contradictory accounts of the country may be given by travellers according to the seasons at which they examined it. There is nothing to denote large permanent lakes; vast masses of water plants and vegetation, requiring both a wet and dry season, exist throughout; but there are no great tracts of deep water. The lake at the Bahr el Gazal entrance is from seven to nine feet deep, by soundings in various places. Anchored the little squadron, as I wait here for observations. Had the *Clumsy*'s yard lowered and examined. Cut a supply of grass for the animals.

"Jan. 6th. – Overhauled the stores. My stock of liquor will last to Gondokoro; after that spot, *vive la misere*. It is curious in African travel to mark the degrees of luxury and misery; how, one by one, the wine, spirits bread, sugar, tea, etc., are dropped like the feathers of a moulting bird, and nevertheless we go ahead contented. My men busy cutting grass, washing, fishing, etc.

"Latitude, by meridian altitude of sun, 9 degrees 29 minutes. Difference of time by observation between this point and the Sobat junction, 4 min. 26 secs., 1 degree 6 minutes 30 seconds distance. Caught some perch, but without the red fin of the European species; also some *boulti* with the net. The latter is a variety of perch growing to about four pounds' weight, and is excellent eating.

"Sailed at 3 p.m. Masses of the beautiful but gloomy Papyrus rush, growing in dense thickets about eighteen feet above the water. I measured the diameter of one head, or crown, four feet one inch.

"Jan. 7th. – Started at 6 a.m.; course E. 10 degrees S.; wind dead against us; the *Clumsy* not in sight. Obliged to haul along by fastening long ropes to the grass about a hundred yards ahead. This is frightful work; the men must swim that distance to secure the rope, and those on board hauling it in gradually, pull the vessel against the stream. Nothing can exceed the labor and tediousness of this operation. From constant work in the water many of my men are suffering from fever. The temperature is much higher than when we left Khartoum; the country, as usual, one vast marsh. At night the hoarse music of hippopotami snorting and playing among the high-flooded reeds, and the singing of countless myriads of mosquitoes – the nightingales of the White Nile. My black fellow,

Richarn, whom I had appointed corporal, will soon be reduced to the ranks; the animal is spoiled by sheer drink. Having been drunk every day in Khartoum, and now being separated from his liquor, he is plunged into a black melancholy. He sits upon the luggage like a sick rook, doing minstrelsy, playing the *rababa* (guitar), and smoking the whole day, unless asleep, which is half that time: he is sighing after the *merissa* (native beer) pots of Egypt. This man is an illustration of missionary success. He was brought up from boyhood at the Austrian mission, and he is a genuine specimen of the average results. He told me a few days ago that he is no longer a Christian. There are two varieties of *convolvolus* growing here; also a peculiar gourd, which, when dry and divested of its shell, exposes a vegetable sponge, formed of a dense but fine network of fibers; the seeds are contained in the center of this fiber. The bright yellow flowers of the ambatch, and of a tree resembling a laburnum, are in great profusion. The men completely done: I served them out a measure of grog. The *Clumsy* not in sight.

"Jan. 8th. – Waited all night for the *Clumsy*. She appeared at 8 a.m., when the *reis* and several men received the whip for laziness. All three vessels now rounded a sharp turn in the river, and the wind being then favorable, we were soon under sail. The clear water of the river from the Bahr el Gazal to this point, does not exceed a hundred and twenty yards in width. The stream runs at one and three-quarter miles per hour, bringing with it a quantity of floating vegetation. The fact of a strong current both above and below the Bahr el Gazal junction, while the lake at that point is dead water, proves that I was right in my surmise, that no water flows from the Bahr el Gazal into the Nile during this season, and that the lake and the extensive marshes at that locality are caused as much by the surplus water of the White Nile flowing into a depression, as they are by the Bahr el Gazal, the water of the latter river being absorbed by the immense marshes.

"Yesterday we anchored at a dry spot, on which grew many mimosas of the red bark variety; the ground was a dead flat, and the river was up to the roots of the trees near the margin; thus the river is quite full at this season, but not flooded. There was no watermark upon the stems of the trees; thus I have little doubt that the actual rise of the water-level during the rainy season is very trifling, as the water extends over a prodigious extent of surface, the river having no banks. The entire country is merely a vast marsh, with a river flowing through the midst. At this season last year I was on the Settite. That great river and the Atbara were then excessively low.

"The Blue Nile was also low at the same time. On the contrary, the White Nile and the Sobat, although not at their highest, are bank-full, while the former two are failing; this proves that the White Nile and the Sobat rise far south, among mountains subject to a rainfall at different seasons, extending over a greater portion of the year than the rainy season of Abyssinia and the neighbouring Galla country.

"It is not surprising that the ancients gave up the exploration of the Nile when they came to the countless windings and difficulties of the marshes; the river is like an entangled skein of thread. Wind light; course S. 20 degrees W. The strong north wind that took us from Khartoum has long since become a mere breath. It never blows in this latitude regularly from the north. The wind commences at between 8 and 9 a.m., and sinks at sunset; thus the voyage through these frightful marshes and windings is tedious and melancholy beyond description. Great numbers of hippopotami this evening, greeting the boats with their loud snorting bellow, which vibrates through the vessels.

"Jan. 9th. – Two natives fishing left their canoe and ran on the approach of our boats. My men wished to steal it, which of course I prevented; it was a simple dome palm hollowed. In the canoe was a harpoon, very neatly made, with only one barb. Both sides of the river from the Bahr el Gazal belong to the Nuehr tribe. Course S.E.; wind very light; windings of river endless; continual hauling. At about half an hour before sunset, as the men were hauling the boat along by dragging at the high reeds from the deck, a man at the mast-head reported a buffalo standing on a dry piece of ground near the river; being in want of meat, the men begged me to shoot him. The buffalo was so concealed by the high grass, that he could not be seen from the deck; I therefore stood upon an *angarep* (bedstead) on the poop, and from this I could just discern his head and shoulders in the high grass, about a hundred and twenty yards off. I fired with No. 1 Reilly rifle, and he dropped apparently dead to the shot. The men being hungry, were mad with delight, and regardless of all but meat, they dashed into the water, and were shortly at him; one man holding him by the tail, another dancing upon him and brandishing his knife, and all shouting a yell of exultation. Presently up jumped the insulted buffalo, and charging through the men, he disappeared in the high grass, falling, as the men declared, in the deep morass. It was dusk, and the men, being rather ashamed of their folly in dancing instead of hamstringing the animal and securing their beef, slunk back to their vessels.

"Jan. 10th. – Early in the morning the buffalo was heard groaning in the marsh, not far from the spot where he was supposed to have fallen. About forty men took their guns and knives, intent upon beefsteaks, and waded knee-deep in mud and water through the high grass of the morass in search. About one hour passed in this way, and, seeing the reckless manner in which the men were wandering about, I went down below to beat the drum to call them back, which the *vakeel* had been vainly attempting. Just at this moment I heard a distant yelling, and shot fired after shot, about twenty times, in quick succession. I saw with the telescope a crowd of men about three hundred yards distant, standing on a white ant-hill raised above the green sea of high reeds, from which elevated point they were keeping up a dropping fire at some object indistinguishable in the high grass. The death-howl was soon raised, and the men rushing down from their secure position, shortly appeared, carrying with them my best *choush*, or sargeant, Sali Achmet – dead. He had come suddenly upon the buffalo, who, although disabled, had caught him in the deep mud and killed him. His gallant comrades bolted, although he called to them for assistance, and they had kept up a distant fire from the lofty anthill, instead of rushing to his rescue. The buffalo lay dead; and a grave was immediately dug for the unfortunate Sali. My journey begins badly with the death of my good man Johann and my best *choush* – added to the constant mishaps of the *Clumsy*. Fortunately I did not start from Khartoum on a Friday, or the unlucky day would have borne the onus of all the misfortunes.

"The graves of the Arabs are an improvement upon those of Europeans. What poor person who cannot afford a vault, has not felt a pang as the clod fell upon the coffin of his relative? The Arabs avoid this. Although there is no coffin, the rude earth does not rest upon the body. The hole being dug similar in shape to a European grave, an extra trench is formed at the bottom of the grave about a foot wide. The body is laid upon its side within this trench, and covered by bricks made of clay which are laid across; thus the body is contained within a narrow vault. Mud is then smeared over the hastily made bricks and nothing is visible; the tomb being made level with the bottom of the large grave. This is filled up with earth, which, resting on the brick covering of the trench cannot press upon the body. In such a grave my best man was laid – the Slave women raising their horrible howling and my men crying loudly, as well explained in the words of Scripture, "and he lifted up his voice and wept." I was glad to see so much external feeling for their comrade, but the grave being filled, their grief, like all loud sorrow, passed quickly away and relapsed into thoughts of buffalo meat; they were soon busily engaged in cutting up the flesh. There are two varieties of buffaloes in this part of Africa – the Bos Caffer, with convex horns, and that with flat horns; this was the latter species. A horn had entered the man's thigh, tearing the whole of the muscles from the bone; there was also a wound from the centre of the throat to the ear, thus completely torn open, severing the jugular vein. One rib was broken, the breastbone. As usual with buffaloes, he had not rested content until he had pounded the breath out of the body, which was found embedded and literally stamped tight into the mud, with only a portion of the head above the marsh. Sali had not even cocked his gun, the hammer being down on the nipples when found. I will not allow these men to come to grief in this way; they are a reckless set of thoughtless cowards, full of noise and bluster, fond of firing off their guns like children, and wasting ammunition uselessly, and in time of danger they can never be relied upon; they deserted their comrade when in need, and cried aloud like infants at his death; they shall not again be allowed to move from the boats.

"In the evening I listened to the men conversing over the whole affair, when I learnt the entire truth. It appears that Richarn and two other men were with the unfortunate Sali when the brute charged him, and the cowards all bolted without firing a shot in defense. There was a large white ant-hill about fifty yards distant, to which they retreated; from the top of this fort they repeatedly saw the man thrown into the air, and heard him calling for assistance. Instead of hastening in a body to his aid, they called to him to keep quiet and the buffalo would leave him. This is a sample of the courage of these Khartoumers. The buffalo was so disabled by my shot of yesterday that he was incapable of leaving the spot, as, with a broken shoulder, he could not get through the deep mud. My Reilly No. 10 bullet was found under the skin of the right shoulder, having passed in at the left shoulder rather above the lungs. The windings of this monotonous river are extraordinary, and during dead calms in these vast marshes the feeling of melancholy produced is beyond description. The White Nile is a veritable Styx. When the wind does happen to blow hard, the navigation is most difficult, owing to the constant windings; the sailors being utterly ignorant, and the rig of the vessel being the usual huge "leg of mutton" sail, there is an amount of screaming and confusion at every attempt to tack which generally ends in our being driven on the lee marsh; this is preferable to a capsize, which is sometimes anything but distant. This morning is one of those days of blowing hard, with the accompaniments of screaming and shouting. Course S.E. Waited half a day for the *Clumsy*, which hove in sight just before dark; the detentions caused by this vessel are becoming serious, a quick voyage being indispensable for the animals. The camels are already suffering from confinement, and I have their legs well swathed in wet bandages.

"This marsh land varies in width. In some portions of the river it appears to extend for about two miles on either side; in other parts farther than the eye can reach. In all cases the main country is a dead flat; now blazing and smoking beyond the limit of marshes, as the natives have fired the dry grass in all directions. Reeds, similar in appearance to bamboos but distinct from them, big watergrass, like sugarcanes, excellent fodder for the cattle, and the everpresent ambatch, cover the morasses. Innumerable mosquitoes.

"Jan. 12th – Fine breeze in the morning, but obliged to wait for the *Clumsy*, which arrived at 10 a.m. How absurd are some descriptions of the White Nile, which state that there is no current! At some parts, like that from just above the Sobat junction to Khartoum, there is but little, but since we have left the Bahr el Gazal the stream runs from one and three-quarters to two and a half miles per hour, varying in localities. Here it is not more than a hundred yards wide in clear water. At 11:20 a.m. got under weigh with a rattling breeze, but scarcely had we been half an hour under sail when crack went the great yard of the *Clumsy* once more. I had her taken in tow. It is of no use repairing the yard again, and, were it not for the donkeys, I would abandon her. Koorshid Aga's boats were passing us in full sail when his diahbiah suddenly carried away her rudder, and went head first into the morass. I serve out grog to the men when the drum beats at sunset, if all the boats are together.

"Jan. 13th. – Stopped near a village on the right bank in company with Koorshid Aga's two diahbiahs. The natives came down to the boats – they are something superlative in the way of savages; the men as naked as they came into the world; their bodies rubbed with ashes, and their hair stained red by a plaster of ashes and cow's urine. These fellows are the most unearthly-looking devils I ever saw – there is no other expression for them. The unmarried women are also entirely naked; the married have a fringe made of grass around their loins. The men wear heavy coils of beads about their necks, two heavy bracelets of ivory on the upper portion of the arms, copper rings upon the wrists, and a horrible kind of bracelet of massive iron armed with spikes about an inch in length, like leopard's claws, which they use for a similar purpose. The chief of the Nuehr village, Joctian, with his wife and daughter, paid me a visit, and asked for all they saw in the shape of beads and bracelets, but declined a knife as useless. They went away delighted with their presents. The women perforate the upper lip, and wear an ornament about four inches long of beads upon an iron wire; this projects like the horn of a rhinoceros; they are very ugly. The men are tall and powerful, armed with lances. They carry pipes that contain nearly a quarter of a pound of tobacco, in which they smoke simple charcoal should the loved tobacco fail. The carbonic acid gas of the charcoal produces a slight feeling of intoxication, which is the effect desired. Koorshid Aga returned them a girl from Khartoum who had been captured by a slave-hunter; this delighted the people, and they immediately brought an ox as an offering. The *Clumsy*'s yard broke in two pieces, thus I was obliged to seek a dry spot for the necessary repairs. I left the village Nuehr Eliab, and in the evening lowered the *Clumsy*'s yard; taking her in tow, we are, this moment, 8:30 p.m., slowly sailing through clouds of mosquitoes looking out for a landing-place in this world of marshes. I took the chief of the Nuehrs' portrait, as he sat in my cabin on the divan; of course he was delighted. He exhibited his wife's arms and back covered with jagged scars, in reply to my question as to the use of the spiked iron bracelet. Charming people are these poor blacks, as they are termed by English sympathisers; he was quite proud of having clawed his wife like a wild beast. In sober earnest, my monkey Wallady looks like a civilized being compared to the Nuehr savages. The chief's forehead was tattooed in horizontal lines that had the appearance of wrinkles. The hair is worn drawn back from the face. Both men and women wear a bag slung from the neck, apparently to contain any presents they may receive, everything being immediately pocketed. Course S.S.E.

"Jan. 14th.- All day occupied in repairing the yard; the buffalo hide of the animal that killed Sali Achmet being most serviceable in lashing. Sailed in the evening in company with a boat belonging to the Austrian mission. River about 120 yards of clear water; current about two miles per hour. Found quantities of natron on the marshy ground bordering the river.

"Had a turkey for dinner, a *cadeau* (gift) from Koorshid Aga, and, as a great wonder, the *kisra*s (a sort of brown pancake in lieu of bread) were free from sand. I must have swallowed a good-sized millstone since I have been in Africa, in the shape of grit rubbed from *the moorhaka*, or grinding-stone. The moorhaka, when new, is a large flat stone, weighing about forty pounds; upon this the corn is ground by being rubbed with a cylindrical stone with both hands. After a few months' use half of the original grinding-stone disappears, the grit being mixed with the flour; thus the grinding-stone is actually eaten. No wonder that hearts become stony in this country!

"Jan. 15th.- We were towing through high reeds this morning, the men invisible, and the rope mowing over the high tops of the grass, when the noise disturbed a hippopotamus from his slumber, and he was immediately perceived close to the boat. He was about half grown, and in an instant about twenty men jumped into the water in search of him, thinking him a mere baby; but as he suddenly appeared, and was about three times as large as they had expected, they were not very eager to close. However, the *reis* Diabb pluckily led the way and seized him by the hind leg, when the crowd of men rushed in, and we had a grand tussle. Ropes were thrown from the vessel, and nooses were quickly slipped over his head, but he had the best of the struggle and was dragging the people into the open river; I was therefore obliged to end the sport by putting a ball through his head. He was scored all over by the tusks of some other hippopotamus that had been bullying him. The men declared that his father had thus misused him; others were of opinion that it was his mother; and the argument ran high, and became hot.

"These Arabs have an extraordinary taste for arguments upon the most trifling points. I have frequently known my men argue throughout the greater part of the night, and recommence the same argument on the following morning. These debates generally end in a fight; and in the present instance the excitement of the hunt only added to the heat of the argument. They at length agreed to refer it to me, and both parties approached, vociferously advancing their theories; one half persisting that the young hippo had been bullied by his father, and the others adhering to the mother as the cause. I, being referee, suggested that perhaps it was his uncle. *Wah Illahi sahe* (by Allah it is true)! Both parties were satisfied with the suggestion; dropping their theory they became practical, and fell to with knives and axes to cut up the cause of the argument. He was as fat as butter, and was a perfect godsend to the people, who divided him with great excitement and good humour.

"We are now a fleet of seven boats, those of several traders having joined us. The *Clumsy's* yard looks much better than formerly. I cut off about ten feet from the end, as it was top heavy. The yard of this class of vessel should look like an immense fishing rod, and should be proportionately elastic, as it tapers gradually to a point. Course S.E. I hear that the Shillook tribe have attacked Chenooda's people, and that his boat was capsized, and some lives lost in the hasty retreat. It serves these slave-hunters right, and I rejoice at their defeat. Exodus 20, v. 16: "And he that stealeth a man, and selleth him, or if he be found in his hand, he shall surely be put to death."

"Jan. 16th. – A new dish! There is no longer mock-turtle soup – "real" turtle is mock hippopotamus. I tried boiling the fat, flesh, and skin together, the result being that the skin assumes the appearance of the green fat of the turtle, but is far superior. A piece of the head thus boiled, and then soused in vinegar, with chopped onions, cayenne pepper, and salt, throws brawn completely in the shade. My men having revelled in a cauldron of hippopotamus soup, I serve out grog at sunset, all ships being together. Great contentment, all appetites being satisfied. The labour of towing through swamps, tugging by the long grass, and poling against a strong current, is dreadful, and there appears to be no end to this horrible country. On dit (one says) that during the dry season there is plenty of game near the river, but at present boundless marshes devoid of life, except in the shape of mosquitoes, and a very few water-fowl, are the only charms of the White Nile. The other day I caught one of the men stealing the salt; Richarn having been aware of daily thefts of this treasure, and having failed to report them, the thief received twenty with the coorbatch, and Richarn is reduced to the ranks, as I anticipated. No possibility of taking observations, as there is no landing-place.

"Jan. 17th. – As usual, marshes, mosquitoes, windings, dead flats, and light winds; the mosquitoes in the cabin give no rest even during the day. Stream about two miles per hour. Course S.E.; the river averaging about one hundred and ten yards in width of clear water.

"Jan. 18th. – Country as usual, but the wind brisker. In company with Koorshid Aga's boats. I have bound the stock of Oswell's old gun with rhinoceros hide. All guns made for sport in wild countries and rough riding, should have steel instead of iron from the breech-socket, extending far back to within six inches of the shoulder-plate; the trigger-guard should likewise be steel, and should be carried back to an equal distance with the above rib; the steel should be of extra thickness, and screwed through to the upper piece; thus the two, being connected by screws above and below, no fall could break the stock.

"Jan. 19th. – At 8 a.m. we emerged from the apparently endless regions of marsh grass, and saw on the right bank large herds of cattle, tended by naked natives, in a country abounding with high grass and mimosa wood. At 9:15 a.m. arrived at the Zareeba, or station of Binder, an Austrian subject, and White Nile trader; here we found five noggurs belonging to him and his partner. Binder's *vakeel* insisted upon giving a bullock to my people. This bullock I resisted for some time, until I saw that the man was affronted. It is impossible to procure from the natives any cattle by purchase. The country is now a swamp, but it will be passable during the dry season. Took equal altitudes of sun producing latitude 7 degrees 5' 46". The misery of these unfortunate blacks is beyond description; they will not kill their cattle, neither do they taste meat unless an animal dies of sickness; they will not work, thus they frequently starve, existing only upon rats, lizards, snakes, and upon such fish as they can spear. The spearing of fish is a mere hazard, as they cast the harpoon at random among the reeds; thus, out of three or four hundred casts, they may, by good luck, strike a fish. The harpoon is neatly made, and is attached to a pliable reed about twenty feet long, secured by a long line. Occasionally they strike a monster, as there are varieties of fish which attain a weight of two hundred pounds. In the event of harpooning such a fish, a long and exciting chase is the result, as he carries away the harpoon, and runs out the entire length of line; they then swim after him, holding their end of the line, and playing him until exhausted. The chief of this tribe (the Kytch) wore a leopard-skin across his shoulders, and a skull-cap of white beads, with a crest of white ostrich-feathers; but the mantle was merely slung over his shoulders, and all other parts of his person were naked. His daughter was the best-looking girl that I have seen among the blacks; she was about sixteen. Her clothing consisted of a little piece of dressed hide about a foot wide slung across her shoulders, all other parts being exposed. All the girls of this country wear merely a circlet of little iron jingling ornaments round their waists. They came in numbers, bringing small bundles of wood to exchange for a few handfuls of corn. Most of the men are tall, but wretchedly thin; the children are mere skeletons, and the entire tribe appears thoroughly starved. The language is that of the Dinka. The chief carried a curious tobacco-box, an iron spike about two feet long, with a hollow socket, bound with iguana-skin; this served for either tobacco-box, club, or dagger. Throughout the whole of this marshy country it is curious to observe the number of white ant-hills standing above the water in the marshes: these Babel towers save their inmates from the deluge; working during the dry season, the white ants carry their hills to so great a height (about ten feet), that they can live securely in the upper stories during the floods. The whole day we are beset by crowds of starving people, bringing small gourd-shells to receive the expected corn. The people of this tribe are mere apes, trusting entirely to the productions of nature for their subsistence; they will spend hours in digging out fieldmice from their burrows, as we should for rabbits. They are the most pitiable set of savages that can be imagined; so emaciated, that they have no visible posteriors; they look as though they had been planed off, and their long thin legs and arms give them a peculiar gnat-like appearance. At night they crouch close to the fires, lying in the smoke to escape the clouds of mosquitoes. At this season the country is a vast swamp, the only dry spots being the white anthills; in such places the natives herd like wild animals, simply rubbing themselves with wood-ashes to keep out the cold.

"Jan. 20th. – The river from this spot turns sharp to the east, but an arm equally broad comes from S. 20 degrees E. to this point. There is no stream from this arm. The main stream runs round the angle with a rapid current of about two and a half miles per hour. The natives say that this arm of dead water extends for three or four days' sailing, and is then lost in the high reeds. My *reis* Diabb declares this to be a mere backwater, and that it is not connected with the main river by any positive channel.

"So miserable are the natives of the Kytch tribe, that they devour both skins and bones of all dead animals; the bones are pounded between stones, and when reduced to powder they are boiled to a kind of porridge; nothing is left even for a fly to feed upon, when an animal either dies a natural death, or is killed. I never pitied poor creatures more than these utterly destitute savages; their method of returning thanks is by holding your hand and affecting to spit upon it; which operation they do not actually perform, as I have seen stated in works upon the White Nile. Their domestic arrangements are peculiar. Polygamy is of course allowed, as in all other hot climates and savage countries; but when a man becomes too old to pay sufficient attention to his numerous young wives, the eldest son takes the place of his father and becomes his substitute. To every herd of cattle there is a sacred bull, which is supposed to exert an influence over the prosperity of the flocks; his horns are ornamented with tufts of feathers, and frequently with small bells, and he invariably leads the great herd to pasture. On starting in the early morning from the cattle kraal the natives address the bull, telling him to watch over the herd; to keep the cows from straying; and to lead them to the sweetest pastures, so that they shall give abundance of milk, etc.

"Jan. 21st. – Last night a sudden squall carried away Koorshid Aga's mast by the deck, leaving him a complete wreck. The weather today is dull, oppressive, and dead calm. As usual, endless marshes and mosquitoes. I never either saw or heard of so disgusting a country as that bordering the White Nile from Khartoum to this point. Course S.E. as nearly as I can judge, but the endless windings, and the absence of any mark as a point, make it difficult to give an accurate course – the river about a hundred yards in width of clear water; alive with floating vegetation, with a current of about two miles per hour.

"Jan. 22d. – The luxuries of the country as usual – malaria, marshes, mosquitoes, misery; far as the eye can reach, vast treeless marshes perfectly lifeless. At times progressing slowly by towing, the men struggling through the water with the rope; at other times by running round the boat in a circle, pulling with their hands at the grass, which thus acts like the cogs of a wheel to move us gradually forward. One of my horses, Filfil, out of pure amusement kicks at the men as they pass, and having succeeded several times in kicking them into the river, he perseveres in the fun, I believe for lack of other employment.

"Hippopotami are heard snorting in the high reeds both day and night, but we see very few. The black women on board are daily quarrelling together and fighting like bull-dogs; little Gaddum Her is a regular black toy terrier, rather old, wonderfully strong, very short, but making up in spirit for what she lacks in stature; she is the quintessence of vice, being ready for a stand-up fight at the shortest notice. On one occasion she fought with her antagonist until both fell down the hold, smashing all my water jars; on another day they both fell into the river. The ennui of this wretched voyage appears to try the temper of both man and beast; the horses, donkeys, and camels are constantly fighting and biting at all around.

"Jan. 23d. – At 8 a.m. arrived at Aboukooka, the establishment of a French trader. It is impossible to describe the misery of the land; in the midst of the vast expanse of marsh is a little plot of dry ground about thirty-five yards square, and within thirty yards of the river, but to be reached only by wading through the swamp. The establishment consisted of about a dozen straw huts, occupied by a wretched fever-stricken set of people; the *vakeel*, and others employed, came to the boats to beg for corn. I stopped for ten minutes at the charming watering place Aboukooka to obtain the news of the country. The current at this point is as usual very strong, being upwards of two and a half miles per hour; the river is quite bank-full although not actually flooding, the windings endless; one moment our course is due north, then east, then again north, and as suddenly due south; in fact, we face every point of the compass within an hour. Frequently the noggurs that are far in the rear appear in advance; it is a heartbreaking river without a single redeeming point; I do not wonder at the failure of all expeditions in this wretched country. There is a breeze today, thus the oppressive heat and stagnated marsh atmosphere is relieved. I have always remarked that when the sky is clouded we suffer more from heat and oppression than when the day is clear; there is a weight in the atmosphere that would be interesting if tested by the barometer.

"The water is excessively bad throughout the White Nile, especially between the Shillook and the Kytch tribes; that of the Bahr Gazal is even worse. The *reis* Diabb tells me that the north wind always fails between the Nuehr and the upper portion of the Kytch. I could not believe that so miserable a country existed as the whole of this land. There is no game to be seen at this season, few birds, and not even crocodiles show themselves; all the water-animals are hidden in the high grass; thus there is absolutely nothing living to be seen, but day after day is passed in winding slowly through the labyrinth of endless marsh, through clouds of mosquitoes.

"At 4:20 a.m. arrived at the Austrian mission- tation of St. Croix, and I delivered a letter to the chief of the establishment, Herr Morlang.

"Jan. 24th. – Took observations of the sun, making latitude 6 degrees 39c.

"The mission station consists of about twenty grass huts on a patch of dry ground close to the river. The church is a small hut, but neatly arranged. Herr Morlang acknowledged, with great feeling, that the mission was absolutely useless among such savages; that he had worked with much zeal for many years, but that the natives were utterly impracticable. They were far below the brutes, as the latter show signs of affection to those who are kind to them; while the natives, on the contrary, are utterly obtuse to all feelings of gratitude. He described the people as lying and deceitful to a superlative degree; the more they receive the more they desire, but in return they will do nothing.

"Twenty or thirty of these disgusting, ash-smeared, stark naked brutes, armed with clubs of hard wood brought to a point, were lying idly about the station. The mission having given up the White Nile as a total failure, Herr Morlang sold the whole village and mission-station to Koorshid Aga this morning for 3,000 piastres (30 pounds)! I purchased a horse of the missionaries for 1,000 piastres, which I christened Priest as coming from the mission; he is a good-looking animal, and has been used to the gun, as the unfortunate Baron Harnier rode him buffalo-hunting. This good sportsman was a Prussian nobleman, who with two European attendants, had for some time amused himself by collecting objects of natural history and shooting in this neighbourhood. Both his Europeans succumbed to marsh fever.

"The end of Baron Harnier was exceedingly tragic. Having wounded a buffalo, the animal charged a native attendant and threw him to the ground; Baron Harnier was unloaded, and with great courage he attacked the buffalo with the butt-end of his rifle to rescue the man then beneath the animal's horns. The buffalo left the man and turned upon his new assailant. The native, far from assisting his master, who had thus jeopardized his life to save him, fled from the spot. The unfortunate baron was found by the missionaries trampled and gored into an undistinguishable mass; and the dead body of the buffalo was found at a short distance, the animal having been mortally wounded. I went to see the grave of this brave Prussian, who had thus sacrificed so noble a life for so worthless an object as a cowardly native. It had been well cared for by the kind hands of the missionaries and was protected by thorn bushes laid around it, but I fear it will be neglected now that the mission has fallen into unholy hands. It is a pitiable sight to witness the self-sacrifice that many noble men have made in these frightful countries without any good results. Near to the grave of Baron Harnier are those of several members of the mission, who have left their bones in this horrid land, while not one convert has been made from the mission of St. Croix.

"The river divides into two branches, about five miles above this station, forming an island. Upon this is a fishing-station of the natives; the native name of the spot is Pomone. The country is swampy and scantily covered with bushes and small trees, but no actual timber. As usual, the entire country is dead flat; it abounds with elephants a few miles inland. Herr Morlang describes the whole of the White Nile traders as a mere colony of robbers, who pillage and shoot the natives at discretion. On the opposite side of the river there is a large neglected garden, belonging to the mission. Although the soil is extremely rich, neither grapes nor pomegranate will succeed; they bear fruit, but of a very acrid flavour. Dates blossom, but will not fruit.

"Jan. 25th. – Started at 7 a.m. Course S.E.

"Jan. 26th. – The Bohr tribe on the east bank. No wind. The current nearly three miles per hour. The river about a hundred and twenty yards wide in clear water. Marshes and flats, as usual. Thermometer throughout the journey, at 6 a.m., 68 degrees Fahr., and at noon 86 to 93 degrees Fahr.

"Jan. 27th. – One day is a repetition of the preceding.

"Jan. 28th. – Passed two bivouacs of the Aliab tribe, with great herds of cattle on the west bank. The natives appeared to be friendly, dancing and gesticulating as the boats passed. The White Nile tribe not only milk their cows, but they bleed their cattle periodically, and boil the blood for food. Driving a lance into a vein in the neck, they bleed the animal copiously, which operation is repeated about once a month.

"Jan. 29th. – Passed a multitude of cattle and natives on a spot on the right bank, in clouds of smoke as a *chasse des moustiques*. They make tumuli of dung, which are constantly on fire, fresh fuel being continually added, to drive away the mosquitoes. Around these heaps the cattle crowd in hundreds, living with the natives in the smoke. By degrees the heaps of ashes become about eight feet high; they are then used as sleeping-places and watch-stations by the natives, who, rubbing themselves all over with the ashes, have a ghastly and devilish appearance that is indescribable. The country is covered with old tumuli formed in this manner. A camp may contain twenty or thirty such, in addition to fresh heaps that are constantly burning. Fires of cow-dung are also made on the leveled tops of the old heaps, and bundles of green canes, about sixteen feet high, are planted on the summit; these wave in the breeze like a plume of ostrich feathers, and give shade to the people during the heat of the day.

"Jan. 30th. – Arrived at the Shir tribe. The men are, as usual in these countries, armed with well-made ebony clubs, two lances, a bow (always strung), and a bundle of arrows; their hands are completely full of weapons; and they carry a neatly-made miniature stool slung upon their backs, in addition to an immense pipe. Thus a man carries all that he most values about his person. The females in this tribe are not absolutely naked; like those of the Kytch, they wear small lappets of tanned leather as broad as the hand; at the back of the belt, which supports this apron, is a tail which reaches to the lower portions of the thighs; this tail is formed of finely-cut strips of leather, and the costume has doubtless been the foundation for the report I had received from the Arabs, that a tribe in Central Africa had tails like horses. The women carry their children very conveniently in a skin slung from their shoulders across the back, and secured by a thong round the waist; in this the young savage sits delightfully. The huts throughout all tribes are circular, with entrances so low that the natives creep both in and out upon their hands and knees. The men wear tufts of cock's feathers on the crown of the head; and their favorite attitude, when standing, is on one leg while leaning on a spear, the foot of the raised leg resting on the inside of the other knee. Their arrows are about three feet long, without feathers, and pointed with hard wood instead of iron, the metal being scarce among the Shir tribe. The most valuable article of barter for this tribe is the iron hoe generally used among the White Nile negroes. In form it is precisely similar to the ace of spades. The finery most prized by the women are polished iron anklets, which they wear in such numbers that they reach nearly half-way up the calf of the leg; the tinkling of these rings is considered to be very enticing, but the sound reminds one of the clanking of convicts' fetters.

"All the tribes of the White Nile have their harvest of the lotus seed. There are two species of waterlily – the large white flower, and a small variety. The seed-pod of the white lotus is like an unblown artichoke, containing a number of light red grains equal in size to mustard-seed, but shaped like those of the poppy, and similar to them in flavour, being sweet and nutty. The ripe pods are collected and strung upon sharp-pointed reeds about four feet in length. When thus threaded they are formed into large bundles, and carried from the river to the villages, where they are dried in the sun, and stored for use. The seed is ground into flour, and made into a kind of porridge. The women of the Shir tribe are very clever at manufacturing baskets and mats from the leaf of the dome palm. They also make girdles and necklaces of minute pieces of river mussel shells threaded upon the hair of the giraffe's tail. This is a work of great time, and the effect is about equal to a string of mother-of-pearl buttons.

"Jan. 31st. – At 1:15 p.m. sighted Gebel Lardo, bearing S. 30 degrees west. This is the first mountain we have seen, and we are at last near our destination, Gondokoro. I observed today a common sand-piper sitting on the head of a hippopotamus; when he disappeared under water the bird skimmed over the surface, hovering near the spot until the animal reappeared, when he again settled.

"Feb. 1st. – The character of the river has changed. The marshes have given place to dry ground; the banks are about four feet above the water-level, and well wooded; the country having the appearance of an orchard, and being thickly populated. The natives thronged to the boats, being astonished at the camels. At one village during the voyage the natives examined the donkeys with great curiosity, thinking that they were the oxen of our country, and that we were bringing them to exchange for ivory.

"Feb. 2nd – The mountain Lardo is about twelve miles west of the river. At daybreak we sighted the mountains near Gondokoro, bearing due south. As yet I have seen no symptoms of hostility in this country. I cannot help, thinking that the conduct of the natives depends much upon that of the traveller. Arrived at Gondokoro. By astronomical observation I determined the latitude, 4 degrees 55 minutes North, Longitude 31 degrees 46 minutes East. Gondokoro is a great improvement upon the interminable marshes; the soil is firm and raised about twenty feet above the river level. Distant mountains relieve the eye accustomed to the dreary flats of the White Nile; and evergreen trees scattered over the face of the landscape, with neat little native villages beneath their shade, form a most inviting landing-place after a long and tedious voyage. This spot was formerly a mission-station. There remain to this day the ruins of the brick establishment and church, and the wreck of what was once a garden; groves of citron and lime-trees still exist, the only signs that an attempt at civilization has been made – "seed cast upon the wayside." There is no town. Gondokoro is merely a station of the ivory traders, occupied for about two months during the year, after which time it is deserted, when the annual boats return to Khartoum and the remaining expeditions depart for the interior. A few miserable grass huts are all that dignify the spot with a name. The climate is unhealthy and hot. The thermometer from 90 to 95 degrees Fahrenheit at noon in the shade.

"I landed the animals from the boats in excellent condition all rejoicing in the freedom of open pasturage."

Chapter II

BAD RECEPTION AT GONDOKORO

All were thankful that the river voyage was concluded; the tedium of the White Nile will have been participated by the reader, upon whom I have inflicted the journal, as no other method of description could possibly convey an idea of the general desolation.

Having landed all my stores, and housed my corn in some granaries belonging to Koorshid Aga, I took a receipt from him for the quantity, and gave him an order to deliver one-half from my depot to Speke and Grant, should they arrive at Gondokoro during my absence in the interior. I was under an apprehension that they might arrive by some route without my knowledge, while I should be penetrating south.

There were a great number of men at Gondokoro belonging to the various traders, who looked upon me with the greatest suspicion; they could not believe that simple travelling was my object, and they were shortly convinced that I was intent upon espionage in their nefarious ivory business and slave-hunting.

In conversing with the traders, and assuring them that my object was entirely confined to a search for the Nile sources, and an inquiry for Speke and Grant, I heard a curious report that had been brought down by the natives from the interior, that at some great distance to the south there were two white men who had been for a long time prisoners of a sultan; and that these men had wonderful fireworks; that both had been very ill, and that one had died. It was in vain that I endeavoured to obtain some further clue to this exciting report. There was a rumour that some native had a piece of wood with marks upon it that had belonged to the white men; but upon inquiry I found that this account was only a report given by some distant tribe. Nevertheless, I attached great importance to the rumour, as there was no white man south of Gondokoro engaged in the ivory trade; therefore there was a strong probability that the report had some connexion with the existence of Speke and Grant. I had heard, when at Khartoum, that the most advanced trading station was about fifteen days' march from Gondokoro, and my plan of operations had always projected a direct advance to that station, where I had intended to leave all my heavy baggage in depot, and to proceed from thence as a *point de depart* to the south. I now understood that the party was expected to arrive at Gondokoro from that station with ivory in a few days, and I determined to wait for their arrival, and to return with them in company. Their ivory porters returning, might carry my baggage, and thus save the backs of my transport animals.

I accordingly amused myself at Gondokoro, exercising my horses in riding about the neighbourhood, and studying the place and people. The native dwellings are the perfection of cleanliness; the domicile of each family is surrounded by a hedge of the impenetrable euphorbia, and the interior of the enclosure generally consists of a yard neatly plastered with a cement of ashes, cow-dung, and sand. Upon this cleanly swept surface are one or more huts surrounded by granaries of neat wicker-work, thatched, resting upon raised platforms. The huts have projecting roofs in order to afford a shade, and the entrance is usually about two feet high. When a member of the family dies he is buried in the yard; a few ox-horns and skulls are suspended on a pole above the spot, while the top of the pole is ornamented with a bunch of cock's feathers. Every man carries his weapons, pipe, and stool, the whole (except the stool) being held between his legs when standing. These natives of Gondokoro are the Bari: the men are well grown, the women are not prepossessing, but the negro-type of thick lips and flat nose is wanting; their features are good, and the woolly hair alone denotes the trace of negro blood. They are tattooed upon the stomach, sides, and back, so closely, that it has the appearance of a broad belt of fish-scales, especially when they are rubbed with red ochre, which is the prevailing fashion. This pigment is made of a peculiar clay, rich in oxide of iron, which, when burnt, is reduced to powder, and then formed into lumps like pieces of soap; both sexes anoint themselves with this ochre, formed into a paste by the admixture of grease, giving themselves the appearance of new red bricks. The only hair upon their persons is a small tuft upon the crown of the head, in which they stick one or more feathers. The women are generally free from hair, their heads being shaved. They wear a neat little lappet, about six inches long, of beads, or of small iron rings, worked like a coat of mail, in lieu of a fig-leaf, and the usual tail of fine shreds of leather or twine, spun from indigenous cotton, pendant behind. Both the lappet and tail are fastened on a belt which is worn round the loins, like those in the Shir tribe; thus the toilette is completed at once. It would be highly useful, could they only wag their tails to whisk off the flies which are torments in this country.

The cattle are very small; the goats and sheep are quite Lilliputian, but they generally give three at a birth, and thus multiply quickly. The people of the country were formerly friendly, but the Khartoumers pillage and murder them at discretion in all directions; thus, in revenge, they will shoot a poisoned arrow at a stranger unless he is powerfully escorted. The effect of the poison used for the arrowheads is very extraordinary. A man came to me for medical aid; five months ago he bad been wounded by a poisoned arrow in the leg, below the calf, and the entire foot had been eaten away by the action of the poison. The bone rotted through just above the ankle, and the foot dropped off. The most violent poison is the produce of the root of a tree, whose milky juice yields a resin that is smeared upon the arrow. It is brought from a great distance, from some country far west of Gondokoro. The juice of the species of euphorbia, common in these countries, is also used for poisoning arrows. Boiled to the consistence of tar, it is then smeared upon the blade. The action of the poison is to corrode the flesh, which loses its fiber, and drops away like jelly, after severe inflammation and swelling. The arrows are barbed with diabolical ingenuity; some are arranged with poisoned heads that fit into sockets; these detach from the arrow on an attempt to withdraw them; thus the barbed blade, thickly smeared with poison, remains in the wound, and before it can be cut out the poison is absorbed by the system. Fortunately the natives are bad archers. The bows are invariably made of the male bamboo, and are kept perpetually strung; they are exceedingly stiff, but not very elastic, and the arrows are devoid of feathers, being simple reeds or other light wood, about three feet long, and slightly knobbed at the base as a hold for the finger and thumb; the string is never drawn with the two forefingers, as in most countries, but is simply pulled by holding the arrow between the middle joint of the forefinger and the thumb. A stiff bow drawn in this manner has very little power; accordingly the extreme range seldom exceeds a hundred and ten yards.

The Bari tribe are very hostile, and are considered to be about the worst of the White Nile. They have been so often defeated by the traders' parties in the immediate neighborhood of Gondokoro, that they are on their best behavior, while within half a mile of the station; but it is not at all uncommon to be asked for beads as a tax for the right of sitting under a shady tree, or for passing through the country. The traders' people, in order to terrify them into submission, were in the habit of binding them, hands and feet, and carrying them to the edge of a cliff about thirty feet high, a little beyond the ruins of the old mission-house: beneath this cliff the river boils in a deep eddy; into this watery grave the victims were remorselessly hurled as food for crocodiles. It appeared that this punishment was dreaded by the natives more than the bullet or rope, and it was accordingly adopted by the trading parties.

Upon my arrival at Gondokoro I was looked upon by all these parties as a spy sent by the British government. Whenever I approached the encampments of the various traders, I heard the clanking of fetters before I reached the station, as the slaves were being quickly driven into hiding-places to avoid inspection. They were chained by two rings secured round the ankles, and connected by three or four links. One of these traders was a Copt, the father of the American Consul at Khartoum; and, to my surprise, I saw the vessels full of brigands arrive at Gondokoro, with the American flag flying at the masthead.

Gondokoro was a perfect hell. It is utterly ignored by the Egyptian authorities, although well known to be a colony of cut-throats. Nothing would be easier than to send a few officers and two hundred men from Khartoum to form a military government, and thus impede the slave trade; but a bribe from the traders to the authorities is sufficient to insure an uninterrupted asylum for any amount of villany. The camps were full of slaves, and the Bari natives assured me that there were large depots of slaves in the interior belonging to the traders that would be marched to Gondokoro for shipment to the Soudan a few hours after my departure. I was the great stumbling block to the trade, and my presence at Gondokoro was considered as an unwarrantable intrusion upon a locality sacred to slavery and iniquity. There were about six hundred of the traders' people at Gondokoro, whose time was passed in drinking, quarrelling, and ill-treating the slaves. The greater number were in a constant state of intoxication, and when in such a state, it was their invariable custom to fire off their guns in the first direction prompted by their drunken instincts; thus, from morning till night, guns were popping in all quarters, and the bullets humming through the air sometimes close to our ears, and on more than one occasion they struck up the dust at my feet. Nothing was more probable than a ball through the head by accident, which might have had the beneficial effect of ridding the traders from a spy. A boy was sitting upon the gunwale of one of the boats, when a bullet suddenly struck him in the head, shattering the skull to atoms. NO ONE HAD DONE IT. The body fell into the water, and the fragments of the skull were scattered on the deck.

After a few days' detention at Gondokoro, I saw unmistakeable signs of discontent among my men, who had evidently been tampered with by the different traders' parties. One evening several of the most disaffected came to me with a complaint that they had not enough meat, and that they must be allowed to make a *razzia* upon the cattle of the natives to procure some oxen. This demand being of course refused, they retired, muttering in an insolent manner their determination of stealing cattle with or without my permission. I said nothing at the time, but early on the following morning I ordered the drum to beat, and the men to fall in. I made them a short address, reminding them of the agreement made at Khartoum to follow me faithfully, and of the compact that had been entered into, that they were neither to indulge in slave-hunting nor in cattle-stealing. The only effect of my address was a great outbreak of insolence on the part of the ringleader of the previous evening. This fellow, named Eesur, was an Arab, and his impertinence was so violent, that I immediately ordered him twenty-five lashes, as an example to the others.

Upon the *vakeel* (Saat) advancing to seize him, there was a general mutiny. Many of the men threw down their guns and seized sticks, and rushed to the rescue of their tall ringleader. Saat was a little man, and was perfectly helpless. Here was an escort: these were the men upon whom I was to depend in hours of difficulty and danger on an expedition in unknown regions; these were the fellows that I had considered to be reduced from wolves to lambs!

I was determined not to be done, and to insist upon the punishment of the ringleader. I accordingly went towards him with the intention of seizing him; but he, being backed by upwards of forty men, had the impertinence to attack me, rushing forward with a fury that was ridiculous. To stop his blow, and to knock him into the middle of the crowd, was not difficult; and after a rapid repetition of the dose, I disabled him, and seizing him by the throat, I called to my *vakeel* Saat for a rope to bind him, but in an instant I had a crowd of men upon me to rescue their leader. How the affair would have ended I cannot say; but as the scene lay within ten yards of my boat, my wife, who was ill with fever in the cabin, witnessed the whole affray, and seeing me surrounded, she rushed out, and in a few moments she was in the middle of the crowd, who at that time were endeavoring to rescue my prisoner. Her sudden appearance had a curious effect, and calling upon several of the least mutinous to assist, she very pluckily made her way up to me. Seizing the opportunity of an indecision that was for the moment evinced by the crowd, I shouted to the drummer boy to beat the drum. In an instant the drum beat, and at the top of my voice I ordered the men to fall in. It is curious how mechanically an order is obeyed if given at the right moment, even in the midst of mutiny. Two-thirds of the men fell in, and formed in line, while the remainder retreated with the ringleader, Eesur, whom they led away, declaring that he was badly hurt. The affair ended in my insisting upon all forming in line, and upon the ringleader being brought forward. In this critical moment Mrs. Baker, with great tact, came forward and implored me to forgive him if he kissed my hand and begged for pardon. This compromise completely won the men, who, although a few minutes before in open mutiny, now called upon their ringleader Eesur to apologize, and that all would be right. I made them rather a bitter speech, and dismissed them.

From that moment I knew that my expedition was fated. This outbreak was an example of what was to follow. Previous to leaving Khartoum I had felt convinced that I could not succeed with such villains for escort as these Khartoumers: thus I had applied to the Egyptian authorities for a few troops, but had been refused. I was now in an awkward position. All my men had received five months' wages in advance, according to the custom of the White Nile; thus I had no control over them. There were no Egyptian authorities in Gondokoro; it was a nest of robbers; and my men had just exhibited so pleasantly their attachment to me, and their fidelity. There was no European beyond Gondokoro, thus I should be the only white man among this colony of wolves; and I had in perspective a difficult and uncertain path, where the only chance of success lay in the complete discipline of my escort, and the perfect organization of the expedition. After the scene just enacted I felt sure that my escort would give me more cause for anxiety than the acknowledged hostility of the natives.

I made arrangements with a Circassian trader, Koorshid Aga, for the purchase of a few oxen, and a fat beast was immediately slaughtered for the men. They were shortly in the best humour, feasting upon masses of flesh cut in strips and laid for a few minutes upon the embers, while the regular meal was being prepared. They were now almost affectionate, vowing that they would follow me to the end of the world; while the late ringleader, in spite of his countenance being rather painted in the late row, declared that no man would be so true as himself, and that every arrow should pass through him before it should reach me in the event of a conflict with the natives. A very slight knowledge of human nature was required to foresee the future with such an escort: if love and duty were dependent upon full bellies, mutiny and disorder would appear with hard fare. However, by having parade every morning at a certain hour, I endeavoured to establish a degree of regularity. I had been waiting at Gondokoro twelve days, expecting the arrival of Debono's party from the south, with whom I wished to return. Suddenly, on the 15th February, I heard the rattle of musketry at a great distance, and a dropping fire from the south. To give an idea of the moment I must extract verbatim from my journal as written at the time:

"Guns firing in the distance; Debono's ivory porters arriving, for whom I have waited. My men rushed madly to my boat, with the report that two white men were with them who had come from the SEA! Could they be Speke and Grant? Off I ran, and soon met them in reality. Hurrah for old England! They had come from the Victoria N'Yanza, from which the Nile springs...The mystery of ages solved. With my pleasure of meeting them is the one disappointment, that I had not met them farther on the road in my search for them; however, the satisfaction is, that my previous arrangements had been such as would have insured my finding them had they been in a fix...My projected route would have brought me vis-a-vis with them, as they had come from the lake by the course I had proposed to take...All my men perfectly mad with excitement: firing salutes as usual with ball cartridge, they shot one of my donkeys; a melancholy sacrifice as an offering at the completion of this geographical discovery."

When I first met them they were walking along the bank of the river towards my boats. At a distance of about a hundred yards I recognised my old friend Speke, and with a heart beating with joy I took off my cap and gave a welcome "hurrah!" as I ran towards him. For the moment he did not recognize me; ten years' growth of beard and moustache had worked a change; and as I was totally unexpected, my sudden appearance in the center of Africa appeared to him incredible. I hardly required an introduction to his companion, as we felt already acquainted, and after the transports of this happy meeting we walked together to my diahbiah; my men surrounding us with smoke and noise by keeping up an unremitting fire of musketry the whole way. We were shortly seated on deck under the awning, and such rough fare as could be hastily prepared was set before these two ragged, careworn specimens of African travel, whom I looked upon with feelings of pride as my own countrymen. As a good ship arrives in harbor, battered and torn by a long and stormy voyage, yet sound in her frame and seaworthy to the last, so both these gallant travelers arrived at Gondokoro. Speke appeared the more worn of the two; he was excessively lean, but in reality he was in good tough condition; he had walked the whole way from Zanzibar, never having once ridden during that wearying march. Grant was in honourable rags; his bare knees projecting through the remnants of trowsers that were an exhibition of rough industry in tailor's work. He was looking tired and feverish, but both men had a fire in the eye that showed the spirit that had led them through.

They wished to leave Gondokoro as soon as possible, en route for England, but delayed their departure until the moon should be in a position for an observation for determining the longitude. My boats were fortunately engaged by me for five months, thus Speke and Grant could take charge of them to Khartoum.

At the first blush on meeting them I had considered my expedition as terminated by having met them, and by their having accomplished the discovery of the Nile source; but upon my congratulating them with all my heart, upon the honour they had so nobly earned, Speke and Grant with characteristic candour and generosity gave me a map of their route, showing that they had been unable to complete the actual exploration of the Nile, and that a most important portion still remained to be determined. It appeared that in N. lat. 2 degrees 17 minutes, they had crossed the Nile, which they had tracked from the Victoria Lake; but the river, which from its exit from that lake had a northern course, turned suddenly to the WEST from Karuma Falls (the point at which they crossed it at lat. 2 degrees 17 minutes). They did not see the Nile again until they arrived in N. lat. 3 deg. 32 min., which was then flowing from the W.S.W. The natives and the King of Unyoro (Kamrasi) had assured them that the Nile from the Victoria N'Yanza, which they had crossed at Karuma, flowed westward for several days' journey, and at length fell into a large lake called the Luta N'Zige; that this lake came from the south, and that the Nile on entering the northern extremity almost immediately made its exit, and as a navigable river continued its course to the north, through the Koshi and Madi countries. Both Speke and Grant attached great importance to this lake Luta N'Zige, and the former was much annoyed that it had been impossible for them to carry out the exploration. He foresaw that stay-at-home geographers, who, with a comfortable armchair to sit in, travel so easily with their fingers on a map, would ask him why he had not gone from such a place to such a place? Why he had not followed the Nile to the Luta N'Zige Lake, and from the lake to Gondokoro? As it happened, it was impossible for Speke and Grant to follow the Nile from Karuma – the tribes were fighting with Kamrasi, and no strangers could have got through the country. Accordingly they procured their information most carefully, completed their map, and laid down the reported lake in its supposed position, showing the Nile as both influent and effluent precisely as had been explained by the natives.

Speke expressed his conviction that the Luta N'Zige must be a second source of the Nile, and that geographers would be dissatisfied that he had not explored it. To me this was most gratifying. I had been much disheartened at the idea that the great work was accomplished, and that nothing remained for exploration; I even said to Speke, "Does not one leaf of the laurel remain for me?" I now heard that the field was not only open, but that an additional interest was given to the exploration by the proof that the Nile flowed out of one great lake, the Victoria, but that it evidently must derive an additional supply from an unknown lake as it entered it at the NORTHERN extremity, while the body of the lake came from the south. The fact of a great body of water such as the Luta N'Zige extending in a direct line from south to north, while the general system of drainage of the Nile was from the same direction, showed most conclusively, that the Luta N'Zige, if it existed in the form assumed, must have an important position in the basin of the Nile.

My expedition had naturally been rather costly, and being in excellent order it would have been heartbreaking to have returned fruitlessly. I therefore arranged immediately for my departure, and Speke most kindly wrote in my journal such instructions as might be useful. I therefore copy them verbatim:

"Before you leave this be sure you engage two men, one speaking the Bari or Madi language, and one speaking Kinyoro, to be your interpreters through the whole journey, for there are only two distinct families of languages in the country, though of course some dialectic differences, which can be easily overcome by anybody who knows the family language...Now, as you are bent on first going to visit Kamrasi M'Kamma, or King of Unyoro, and then to see as much of the western countries bordering on the little Luta N'Zige, or `dead locust' lake, as possible, go in company with the ivory hunters across the Asua River to Apuddo eight marches, and look for game to the east of that village. Two marches further on will bring you to Panyoro, where there are antelopes in great quantity; and in one march more the Turks' farthest outpost, Faloro, will be reached, where you had better form a depot, and make a flying trip across the White Nile to Koshi for the purpose of inquiring what tribes live to west and south of it, especially of the Wallegga; how the River comes from the south, and where it is joined by the little Luta N'Zige. Inquire also after the country of Chopi, and what difficulties or otherwise you would have to overcome if you followed up the left bank of the White River to Kamrasi's; because, if found easy, it would be far nearer and better to reach Kamrasi that way than going through the desert jungles of Ukidi, as we went. This is the way I should certainly go myself, but if you do not like the look of it, preserve your information well; and after returning to Faloro, make Koki per Chougi in two marches, and tell old Chougi you wish to visit his M'Kamma Kamrasi, for Chougi was appointed Governor-general of that place by Kamrasi to watch the Wakidi who live between his residence and Chopi, which is the next country you will reach after passing through the jungles of Ukidi and crossing the Nile below Karuma Falls. Arrived at Chopi, inquire for the residence of the Katikiro or commander-in-chief, who will show you great respect, give you cows and pombe, and send messengers on to Kamrasi to acquaint him of your intention to visit him. This is the richest part of Kamrasi's possessions, and by a little inquiry you will learn much about the lake. Kamrasi's brother Rionga lives on a River island within one march of this. They are deadly enemies and always fighting, so if you made a mistake and went to Rionga's first, as the Turks would wish you to do, all travelling in Unyoro would be cut off. Tell the Katikiro all your plans frankly, and remark earnestly upon my great displeasure at Kamrasi's having detained me so long in his country without deigning to see me, else he may be assured no other white man will ever take the trouble to see him. We came down the River in boats from Kamrasi's to Chopi, but the boatmen gave much trouble, therefore it would be better for you to go overland. Kamrasi will most likely send Kidgwiga, an excellent officer, to escort you to his palace, but if he does not, ask after him; you could not have a better man.

"Arrive at Kamrasi's, insist upon seeing all his fat wives and brothers. Find out all you can about his pedigree, and ask for leave to follow up the lake from its junction with the Nile to Utumbi, and then crossing to its northern bank follow it down to Ullegga and Koshi. If you are so fortunate as to reach Utumbi, and don't wish to go farther south, inquire well about Ruanda, the M'Fumbiro mountains, if there is any copper in Rwanda, and whether or not the people of those countries receive *simbi* (the cowrie shell) or any other articles of merchandise from the west coast, guarding well that no confusion is made with the trade of *Karagwe*, for Rumanika sends men to Utumbi ivory-hunting continually. Remember well that the Wahuma are most likely Gallas; this question is most interesting, and the more you can gather of their history, since they crossed the White Nile, the better. Formerly Unyoro, Uganda, and Uddhu were all united in one vast kingdom called Kittara, but this name is now only applied to certain portions of that kingdom.

"Nothing is known of the Mountains of the Moon to the westward of Ruanda. In Unyoro the king will feed you; beyond that I suspect you will have to buy food with beads."

Such was the information most kindly written by Speke, which, in addition to a map drawn by Captain Grant, and addressed to the Secretary of the Royal Geographical Society, was to be my guide in the important exploration resolved upon. I am particular in publishing these details, in order to show the perfect freedom from jealousy of both Captains Speke and Grant. Unfortunately, in most affairs of life, there is not only fair emulation, but ambition is too often combined with intense jealousy of others. Had this miserable feeling existed in the minds of Speke and Grant, they would have returned to England with the sole honour of discovering the source of the Nile; but in their true devotion to geographical science and especially to the specific object of their expedition they gave me all information to assist in the completion of the great problem – the Nile sources.

We were all ready to start. Speke and Grant, an their party of twenty-two people, for Egypt, and I in the opposite direction. At this season there were many boats at Gondokoro belonging to the traders' parties, among which were four belonging to Mr. Petherick, three of which were open cargo boats, and one remarkably nice diahbiah, named the *Kathleen*, that was waiting for Mrs. Petherick and her husband, who were supposed to be at their trading station, the Niambara, about seventy miles west of Gondokoro; but no accounts had been heard of them. On the 20th February they suddenly arrived from the Niambara, with their people and ivory and were surprised at seeing so large a party of English in so desolate a spot. It is a curious circumstance, that although many Europeans had been as far south as Gondokoro, I was the first Englishman that had ever reached it. We now formed a party of four.

Gondokoro has a poor and sandy soil, so unproductive that corn is in the greatest scarcity and is always brought from Khartoum by the annual boats for the supply of the traders' people, who congregate there from the interior, in the months of January and February, to deliver the ivory for shipment to Khartoum. Corn is seldom or never less than eight times the price at Khartoum; this is a great drawback to the country, as each trading party that arrives with ivory from the interior brings with it five or six hundred native porters, all of whom have to be fed during their stay at Gondokoro, and in many cases, in times of scarcity, they starve. This famine has given a bad name to the locality, and it is accordingly difficult to procure porters from the interior, who naturally fear starvation.

I was thus extremely sorry that I was obliged to refuse a supply of corn to Mr. Petherick upon his application – an act of necessity, but not of ill-nature upon my part, as I was obliged to leave a certain quantity in depot at Gondokoro, in case I should be driven back from the interior, in the event of which, without a supply in depot, utter starvation would have been the fate of my party. Mr. Petherick accordingly despatched one of his boats to the Shir tribe down the White Nile to purchase corn in exchange for molotes (native hoes). The boat returned with corn on the 11th of March. On the 26th February, Speke and Grant sailed from Gondokoro. Our hearts were too full to say more than a short "God bless you!" They had won their victory; my work lay all before me. I watched their boat until it turned the corner, and wished them in my heart all honor for their great achievement. I trusted to sustain the name they had won for English perseverance, and I looked forward to meeting them again in dear old England, when I should have completed the work we had so warmly planned together.

Chapter III

GUN ACCIDENT

A day before the departure of Speke and Grant from Gondokoro, an event occurred which appeared as a bad omen to the superstitions of my men. I had ordered the diahbiah to be prepared for sailing: thus, the cargo having been landed and the boat cleared and washed, we were sitting in the cabin, when a sudden explosion close to the windows startled us from our seats, and the consternation of a crowd of men who were on the bank, showed that some accident had happened. I immediately ran out, and found that the servants had laid all my rifles upon a mat upon the ground, and that one of the men had walked over the guns; his foot striking the hammer of one of the No. 10 Reilly rifles, had momentarily raised it from the nipple, and an instantaneous explosion was the consequence. The rifle was loaded for elephants, with seven drachms of powder. There was a quantity of luggage most fortunately lying before the muzzle, but the effects of the discharge were extraordinary. The ball struck the steel scabbard of a sword, tearing off the ring; it then passed obliquely through the stock of a large rifle, and burst through the shoulder-plate; entering a packing-case of inch-deal, it passed through it and through the legs of a man who was sitting at some distance, and striking the hip-bone of another man, who was sitting at some paces beyond, it completely smashed both hips, and fortunately being expended, it lodged in the body. Had it not been for the first objects happily in the route of the ball, it would have killed several men, as they were sitting in a crowd exactly before the muzzle.

Dr. Murie, who had accompanied Mr. Petherick, very kindly paid the wounded men every attention, but he with the smashed hip died in a few hours, apparently without pain.

After the departure of Speke and Grant, I moved my tent to the high ground above the River; the effluvium from the filth of some thousands of people was disgusting, and fever was prevalent in all quarters. Both of us were suffering; also Mr. and Mrs. Petherick, and many of my men, one of whom died. My animals were all healthy, but the donkeys and camels were attacked by a bird, about the size of a thrush, which caused them great uneasiness. This bird is of a greenish-brown colour, with a powerful red beak, and excessively strong claws. It is a perfect pest to the animals, and positively eats them into holes. The original object of the bird in settling upon the animal is to search for vermin, but it is not contented with the mere insects, and industriously pecks holes in all parts of the animal, more especially on the back. A wound once established, adds to the attraction, and the unfortunate animal is so pestered that it has no time to eat. I was obliged to hire little boys to watch the donkeys, and to drive off these plagues; but so determined and bold were the birds, that I have constantly seen them run under the body of the donkey, clinging to the belly with their feet, and thus retreating to the opposite side of the animal when chased by the watch-boys. In a few days my animals were full of wounds, excepting the horses, whose long tails were effectual whisks. Although the temperature was high, 95 degrees Fahrenheit, it was frequently cold at about three o'clock in the morning, and one of my horses, Priest, that I had lately purchased of the mission, became paralysed, and could not rise from the ground. After several days' endeavours to cure him, I was obliged to shoot him, as the poor animal could not eat.

I now weighed all my baggage, and found that I had fifty-four *cantars* (100 lbs. each). The beads, copper, and ammunition were the terrible onus. I therefore applied to Mahommed, the *vakeel* of Andrea Debono, who had escorted Speke and Grant, and I begged his co-operation in the expedition. These people had brought down a large quantity of ivory from the interior, and had therefore a number of porters who would return empty-handed; I accordingly arranged with Mahommed for fifty porters, who would much relieve the backs of my animals from Gondokoro to the station at Faloro, about twelve days' march. At Faloro I intended to leave my heavy baggage in depot, and to proceed direct to Kamrasi's country.

I promised Mahommed that I would use my influence in all new countries that I might discover, to open a road for his ivory trade, provided that he would agree to conduct it by legitimate purchase, and I gave him a list of the quality of beads most desirable for Kamrasi's country, according to the description I had received from Speke.

Mahommed promised to accompany me, not only to his camp at Faloro, but throughout the whole of my expedition, provided that I would assist him in procuring ivory, and that I would give him a handsome present. All was agreed upon, and my own men appeared in high spirits at the prospect of joining so large a party as that of Mahommed, which mustered about two hundred men.

At that time I really placed dependence upon the professions of Mahommed and his people; they had just brought Speke and Grant with them, and had received from them presents of a first-class double-barrelled gun and several valuable rifles. I had promised not only to assist them in their ivory expeditions, but to give them something very handsome in addition, and the fact of my having upwards of forty men as escort was also an introduction, as they would be an addition to the force, which is a great advantage in hostile countries. Everything appeared to be in good train, but I little knew the duplicity of these Arab scoundrels. At the very moment that they were most friendly, they were plotting to deceive me, and to prevent me from entering the country. They knew, that should I penetrate the interior, the ivory trade of the White Nile would be no longer a mystery, and that the atrocities of the slave trade would be exposed, and most likely be terminated by the intervention of European Powers; accordingly they combined to prevent my advance, and to overthrow my expedition completely. The whole of the men belonging to the various traders were determined that no Englishman should penetrate into the country; accordingly they fraternised with my escort, and persuaded them that I was a Christian dog, that it was a disgrace for a Mahommedan to serve; that they would be starved in my service, as I would not allow them to steal cattle; that they would have no slaves; and that I should lead them – God knew where – to the sea, from whence Speke and Grant had started; that they had left Zanzibar with two hundred men, and had only arrived at Gondokoro with eighteen, thus the remainder must have been killed by the natives on the road; that if they followed me, and arrived at Zanzibar, I should find a ship waiting to take me to England, and I should leave them to die in a strange country. Such were the reports circulated to prevent my men from accompanying me, and it was agreed that Mahommed should fix a day for our pretended start in company, but that he would in reality start a few days before the time appointed; and that my men should mutiny, and join his party in cattle-stealing and slave-hunting. This was the substance of the plot thus carefully concocted.

My men evinced a sullen demeanour, neglected all orders, and I plainly perceived a settled discontent upon their general expression. The donkeys and camels were allowed to stray, and were daily missing, and recovered with difficulty; the luggage was overrun with white ants instead of being attended to every morning; the men absented themselves without leave, and were constantly in the camps of the different traders. I was fully prepared for some difficulty, but I trusted that when once on the march I should be able to get them under discipline. Among my people were two blacks: one, Richarn, already described as having been brought up by the Austrian mission at Khartoum; the other, a boy of twelve years old, Saat. As these were the only really faithful members of the expedition, it is my duty to describe them. Richarn was a habitual drunkard, but he had his good points; he was honest, and much attached to both master and mistress. He had been with me for some months, and was a fair sportsman, and being of an entirely different race to the Arabs, he kept himself apart from them, and fraternised with the boy Saat.

Saat was a boy that would do no evil; he was honest to a superlative degree, and a great exception to the natives of this wretched country. He was a native of Fertit, and was minding his father's goats, when a child of about six years old, at the time of his capture by the Baggera Arabs. He described vividly how men on camels suddenly appeared while he was in the wilderness with his flock, and how he was forcibly seized and thrust into a large gum sack, and slung upon the back of a camel. Upon screaming for help, the sack was opened, and an Arab threatened him with a knife should he make the slightest noise. Thus quieted, he was carried hundreds of miles through Kordofan to Dongola on the Nile, at which place he was sold to slave-dealers, and taken to Cairo to be sold to the Egyptian government as a drummer-boy. Being too young he was rejected, and while in the dealer's hands he heard from another slave, of the Austrian mission at Cairo, that would protect him could he only reach their asylum. With extraordinary energy for a child of six years old, he escaped from his master, and made his way to the mission, where he was well received, and to a certain extent disciplined and taught as much of the Christian religion as he could understand. In company with a branch establishment of the mission, he was subsequently located at Khartoum, and from thence was sent up the White Nile to a mission-station in the Shillook country. The climate of the White Nile destroyed thirteen missionaries in the short space of six months, and the boy Saat returned with the remnant of the party to Khartoum, and was re-admitted into the Mission. The establishment was at that time swarming with little black boys from the various White Nile tribes, who repaid the kindness of the missionaries by stealing everything they could lay their hands upon. At length the utter worthlessness of the boys, their moral obtuseness, and the apparent impossibility of improving them, determined the chief of the mission to purge his establishment from such imps, and they were accordingly turned out. Poor little Saat, the one grain of gold amidst the mire, shared the same fate.

It was about a week before our departure from Khartoum that Mrs. Baker and I were at tea in the middle of the court-yard, when a miserable boy about twelve years old came uninvited to her side, and knelt down in the dust at her feet. There was something so irresistibly supplicating in the attitude of the child, that the first impulse was to give him something from the table. This was declined, and he merely begged to be allowed to live with us, and to be our boy. He said that he had been turned out of the Mission, merely because the Bari boys of the establishment were thieves, and thus he suffered for their sins. I could not believe it possible that the child had been actually turned out into the streets, and believing that the fault must lay in the boy, I told him I would inquire. In the meantime he was given in charge of the cook.

It happened that, on the following day, I was so much occupied that I forgot to inquire at the Mission; and once more the cool hour of evening arrived when, after the intense heat of the day, we sat at table in the open court-yard; it was refreshed by being plentifully watered. Hardly were we seated, when again the boy appeared, kneeling in the dust, with his head lowered at my wife's feet, and imploring to be allowed to follow us. It was in vain that I explained that we had a boy, and did not require another; that the journey was long and difficult, and that he might perhaps die. The boy feared nothing, and craved simply that he might belong to us. He had no place of shelter, no food; had been stolen from his parents, and was a helpless outcast.

The next morning, accompanied by Mrs. Baker, I went to the mission and heard that the boy had borne an excellent character, and that it must have been by mistake that he had been turned out with the others. This being conclusive, Saat was immediately adopted. Mrs. Baker was shortly at work making him some useful clothes, and in an incredibly short time a great change was effected. As he came from the hands of the cook – after a liberal use of soap and water, and attired in trowsers, blouse, and belt – the new boy appeared in a new character.

From that time he considered himself as belonging absolutely to his mistress. He was taught by her to sew; Richarn instructed him in the mysteries of waiting at table, and washing plates, etc.; while I taught him to shoot, and gave him a light double-barrelled gun. This was his greatest pride.

In the evening, when the day's work was done, Saat was allowed to sit near his mistress; and he was at times amused and instructed by stories of Europe and Europeans, and anecdotes from the Bible adapted to his understanding, combined with the first principles of Christianity. He was very ignorant, notwithstanding his advantages in the mission, but he possessed the first grand rudiments of all religion – honesty of purpose. Although a child of only twelve years old, he was so perfectly trustworthy that, at the period of our arrival at Gondokoro, he was more to be depended upon than my *vakeel*, and nothing could occur among my mutinous escort without the boy's knowledge: thus he reported the intended mutiny of the people when there was no other means of discovering it, and without Saat I should have had no information of their plots.

Not only was the boy trustworthy, but he had an extraordinary amount of moral in addition to physical courage. If any complaint were made, and Saat was called as a witness – far from the shyness too often evinced when the accuser is brought face to face with the accused – such was Saat's proudest moment; and, no matter who the man might be, the boy would challenge him, regardless of all consequences. We were very fond of this boy; he was thoroughly good; and in that land of iniquity, thousands of miles away from all except what was evil, there was a comfort in having some one innocent and faithful, in whom to trust.

We were to start upon the following Monday. Mahommed had paid me a visit, assuring me of his devotion, and begging me to have my baggage in marching order, as he would send me fifty porters on the Monday, and we would move off in company. At the very moment that he thus professed, he was coolly deceiving me. He had arranged to start without me on the Saturday, while he was proposing to march together on the Monday. This I did not know at the time.

One morning I had returned to the tent after having, as usual, inspected the transport animals, when I observed Mrs. Baker looking extraordinarily pale, and immediately upon my arrival she gave orders for the presence of the *vakeel* (headman). There was something in her manner, so different to her usual calm, that I was utterly bewildered when I heard her question the *vakeel*, whether the men were willing to march. "Perfectly ready," was the reply. "Then order them to strike the tent, and load the animals; we start this moment." The man appeared confused, but not more so than I. Something was evidently on foot, but what I could not conjecture. The *vakeel* wavered, and to my astonishment I heard the accusation made against him, that, during the night, the whole of the escort had mutinously conspired to desert me, with my arms and ammunition that were in their hands, and to fire simultaneously at me should I attempt to disarm them. At first this charge was indignantly denied until the boy Saat manfully stepped forward, and declared that the conspiracy was entered into by the whole of the escort, and that both he and Richarn, knowing that mutiny was intended, had listened purposely to the conversation during the night; at daybreak the boy reported the fact to his mistress. Mutiny, robbery, and murder were thus deliberately determined.

I immediately ordered an *angarep* (travelling bedstead) to be placed outside the tent under a large tree; upon this I laid five double-barrelled guns loaded with buckshot, a revolver, and a naked sabre as sharp as a razor. A sixth rifle I kept in my hands while I sat upon the *angarep*, with Richarn and Saat both with double-barrelled guns behind me. Formerly I had supplied each of my men with a piece of mackintosh waterproof to be tied over the locks of their guns during the march. I now ordered the drum to be beat, and all the men to form in line in marching order, with their locks tied up in the waterproof. I requested Mrs. Baker to stand behind me, and to point out any man who should attempt to uncover his locks, when I should give the order to lay down their arms. The act of uncovering the locks would prove his intention, in which event I intended to shoot him immediately, and take my chance with the rest of the conspirators. I had quite determined that these scoundrels should not rob me of my own arms and ammunition, if I could prevent it.

The drum beat, and the *vakeel* himself went into the men's quarters, and endeavoured to prevail upon them to answer the call. At length fifteen assembled in line; the others were nowhere to be found. The locks of the arms were secured by mackintosh as ordered; it was thus impossible for any man to fire at me until he should have released his locks.

Upon assembling in line I ordered them immediately to lay down their arms. This, with insolent looks of defiance, they refused to do. "Down with your guns this moment," I shouted, "sons of dogs!" And at the sharp click of the locks, as I quickly cocked the rifle that I held in my hands, the cowardly mutineers widened their line and wavered. Some retreated a few paces to the rear; others sat down, and laid their guns on the ground; while the remainder slowly dispersed, and sat in twos, or singly, under the various trees about eighty paces distant. Taking advantage of their indecision, I immediately rose and. ordered my *vakeel* and Richarn to disarm them as they were thus scattered. Foreseeing that the time had arrived for actual physical force, the cowards capitulated, agreeing to give up their arms and ammunition if I would give them their written discharge. I disarmed them immediately, and the *vakeel* having written a discharge for the fifteen men present, I wrote upon each paper the word "mutineer" above my signature. None of them being able to read, and this being written in English, they unconsciously carried the evidence of their own guilt, which I resolved to punish should I ever find them on my return to Khartoum.

Thus disarmed, they immediately joined other of the traders' parties. These fifteen men were the Jalyns of my party, the remainder being Dongolowas: both Arabs of the Nile, north of Khartoum. The Dongolowas had not appeared when summoned by the drum, and my *vakeel* being of their nation, I impressed upon him his responsibility for the mutiny, and that he would end his days in prison at Khartoum should my expedition fail.

The boy Saat and Richarn now assured me that the men had intended to fire at me, but that they were frightened at seeing us thus prepared, but that I must not expect one man of the Dongolowas to be any more faithful than the Jalyns. I ordered the *vakeel* to hunt up the men, and to bring me their guns, threatening that if they refused I would shoot any man that I found with one of my guns in his hands.

There was no time for mild measures. I had only Saat (a mere child), and Richarn, upon whom I could depend; and I resolved with them alone to accompany Mahommed's people to the interior, and to trust to good fortune for a chance of proceeding.

I was feverish and ill with worry and anxiety, and I was lying down upon my mat, when I suddenly heard guns firing in all directions, drums beating, and the customary signs of either an arrival or departure of a trading party. Presently a messenger arrived from Koorshid Aga, the Circassian, to announce the departure of Mahommed's party without me, and my *vakeel* appeared with a message from the same people, that if I followed on their road (my proposed route), they would fire upon me and my party, as they would allow no English spies in their country.

My *vakeel* must have known of this preconcerted arrangement. I now went to the Circassian, Koorshid, who had always been friendly personally. In an interview with him, I made him understand that nothing should drive me back to Khartoum, but that, as I was now helpless, I begged him to give me ten elephant-hunters; that I would pay one-half of their wages, and amuse myself in hunting and exploring in any direction until the following year, he to take the ivory; by which time I could receive thirty black soldiers from Khartoum, with whom I should commence my journey to the lake. I begged him to procure me thirty good blacks at Khartoum, and to bring them with him to Gondokoro next season, where I arranged to meet him. This he agreed to, and I returned to my tent delighted at a chance of escaping complete failure, although I thus encountered a delay of twelve months before I could commence my legitimate voyage. That accomplished, I was comparatively happy; the disgrace of returning to Khartoum beaten would have been insupportable.

That night I slept well, and we sat under our shady tree by the tent-door at sunrise on the following morning, drinking our coffee with contentment. Presently, from a distance, I saw Koorshid, the Circassian, approaching with his partner. Coffee and pipes were ready instanter: both the boy Saat and Richarn looked upon him as a friend and ally, as it was arranged that ten of his hunters were to accompany us. Before he sipped his coffee he took me by the hand, and with great confusion of manner he confessed that he was ashamed to come and visit me. "The moment you left me yesterday," said he, "I called my *vakeel* and headman, and ordered them to select the ten best men of my party to accompany you; but instead of obeying me as usual, they declared that nothing would induce them to serve under you; that you were a spy who would report their proceedings to the government, and that they should all be ruined; that you were not only a spy on the slave-trade, but that you were a madman, who would lead them into distant and unknown countries, where both you and your wife and they would all be murdered by the natives; thus they would mutiny immediately, should you be forced upon them." My last hope was gone. Of course I thanked Koorshid for his good-will, and explained that I should not think of intruding myself upon his party, but that at the same time they should not drive me out of the country. I had abundance of stores and ammunition, and now that my men had deserted me, I had sufficient corn to supply my small party for twelve months; I had also a quantity of garden-seeds, that I had brought with me in the event of becoming a prisoner in the country; I should therefore make a *zareeba* or camp at Gondokoro, and remain there until I should receive men and supplies in the following season. I now felt independent, having preserved my depot of corn. I was at least proof against famine for twelve months. Koorshid endeavoured to persuade me that my party of only a man and a boy would be certainly insulted and attacked by the insolent natives of the Bari tribe should I remain alone at Gondokoro after the departure of the traders' parties. I told him that I preferred the natives to the traders' people, and that I was resolved; I merely begged him to lend me one of his little slave boys as an interpreter, as I had no means of communicating with the natives. This he promised to do.

After Koorshid's departure, we sat silently for some minutes, both my wife and I occupied by the same thoughts.

No expedition had ever been more carefully planned; everything had been well arranged to insure success. My transport animals were in good condition; their saddles and pads had been made under my own inspection; my arms, ammunition, and supplies were abundant, and I was ready to march at five minutes' notice to any part of Africa; but the expedition, so costly, and so carefully organized, was completely ruined by the very people whom I had engaged to protect it. They had not only deserted, but they had conspired to murder. There was no law in these wild regions but brute force; human life was of no value; murder was a pastime, as the murderer could escape all punishment. Mr. Petherick's *vakeel* had just been shot dead by one of his own men, and such events were too common to create much attention. We were utterly helpless; the whole of the people against us, and openly threatening. For myself personally I had no anxiety, but the fact of Mrs. Baker being with me was my greatest care. I dared not think of her position in the event of my death amongst such savages as those around her. These thoughts were shared by her; but she, knowing that I had resolved to succeed, never once hinted an advice for retreat.

Richarn was as faithful as Saat, and I accordingly confided in him my resolution to leave all my baggage in charge of a friendly chief of the Bari's at Gondokoro, and to take two fast dromedaries for him and Saat, and two horses for Mrs. Baker and myself, and to make a push through the hostile tribe for three days, to arrive among friendly people at Moir, from which place I trusted to fortune. I arranged that the dromedaries should carry a few beads, ammunition, and the astronomical instruments. Richarn said the idea was very mad; that the natives would do nothing for beads; that he had had great experience on the White Nile when with a former master, and that the natives would do nothing without receiving cows as payment; that it was of no use being good to them, as they had no respect for any virtue but force; that we should most likely be murdered; but that if I ordered him to go, he was ready to obey.

"Master, go on, and I will follow thee, to the last gasp, with truth and loyalty."

I was delighted with Richarn's rough and frank fidelity. Ordering the horses to be brought, I carefully pared their feet – their hard flinty hoofs, that had never felt a shoe, were in excellent order for a gallop if necessary. All being ready, I sent for the chief of Gondokoro. Meanwhile a Bari boy arrived from Koorshid to act as my interpreter.

The Bari chief was, as usual, smeared all over with red ochre and fat, and had the shell of a small land tortoise suspended to his elbow as an ornament. He brought me a large jar of *merissa* and said he had been anxious to see the white man who did not steal cattle, neither kidnap slaves, but that I should do no good in that country, as the traders did not wish me to remain. He told me that all people were bad, both natives and traders, and that force was necessary in this country. I tried to discover whether he had any respect for good and upright conduct. "Yes," he said; "all people say that you are different to the Turks and traders, but that character will not help you; it is all very good and very right, but you see your men have all deserted, thus you must go back to Khartoum; you can do nothing here without plenty of men and guns." I proposed to him my plan of riding quickly through the Bari tribe to Moir; he replied, "Impossible! If I were to beat the great *nogaras* (drums), and call my people together to explain who you were, they would not hurt you; but there are many petty chiefs who do not obey me, and their people would certainly attack you when crossing some swollen torrent, and what could you do with only a man and a boy?"

His reply to my question concerning the value of beads corroborated Richarn's statement; nothing could be purchased for anything but cattle; the traders had commenced the system of stealing herds of cattle from one tribe to barter with the next neighbour; thus the entire country was in anarchy and confusion, and beads were of no value. My plan for a dash through the country was impracticable.

I therefore called my *vakeel*, and threatened him with the gravest punishment on my return to Khartoum. I wrote to Sir R. Colquhoun, H.M. Consul-General for Egypt, which letter I sent by one of the return boats; and I explained to my *vakeel* that the complaint to the British authorities would end in his imprisonment, and that in case of my death through violence he would assuredly be hanged. After frightening him thoroughly, I suggested that he should induce some of the mutineers, who were Dongolowas (his own tribe), many of whom were his relatives, to accompany me, in which case I would forgive them their past misconduct.

In the course of the afternoon he returned with the news, that he had arranged with seventeen of the men, but that they refused to march towards the south, and would accompany me to the east if I wished to explore that part of the country. Their plea for refusing a southern route was the hostility of the Bari tribe. They also proposed a condition, that I should leave all my transport animals and baggage behind me. To this insane request, which completely nullified their offer to start, I only replied by vowing vengeance against the *vakeel*.

Their time was passed in vociferously quarrelling among themselves during the day, and in close conference with the *vakeel* during the night, the substance of which was reported on the following morning by the faithful Saat. The boy recounted their plot. They agreed to march to the east, with the intention of deserting me at the station of a trader named Chenooda, seven days' march from Gondokoro, in the Latooka country, whose men were, like themselves, Dongolowas; they had conspired to mutiny at that place, and to desert to the slave-hunting party with my arms and ammunition, and to shoot me should I attempt to disarm them. They also threatened to shoot my *vakeel*, who now, through fear of punishment at Khartoum, exerted his influence to induce them to start. Altogether, it was a pleasant state of things.

That night I was asleep in my tent, when I was suddenly awoke by loud screams, and upon listening attentively I distinctly heard the heavy breathing of something in the tent, and I could distinguish a dark object crouching close to the head of my bed. A slight pull at my sleeve showed me that my wife also noticed the object, as this was always the signal that she made if anything occured at night that required vigilance. Possessing a share of sangfroid admirably adapted for African travel, Mrs. Baker was not a screamer, and never even whispered; in the moment of suspected danger, a touch of my sleeve was considered a sufficient warning. My hand had quietly drawn the revolver from under my pillow and noiselessly pointed it within two feet of the dark crouching object, before I asked, "Who is that?" No answer was given – until, upon repeating the question, with my finger touching gently upon the trigger ready to fire, a voice replied, "Fadeela." Never had I been so near to a fatal shot! It was one of the black women of the party, who had crept into the tent for an asylum. Upon striking a light I found that the woman was streaming with blood, being cut in the most frightful manner with the *coorbatch* (whip of hippopotamus' hide). Hearing the screams continued at some distance from the tent, I found my angels in the act of flogging two women; two men were holding each woman upon the ground by sitting upon her legs and neck, while two men with powerful whips operated upon each woman alternately. Their backs were cut to pieces, and they were literally covered with blood. The brutes had taken upon themselves the task of thus punishing the women for a breach of discipline in being absent without leave. Fadeela had escaped before her punishment had been completed, and narrowly escaped being shot by running to the tent without giving warning. Seizing the *coorbatch* from the hands of one of the executioners, I administered them a dose of their own prescription, to their intense astonishment, as they did not appear conscious of any outrage; they were only slave women. In all such expeditions it is necessary to have women belonging to the party to grind the corn and prepare the food for the men; I had accordingly hired several from their proprietors at Khartoum, and these had been maltreated as described.

I was determined at all hazards to start from Gondokoro for the interior. From long experience with natives of wild countries, I did not despair of obtaining an influence over my men, however bad, could I once quit Gondokoro, and lead them among the wild and generally hostile tribes of the country; they would then be separated from the contagion of the slave-hunting parties, and would feel themselves dependent upon me for guidance. Accordingly I professed to believe in their promises to accompany me to the east, although I knew of their conspiracy; and I trusted that by tact and good management I should eventually thwart all their plans, and, although forced out of my intended course, I should be able to alter my route, and to work round from the east to my original plan of operations south. The interpreter given by Koorshid Aga had absconded: this was a great loss, as I had no means of communication with the natives except by casually engaging a Bari in the employment of the traders, to whom I was obliged to pay exorbitantly in copper bracelets for a few minutes' conversation.

A party of Koorshid's people had just arrived with ivory from the Latooka country, bringing with them a number of that tribe as porters. These people were the most extraordinary that I had seen – wearing beautiful helmets of glass beads, and being remarkably handsome. The chief of the party, Adda, came to my tent, accompanied by a few of his men. He was one of the finest men I ever saw, and he gave me much information concerning his country, and begged me to pay him a visit. He detested the Turks, but he was obliged to serve them, as he had received orders from the great chief Commoro to collect porters, and to transport their ivory from Latooka to Gondokoro. I took his portrait, to his great delight, and made him a variety of presents of copper bracelets, beads, and a red cotton handkerchief; the latter was most prized, and he insisted upon wearing it upon his person. He had no intention of wearing his new acquisition for the purpose of decency, but he carefully folded it so as to form a triangle, and then tied it round his waist, so that the pointed end should hang exactly straight BEHIND him. So particular was he, that he was quite half an hour in arranging this simple appendage; and at length he departed with his people, always endeavouring to admire his new finery, by straining his neck in his attempts to look behind him.

From morning till night natives of all ranks surrounded the tent to ask for presents; these being generally granted, as it was highly necessary to create a favourable impression. Koorshid's party, who had arrived from Latooka, were to return shortly, but they not only refused to allow me to accompany them, but they declared their intention of forcibly repelling me, should I attempt to advance by their route. This was a grand excuse for my men, who once more refused to proceed. By pressure upon the *vakeel* they again yielded, but on condition that I would take one of the mutineers named Bellaal, who wished to join them, but whose offer I had refused, as he had been a notorious ringleader in every mutiny. It was a sine qua non that he was to go; and knowing the character of the man, I felt convinced that it had been arranged that he should head the mutiny conspired to be enacted upon our arrival at Chenooda's camp in the Latooka country. The *vakeel* of Chenooda, one Mahommed Her, was in constant communication with my men, which tended to confirm the reports I had heard from the boy Saat. This Mahommed Her started from Gondokoro for Latooka. Koorshid's men would start two days later; these were rival parties, both antagonistic, but occupying the same country, the Latooka; both equally hostile to me, but as the party of Mahommed Her were Dongolowas, and that of Koorshid were Jalyns and Soodanes, I trusted eventually to turn their disputes to my own advantage.

The plan that I had arranged was to leave all the baggage not indispensable with Koorshid Aga at Gondokoro, who would return it to Khartoum. I intended to wait until Koorshid's party should march, when I resolved to follow them, as I did not believe they would dare to oppose me by force, their master himself being friendly. I considered their threats as mere idle boasting, to frighten me from an attempt to follow them; but there was another more serious cause of danger to be apprehended.

On the route, between Gondokoro and Latooka, there was a powerful tribe among the mountains of Ellyria. The chief of that tribe (Legge) had formerly massacred a hundred and twenty of a trader's party. He was an ally of Koorshid's people, who declared that they would raise the tribe against me, which would end in the defeat or massacre of my party. There was a difficult pass through the mountains of Ellyria, which it would be impossible to force; thus my small party of seventeen men would be helpless. It would be merely necessary for the traders to request the chief of Ellyria to attack my party to insure its destruction, as the plunder of the baggage would be an ample reward.

There was no time for deliberation. Both the present and the future looked as gloomy as could be imagined; but I had always expected extraordinary difficulties, and they were, if possible, to be surmounted. It was useless to speculate upon chances; there was no hope of success in inaction; and the only resource was to drive through all obstacles without calculating the risk.

Once away from Gondokoro we should be fairly launched on our voyage, the boats would have returned to Khartoum, thus retreat would be cut off; it only remained to push forward, trusting in Providence and good fortune. I had great faith in presents. The Arabs are all venal; and, having many valuable effects with me, I trusted, when the proper moment should arrive, to be able to overcome all opposition by an open hand. The day arrived for the departure of Koorshid's people. They commenced firing their usual signals; the drums beat; the Turkish ensign led the way; and they marched at 2 o'clock p.m., sending a polite message daring me to follow them.

I immediately ordered the tent to be struck, the luggage to be arranged, the animals to be collected, and everything to be ready for the march. Richarn and Saat were in high spirits, even my unwilling men were obliged to work, and by 7 p.m. we were all ready. The camels were too heavily loaded, carrying about seven hundred pounds each. The donkeys were also overloaded, but there was no help for it. Mrs. Baker was well mounted on my good old Abyssinian hunter Tetel, ("hartebeest") and was carrying several leather bags slung to the pommel, while I was equally loaded on my horse Filfil ("pepper"); in fact, we were all carrying as much as we could stow.

We had neither guide, nor interpreter. Not one native was procurable, all being under the influence of the traders, who had determined to render our advance utterly impossible by preventing the natives from assisting us. All had been threatened, and we, perfectly helpless, commenced the desperate journey in darkness about an hour after sunset.

"Where shall we go?" said the men, just as the order was given to start. "Who can travel without a guide? No one knows the road." The moon was up, and the mountain of Belignan was distinctly visible about nine miles distant. Knowing that the route lay on the east side of that mountain, I led the way, Mrs. Baker riding by my side, and the British flag following close behind us as a guide for the caravan of heavily laden camels and donkeys. We shook hands warmly with Dr. Murie, who had come to see us off, and thus we started on our march in Central Africa on the 26th of March, 1863.

Chapter IV

FIRST NIGHT'S MARCH

The country was park-like, but much parched by the dry weather. The ground was sandy, but firm, and interspersed with numerous villages, all of which were surrounded with a strong fence of euphorbia. The country was well wooded, being free from bush or jungle, but numerous trees, all evergreens, were scattered over the landscape. No natives were to be seen, but the sound of their drums and singing in chorus was heard in the far distance. Whenever it is moonlight the nights are passed in singing and dancing, beating drums, blowing horns, and the population of whole villages thus congregate together.

After a silent march of two hours we saw watch fires blazing in the distance, and upon nearer approach we perceived the trader's party bivouacked. Their custom is to march only two or three hours on the first day of departure, to allow stragglers who may have lagged behind in Gondokoro to rejoin the party before morning.

We were roughly challenged by their sentries as we passed, and were instantly told not to remain in their neighbourhood. Accordingly we passed on for about half a mile in advance, and bivouacked on some rising ground above a slight hollow in which we found water. All were busy collecting firewood and cutting grass for the donkeys and horses who were picketed near the fires. The camels were hobbled, and turned to graze upon the branches of a large mimosa. We were not hungry; the constant anxiety had entirely destroyed all appetite. A cup of strong black coffee was the greatest luxury, and not requiring a tent in the clear still night, we were soon asleep on our simple *angareps*. Before daylight on the following morning the drum beat; the lazy soldiers, after stretching and yawning, began to load the animals, and we started at six o'clock. In these climates the rising of the sun is always dreaded. For about an hour before sunrise the air is deliciously cool and invigorating, but the sun is regarded as the common enemy. There is, nevertheless, a difficulty in starting before sunrise-the animals cannot be properly loaded in the darkness, and the operation being tedious, the cool hour of morning is always lost. The morning was clear, and the mountain of Belignan, within three or four miles, was a fine object to direct our course. I could distinctly see some enormous trees at the foot of the mountain near a village, and I hastened forward, as I hoped to procure a guide who would also act as interpreter, many of the natives in the vicinity of Gondokoro having learnt a little Arabic from the traders. We cantered on ahead of the party, regardless of the assurance of our unwilling men that the natives were not to be trusted, and we soon arrived beneath the shade of a cluster of most superb trees. The village was within a quarter of a mile, situated at the very base of the abrupt mountain; the natives seeing us alone had no fear, and soon thronged around us.

The chief understood a few words of Arabic, and I offered a large payment of copper bracelets and beads for a guide. After much discussion and bargaining, a bad-looking fellow offered to guide us to Ellyria, but no farther. This was about twenty-eight or thirty miles distant, and it was of vital importance that we should pass through that tribe before the trader's party should raise them against us. I had great hopes of outmarching them, as they would be delayed in Belignan by ivory transactions with the chief. While negotiations were pending with the guide, the trader's party appeared in the distance, and avoiding us, they halted on the opposite side of the village. I now tried conciliatory measures, and I sent my *vakeel* to their headman Ibrahim to talk with him confidentially, and to try to obtain an interpreter in return for a large present.

My *vakeel* was in an awkward position – he was afraid of me; also mortally afraid of the government in Khartoum; and frightened out of his life at his own men, whose conspiracy to desert he was well aware of. With the cunning of an Arab he started on his mission, accompanied by several of the men, including the arch-mutineer Bellaal. He shortly returned, saying, that it was perfectly impossible to proceed to the interior; that Ibrahim's party were outrageous at my having followed on their route; that he would neither give an interpreter, nor allow any of the natives to serve me; and that he would give orders to the great chief of Ellyria to prevent me from passing through his country. At that time the Turks were engaged in business transactions with the natives; it therefore was all important that I should start immediately, and by a forced march arrive at Ellyria, and get through the pass, before they should communicate with the chief. I had no doubt that, by paying black mail, I should be able to clear Ellyria, provided I was in advance of the Turks, but should they outmarch me there would be no hope; a fight and defeat would be the climax. I accordingly gave orders for an immediate start. "Load the camels, my brothers!" I exclaimed to the sullen ruffians around me; but not a man stirred except Richarn and a fellow named Sali, who began to show signs of improvement. Seeing that the men intended to disobey, I immediately set to work myself loading the animals, requesting my men not to trouble themselves, and begging them to lie down and smoke their pipes while I did the work. A few rose from the ground ashamed, and assisted to load the camels, while the others declared the impossibility of camels travelling by the road we were about to take, as the Turks had informed them that not even the donkeys could march through the thick jungles between Belignan and Ellyria.

"All right, my brothers!" I replied; "then we'll march as far as the donkeys can go, and leave both them and the baggage on the road when they can go no farther; but I go FORWARD."

With sullen discontent the men began to strap on their belts and cartouche boxes, and prepare for the start. The animals were loaded, and we moved slowly forward at 4:30 p.m. The country was lovely. The mountain of Belignan, although not exceeding 1,200 feet, is a fine mass of gneiss and syenite, ornamented in the hollows with fine trees, while the general appearance of the country at the base was that of a beautiful English park well timbered and beautified with distant mountains. We had just started with the Bari guide that I had engaged at Belignan, when we were suddenly joined by two of the Latookas whom I had seen when at Gondokoro, and to whom I had been very civil. It appeared that these fellows, who were acting as porters to the Turks, had been beaten, and had therefore absconded and joined me. This was extraordinary good fortune, as I now had guides the whole way to Latooka, about ninety miles distant. I immediately gave them each a copper bracelet and some beads, and they very good-naturedly relieved the camels of one hundred pounds of copper rings, which they carried in two baskets on their heads.

We now crossed the broad dry bed of a torrent, and the banks being steep, a considerable time was occupied in assisting the loaded animals in their descent. The donkeys were easily aided, their tails being held by two men, while they shuffled and slid down the sandy banks; but every camel fell, and the loads had to be carried up the opposite bank by the men, and the camels to be reloaded on arrival. Here again the donkeys had the advantage, as without being unloaded they were assisted up the steep ascent by two men in front pulling at their ears, while others pushed behind. Altogether, the donkeys were far more suitable for the country, as they were more easily loaded. I had arranged their packs and saddles so well, that they carried their loads with the greatest comfort. Each animal had an immense pad well stuffed with goats' hair; this reached from the shoulder to the hip-bones; upon this rested a simple form of saddle made of two forks of boughs inverted, and fastened together with rails – there were no nails in these saddles, all the fastenings being secured with thongs of raw hide. The great pad, projecting far both in front, behind, and also below the side of the saddle, prevented the loads from chafing the animal. Every donkey carried two large bags made of the hides of antelopes that I had formerly shot on the frontier of Abyssinia, and these were arranged with toggles on the one to fit into loops on the other, so that the loading and unloading was exceedingly simple. The success of an expedition depends mainly upon the perfection of the details, and where animals are employed for transport, the first consideration should be bestowed upon saddles and packs. The facility of loading is all important, and I now had an exemplification of its effect upon both animals and men; the latter began to abuse the camels and to curse the father of this, and the mother of that, because they had the trouble of unloading them for the descent into the river's bed, while the donkeys were blessed with the endearing name of "my brother," and alternately whacked with the stick. It was rather a bad commencement of a forced march, and the ravine we had crossed had been a cause of serious delay. Hardly were the animals reloaded and again ready for the march, when the men remembered that they had only one waterskin full. I had given orders before the start from Belignan that all should be filled. This is the unexceptional rule in African traveling: fill your *girbas* before starting. Never mind what the natives may tell you concerning the existence of water on the road; believe nothing; but resolutely determine to fill the girbas – should you find water, there is no harm done if you are already provided: but nothing can exceed the improvidence of the people. To avoid the trouble of filling the girbas before starting, the men will content themselves with *"Inshallah* (please God), we shall find water on the road," and they frequently endure the greatest suffering from sheer idleness in neglecting a supply.

They had in this instance persuaded themselves that the River we had just crossed would not be dry. Several of them had been employed in this country formerly, and because they had at one time found water in the sandy bed, they had concluded that it existed still. Accordingly they now wished to send parties to seek for water; this would entail a further delay, at a time when every minute was precious, as our fate depended upon reaching and passing through Ellyria before the arrival of the Turks. I was very anxious, and determined not to allow a moment's hesitation; I therefore insisted upon an immediate advance, and resolved to march without stopping throughout the night. The Latooka guides explained by signs that if we marched all night we should arrive at water on the following morning. This satisfied the men; and we started. For some miles we passed through a magnificent forest of large trees: the path being remarkably good, the march looked propitious – this good fortune, however, was doomed to change. We shortly entered upon thick thorny jungles; the path was so overgrown that the camels could scarcely pass under the overhanging branches, and the leather bags of provisions piled upon their backs were soon ripped by the hooked thorns of the mimosa – the salt, rice, and coffee bags all sprang leaks, and small streams of these important stores issued from the rents, which the men attempted to repair by stuffing dirty rags into the holes. These thorns were shaped like fish-hooks, thus it appeared that the perishable baggage must soon become an utter wreck, as the great strength and weight of the camels bore all before them, and sometimes tore the branches from the trees, the thorns becoming fixed in the leather bags. Meanwhile the donkeys walked along in comfort, being so short that they and their loads were below the branches.

I dreaded the approach of night. We were now at the foot of a range of high rocky hills, from which the torrents during the rainy season had torn countless ravines in their passage through the lower ground; we were marching parallel to the range at the very base, thus we met every ravine at right angles. Down tumbled a camel; and away rolled his load of bags, pots, pans, boxes, etc. into the bottom of a ravine in a confused ruin. Halt! And the camel had to be raised and helped up the opposite bank, while the late avalanche of luggage was carried piecemeal after him to be again adjusted. To avoid a similar catastrophe the remaining three camels had to be unloaded, and reloaded when safe upon the opposite bank. The operation of loading a camel with about 700 lbs. of luggage of indescribable variety is at all times tedious; but no sooner had we crossed one ravine with difficulty than we arrived at another, and the same fatiguing operation had to be repeated, with frightful loss of time at the moment when I believed the Turks were following on our path.

My wife and I rode about a quarter of a mile at the head of the party as an advance guard, to warn the caravan of any difficulty. The very nature of the country declared that it must be full of ravines, and yet I could not help hoping against hope that we might have a clear mile of road without a break. The evening had passed, and the light faded. What had been difficult and tedious during the day, now became most serious; we could not see the branches of hooked thorns that overhung the broken path; I rode in advance, my face and arms bleeding with countless scratches, while at each rip of a thorn I gave a warning shout – "Thorn!" – for those behind, and a cry of "Hole!" for any deep rut that lay in the path. It was fortunately moonlight, but the jungle was so thick that the narrow track was barely perceptible; thus both camels and donkeys ran against the trunks of trees, smashing the luggage, and breaking all that could be broken; nevertheless, the case was urgent; march we must, at all hazards.

My heart sank whenever we came to a deep ravine, or *hor*; the warning cry of "Halt!" told those in the rear that once more the camels must be unloaded, and the same fatiguing operation must be repeated. For hours we marched: the moon was sinking; the path, already dark, grew darker; the animals, overloaded even for a good road, were tired out; and the men were disheartened, thirsty, and disgusted. I dismounted from my horse and loaded him with sacks, to relieve a camel that was perfectly done – but on we marched. Every one was silent; the men were too tired to speak; and through the increasing gloom we crept slowly forward Suddenly another ravine, but not so deep; and we trusted that the camels might cross it without the necessity of unloading; down went the leading camel, rolling completely over with his load to the bottom. Now, the boy Saat was the drummer; but being very tired, he had come to the conclusion that the drum would travel quite as easily upon a camel's back as upon his shoulders; he had accordingly slung it upon the very camel that had now performed a somersault and solo on the drum. The musical instrument was picked up in the shape of a flat dish, and existed no longer as a drum, every note having been squeezed out of it. The donkey is a much more calculating animal than the camel, the latter being an excessively stupid beast, while the former is remarkably clever – at least I can answer for the ability of the Egyptian species. The expression "what an ass" is in Europe supposed to be slightly insulting, but a comparison with the Egyptian variety would be a compliment. Accordingly my train of donkeys, being calculating and reasoning creatures, had from thus night's experience come to the conclusion that the journey was long; that the road was full of ravines; that the camels who led the way would assuredly tumble into these ravines unless unloaded; and that as the reloading at each ravine would occupy at least half an hour, it would be wise for them (the donkeys) to employ that time in going to sleep – therefore, as it was just as cheap to lie down as to stand, they preferred a recumbent posture, and a refreshing roll upon the sandy ground. Accordingly, whenever the word "halt" was given, the clever donkeys thoroughly understood their advantage, and the act of unloading a camel on arrival at a ravine was a signal sufficient to induce each of twenty-one donkeys to lie down. It was in vain that the men beat and swore at them to keep them on their legs; the donkeys were determined, and lie down they would. This obstinacy on their part was serious to the march – every time that they lay down they shifted their loads; some of the most wilful persisted in rolling, and of course upset their packs. There were only seventeen men, and these were engaged in assisting the camels; thus the twenty-one donkeys had it all their own way; and what added to the confusion was the sudden cry of hyenas in close proximity, which so frightened the donkeys that they immediately sprang to their feet, with their packs lying discomfited, entangled among their legs. Thus, no sooner were the camels reloaded on the other side of the ravine, than all the donkeys had to undergo the same operation; during which time the camels, however stupid, having observed the donkeys' dodge, took the opportunity of lying down also, and necessarily shifted their loads. The women were therefore ordered to hold the camels, to prevent them from lying down while the donkeys were being reloaded; but the women were dead tired, as they had been carrying loads; they themselves laid down, and it being dark, they were not observed until a tremendous scream was heard, and we found that a camel had lain down on the top of a woman who had been placed to watch it, but who had herself fallen asleep. The camel was with difficulty raised, and the woman dragged from beneath. Everything was tired out. I had been working like a slave to assist, and to cheer the men; I was also fatigued. We had marched from 4:30 p.m. – it was now 1 a.m.; we had thus been eight hours and a half struggling along the path. The moon had sunk, and the complete darkness rendered a further advance impossible; I therefore, on arrival at a large plateau of rock, ordered the animals to be unloaded, and both man and beast to rest. The people had no water; I had a girba full for Mrs. Baker and myself, which was always slung on my saddle; this precaution I never neglected.

The men were hungry. Before leaving Gondokoro I had ordered a large quantity of *kisra*s (black pancakes) to be prepared for the march, and they were packed in a basket that had been carried on a camel; unfortunately Mrs. Baker's pet monkey had been placed upon the same camel, and he had amused himself during the night's march by feasting and filling his cheeks with the *kisra*s, and throwing the remainder away when his hunger was satisfied. There literally was not a *kisra* remaining in the basket.

Every one lay down supperless to sleep. Although tired, I could not rest until I had arranged some plan for the morrow. It was evident that we could not travel over so rough a country with the animals thus overloaded; therefore determined to leave in the jungle such articles as could be dispensed with, and to rearrange all the loads.

At 4 a.m. I woke, and lighting a lamp, I tried in vain to wake any of the men who lay stretched upon the ground, like so many corpses, sound asleep. At length Saat sat up, and after rubbing his eyes for about ten minutes, he made a fire, and began to boil the coffee; meanwhile I was hard at work lightening the ship. I threw away about 100 lbs. of salt; divided the heavy ammunition more equally among the animals; rejected a quantity of odds and ends that, although most useful, could be forsaken; and by the time the men woke, a little before sunrise, I had completed the work. We now reloaded the animals, who showed the improvement by stepping out briskly. We marched well for three hours at a pace that bid fair to keep us well ahead of the Turks, and at length we reached the dry bed of a stream, where the Latooka guides assured us we should obtain water by digging. This proved correct; but the holes were dug deep in several places, and hours passed before we could secure a sufficient supply for all the men and animals. The great sponging-bath was excessively useful, as it formed a reservoir out of which all the animals could drink.

While we were thus engaged some natives appeared carrying with them the head of a wild boar in a horrible state of decomposition, and alive with maggots. On arrival at the drinking-place they immediately lighted a fire, and proceeded to cook their savoury pork by placing it in the flames. The skull becoming too hot for the inmates, crowds of maggots rushed pele-mele from the ears and nostrils like people escaping from the doors of a theatre on fire. The natives merely tapped the skull with a stick to assist in their exit, and proceeded with their cooking until completed; after which they ate the whole, and sucked the bones. However putrid meat may be, it does not appear to affect the health of these people.

My animals requiring rest and food, I was obliged to wait unwillingly until 4:30 p.m. The natives having finished their boar's head, offered to join us; and accordingly we rode on a considerable distance ahead of our people with our active guides, while the caravan followed slowly behind us. After ascending for about a mile through jungle, we suddenly emerged upon an eminence, and looked down upon the valley of Tollogo. This was extremely picturesque. An abrupt wall of grey granite rose on the east side of the valley to a height of about a thousand feet: from this perpendicular wall huge blocks had fallen, strewing the base with a confused mass of granite lumps ten to forty feet in diameter; and among these natural fortresses of disjointed masses were numerous villages. The bottom of the valley was a meadow, in which grew several enormous fig trees by the side of a sluggish, and in some places stagnant, brook. The valley was not more than half a mile wide, and was also walled in by mountains on the west, having the appearance of a vast street.

We were now about a mile ahead of our party; but accompanied by our two Latooka guides, and upon descending to the valley and crossing a deep gully, we soon arrived beneath a large fig tree at the extremity of the vale. No sooner was our presence observed than crowds of natives issued from the numerous villages among the rocks, and surrounded us. They were all armed with bows and arrows and lances, and were very excited at seeing the horses, which to them were unknown animals. Dismounting, I fastened the horses to a bush, and we sat down on the grass under a tree.

There were five or six hundred natives pressing round us. They were excessively noisy, hallooing to us as though we were deaf, simply because we did not understand them. Finding that they were pressing rudely around us, I made signs to them to stand off; when at that moment a curiously ugly, short, humped-back fellow came forward and addressed me in broken Arabic. I was delighted to find an interpreter, and requesting him to tell the crowd to stand back, I inquired for their chief. The humpback spoke very little Arabic, nor did the crowd appear to heed him, but they immediately stole a spear that one of my Latooka guides had placed against the tree under which we were sitting. It was getting rather unpleasant; but having my revolver and a double-barrelled rifle in my hands, there was no fear of their being stolen.

In reply to a question to the humpback, he asked me who I was. I explained that I was a traveller. "You want ivory?" he said. "No," I answered, "it is of no use to me." "Ah, you want slaves!" he replied. "Neither do I want slaves," I answered. This was followed by a burst of laughter from the crowd, and the humpback continued his examination. "Have you got plenty of cows?" "Not one; but plenty of beads and copper." "Plenty? Where are they?" "Not far off; they will be here presently with my men," and I pointed to the direction from which they would arrive. "What countryman are you?" "An Englishman." He had never heard of such people. "You are a Turk?" "All right," I replied; "I am anything you like." "And that is your son (pointing at Mrs. Baker)?" "No, she is my wife." "Your wife! What a lie! He is a boy." "Not a bit of it," I replied; "she is my wife, who has come with me to see the women of this country." "What a lie!" he again politely re-joined in the one expressive Arabic word, "*katab*." After this charmingly frank conversation he addressed the crowd, explaining, I suppose, that I was endeavouring to pass off a boy for a woman. Mrs. Baker was dressed similarly to myself, in a pair of loose trousers and gaiters, with a blouse and belt – the only difference being that she wore long sleeves, while my arms were bare from a few inches below the shoulder. I always kept my arms bare, as being cooler than if covered.

The curiosity of the crowd was becoming impertinent, when at an opportune moment the chief appeared. To my astonishment I recognised him as a man who had often visited me at Gondokoro, to whom I had given many presents without knowing his position.

In a few moments he drove away the crowd, screaming and gesticulating at there as though greatly insulted; re serving the humpback as interpreter, he apologized for the rudeness of his people. Just at this instant I perceived, in the distance, the English flag leading the caravan of camels and donkeys from the hillside into the valley, and my people and baggage shortly arrived. The chief now brought me a large pumpkin-shell containing about a gallon of *merissa*, which was most refreshing. He also brought a gourd-bottle full of honey, and an elephant's tusk; the latter I declined, as ivory was not required.

We were now within six miles of Ellyria, and by means of the humpback I explained to Tombe, the chief, that we wished to start the first thing in the morning, and that I would engage the humpback as interpreter. This was agreed upon, and I now had hopes of getting through Ellyria before the arrival of the Turks. My caravan having arrived, the interest first bestowed upon the horses, as being a new kind of animal, was now transferred to the camels. The natives crowded round them, exclaiming, "that they were the giraffes of our country." They were amazed at the loads that they carried, and many assisted in unloading.

I noticed, however, that they stuck their fingers through the baskets to investigate the contents; and when they perceived twenty baskets full of beads, and many of copper bracelets – the jingling of which betrayed the contents – they became rather too eager in lending a helping hand; therefore I told the chief to order his men to retire while I opened one bag of beads to give him a present. I had a bag always in reserve that contained a variety of beads and bracelets, which obviated the necessity of opening one of the large baskets on the road. I accordingly made the chief happy, and also gave a present to the humpback. The crowd now discovered an object of fresh interest, and a sudden rush was made to the monkey, which, being one of the red variety from Abyssinia, was quite unknown to them. The monkey, being far more civilized than these naked savages, did not at all enjoy their society; and attacking the utterly unprotected calves of their legs, Wallady soon kept his admirers at a distance, and amused himself by making insulting grimaces, which kept the crowd in a roar of laughter. I often found this monkey of great use in diverting the attention of the savages from myself. He was also a guarantee of my peaceful intentions, as no one intending hostility would travel about with a monkey as one of the party. He was so tame and affectionate to both of us that he was quite unhappy if out of sight of his mistress: but he frequently took rough liberties with the blacks, for whom he had so great an aversion and contempt that he would have got into sad trouble at Exeter Hall. Wallady had no idea of a naked savage being a man and a brother.

That night we slept soundly, both men and beasts being thoroughly fatigued. The natives seemed to be aware of this, and a man was caught in the act of stealing copper bracelets from a basket. He had crept like a cat upon hands and knees to the spot where the luggage was piled, and the sleepy sentry bad not observed him.

There was no drum-call on the following morning, that useful instrument having been utterly smashed by the camel; but I woke the men early, and told them to be most careful in arranging the loads securely, as we had to thread the rocky pass between Tollogo and Ellyria. I felt sure that the Turks could not be far behind us, and I looked forward with anxiety to getting through the pass before them.

The natives of both Tollogo and Ellyria are the same in appearance and language as the Bari; they are very brutal in manner, and they collected in large crowds on our departure, with by no means a friendly aspect. Many of them ran on ahead under the base of the rocks, apparently to give notice at Ellyria of our arrival. I had three men as an advance guard, – five or six in the rear, – while the remainder drove the animals. Mrs. Baker and I rode on horseback at the head of the party. On arriving at the extremity of the narrow valley we had to thread our way through the difficult pass. The mountain of Ellyria, between two and three thousand feet high, rose abruptly on our left, while the base was entirely choked with enormous fragments of grey granite that, having fallen from the face of the mountain, had completely blocked the pass. Even the horses had great difficulty in threading their way through narrow alleys formed of opposing blocks, and it appeared impossible for loaded camels to proceed. The path was not only thus obstructed, but was broken by excessively deep ravines formed by the torrents that during the rains tore everything before them in their impetuous descent from the mountains. To increase the difficulties of the pass many trees and bushes were growing from the interstices of the rocks; thus in places where the long legs of the camels could have cleared a narrow cleft, the loads became jammed between the trees. These trees were for the most part intensely hard wood, a species of *lignum vitae*, called by the Arabs "babanoose," and were quite proof against our axes. Had the natives been really hostile they could have exterminated us in five minutes, as it was only necessary to hurl rocks from above to insure our immediate destruction. It was in this spot that a trader's party of 126 men, well armed, had been massacred to a man the year previous.

Bad as the pass was, we had hope before us, as the Latookas explained that beyond this spot there was level and unbroken ground the whole way to Latooka. Could we only clear Ellyria before the Turks I had no fear for the present; but at the very moment when success depended upon speed, we were thus baffled by the difficulties of the ground. I therefore resolved to ride on in advance of my party, leaving them to overcome the difficulties of the pass by constantly unloading the animals, while I would reconnoitre in front, as Ellyria was not far distant. My wife and I accordingly rode on, accompanied only by one of the Latookas as a guide. After turning a sharp angle of the mountain, leaving the cliff abruptly rising to the left from the narrow path, we descended a ravine worse than any place we had previously encountered, and we were obliged to dismount, in order to lead our horses up the steep rocks on the opposite side. On arrival on the summit, a lovely view burst upon us. The valley of Ellyria was about four hundred feet below, at about a mile distant. Beautiful mountains, some two or three thousand feet high, of grey granite, walled in the narrow vale; while the landscape of forest and plain was bounded at about fifty or sixty miles' distance to the east by the blue mountains of Latooka. The mountain of Ellyria was the commencement of the fine range that continued indefinitely to the south. We were now in the very gorge of that chain. Below us, in the valley, I observed some prodigious trees growing close to a Hor (ravine), in which was running water, and the sides of the valley under the mountains being as usual a mass of debris of huge detached rocks, were thronged with villages, all strongly fortified with thick bamboo palisades. The whole country was a series of natural forts, occupied by a large population.

A glance at the scene before me was quite sufficient; to fight a way through a valley a quarter of a mile wide, hemmed in by high walls of rock and bristling with lances and arrows, would be impossible with my few men, encumbered by transport animals. Should the camels arrive, I could march into Myria in twenty minutes, make the chief a large present, and pass on without halting until I cleared the Ellyria valley. At any rate I was well before the Turks, and the forced march at night, however distressing, had been successful. The great difficulty now lay in the ravine that we had just crossed; this would assuredly delay the caravan for a considerable time.

Tying our horses to a bush, we sat upon a rock beneath the shade of a small tree within ten paces of the path, and considered the best course to pursue. I hardly liked to risk an advance into Ellyria alone, before the arrival of my whole party, as we had been very rudely received by the Tollogo people on the previous evening; nevertheless I thought it might be good policy to ride unattended into Ellyria, and thus to court an introduction to the chief. However, our consultation ended in a determination to wait where we then were, until the caravan should have accomplished the last difficulty by crossing the ravine; when we would all march into Ellyria in company. For a long time we sat gazing at the valley before us in which our fate lay hidden, feeling thankful that we had thus checkmated the brutal Turks. Not a sound was heard of our approaching camels; the delay was most irksome.

There were many difficult places that we had passed through, and each would be a source of serious delay to the animals. At length we heard them in the distance. We could distinctly hear the men's voices; and we rejoiced that they were approaching the last remaining obstacle; that one ravine passed through, and all before would be easy. I heard the rattling of the stones as they drew nearer; and, looking towards the ravine, I saw emerge from the dark foliage of the trees within fifty yards of us the hated red flag and crescent, leading the Turks' party! We were outmarched! One by one, with scowling looks, the insolent scoundrels filed by us within a few feet, without making the customary salaam; neither noticing us in any way, except by threatening to shoot the Latooka, our guide, who had formerly accompanied them.

Their party consisted of a hundred and forty men armed with guns; while about twice as many Latookas acted as porters, carrying beads, ammunition, and the general effects of the party. It appeared that we were hopelessly beaten.

However, I determined to advance, at all hazards, on the arrival of my party; and should the Turks incite the Ellyria tribe to attack us, I intended, in the event of a fight, to put the first shot through the leader.

To be thus beaten, at the last moment, was unendurable. Boiling with indignation as the insolent wretches filed past, treating me with the contempt of a dog, I longed for the moment of action, no matter what were the odds against us. At length their leader, Ibrahim, appeared in the rear of the party. He was riding on a donkey, being the last of the line, behind the flag that closed the march.

I never saw a more atrocious countenance than that exhibited in this man. A mixed breed, between a Turk sire and Arab mother, he had the good features and bad qualities of either race. The fine, sharp, high-arched nose and large nostril; the pointed and projecting chin; rather high cheek-bones and prominent brow, overhanging a pair of immense black eyes full of expression of all evil. As he approached he took no notice of us, but studiously looked straight before him with the most determined insolence.

The fate of the expedition was, at this critical moment, retrieved by Mrs. Baker. She implored me to call him, to insist upon a personal explanation, and to offer him some present in the event of establishing amicable relations. I could not condescend to address the sullen scoundrel. He was in the act of passing us, and success depended upon that instant. Mrs. Baker herself called him. For the moment he made no reply; but, upon my repeating the call in a loud key, he turned his donkey towards us and dismounted. I ordered him to sit down, as his men were ahead and we were alone.

The following dialogue passed between us after the usual Arab mode of greeting. I said, "Ibrahim, why should we be enemies in the midst of this hostile country? We believe in the same God, why should we quarrel in this land of heathens, who believe in no God? You have your work to perform; I have mine. You want ivory; I am a simple traveller; why should we clash? If I were offered the whole ivory of the country, I would not accept a single tusk, nor interfere with you in any way. Transact your business, and don't interfere with me: the country is wide enough for us both. I have a task before me, to reach a great lake – the head of the Nile. Reach it I will (*Inshallah*). No power shall drive me back. If you are hostile, I will imprison you in Khartoum; if you assist me, I will reward you far beyond any reward you have ever received. Should I be killed in this country, you will be suspected; you know the result; the government would hang you on the bare suspicion. On the contrary, if you are friendly, I will use my influ3ence in any country that I discover, that you may procure its ivory for the sake of your master Koorshid, who was generous to Captains Speke and Grant, and kind to me. Should you be hostile, I shall hold your master responsible as your employer. Should you assist me, I will befriend you both. Choose your course frankly, like a man – friend or enemy?"

Before he had time to reply, Mrs. Baker addressed him much in the same strain, telling him that he did not know what Englishmen were; that nothing would drive them back; that the British government watched over them wherever they might be, and that no outrage could be committed with impunity upon a British subject. That I would not deceive him in any way; that I was not a trader; and that I should be able to assist him materially by discovering new countries rich in ivory, and that he would benefit himself personally by civil conduct.

He seemed confused, and wavered. I immediately promised him a new double-barrelled gun and some gold, when my party should arrive, as an earnest of the future.

He replied, that he did not himself wish to be hostile, but that all the trading parties, without one exception, were against me, and that the men were convinced that I was a consul in disguise, who would report to the authorities at Khartoum all the proceedings of the traders. He continued that he believed me, but that his men would not; that all people told lies in their country, therefore no one was credited for the truth. "However," said he, "do not associate with my people, or they may insult you, but go and take possession of that large tree (pointing to one in the valley of Ellyria) for yourself and people, and I will come there and speak with you. I will now join my men, as I do not wish them to know that I have been conversing with you." He then made a salaam, mounted his donkey, and rode off.

I had won him. I knew the Arab character so thoroughly that I was convinced that the tree he had pointed out, followed by the words, "I will come there and speak to you," was to be the rendezvous for the receipt of the promised gun and money.

I did not wait for the arrival of my men, but, mounting our horses, my wife and I rode down the hillside with lighter spirits than we had enjoyed for some time past; I gave her the entire credit of the ruse. Had I been alone, I should have been too proud to have sought the friendship of the sullen trader, and the moment on which success depended would have been lost.

On arrival at the grassy plain at the foot of the mountain, there was a crowd of the trader's ruffians quarrelling for the shade of a few large trees that grew on the banks of the stream. We accordingly dismounted, and turning the horses to graze, we took possession of a tree at some distance, under which a number of Latookas were already sitting. Not being very particular as to our society, we sat down and waited for the arrival of our party. The valley of Ellyria was a lovely spot in the very bosom of the mountains. Close to where we sat were the great masses of rock that had fallen from the cliffs, and upon examination I found them to be the finest quality of grey granite, the feldspar being in masses several inches square and as hard as a flint. There was no scaling upon the surface, as is common in granite rocks.

No sooner had the trader's party arrived than crowds of natives issued from the palisaded villages on the mountain; and descending to the plain, they mingled with the general confusion. The baggage was piled beneath a tree, and a sentry placed on guard.

The natives were entirely naked, and precisely the same as the Bari. Their chief, Legge, was among them, and received a present from Ibrahim of a long red cotton shirt, and he assumed an air of great importance. Ibrahim explained to him who I was, and he immediately came to ask for the tribute he expected to receive as blackmail for the right of entree into his country. Of all the villanous countenances that I have ever seen, that of Legge excelled.

Ferocity, avarice, and sensuality were stamped upon his face, and I immediately requested him to sit for his portrait, and in about ten minutes I succeeded in placing within my portfolio an exact likeness of about the greatest rascal that exists in Central Africa.

I had, now the satisfaction of seeing my caravan slowly winding down the hillside in good order, having surmounted all their difficulties.

Upon arrival, my men were perfectly astonished at seeing us so near the trader's party, and still more confounded at my sending for Ibrahim to summon him to my tree, where I presented him with some English sovereigns, and a double-barrelled gun. Nothing escapes the inquisitiveness of these Arabs; and the men of both parties quickly perceived that I had established an alliance in some unaccountable manner with Ibrahim. I saw the gun, lately presented to him, being handed from one to the other for examination; and both my *vakeel* and men appeared utterly confused at the sudden change.

The chief of Ellyria now came to inspect my luggage, and demanded fifteen heavy copper bracelets and a large quantity of beads. The bracelets most in demand are simple rings of copper five-eighths of an inch thick, and weighing about a pound; those of smaller size not being so much valued. I gave him fifteen such rings, and about ten pounds of beads in varieties, the red coral porcelain (*dimiriaf*) being the most acceptable. Legge was by no means satisfied: he said his belly was very big and it must be filled, which signified, that his desire was great and must be gratified. I accordingly gave him a few extra copper rings; but suddenly he smelt spirits, one of the few bottles that I possessed of spirits of wine having broken in the medicine chest. Ibrahim begged me to give him a bottle to put him in a good humour, as he enjoyed nothing so much as *araki*; I accordingly gave him a pint bottle of the strongest spirits of wine. To my amazement he broke off the neck, and holding his head well back, he deliberately allowed the whole of the contents to trickle down his throat as innocently as though it had been simple water. He was thoroughly accustomed to it, as the traders were in the habit of bringing him presents of araki every season. He declared this to be excellent, and demanded another bottle. At that moment a violent storm of thunder and rain burst upon us with a fury well known in the tropics; the rain fell like a waterspout, and the throng immediately fled for shelter. So violent was the storm, that not a man was to be seen: some were sheltering themselves under the neighbouring rocks; while others ran to their villages that were close by; the trader's people commenced a fusilade, firing off all their guns lest they should get wet and miss fire. I could not help thinking how completely they were at the mercy of the natives at that moment, had they chosen to attack them; the trader's party were lying under their untanned ox-hides with their empty guns.

Each of my men was provided with a piece of mackintosh, with which his gunlocks were secured. We lay upon an *angarep* covered with a bull's hide until the storm was over. The thunder was magnificent, exploding on the peak of the mountain exactly above us, and in the course of a quarter of an hour torrents were rushing down the ravines among the rocks, the effects of the violent storm that had passed away as rapidly as it had arrived.

No sooner had it ceased than the throng again appeared. Once more the chief, Legge, was before us begging for all that we had. Although the natives asked for beads, they would give nothing in exchange, and we could purchase nothing for any article except *molotes*. These iron hoes are made principally in this country: thus it appeared strange that they should demand them. Legge does a large business with these hoes, sending them into the Berri and Galla countries to the east, with various beads and copper bracelets, to purchase ivory. Although there are very few elephants in the neighbourhood of Ellyria, there is an immense amount of ivory, as the chief is so great a trader that he accumulates it to exchange with the Turks for cattle. Although he sells it so dear that he demands twenty cows for a large tusk, it is a convenient station for the traders, as, being near to Gondokoro, there is very little trouble in delivering the ivory on shipboard.

Although I had presented Legge with what he desired, he would give nothing in return, neither would he sell either goats or fowls; in fact, no provision was procurable except honey. I purchased about eight pounds of this luxury for a hoe. My men were starving, and I was obliged to serve them out rice from my sacred stock, as I had nothing else to give them. This they boiled and mixed with honey, and they were shortly sitting round an immense circular bowl of this rarity, enjoying themselves thoroughly, but nevertheless grumbling as usual. In the coolest manner possible the great and greedy chief, Legge, who had refused to give or even to sell anything to keep us from starving, no sooner saw the men at their novel repast than he sat down among them and almost choked himself by cramming handfuls of the hot rice and honey into his mouth, which yawned like that of an old hippopotamus. The men did not at all approve of this assistance, but as it is the height of bad manners in Arab etiquette to repel a self-invited guest from the general meal, he was not interfered with, and was thus enabled to swallow the share of about three persons.

Legge, although worse than the rest of his tribe, had a similar formation of head. The Bari and those Tollogo and Ellyria have generally bullet-shaped heads, low foreheads, skulls heavy behind the ears and above the nape of the neck: altogether their appearance is excessively brutal, and they are armed with bows six feet long and arrows horribly barbed and poisoned.

Chapter V

LEAVE ELLYRIA

Although Ellyria was a rich and powerful country, we had not been able to procure any provisions – the natives refused to sell, and their general behaviour was such that assured me of their capability of any atrocity had they been prompted to attack us by the Turks. Fortunately we had a good supply of meal that had been prepared for the journey prior to our departure from Gondokoro: thus we could not starve. I also had a sack of corn for the animals, a necessary precaution, as at this season there was not a blade of grass; all in the vicinity of the route having been burnt.

We started on the 30th March, at 7:30 a.m., and opened from the valley of Ellyria upon a perfectly flat country interspersed with trees. After an hour's march we halted at a small stream of bad water. We had *kisra*s and honey for breakfast; but, for several days not having tasted meat, I took the rifle for a stroll through the forest in search of game. After an hour's ramble I returned without having fired a shot. I had come upon fresh tracks of Tetel ("hartebeest") and guinea fowl, but they had evidently come down to the stream to drink, and had wandered back into the interior. If game was scarce, fruit was plentiful – both Richarn and I were loaded with a species of yellow plum as large as an egg; these grew in prodigious numbers upon fine forest trees, beneath which the ground was yellow with the quantities that had fallen from the boughs; these were remarkably sweet, and yet acid, with much juice, and a very delicious flavour.

At 11:25 we again started for a long march, our course being east. The ground was most favourable for the animals, being perfectly flat and free from ravines. We accordingly stepped along at a brisk pace, and the intense heat of the sun throughout the hottest hours of the day made the journey fatiguing for all but the camels. The latter were excellent of their class, and now far excelled the other transport animals, marching along with ease under loads of about 600 lbs. each.

My caravan was at the rear of the trader's party; but the ground being good, we left our people and cantered on to the advanced flag. It was curious to witness the motley assemblage in single file extending over about half a mile of ground: – several of the people were mounted on donkeys; some on oxen: the most were on foot, including all the women to the number of about sixty, who were the slaves of the trader's people. These carried heavy loads; and many, in addition to the burdens, carried children strapped to their backs in leather slings.

After four or five hours' march during the intense heat many of the overloaded women showed symptoms of distress, and became footsore; the grass having been recently burnt had left the sharp charred stumps, which were very trying to those whose sandals were not in the best condition. The women were forced along by their brutal owners with sharp blows of the *coorbatch*; and one who was far advanced in pregnancy could at length go no farther. Upon this the savage to whom she belonged belaboured her with a large stick, and not succeeding in driving her before him, he knocked her down and jumped upon her. The woman's feet were swollen and bleeding, but later in the day again saw her hobbling along in the rear by the aid a bamboo.

The traders march in good form; one flag leads the party, guarded by eight or ten men, while a native carries a box of five hundred cartridges for their use in case of an attack. The porters and baggage follow in single file, soldiers being at intervals to prevent them from running away; in which case the runner is invariably fired at The supply of ammunition is in the centre, carried generally by about fifteen natives, and strongly escorted by guards. The rear of the party is closed by another flag behind which no straggler is permitted. The rear flag is also guarded by six or eight men, with a box of spare ammunition. With these arrangements the party is always ready to support an attack.

Ibrahim, my new ally, was now riding in front of the line, carrying on his saddle before him a pretty little girl, his daughter, a child of a year and a half old; her mother, a remarkably pretty Bari girl, one of his numerous wives, was riding behind him on an ox. We soon got into conversation; a few pieces of sugar given to the child and mother by Mrs. Baker was a sweet commencement; and Ibrahim then told me to beware of my own men, as he knew they did not intend to remain with me; that they were a different tribe from his men, and they would join Chenooda's people and desert me on our arrival at their station in Latooka. This was a corroboration of all I had heard previous to leaving Gondokoro, therefore I had the promised mutiny in perspective. I had noticed that my men were even more sullen than usual since I had joined Ibrahim; however, I succeeded in convincing him that he would benefit so decidedly by an alliance with me, that he now frankly told me that I should receive no opposition from his party. So far all had prospered beyond my most sanguine expectations. We were fairly launched upon our voyage, and now that we were in the wild interior, I determined to crush the mutiny with an iron hand should the rascals attempt to carry their murderous threats into execution. Two or three of the men appeared willing, but the original ringleader, Bellaal, would literally do nothing, not even assisting at loading the animals; but swaggering about with the greatest insolence.

After a fatiguing march of eight hours and ten minutes through a perfectly flat country interspersed with trees, we halted at a little well of excessively bad water at 7:35 p.m. The horses were so much in advance that the main party did not arrive until 11 p.m. completely fatigued. The night being fine, we slept on a hillock of sand a few yards from the well, rejoiced to be away from the mosquitoes of Gondokoro.

On the following morning we started at sunrise, and in two hours' fast marching we arrived at the Kanieti River Although there had been no rain, the stream was very rapid and up to the girths of the horses at the ford. The banks were very abrupt and about fifteen feet deep, the bed between forty and fifty yards wide; thus a considerable volume of water is carried down to the river Sobat by this river during the rains. The whole drainage of the country, tends to the east, and accordingly flows into the Sobat.

The range of mountains running south from Ellyria is the watershed between the east and west drainage; the Sobat receiving it on the one hand, and the White Nile on the other, while the Nile eventually receives the entire flow by the Sobat, as previously mentioned, in lat. 9 degrees 22 minutes. Having scrambled up the steep bank of the Kanieti River, we crossed a large field of dhurra, and arrived at the village of Wakkala. The village, or town, is composed of about seven hundred houses, the whole being most strongly protected by a system of palisades formed of *babanoose*, the hard ironwood of the country. Not only is it thus fortified, but the palisades are also protected by a hedge of impervious thorns that grow to a height of about twenty feet. The entrance to this fort is a curious archway, about ten feet deep, formed of the iron-wood palisades, with a sharp turn to the right and left forming a zigzag. The whole of the village thus fenced is situated in the midst of a splendid forest of large timber. The inhabitants of Wakkala are the same as the Ellyria, but governed by an independent chief. They are great hunters; and as we arrived I saw several parties returning from the forest with portions of wild boar and buffalo. From Gondokoro to this spot I had not seen a single head of game, but the immediate neighbourhood of Wakkala was literally trodden down by the feet of elephants, giraffes, buffaloes, rhinoceros, and varieties of large antelopes.

Having examined the village, I ordered my people to unload the animals in the forest about a quarter of a mile from the entrance. The soil was extremely rich, and the ground being shaded from the scorching rays of the sun by the large trees, there was abundance of fine grass, which accounted for the presence of the game: good pasturage, extensive forests, and a plentiful supply of water insuring the supply of wild animals.

In a few minutes my horses and donkeys were luxuriating on the rich herbage, not having tasted grass for some days; the camels revelled in the foliage of the dark green mimosas; and the men, having found on the march a buffalo that had been caught in a trap and there killed by a lion, obtained some meat, and the whole party were feeding. We had formed a kind of arbour by hacking out with a sabre a delightful shady nook in the midst of a dense mass of creepers, and there we feasted upon a couple of roast fowls that we had procured from the natives for glass beads. This was the first meat we had tasted since we had quitted Gondokoro.

At 5:10 p.m. we left this delightful spot, and marched. Emerging from the forest we broke upon a beautiful plain of fine low grass, bounded on our right hand by jungle. This being the cool hour of evening, the plain was alive with game, including buffaloes, zebras, and many varieties of large antelopes. It was a most enlivening sight to see them scouring over the plain as we advanced; but our large party, and three red flags streaming in the breeze, effectually prevented us from getting sufficiently near for a shot.

I was sorely tempted to remain in this Elysium for a few days' shooting, but the importance of an advance was too great to permit of any thoughts of amusement; thus, I could only indulge a sportsman's feelings by feasting my eyes upon the beautiful herds before me.

At a quarter past seven we bivouacked in thick jungle. In the middle of the night, the watch-fires still blazing, I was awoke by a great noise, and upon arrival at the spot I found a number of the Turks with firebrands, searching upon the ground, which was literally strewed with beads and copper bracelets. The Latooka porters had broken open the bags and baskets containing many hundredweight of these objects, and, loading themselves, had intended to desert with their stolen prize; but the sentries having discovered them, they were seized by the soldiers.

There fellows, the Latookas, had exhibited the folly of monkeys in so rashly breaking open the packages while the sentries were on guard. Several who had been caught in the act were now pinioned by the Turks, and were immediately condemned to be shot; while others were held down upon the ground and well chastised with the *coorbatch* I begged that the punishment of death might be commuted for a good flogging; at first I implored in vain, until I suggested, that if the porters were shot, there would be no one to carry their loads: – this practical argument saved them, and after receiving a severe thrashing, their arms were pinioned, and a guard set over them until the morning.

We marched at 5:25 on the following morning. For several hours the path led through thick jungle in which we occasionally caught glimpses of antelopes. At length quitting the jungle we arrived at an open marshy plain, upon which I discerned at a great distance a number of antelopes. Having nothing to eat I determined to stalk them, as I heard from the people that we were not far from our halting-place for the day.

Accordingly I left Mrs. Baker with my horse and a spare rifle to wait, while the party marched straight on; I intended to make a circuit through the jungle and to wait for the entrance of the herd, which she was to drive, by simply riding through the plain and leading my horse; she was to bring the horse to me should I fire a shot. After walking for about a mile in the jungle parallel with the plain, I saw the herd of about two hundred Tetel going at full gallop from the open ground into the jungle, having been alarmed by the red bags and the Turks, who had crossed over the marsh. So shy were these antelopes that there was no possibility of stalking them. I noticed however that there were several waterbucks in the very centre of the marsh, and that two or three trees afforded the possibility of a stalk. Having the wind all right, I succeeded in getting to a tree within about two hundred and fifty yards of the largest buck, and lying down in a dry trench that in the wet season formed a brook, I crept along the bottom until I reached a tall tuft of grass that was to be my last point of cover. Just as I raised myself slowly from the trench I found the buck watching me most attentively. A steady shot with my little No. 24 rifle took no effect-it was too high: the buck did not even notice the shot, which was, I suppose, the first he had ever heard;-he was standing exactly facing me; this is at all tines an unpleasant position for a shot. Seeing that he did not seem disposed to move, I reloaded without firing my left-hand barrel. I now allowed for the high range of the last shot; a moment after the report he sprang into the air, then fell upon his knees and galloped off on three legs; one of the fore-legs being broken. I had heard the sharp sound of the bullet, but the shot was not very satisfactory. Turning to look for my horse, I saw Mrs. Baker galloping over the plain towards me, leading Filfil, while Richard ran behind at his best speed.

Upon her arrival I mounted Filfil, who was a fast horse, and with my little No. 24 rifle in my hand I rode slowly towards the wounded waterbuck, who was now standing watching us at about a quarter of a mile distant. However, before I had decreased my distance by a hundred yards he started off at full gallop. Putting Filfil into a canter I increased the pace until I found that I must press him at full speed, as the waterbuck, although on only three legs, had the best of it. The ground was rough, having been marshy and trodden into ruts by the game, but now dried by the sun; bad for both horse and antelope, but especially for the former: however, after a race of about a mile I found myself gaining so rapidly that in a few moments I was riding on his left flank within three yards of him, and holding the rifle with one hand like a pistol I shot him dead through the shoulder. This little double rifle is an exceedingly handy weapon; it was made for me about nine years ago by Thomas Fletcher, gunmaker of Gloucester, and is of most perfect workmanship. I have shot with it most kinds of large game; although the bore is so small as No. 24, I have bagged with it rhinoceros, hippopotamus, lions, buffaloes, and all the heavy game except elephants and giraffes; upon the latter I have never happened to try it. Weighing only eight pounds and three-quarters it is most convenient to carry on horseback, and although I have had frequent accidents through my horse falling in full gallop, the stock is perfectly sound to this day. The best proof of thorough honest workmanship is, that in many years of hard work it has never been out of order, nor has it ever been in a gunmaker's hands.

The operation of cutting the waterbuck into four quarters, and then stringing them on to a strip of its own hide, was quickly performed, and with Richarn's assistance I slung it across my saddle, and led my horse, thus heavily laden, towards the path. After some difficulty in crossing muddy hollows and gullies in the otherwise dried marsh, we at length succeeded in finding the tracks of the party that had gone on ahead.

We had been steering from Ellyria due east towards the high peak of Gebel Lafeet, that rose exactly above one of the principal towns of Latooka. With this fine beacon now apparently just before us, we had no difficulty in finding our way. The country was now more open, and the ground sandy and interspersed with the hegleek trees, which gave it the appearance of a vast orchard of large pear trees. The *hegleek* is peculiarly rich in potash; so much so that the ashes of the burnt wood will blister the tongue. It bears a fruit about the size and shape of a date; this is very sweet and aromatic in flavour, and is also so rich in potash that it is used as a substitute for soap.

After an hour's walk always on the tracks of the party, we saw a large Latooka town in the distance, and upon a nearer approach we discovered crowds of people collected under two enormous trees. Presently guns fired, the drums beat, and as we drew nearer we perceived the Turkish flags leading a crowd of about a hundred men, who approached us with the usual salutes, every man firing off ball cartridge as fast as he could reload. My men were already with this lot of ragamuffins, and this was the ivory or slave trading party that they had conspired to join. They were marching towards me to honour me with a salute, which, upon close approach, ended by their holding their guns, muzzle downwards, and firing them almost into my feet. I at once saw through their object in giving me this reception; they had already heard from the other party exaggerated accounts of presents that their leader had received, and they were jealous at the fact of my having established confidence with a party opposed to them. The *vakeel* of Chenooda was the man who had from the first instigated my men to revolt and to join his party, and he at that moment had two of my deserters with him that had mutinied and joined him at Gondokoro. It had been agreed that the remainder of my men were to mutiny at this spot and to join him with my arms and ammunition. This was to be the stage for the outbreak. The apparent welcome was only to throw me off my guard.

I was coldly polite, and begging them not to waste their powder, I went to the large tree that threw a beautiful shade, and we sat down, surrounded by a crowd of both natives and trader's people. Mahommed Her sent me immediately a fat ox for my people: not to be under any obligation I immediately gave him a double-barrelled gun. The ox was slaughtered, and the people preferring beef to antelope venison, I gave the flesh of the waterbuck to the Latooka porters belonging to Ibrahim's party. Thus all teeth were busy. Ibrahim and his men occupied the shade of another enormous tree at about a hundred and fifty yards' distance.

The town was Latome, one of the principal places in the Latooka country, and was strongly palisaded, like the town of Wakkala. I did not go through the entrance, but contented myself with resting under my tree and writing up the journal from my notebook. Before we had been there many hours the two parties of Ibrahim and Mahommed Her were engaged in a hot contention. Mahommed Her declared that no one had a right of way through that country, which belonged to him according to the customs of the White Nile trade; that he would not permit the party of Ibrahim to proceed, and that, should they persist in their march, he would resist them by force.

Words grew high; Ibrahim was not afraid of force, as he had a hundred and forty men against Mahommed Her's hundred and five; insults and abuse were liberally exchanged, while the natives thronged around, enjoying the fun, until at last Mahommed Her's temper becoming outrageous, he was seized by the throat by Sulieman, a powerful *choush* of Ibrahim's party, and hurled away from the select society who claimed the right of road. Great confusion arose, and both parties prepared for a fight, which after the usual bluster died away to nothing. However, I noticed that my men most unmistakeably took the part of Mahommed Her against Ibrahim; they belonging to his tribe.

The evening arrived, and my *vakeel*, with his usual cunning, came to ask me whether I intended to start to-morrow. He said there was excellent shooting in this neighbourhood, and that Ibrahim's camp not being more than five hours' march beyond, I could at any time join him, should I think proper. Many of my men were sullenly listening to my reply, which was, that we should start in company with Ibrahim. The men immediately turned their backs, and swaggered insolently to the town, muttering something that I could not distinctly understand. I gave orders directly, that no man should sleep in the town, but that all should be at their posts by the luggage under the tree that I occupied. At night several men were absent, and were with difficulty brought from the town by the *vakeel*. The whole of the night was passed by the rival parties quarrelling and fighting. At 5:30 on the following morning the drum of Ibrahim's party beat the call, and his men with great alacrity got their porters together and prepared to march.

My *vakeel* was not to be found; my men were lying idly in the positions where they had slept; and not a man obeyed when I gave the order to prepare to start except Richarn and Sali. I saw that the moment had arrived. Again I gave the order to the men, to get up and load the animals; – not a man would move, except three or four who slowly rose from the ground, and stood resting on their guns. In the meantime Richarn and Sali were bringing the camels and making them kneel by the luggage. The boy Saat was evidently expecting a row, and although engaged with the black women in packing, he kept his eyes constantly upon me.

I now observed that Bellaal was standing very near me on my right, in advance of the men who had risen from the ground, and employed himself in eyeing me from head to foot with the most determined insolence. The fellow had his gun in his hand, and he was telegraphing by looks with those who were standing near him, while not one of the others rose from the ground, although close to me. Pretending not to notice Bellaal who was now as I had expected once more the ringleader, for the third time I ordered the men to rise immediately, and to load the camels. Not a man moved, but the fellow Bellaal marched up to me, and looking me straight in the face dashed the butt-end of his gun in defiance on the ground, and led the mutiny. "Not a man shall go with you! Go where you like with Ibrahim, but we won't follow you, nor move a step farther. The men shall not load the camels; you may employ the 'niggers' to do it, but not us."

I looked at this mutinous rascal for a moment; this was the burst of the conspiracy, and the threats and insolence that I had been forced to pass over for the sake of the expedition all rushed before me. "Lay down your gun!" I thundered, "and load the camels!" "I won't" was his reply. "Then stop here!" I answered; at the same time lashing out as quick as lightning with my right hand upon his jaw.

He rolled over in a heap, his gun flying some yards from his hand; and the late ringleader lay apparently insensible among the luggage, while several of his friends ran to him, and did the good Samaritan. Following up on the moment the advantage I had gained by establishing a panic, I seized my rifle and rushed into the midst of the wavering men, catching first one by the throat, and then another, and dragging them to the camels, which I insisted upon their immediately loading. All except three, who attended to the ruined ringleader, mechanically obeyed. Richarn and Sali both shouted to them to "burry," and the *vakeel* arriving at this moment and seeing how matters stood, himself assisted, and urged the men to obey.

Ibrahim's party had started. The animals were soon loaded, and leaving the *vakeel* to take them in charge, we cantered on to overtake Ibrahim, having crushed the mutiny, and given such an example, that in the event of future conspiracies my men would find it difficult to obtain a ringleader. So ended the famous conspiracy that had been reported to me by both Saat and Richarn before we left Gondokoro; and so much for the threat of firing simultaneously at me and deserting my wife in the jungle. In those savage countries success frequently depends upon one particular moment; you may lose or win according to your action at that critical instant. We congratulated ourselves upon the termination of this affair, which I trusted would be the last of the mutinies.

The country was now lovely; we were at the base of the mountain Lafeet, which rose abruptly on our left to the height of about 3,000 feet, the highest peak of the eastern chain that formed the broad valley of Latooka. The course of the valley was from S.E. to N.W.; about forty miles long by eighteen miles wide; the flat bottom was diversified by woods, thick jungles, open plains, and the ever-present hegleek trees, which in some places gave the appearance of forest. The south side of the valley was bounded by a high range of mountains, rising to six or seven thousand feet above the general level of Latooka, while the extreme end was almost blocked by a noble but isolated mountain of about 5,000 feet.

Our path being at the foot of the Lafeet chain, the ground was sandy but firm, being composed of disintegrated portions of the granite rocks that had washed down from the mountains, and we rode quickly along a natural road, equal to the best highway in England. We soon overtook Ibrahim and his party, and recounted the affair of mutiny.

The long string of porters now closed together as we were approaching a rebel town of Latooka that was hostile to both Turks and others. Suddenly one of the native porters threw down his load and bolted over the open ground towards the village at full speed. The fellow bounded along like an antelope, and was immediately pursued by half a dozen Turks. "Shoot him! Shoot him! Knock him over!" was shouted from the main body; and twenty guns were immediately pointed at the fugitive, who distanced his pursuers as a horse would outstrip an ox.

To save the man I gave chase on Filfil, putting myself in the line between him and the guns, to prevent them from firing. After a short course I overtook him, but he still continued running, and upon my closing with him he threw his spear on the ground, but still ran. Not being able to speak his language, I made signs that he should hold the mane of my horse, and that no one should hurt him. He at once clutched with both hands the horse's mane, and pushed himself almost under my knee in his efforts to keep close to me for protection. The Turks arrived breathless, and the native appeared as terrified as a hare at the moment it is seized by the greyhound. "Shoot him!" they one and all shouted. "Well done, *Hawaga!* You caught him beautifully! We never could have caught him without your horse. Pull him out! We'll shoot him as an example to the others!" I explained that he was my man, and belonged to me as I had caught him, therefore I could not allow him to be shot. "Then we'll give him five hundred with the *coorbatch!*" they cried. Even this generous offer I declined, and I insisted that he should accompany me direct to Ibrahim, into whose hands I should myself deliver him. Accordingly, still clutching to my horse's mane, the captive followed, and was received by the main body on arrival with shouts of derision.

I told Ibrahim that he must forgive him this time, if he promised to carry his load to the end of the journey. He immediately picked up his heavy burden as though it were a feather, and balancing it on his head, stepped along in the line of porters as though nothing had occurred.

Trifling as this incident may appear, it was of much service to me, as it served as an introduction to both Turks and natives. I heard the former conversing together, praising the speed of the horse, and congratulating themselves on the impossibility of the porters escaping now that they had seen how quickly they could be overtaken. Another remarked, "*Wah Illahi*, I should not like to chase a nigger so closely while a lance was in his hand. I expected he would turn sharp round and throw it through the *Hawaga*." Thus I was now looked upon by the Turks as an ally, and at the same time I was regarded by the Latookas as their friend for having

saved their man; and they grinned their approbation in the most
unmistakeable manner as I rode past their line, shouting, "*Morrte,
morrte mattat* (welcome, welcome, chief)!" On arriving at a large
town named Kattaga, we rested under the shade of an immense
tamarind tree. There was no sign of my men and animals, and I
began to think that something had gone wrong. For two hours we
waited for their arrival. Ascending some rising ground, I at length
observed my caravan approaching in the distance, and every one of
my men, except Richarn, mounted upon my donkeys, although the
poor animals were already carrying loads of 150 lbs. each. Upon
observing me, the dismount was sudden and general. On their
arrival I found that three of the men had deserted, including Bellaal,
and had joined the party of Mahommed Her, taking with them my
guns and ammunition. Two had previously joined that party; thus
five of my men were now engaged by those slavehunters, and I little doubted that my remaining men would abscond likewise.

On the arrival of my *vakeel* he told me, in face of the men, that
so many had deserted, and that the others had refused to assist him
in taking the guns from them; thus my arms and ammunition had
been forcibly stolen. I abused both the *vakeel* and the men most
thoroughly; and "...as for the mutineers who have joined the slave-
hunters, *Inshallah*, the vultures shall pick their bones!" This chari-
table wish – which, I believe, I expressed with intense hatred – was
never forgotten either by my own men or by the Turks. Believing
firmly in the evil eye, their superstitious fears were immediately
excited. Continuing the march along the same style of country we
shortly came in view of Tarrangolle, the chief town of Latooka, at
which point was the station of Ibrahim. We had marched thirteen
miles from Latome, the station of Mahommed Her, at which place
my men had deserted, and we were now 101 miles from Gondokoro by dead reckoning.

There were some superb trees situated close to the town, under
which we camped until the natives could prepare a hut for our
reception. Crowds of people now surrounded us, amazed at the two
great objects of interest – the camels, and a white woman. They did
not think me very peculiar, as I was nearly as brown as an Arab.

The Latookas are the finest savages I have ever seen. I measured a number of them as they happened to enter my tent, and

allowing two inches for the thickness of their felt helmets, the average height was 5 ft. 11 1/2 in. Not only are they tall, but they possess a wonderful muscular development, having beautifully proportioned legs and arms; and although extremely powerful, they are never fleshy or corpulent. The formation of head and general physiognomy is totally different from all other tribes that I have met with in the neighbourhood of the White Nile. They have high foreheads, large eyes, rather high cheekbones, mouths not very large, well shaped, and the lips rather full. They all have a remarkably pleasing cast of countenance, and are a great contrast to the other tribes in civility of manner. Altogether their appearance denotes a Galla origin, and it is most probable that, at some former period, an invasion by the Gallas of this country originated the settlement of the Latookas.

One of the principal channels, if not the main stream of the river Sobat, is only four days' march or fifty miles east of Latooka, and is known to the natives as the Chol. The east bank of that stream is occupied by the Gallas, who have frequently invaded the Latooka country. There is an interesting circumstance connected with these invasions, that the Gallas were invariably mounted upon mules. Neither horse, camel, nor other beast of burden is known to any of the White Nile tribes, therefore the existence of mules on the east bank of the Chol is a distinguishing feature. Both Abyssinia and the Galla being renowned for a fine breed of mules, affords good circumstantial evidence that the Akkara tribe of the Chol are true Gallas, and that the Latookas may be derived from a similar origin by settlements after conquest.

The great chief of the Latookas, Moy, assured me that his people could not withstand the cavalry of the Akkara, although they were superior to all other tribes on foot.

I have heard the traders of Khartoum pretend that they can distinguish the tribes of the White Nile by their individual type. I must confess my inability on this point. In vain I have attempted to trace an actual difference. To me the only distinguishing mark between the tribes bordering the White River is a peculiarity in either dressing the hair, or in ornament. The difference of general appearance caused by a variety of hairdressing is most perplexing, and is apt to mislead a traveller who is only a superficial observer; but from the commencement of the negro tribes in N. lat. 12 degrees to Ellyria in lat. 4 degrees 30 minutes I have found no specific difference in the people. The actual change takes place suddenly on arrival in Latooka, and this is accounted for by an admixture with the Gallas.

The Latookas are a fine, frank, and warlike race. Far from being the morose set of savages that I had hitherto seen, they were excessively merry, and always ready for either a laugh or a fight. The town of Tarrangolle contained about three thousand houses, and was not only surrounded by iron-wood palisades, but every house was individually fortified by a little stockaded courtyard. The cattle were kept in large kraals in various parts of the town, and were most carefully attended to, fires being lit every night to protect them from flies; and high platforms, in three tiers, were erected in many places, upon which sentinels watched both day and night to give the alarm in case of danger. The cattle are the wealth of the country, and so rich are the Latookas in oxen, that ten or twelve thousand head are housed in every large town; thus the natives are ever on the watch, fearing the attacks of the adjacent tribes.

The houses of the Latookas are generally bell-shaped, while others are precisely like huge candle-extinguishers, about twenty-five feet high. The roofs are neatly thatched, at an angle of about 75 degrees, resting upon a circular wall about four feet high; thus the roof forms a cap descending to within two feet and a half of the ground. The doorway is only two feet and two inches high, thus an entrance must be effected upon all-fours. The interior is remarkably clean, but dark, as the architects have no idea of windows. It is a curious fact that the circular form of but is the only style of architecture adopted among all the tribes of Central Africa, and also among the Arabs of Upper Egypt; and that, although these differ more or less in the form of the roof, no tribe has ever yet sufficiently advanced to construct a window. The town of Tarrangolle is arranged with several entrances, in the shape of low archways through the palisades; these are closed at night by large branches of the hooked thorn of the *kittur* bush (a species of mimosa). The main street is broad, but all others are studiously arranged to admit of only one cow, in single file, between high stockades; thus, in the event of an attack, these narrow passages could be easily defended, and it would be impossible to drive off their vast herds of cattle unless by the main street. The large cattle kraals are accordingly arranged in various quarters in connexion with the great road, and the entrance of each kraal is a small archway in the strong iron-wood fence sufficiently wide to admit one ox at a time.

Suspended from the arch is a bell, formed of the shell of the Dolape palm-nut, against which every animal must strike either its horns or back, on entrance.

Every tinkle of the bell announces the passage of an ox into the kraal, and they are thus counted every evening when brought home from pasture. I had noticed, during the march from Latome, that the vicinity of every town was announced by heaps of human remains. Bones and skulls formed a Golgotha within a quarter of a mile of every village. Some of these were in earthenware pots, generally broken; others lay strewn here and there; while a heap in the centre showed that some form had originally been observed in their disposition. This was explained by an extraordinary custom most rigidly observed by the Latookas. Should a man be killed in battle the body is allowed to remain where it fell, and is devoured by the vultures and hyenas; but should he die a natural death, he or she is buried in a shallow grave within a few feet of his own door, in the little courtyard that surrounds each dwelling. Funeral dances are then kept up in memory of the dead for several weeks; at the expiration of which time, the body being sufficiently decomposed, is exhumed. The bones are cleaned, and are deposited in an earthenware jar, and carried to a spot near the town which is regarded as the cemetery. I observed that they were not particular in regarding the spot as sacred, as signs of nuisances were present even upon the bones, that in civilized countries would have been regarded as an insult.

There is little difficulty in describing the toilette of the native – that of the men being simplified by the sole covering of the head, the body being entirely nude. It is curious to observe among these wild savages the consummate vanity displayed in their headdresses. Every tribe has a distinct and unchanging fashion for dressing the hair; and so elaborate is the coiffure that hairdressing is reduced to a science. European ladies would be startled at the fact, that to perfect the coiffure of a man requires a period of from eight to ten years! However tedious the operation, the result is extraordinary.

The Latookas wear most exquisite helmets, all of which are formed of their own hair; and are, of course, fixtures. At first sight it appears incredible, but a minute examination shows the wonderful perseverance of years in producing what must be highly inconvenient. The thick, crisp wool is woven with fine twine, formed from the bark of a tree, until it presents a thick network of felt. As the hair grows through this matted substance it is subjected to the same process, until, in the course of years, a compact substance is formed like a strong felt, about an inch and a half thick, that has been trained into the shape of a helmet. A strong rim, of about two inches deep, is formed by sewing it together with thread; and the front part of the helmet is protected by a piece of polished copper; while a piece of the same metal, shaped like the half of a bishop's mitre and about a foot in length, forms the crest. The framework of the helmet being at length completed, it must be perfected by an arrangement of beads, should the owner of the head be sufficiently rich to indulge in the coveted distinction. The beads most in fashion are the red and the blue porcelain, about the size of small peas. These are sewn on the surface of the felt, and so beautifully arranged in sections of blue and red that the entire helmet appears to be formed of beads; and the handsome crest of polished copper, surmounted by ostrich-plumes, gives a most dignified and martial appearance to this elaborate headdress. No helmet is supposed to be complete without a row of cowrie-shells stitched around the rim so as to form a solid edge.

The Latookas have neither bows nor arrows, their weapons consisting of the lance, a powerful iron-headed mace, a long-bladed knife or sword, and an ugly iron bracelet, armed with knife-blades about four inches long by half an inch broad: the latter is used to strike with if disarmed, and to tear with when wrestling with an enemy. Their shields are either of buffaloes' hide or of giraffes', the latter being highly prized as excessively tough although light, and thus combining the two requisite qualities of a good shield; they are usually about four feet six inches long by two feet wide, and are the largest I have seen. Altogether, everything in Latooka looks like fighting. Although the men devote so much attention to their head-dress, the women are extremely simple. It is a curious fact, that while the men are remarkably handsome, the women are exceedingly plain; they are immense creatures, few being under five feet seven in height, with prodigious limbs. Their superior strength to that of other tribes may be seen in the size of their water jars, which are nearly double as large as any I have seen elsewhere, containing about ten gallons; in these they fetch water from the stream about a mile distant from the town. They wear exceedingly long tails, precisely like those of horses, but made of fine twine and rubbed with red ochre and grease. They are very convenient when they creep into their huts on bands and knees. In addition to the tails, they wear a large flap of tanned leather in front. Should I ever visit that country again, I should take a great number of "freemasons" aprons for the women; these would be highly prized, and would create a perfect furor. The only really pretty women that I saw in Latooka were Bokke, the wife of the chief, and her daughter; they were facsimiles of each other, the latter having the advantage of being the second edition. Both women and men were extremely eager for beads of all kinds, the most valuable being the red and blue porcelain for helmets, and the large opalescent bead, the size of a child's marble.

The day after my arrival in Latooka I was accommodated by the chief with a hut in a neat courtyard, beautifully clean and cemented with clay, ashes, and cow-dung. Not patronising the architectural advantages of a doorway of two feet high, I pitched my large tent in the yard and stowed all my baggage in the hut. All being arranged, I had a large Persian carpet spread upon the ground, and received the chief of Latooka in state. He was introduced by Ibrahim, and I had the advantage of his interpreter.

I commenced the conversation by ordering a present to be laid on the carpet of several necklaces of valuable beads, copper bars, and coloured cotton handkerchief. It was most amusing to witness his delight at a string of fifty little *berrets* (opal beads the size of marbles) which I had brought into the country for the first time, and were accordingly extremely valuable. No sooner had he surveyed them with undisguised delight than he requested me to give him another string of opals for his wife, or she would be in a bad humour; accordingly a present for the lady was added to the already large pile of beads that lay heaped upon the carpet before him. After surveying his treasures with pride, he heaved a deep sigh, and turning to the interpreter he said, "What a row there will be in the family when my other wives see Bokke (his head wife) dressed up with this finery. Tell the Mattat that unless he gives necklaces for each of my other wives, they will fight!" Accordingly I asked him the number of ladies that made him anxious. He deliberately began to count upon his fingers, and having exhausted the digits of one hand, I compromised immediately, begging him not to go through the whole of his establishment, and presented him with about three pounds of various beads, to be divided among them. He appeared highly delighted, and declared his intention of sending all his wives to pay Mrs. Baker a visit. This was an awful visitation, as each wife would expect a present for herself, and would assuredly have either a child or a friend for whom she would beg an addition. I therefore told him that the heat was so great that we could not bear too many in the tent, but that if Bokke, his favourite, would appear, we should be glad to see her.

Accordingly he departed, and shortly we were honoured by a visit. Bokke and her daughter were announced, and a prettier pair of savages I never saw. They were very clean; their hair was worn short, like all the women of the country, and plastered with red ochre and fat, so as to look like vermilion; their faces were slightly tattooed on the cheeks and temples; and they sat down on the many-coloured carpet with great surprise, and stared at the first white man and woman they had ever seen. We gave them both a number of necklaces of red and blue beads, and I secured Bokke's portrait in my sketchbook, obtaining a very correct likeness. She told us that Mahommed Her's men were very bad people; that they had burnt and plundered one of her villages; and that one of the Latookas who had been wounded in the fight by a bullet had just died, and they were to dance for him to-morrow, if we would like to attend. She asked many questions – how many wives I had – and was astonished to hear that I was contented with one. This seemed to amuse her immensely, and she laughed heartily with her daughter at the idea. She said that my wife would be much improved if she would extract her four front teeth from the lower jaw, and wear the red ointment on her hair, according to the fashion of the country; she also proposed that she should pierce her under lip, and wear the long pointed polished crystal, about the size of a drawing pencil, that is the "thing" in the Latooka country. No woman among the tribe who has any pretensions to be a "swell" would be without this highly-prized ornament, and one of my thermometers having come to an end I broke the tube into three pieces, and they were considered as presents of the highest value, to be worn through the perforated under lip. Lest the piece should slip through the hole in the lip, a kind of rivet is formed by twine bound round the inner extremity, and this protruding into the space left by the extraction of the four front teeth of the lower jaw, entices the tongue to act upon the extremity, which gives it a wriggling motion, indescribably ludicrous during conversation.

I cannot understand for what reason all the White Nile tribes extract the four front teeth of the lower jaw. Were the meat of the country tender, the loss of teeth might be a trifle; but I have usually found that even a good set of grinders are sometimes puzzled to go through the operation needful to a Latooka beefsteak. It is difficult to explain real beauty; a defect in one country is a desideratum in another; scars upon the face are, in Europe, a blemish; but here and in the Arab countries no beauty can be perfect until the cheeks or temples have been gashed.

The Arabs make three gashes upon each cheek, and rub the wounds with salt and a kind of porridge (*asida*) to produce proud flesh; thus every female slave, captured by the slave-hunters, is marked to prove her identity, and to improve her charms. Each tribe has its peculiar fashion as to the position and form of the cicatrix.

The Latookas gash the temples and cheeks of their women, but do not raise the scar above the surface, as is the custom of the Arabs.

Polygamy is, of course, the general custom; the number of a man's wives depending entirely upon his wealth, precisely as would the number of his horses in England. There is no such thing as love in these countries: the feeling is not understood, nor does it exist in the shape in which we understand it. Everything is practical, without a particle of romance. Women are so far appreciated as they are valuable animals. They grind the corn, fetch the water, gather firewood, cement the floors, cook the food, and propagate the race; but they are mere servants, and as such are valuable. The price of a good-looking, strong young wife, who could carry a heavy jar of water, would be ten cows; thus a man, rich in cattle, would be rich in domestic bliss, as he could command a multiplicity of wives. However delightful may be a family of daughters in England, they nevertheless are costly treasures; but in Latooka, and throughout savage lands, they are exceedingly profitable. The simple rule of proportion will suggest that if one daughter is worth ten cows, ten daughters must be worth a hundred, therefore a large family is the source of wealth; the girls produce the cows, and the boys milk them. All being perfectly naked (I mean the girls and the boys), there is no expense, and the children act as herdsmen to the flocks as in the patriarchal times. A multiplicity of wives thus increases wealth by the increase of family. I am afraid this practical state of affairs will be a strong barrier to missionary enterprise.

A savage holds to his cows, and his women, but especially to his cows. In a *razzia* fight he will seldom stand for the sake of his wives, but when he does fight it is to save his cattle. I had now a vivid exemplification of this theory.

One day, at about 3 p.m., the men of Ibrahim started upon some mysterious errand, but returned equally mysterious at about midnight. On the following morning I heard that they had intended to attack some place upon the mountains, but they had heard that it was too powerful; and as "discretion is the better part of valour," they had returned.

On the day following I heard that there had been some disaster, and that the whole of Mahommed Her's party had been massacred. The natives seemed very excited, and messenger succeeded messenger, all confirming the account that Mahommed Her had attacked a village on the mountains, the same that Ibrahim had intended to attack, and that the natives had exterminated their whole party.

On the following morning I sent ten of my men with a party of Ibrahim's to Latome to make inquiries. They returned on the following afternoon, bringing with them two wounded men.

It appeared that Mahommed Her had ordered his party of 110 armed men, in addition to 300 natives, to make a *razzia* upon a certain village among the mountains for slaves and cattle. They had succeeded in burning a village, and in capturing a great number of slaves. Having descended the pass, a native gave them the route that would lead to the capture of a large herd of cattle that they had not yet discovered. They once more ascended the mountain by a different path, and arriving at the kraal, they commenced driving off the vast herd of cattle. The Latookas, who had not fought while their wives and children were being carried into slavery, now fronted bravely against the muskets to defend their herds, and charging the Turks, they drove them down the pass.

It was in vain that they fought; every bullet aimed at a Latooka struck a rock, behind which the enemy was hidden. Rocks, stones, and lances were hurled at them from all sides and from above; they were forced to retreat.

The retreat ended in a panic and precipitate flight. Hemmed in on all sides, amidst a shower of lances and stones thrown from the mountain above, the Turks fled pele-mele down the rocky and precipitous ravines. Mistaking their route, they came to a precipice from which there was no retreat. The screaming and yelling savages closed round them. Fighting was useless; the natives, under cover of the numerous detached rocks, offered no mark for an aim; while the crowd of armed savages thrust them forward with wild yells to the very verge of the great precipice about five hundred feet below. Down they fell, hurled to utter destruction by the mass of Latookas pressing onward! A few fought to the last; but one and all were at length forced, by sheer pressure, over the edge of the cliff, and met a just reward for their atrocities.

My men looked utterly cast down, and a feeling of horror pervaded the entire party. No quarter had been given by the Latookas; and upwards of 200 natives who had joined the slave-hunters in the attack, had also perished with their allies. Mahommed Her had not him self accompanied his people, both he and Bellaal, my late ringleader, having remained in camp; the latter having, fortunately for him, been disabled, and placed hors de combat by the example I had made during the mutiny.

My men were almost green with awe, when I asked them solemnly, "Where were the men who had deserted from me?" Without answering a word they brought two of my guns and laid them at my feet. They were covered with clotted blood mixed with sand, which had hardened like cement over the locks and various portions of the barrels. My guns were all marked. As I looked at the numbers upon the stocks, I repeated aloud the names of the owners. "Are they all dead?" I asked. "All dead," the men replied. "Food for the vultures?" I asked. "None of the bodies can be recovered," faltered my *vakeel*. "The two guns were brought from the spot by some natives who escaped, and who saw the men fall. They are all killed." "Better for them had they remained with me and done their duty. The hand of God is heavy," I replied. My men slunk away abashed, leaving the gory witnesses of defeat and death upon the ground. I called Saat and ordered him to give the two guns to Richarn to clean.

Not only my own men but the whole of Ibrahim's party were of opinion that I had some mysterious connexion with the disaster that had befallen my mutineers. All remembered the bitterness of my prophecy – "he vultures will pick their bones" – and this terrible mishap having occurred so immediately afterwards took a strong hold upon their superstitious minds. As I passed through the camp, the men would quietly exclaim, "*Wah Illahi Hawaga* (My God! Master)!" To which I simply replied, "*Robinee fe* (There is a God)!" From that moment I observed an extraordinary change in the manner of both my people and those of Ibrahim, all of whom now paid us the greatest respect.

Unfortunately a great change had likewise taken place in the manner of the Latookas. The whole town was greatly excited, drums were beating and horns blowing in all quarters, every one rejoicing at the annihilation of Mahommed Her's party. The natives no longer respected the superior power of guns; in a hand-to-hand fight they had proved their own superiority, and they had not the sense to distinguish the difference between a struggle in a steep mountain pass and a battle on the open plain. Ibrahim was apprehensive of a general attack on his party by the Latookas.

This was rather awkward, as it was necessary for him to return to Gondokoro for a large supply of ammunition which had been left there for want of porters to convey it, when he had started for the interior. To march to Gondokoro, and to guard the ammunition, would require a large force in the present disturbed state of the country; thus we should be a much-reduced party, which might induce the Latookas to attack us after his departure. However, it was necessary that he should start. I accordingly lent him a couple of donkeys to convey his powder, in case he should not be able to procure porters.

After the departure of Ibrahim, the force of his party remaining at Tarrangolle was reduced to thirty-five men, under the command of his lieutenant, Suleiman. This was a weak detachment in the event of an attack, especially as they had no separate camp, but were living in the native town, the men quartered in detached huts, and accordingly at the mercy of the natives if surprised. The brutality of the Turks was so inseparable from their nature, that they continually insulted the native women to such an extent that I felt sure they would provoke hostilities in the present warlike humour of the Latookas. The stream being nearly a mile distant, there was a difficulty in procuring water. The Turks being far too lazy to carry it for themselves, seized upon the water-jars when the women returned from the stream, and beat them severely upon their refusal to deliver them without payment. I found no difficulty, as I engaged a woman to bring a regular supply for a daily payment in beads. Much bartering was going on between the Turks and the natives for provisions, in which the latter were invariably cheated, and beaten if they complained. I felt sure that such conduct must end in disagreement, if not in actual fight, in the event of which I knew that I should be dragged into the affair, although perfectly innocent, and having nothing to do with the Turks.

My quarters in the town were near an open quadrangular space about eighty yards square, inclosed upon all sides, but having a narrow entrance to the main street. The Turks were scattered about in the neighbouring lanes, their time passed in drinking *merissa*, and quarrelling with the natives and with each other.

The day after Ibrahim's departure, the Turks seized some jars of water by force from the women on their return from the stream. A row ensued, and ended by one of the women being shamefully maltreated; and a Latooka, who came to her assistance, was severely beaten. This I did not see, but it was reported to me. I called Suleiman, and told him that if such things were permitted it would entail a fight with the natives, in which I should not allow my men to join; that I prohibited my men from taking anything from the Latookas without just payment: thus, should a fight be caused by the conduct of his people, they must get out of it as they best could.

A bad feeling already existed between the natives and his people, owing to the defeat of the party of Mahommed Her. Much good management was required to avoid a collision, and the reverse was certain to cause an outbreak. Shortly before dusk the women were again assaulted on their return with water from the stream. One of Ibrahim's soldiers threatened a powerful-looking Amazon with his stick because she refused to deliver up her jar of water that she had carried about a mile for her own requirements. Upon seeing this my pretty friend, Bokke, the chief's wife, seized the soldier by the throat, wrested the stick from him, while another woman disarmed him of his gun. Other women then set upon him, and gave him a most ignominious shaking; while some gathered up mud from the gutter and poured it down the barrel of his gun until they effectually choked it; not content with this, they plastered large masses of mud over the locks and trigger.

I looked on with enjoyment at the thorough discomfiture of the Turk. The news quickly spread, and in revenge for his disgrace his comrades severely beat some women at some distance from the camp. I heard screams, and shouts, and a confused noise; and upon my arrival outside the town, I saw large numbers of natives running from all quarters, and collecting together with lances and shields. I felt sure that we were to be involved in a general outbreak. However, the Turks beat the drum, and collected their men, so that in a few minutes no straggler was in the town.

It was remarkably unpleasant to be dragged into a row by the conduct of these brutal traders, with whom I had nothing in common, and who, should a fight actually occur, would be certain to behave as cowards. The Latookas would make no distinction between me and them, in the event of an attack, as they would naturally class all strangers and new comers with the hated Turks.

It was about 5 p.m. one hour before sunset. The woman who usually brought us water delivered her jar, but disappeared immediately after without sweeping the courtyard as was her custom. Her children, who usually played in this inclosure, had vanished. On searching her hut, which was in one corner of the yard, no one was to be found, and even the grinding-stone was gone. Suspecting that something was in the wind, I sent Karka and Gaddum Her, the two black servants, to search in various huts in the neighbourhood to observe if the owners were present, and whether the women were in their houses. Not a woman could be found. Neither woman nor child remained in the large town of Tarrangolle. There was an extraordinary stillness where usually all was noise and chattering. All the women and children had been removed to the mountains about two miles distant, and this so quickly and noiselessly that it appeared incredible. I immediately sent to the house of the chief, and requested his attendance. There were two chiefs, brothers; Moy was the greater in point of rank, but his brother, Commoro, had more actual authority with the people. I was glad that the latter appeared.

I sent to request an interpreter from the Turks, and upon his arrival I asked Commoro why the women and children had been removed. He replied that the Turks were so brutal that he could not prevail upon his people to endure it any longer; their women were robbed and beaten, and they were all so ill-treated, that he, as their chief, had no longer any control over them; and that the odium of having introduced the Turks to Latooka was thrown upon him. I asked him whether any of my men had misbehaved. I explained that I should flog any one of my men who should steal the merest trifle from his people, or insult any women. All my men were in dark-brown uniforms. He said that none of the men with the brown clothes had been complained of, but that his people had taken a dislike to all strangers, owing to the conduct of the Turks, and that he could not answer for the consequences.

There was a division among his own people, some wishing to fight and to serve the Turks as the Latookas had served the party of Mahommed Her, and others yielding to his advice, and agreeing to remain quiet.

I inquired whether the chief, Moy, intended peace or war. He said that Bokke, his wife, had made him very angry against the Turks by describing their conduct towards the women.

This was rather an unsatisfactory state of things. Commoro departed, frankly admitting that the natives were much excited and wished to attack, but that he would do his best with them.

These rascally traders set every country in a blaze by their brutal conduct, and rendered exploring, not only most dangerous but next to impossible, without an exceedingly powerful force.

The sun set; and, as usual in tropical climates, darkness set in within half an hour. Not a woman had returned to the town, nor was the voice of a man to be heard. The natives had entirely forsaken the portion of the town that both I and the Turks occupied. The night was perfectly calm, and the stars shone so brightly, that I took an observation for the latitude – 4 degrees 30 minutes. There was a death-like stillness in the air. Even the Turks, who were usually uproarious, were perfectly quiet, and although my men made no remark, it was plain that we were all occupied by the same thoughts, and that an attack was expected.

It was about 9 o'clock, and the stillness had become almost painful. There was no cry of a bird; not even the howl of a hyena: the camels were sleeping; but every man was wide awake, and the sentries well on the alert. We were almost listening at the supernatural stillness, if I may so describe the perfect calm, when, suddenly, every one startled at the deep and solemn boom of the great war-drum, or *nogara*. Three distinct beats, at slow intervals, rang through the apparently deserted town, and echoed loudly from the neighbouring mountain. It was the signal! A few minutes elapsed, and like a distant echo from the north the three mournful tones again distinctly sounded. Was it an echo? Impossible. Now from the south, far distant, but unmistakeable, the same three regular beats came booming through the still night air. Again and again, from every quarter, spreading far and wide, the signal was responded; and the whole country echoed those three solemn notes so full of warning. Once more the great *nogara* of Tarrangolle sounded the original alarm within a few hundred paces of our quarters. The whole country was up.

There was no doubt about the matter. The Turks well knew those three notes were the war-signal of the Latookas. I immediately called Suleiman. It was necessary to act in unison. I ordered him to beat the drum loudly for about five minutes to answer the *nogara*. His men were all scattered in several small inclosures. I called them all out into the open quadrangle; in the centre of which I placed the baggage, and planted the English ensign in the middle, while the Turks fixed their flag within a few paces. Posting sentries at each corner of the square, I stationed patrols in the principal street. In the meantime Mrs. Baker had laid out upon a mat several hundred cartridges of buck-shot, powder-flasks, wadding, and opened several boxes of caps, all of which were neatly arranged for a reserve of ammunition; while a long row of first-class double guns and rifles lay in readiness. The boy Saat was full of fight, and immediately strapped on his belt and cartouche-box, and took his stand among the men.

I ordered the men, in the event of an attack, to immediately set fire to all the huts around the quadrangle; in which case the sudden rush of a large body of men would be impossible, and the huts being of straw, the town would be quickly in a blaze.

Everything was in order to resist an attack in five minutes from the sounding of the *nogara*.

The patrols shortly reported that large bodies of men were collecting outside the town. The great *nogara* again beat, and was answered at intervals as before from the neighbouring villages; but the Turks' drum kept up an uninterrupted roll as a challenge whenever the *nogara* sounded. Instead of the intense stillness that had formerly been almost painful, a distinct hum of distant voices betokened the gathering of large bodies of men. However, we were well fortified; and the Latookas knew it. We occupied the very stronghold that they had themselves constructed for the defence of their town; and the square being surrounded with strong iron-wood palisades with only a narrow entrance, would be impregnable when held, as now, by fifty men well armed with guns against a mob whose best weapons were only lances. I sent men up the watchmen's stations; these were about twenty-five feet high; and the night being clear, they could distinctly report the movements of a dark mass of natives that were ever increasing on the outside of the town at about two hundred yards' distance. The rattle of the Turks' drum repeatedly sounded in reply to the *nogara*, and the intended attack seemed destined to relapse into a noisy but empty battle of the drums.

A few hours passed in uncertainty, when, at about midnight, the chief Commoro came fearlessly to the patrol, and was admitted to the quadrangle. He seemed greatly struck with the preparations for defence, and explained that the *nogara* had been beaten without his orders, and accordingly the whole country had risen; but that he had explained to the people that I had no hostile intentions, and that all would be well if they only kept the peace. He said they certainly had intended to attack us, and were surprised that we were prepared, as proved by the immediate reply of the Turks' drum to their *nogara*. He assured us that he would not sleep that night, but would watch that nothing should happen. I assured him that we should also keep awake, but should the *nogara* sound once more I should give orders to my men to set fire to the town, as I should not allow the natives to make use of such threats with impunity. I agreed to use what little interest I had to keep the Turks in order, but that I must not be held responsible by the natives for their proceedings, as I was not of their country, neither had I anything to do with them. I explained, that upon Ibrahim's return from Gondokoro things might improve, as he was the captain of the Turks, and might be able to hold his men in command. Commoro departed, and about 2 a.m. the dense crowds of armed men that had accumulated outside the town began to disperse.

The morning broke and saw the men still under arms, but the excitement had passed. The women soon reappeared with their water jars as usual, but on this occasion they were perfectly unmolested by the Turks, who, having passed the night in momentary expectation of an attack, were now upon their best behaviour. However, I heard them muttering among themselves, "Wait until Ibrahim returns with reinforcements and ammunition, and we will pay the Latookas for last night."

The town filled; and the Latookas behaved as though nothing out of the common had occurred; but when questioned, they coolly confessed that they had intended to surprise us, but that we were too wide awake. It is extraordinary that these fellows are so stupid as to beat the drum or *nogara* before the attack, as it naturally gives the alarm, and renders a surprise impossible; nevertheless, the war-drum is always a preliminary step to hostilities. I now resolved to camp outside the town, so as not to be mixed up in any way with the Turks, whose presence was certain to create enmity. Accordingly I engaged a number of natives to cut thorns, and to make a zareeba, or camp, about four hundred yards from the main entrance of the town, on the road to the stream of water. In a few days it was completed, and I constructed houses for my men, and two good huts for ourselves. Having a supply of garden seeds, I arranged a few beds, which I sowed with onions, cabbages, and radishes. My camp was eighty yards long, and forty wide. My horses were pic-queted in two corners, while the donkeys and camels occupied the opposite extremity. We now felt perfectly independent. I had masses of supplies, and I resolved to work round to the south-west whenever it might be possible, and thus to recover the route that I had originally proposed for my journey south. My present difficulty was the want of an interpreter. The Turks had several, and I hoped that on the return of Ibrahim from Gondokoro I might induce him to lend me a Bari lad for some consideration. For the present I was obliged to send to the Turks' camp and borrow an interpreter when-ever I required one, which was both troublesome and expensive.

Although I was willing to purchase all supplies with either beads or copper bracelets, I found it was impossible to procure meat. The natives refused to sell either cattle or goats. This was most tantalizing, as not less than 10,000 head of cattle filed by my camp every morning as they were driven from the town to pastur-age. All this amount of beef paraded before me, and did not pro-duce a steak! Milk was cheap and abundant; fowl were scarce; corn was plentiful; vegetables were unknown; not even pumpkins were grown by the Latookas.

Fortunately there was an abundance of small game in the shape of wild ducks, pigeons, doves; and a great variety of birds such as herons, cranes, spoonbills, etc. Travellers should always take as large a supply of shot as possible. I had four hundred weight, and prodigious quantities of powder and caps: thus I could at all times kill sufficient game for ourselves and people. There were a series of small marshy pools scattered over the country near the stream that ran through the valley; these were the resort of numerous ducks, which afforded excellent sport. The town of Tarrangolle is situated at the foot of the mountain, about a mile from the stream, which is about eighty yards wide, but shallow. In the dry weather, water is obtained by wells dug in the sandy bed, but during the rains it is a simple torrent not exceeding three feet in depth. The bed being sandy, the numerous banks, left dry by the fluctuations of the stream, are most inviting spots for ducks; and it was only necessary to wait under a tree, on the river's bank, to obtain thirty or forty shots in one morning as the ducks flew down the course of the stream. I found two varieties: the small brown duck with a grey head; and a magnificent variety, as large as the Muscovy, having a copper-and-blue coloured tinselled back and wings, with a white but speckled head and neck. This duck had a curious peculiarity in a fleshy protuberance on the beak about as large as a half-crown. This stands erect, like a cock's comb. Both this, and the smaller variety, were delicious eating. There were two varieties of geese – the only two that I have ever seen on the White Nile – the common Egyptian grey goose, and a large black and white bird with a crimson head and neck, and a red and yellow horny protuberance on the top of the head. This variety has a sharp spur upon the wing an inch long, and exceedingly powerful; it is used as a weapon of defence for striking, like the spurred wing of the plover.

I frequeutly shot ten or twelve ducks, and as many cranes, before breakfast; among others the beautiful crested crane, called by the Arabs *garranook*. The black velvet head of this crane, surrounded by a golden crest, was a favourite ornament of the Latookas, and they were immediately arranged as crests for their helmets. The neighbourhood of my camp would have made a fortune for a feather-dealer; it was literally strewn with down and plumes. I was always attended every morning by a number of Latooka boys, who were eager sportsmen, and returned to camp daily laden with ducks and geese.

No sooner did we arrive in camp than a number of boys volunteered to pluck the birds, which they did for the sake of the longest feathers, with which they immediately decked their woolly heads. Crowds of boys were to be seen with heads like cauliflowers, all dressed with the feathers of cranes and wild ducks. It appears to be accepted, both by the savage and civilized, that birds' feathers are specially intended for ornamenting the human head.

It was fortunate that Nature had thus stocked Latooka with game. It was impossible to procure any other meat; and not only were the ducks and geese to us what the quails were to the Israelites in the desert, but they enabled me to make presents to the natives that assured them of our good will.

Although the Latookas were far better than other tribes that I had met, they were sufficiently annoying; they gave me no credit for real good will, but they attributed my forbearance to weakness.

On one occasion Adda, one of the chiefs, came to ask me to join him in attacking a village to procure *molotes* (iron hoes); he said, "Come along with me, bring your men and guns, and we will attack a village near here, and take their molotes and cattle; you keep the cattle, and I will have the molotes." I asked him whether the village was in an enemy's country. "Oh no!" he replied, "it is close here; but the people are rather rebellious, and it will do them good to kill a few, and to take their molotes. If you are afraid, never mind, I will ask the Turks to do it." Thus forbearance on my part was supposed to be caused from weakness, and it was difficult to persuade them that it originated in a feeling of justice. This Adda most coolly proposed that we should plunder one of his own villages that was rather too liberal in its views. Nothing is more heartbreaking than to be so thoroughly misunderstood, and the obtuseness of the savages was such, that I never could make them understand the existence of good principle; their one idea was power – force that could obtain all – the strong hand that could wrest from the weak. In disgust I frequently noted the feelings of the moment in my journal – a memorandum from which I copy as illustrative of the time:

"1863, 10th April, Latooka. I wish the black sympathisers in England could see Africa's inmost heart as I do, much of their sympathy would subside. Human nature viewed in its crude state as pictured amongst African savages is quite on a level with that of the brute, and not to be compared with the noble character of the dog. There is neither gratitude, pity, love, nor self-denial; no idea of duty; no religion; but covetousness, ingratitude, selfishness and cruelty. All are thieves, idle, envious, and ready to plunder and enslave their weaker neighbours."

Chapter VI

THE FUNERAL DANCE

Drums were beating, horns blowing, and people were seen all running in one direction; the cause was a funeral dance, and I joined the crowd, and soon found myself in the midst of the entertainment. The dancers were most grotesquely got up. About a dozen huge ostrich feathers adorned their helmets; either leopard or the black and white monkey skins were suspended from their shoulders, and a leather tied round the waist covered a large iron bell which was strapped upon the loins of each dancer, like a woman's old-fashioned bustle: this they rung to the time of the dance by jerking their posteriors in the most absurd manner. A large crowd got up in this style created an indescribable hubbub, heightened by the blowing of horns and the beating of seven *nogaras* of various notes. Every dancer wore an antelope's horn suspended round the neck, which he blew occasionally in the height of his excitement. These instruments produced a sound partaking of the braying of a donkey and the screech of an owl. Crowds of men rushed round and round in a sort of *galop infernel*, brandishing their lances and iron-headed maces, and keeping tolerably in line five or six deep, following the leader who headed them, dancing backwards. The women kept outside the line, dancing a slow stupid step, and screaming a wild and most inharmonious chant; while a long string of young girls and small children, their heads and necks rubbed with red ochre and grease, and prettily ornamented with strings of beads around their loins, kept a very good line, beating the time with their feet, and jingling the numerous iron rings which adorned their ankles to keep time with the drums. One woman attended upon the men, running through the crowd with a gourd full of wood-ashes, handfuls of which she showered over their heads, powdering them like millers; the object of the operation I could not understand. The *premiere danseuse* was immensely fat; she had passed the bloom of youth, but, *malgre* [inspite of] her unwieldy state, she kept up the pace to the last, quite unconscious of her general appearance, and absorbed with the excitement of the dance.

These festivities were to be continued in honour of the dead; and as many friends had recently been killed, music and dancing would be in fashion for some weeks.

There was an excellent interpreter belonging to Ibrahim's party – a Bari lad of about eighteen. This boy had been in their service for some years, and had learnt Arabic, which he spoke fluently, although with a peculiar accent, owing to the extraction of the four front teeth of the lower jaw, according to the general custom. It was of great importance to obtain the confidence of Loggo, as my success depended much upon information that I might obtain from the natives; therefore, whenever I sent for him to hold any conversation with the people, I invariably gave him a little present at parting. Accordingly he obeyed any summons from me with great alacrity, knowing that the interview would terminate with a *baksheesh* (present). In this manner I succeeded in establishing confidence, and he would frequently come uncalled to my tent and converse upon all manner of subjects. The Latooka language is different to the Bari, and a second interpreter was necessary; this was a sharp lad about the same age: thus the conversation was somewhat tedious, the medium being Bari and Latooka.

The chief Commoro (the "Lion") was one of the most clever and common sense savages that I had seen in these countries, and the tribe paid far more deference to his commands than to those of his brother, Moy, although the latter was the superior in rank.

One day I sent for Commoro after the usual funeral dance was completed, and, through my two young interpreters, I had a long conversation with him on the customs of his country. I wished if possible to fathom the origin of the extraordinary custom of exhuming the body after burial, as I imagined that in this act some idea might be traced to a belief in the resurrection.

Commoro was, like all his people, extremely tall. Upon entering my tent he took his seat upon the ground, the Latookas not using stools like the other White Nile tribes. I commenced the conversation by complimenting him on the perfection of his wives and daughters in the dance, and on his own agility in the performance; and inquired for whom the ceremony had been performed.

He replied, that it was for a man who had been recently killed, but no one of great importance, the same ceremony being observed for every person without distinction. I asked him why those slain in battle were allowed to remain unburied. He said, it had always been the custom, but that he could not explain it.

"But," I replied, "why should you disturb the bones of those whom you have already buried, and expose them on the outskirts of the town?"

"It was the custom of our forefathers," he answered, "therefore we continue to observe it."

"Have you no belief in a future existence after death? Is not some idea expressed in the act of exhuming the bones after the flesh is decayed?"

Commoro (loq.) – "Existence AFTER death! How can that be? Can a dead man get out of his grave, unless we dig him out?"

"Do you think man is like a beast, that dies and is ended?"

Commoro – "Certainly; an ox is stronger than a man; but he dies, and his bones last longer; they are bigger. A man's bones break quickly – he is weak."

"Is not a man superior in sense to an ox? Has he not a mind to direct his actions?"

Commoro – "Some men are not so clever as an ox. Men must sow corn to obtain food, but the ox and wild animals can procure it without sowing."

"Do you not know that there is a spirit within you more than flesh? Do you not dream and wander in thought to distant places in your sleep? Nevertheless, your body rests in one spot. How do you account for this?"

Commoro (laughing) – "Well, how do YOU account for it? It is a thing I cannot understand; it occurs to me every night."

"The mind is independent of the body; the actual body can be fettered, but the mind is uncontrollable; the body will die and will become dust, or be eaten by vultures, but the spirit will exist for ever."

Commoro – "Where will the spirit live?"

"Where does fire live? Cannot you produce a fire (The natives always produce fire by rubbing two sticks together.) by rubbing two sticks together, yet you SEE not the fire in the wood. Has not that fire, that lies harmless and unseen in the sticks, the power to consume the whole country? Which is the stronger, the small stick that first produces the fire, or the fire itself? So is the spirit the element within the body, as the element of fire exists in the stick; the element being superior to the substance."

Commoro – "Ha! Can you explain what we frequently see at night when lost in the wilderness? I have myself been lost, and wandering in the dark, I have seen a distant fire; upon approaching, the fire has vanished, and I have been unable to trace the cause – nor could I find the spot."

"Have you no idea of the existence of spirits superior to either man or beast? Have you no fear of evil except from bodily causes?"

Commoro – "I am afraid of elephants and other animals when in the jungle at night, but of nothing else."

"Then you believe in nothing; neither in a good nor evil spirit! And you believe that when you die it will be the end of body and spirit; that you are like other animals; and that there is no distinction between man and beast; both disappear, and end at death?"

Commoro – "Of course they do."

"Do you see no difference in good and bad actions?"

Commoro – "Yes, there are good and bad in men and beasts."

"Do you think that a good man and a bad must share the same fate, and alike die, and end?"

Commoro – "Yes; what else can they do? How can they help dying? Good and bad all die."

"Their bodies perish, but their spirits remain; the good in happiness, the bad in misery. If you have no belief in a future state, why should a man be good? Why should he not be bad, if he can prosper by wickedness?"

Commoro – "Most people are bad; if they are strong they take from the weak. The good people are all weak; they are good because they are not strong enough to be bad."

Some corn had been taken out of a sack for the horses, and a few grains lying scattered on the ground, I tried the beautiful metaphor of St. Paul as an example of a future state. Making a small hole with my finger in the ground, I placed a grain within it. "That," I said, "represents you when you die." Covering it with earth, I continued, "That grain will decay, but from it will rise the plant that will produce a reappearance of the original form."

Commoro – "Exactly so; that I understand. But the original grain does not rise again; it rots like the dead man, and is ended; the fruit produced is not the same grain that we buried, but the production of that grain: so it is with man – I die, and decay, and am ended; but my children grow up like the fruit of the grain. Some men have no children, and some grains perish without fruit; then all are ended."

I was obliged to change the subject of conversation. In this wild naked savage there was not even a superstition upon which to found a religious feeling; there was a belief in matter; and to his understanding everything was material. It was extraordinary to find so much clearness of perception combined with such complete obtuseness to anything ideal.

Giving up the religious argument as a failure, I resolved upon more practical inquiries.

The Turks had only arrived in the Latooka country in the preceding year. They had not introduced the cowrie shell; but I observed that every helmet was ornamented with this species; it therefore occurred to me that they must find their way into the country from Zanzibar.

In reply to my inquiries, Commoro pointed to the south, from which he said they arrived in his country, but he had no idea from whence they came. The direction was sufficient to prove that they must be sent from the east coast, as Speke and Grant had followed the Zanzibar traders as far as Karagwe, the 2 degrees S. lat.

Commoro could not possibly understand my object in visiting the Latooka country; it was in vain that I attempted to explain the intention of my journey. He said, "Suppose you get to the great lake; what will you do with it? What will be the good of it? If you find that the large river does flow from it, what then? What's the good of it?"

I could only assure him, that in England we had an intimate knowledge of the whole world, except the interior of Africa, and that our object in exploring was to benefit the hitherto unknown countries by instituting legitimate trade, and introducing manufactures from England in exchange for ivory and other productions. He replied that the Turks would never trade fairly; that they were extremely bad people, and that they would not purchase ivory in any other way than by bartering cattle, which they stole from one tribe to sell to another.

Our conversation was suddenly terminated by one of my men running in to the tent with the bad news that one of the camels had dropped down and was dying. The report was too true. He was poisoned by a well-known plant that he had been caught in the act of eating. In a few hours he died. There is no more stupid animal than the camel. Nature has implanted in most animals an instinctive knowledge of the plants suitable for food, and they generally avoid those that are poisonous: but the camel will eat indiscriminately anything that is green; and if in a country where the plant exists that is well known by the Arabs as the "camel poison," watchers must always accompany the animals while grazing. The most fatal plant is a creeper, very succulent, and so beautifully green that its dense foliage is most attractive to the stupid victim. The stomach of the camel is very subject to inflammation, which is rapidly fatal. I have frequently seen them, after several days of sharp desert marching, arrive in good pasture, and die, within a few hours, of inflammation caused by repletion. It is extraordinary how they can exist upon the driest and apparently most innutritious food. When other animals are starving, the camel manages to pick up a subsistence, eating the ends of barren, leafless twigs, the dried sticks of certain shrubs, and the tough dry paper-like substance of the dome palm, about as succulent a breakfast as would be a green umbrella and a Times newspaper. With intense greediness the camel, although a hermit in simplicity of fare in hard times, feeds voraciously when in abundant pasture, always seeking the greenest shrubs. The poison-bush becomes a fatal bait.

The camel is by no means well understood in Europe. Far from being the docile and patient animal generally described, it is quite the reverse, and the males are frequently dangerous. They are exceedingly perverse; and are, as before described, excessively stupid. For the great deserts they are wonderfully adapted, and without them it would be impossible to cross certain tracts of country for want of water.

Exaggerated accounts have been written respecting the length of time that a camel can travel without drinking. The period that the animal can subsist without suffering from thirst depends entirely upon the season and the quality of food. Precisely as in Europe sheep require but little water when fed upon turnips, so does the camel exist almost without drinking during the rainy season when pastured upon succulent and dewy herbage. During the hottest season, when green herbage ceases to exist in the countries inhabited by camels, they are led to water every alternate day, thus they are supposed to drink once in forty-eight hours; but when upon the march across deserts, where no water exists, they are expected to carry a load of from five to six hundred pounds, and to march twenty-five miles per day, for three days, without drinking, but to be watered on the fourth day. Thus a camel should drink the evening before the start, and he will carry his load one hundred miles without the necessity of drinking; not, however, without suffering from thirst. On the third day's march, during the hot simoom, the camel should drink if possible; but he can endure the fourth day.

This peculiarity of constitution enables the camel to overcome obstacles of nature that would otherwise be insurmountable. Not only can he travel over the scorching sand of the withering deserts, but he never seeks the shade. When released from his burden he kneels by his load in the burning sand, and luxuriates in the glare of a sun that drives all other beasts to shelter. The peculiar spongy formation of the foot renders the camel exceedingly sure, although it is usual to believe that it is only adapted for flat, sandy plains. I have travelled over mountains so precipitous that no domestic animal but the camel could have accomplished the task with a load. This capability is not shared generally by the race, but by a breed belonging to the Hadendowa Arabs, between the Red Sea and Taka. There is quite as great a variety in the breeds of camels as of horses. Those most esteemed in the Soudan are the Bishareen; they are not so large as others, but are exceedingly strong and enduring.

The average value of a baggage camel among the Soudan Arabs is fifteen dollars, but a good *hygeen*, or riding dromedary, is worth from fifty to a hundred and fifty dollars, according to his capabilities. A thoroughly good hygeen is supposed to travel fifty miles a day, and to continue this pace for five days, carrying only his rider and a small water-skin or girba. His action should be so easy that his long ambling trot should produce that peculiar movement adopted by a nurse when hushing a child to sleep upon her knee. This movement is delightful, and the quick elastic step of a first-class animal imparts an invigorating spirit to the rider; and were it not for the intensity of the sun, he would willingly ride forever. The difference of action and of comfort to the rider between a common camel and a high-class hygeen is equal to that between a thoroughbred and a heavy dray-horse.

However, with all the good qualities of a Bishareen, my best camel was dead. This was a sad loss. So long as my animals were well I felt independent, and the death of this camel was equal to minus five cwt. of luggage. My men were so idle that they paid no attention to the animals, and the watcher who had been appointed to look after the four camels had amused himself by going to the Latooka dance. Thus was the loss of my best animal occasioned.

So well had all my saddles and pads been arranged at Khartoum, that although we had marched seven days with exceedingly heavy loads, not one of the animals had a sore back. The donkeys were exceedingly fresh, but they had acquired a most disgusting habit. The Latookas are remarkably clean in their towns, and nothing unclean is permitted within the stockade or fence. Thus the outside, especially the neighbourhood of the various entrances, was excessively filthy, and my donkeys actually fattened as scavengers, like pigs. I remembered that my unfortunate German Johann Schmidt had formerly told me that he was at one time shooting in the Base country, where the grass had been burnt, and not a blade of vegetation was procurable. He had abundance of sport, and he fed his donkey upon the flesh of antelopes, which he ate with avidity, and throve exceedingly. It is a curious fact that donkeys should under certain circumstances become omnivorous, while horses remain clean feeders.

Chapter VII

LATOOKA

The country in the immediate neighbourhood of Latooka was parched, as there had been no rain for some time. The latitude was 4 degrees 35', longitude 32 degrees 55' E.; the rains had commenced in February on the mountains on the south side of the valley, about eighteen miles distant. Every day there was an appearance of a storm; the dark clouds gathered ominously around the peak of the Gebel Lafeet above the town, but they were invariably attracted by the higher range on the opposite and south side of the valley, where they daily expended themselves at about 3 p.m. On that side of the valley the mountains rose to about 6,000 feet, and formed a beautiful object seen from my camp. It was most interesting to observe the embryo storms travel from Tarrangolle in a circle, and ultimately crown the higher range before us, while the thunder roared and echoed from rock to rock across the plain.

The Latookas assured me that at the foot of those mountains there were elephants and giraffes in abundance; accordingly, I determined to make a reconnaissance of the country.

On the following morning I started on horseback, with two of my people mounted, and a native guide, and rode through the beautiful valley of Latooka to the foot of the range. The first five or six miles were entirely de-pastured by the enormous herds of the Latookas who were driven to that distance from the towns daily, all the country in the immediate vicinity being dried up. The valley was extremely fertile, but totally unoccupied and in a state of nature, being a wilderness of open plains, jungles, patches of forest and gullies, that although dry evidently formed swamps during the wet season. When about eight miles from the town we came upon tracks of the smaller antelopes, which, although the weakest, are the most daring in approaching the habitations of man. A few miles farther on, we saw buffaloes and hartebeest, and shortly came upon tracks of giraffes. Just at this moment the inky clouds that as usual had gathered over Tarrangolle came circling around us, and presently formed so dense a canopy that the darkness was like a partial eclipse. The thunder warned us with tremendous explosions just above us, while the lightning flashed almost at our feet with blinding vividness. A cold wind suddenly rushed through the hitherto calm air; this is the certain precursor of rain in hot climates, the heavier cold air of the raincloud falling into the stratum of warmer and lighter atmosphere below.

It did rain – in such torrents as only the inhabitants of tropical countries can understand. "Cover up the gun-locks!" And the pieces of mackintosh for that purpose were immediately secured in their places. Well, let it rain! It is rather pleasant to be wet through in a country where the thermometer is seldom below 92 degrees Fahr., especially when there is no doubt of getting wet through – not like the wretched drizzling rain of England, that chills you with the fear that perhaps your great-coat is not waterproof, but a regular douche bath that would beat in the crown of a cheap hat. How delightful to be really cool in the centre of Africa! I was charmingly wet – the water was running out of the heels of my shoes, which were overflowing; the wind howled over the flood that was pouring through the hitherto dry gullies, and in the course of ten minutes the whole scene had changed. It was no longer the tropics; the climate was that of old England restored to me: the chilled air refreshed me, and I felt at home again. "How delightful!" I exclaimed, as I turned round to see how my followers were enjoying it.

Dear me! I hardly knew my own people. Of all the miserable individuals I ever saw, they were superlative – they were not enjoying the change of climate in the least – with heads tucked down and streams of water running from their nasal extremities, they endeavoured to avoid the storm. Perfectly thoughtless of all but self in the extremity of their misery, they had neglected the precaution of lowering the muzzles of their guns, and my beautiful No. 10 rifles were full of water. "Charming day!" I exclaimed to my soaked and shivering followers, who looked like kittens in a pond. They muttered something that might be interpreted "What's fun to you is death to us." I comforted them with the assurance that this was an English climate on a midsummer day. If my clothed Arabs suffered from cold, where was my naked guide? He was the most pitiable object I ever saw; with teeth chattering and knees knocking together with cold, he crouched under the imaginary shelter of a large tamarind tree; he was no longer the clean black that had started as my guide, but the cold and wet had turned him grey, and being thin, he looked like an exaggerated slate-pencil. Not wishing to discourage my men, I unselfishly turned back just as I was beginning to enjoy myself, and my people regarded me as we do the Polar bear at the Zoological Gardens, who begins to feel happy on the worst day in our English winter.

We returned home by a different route, not being able to find the path in the trackless state of the country during the storm. There were in some places unmistakeable evidences of the presence of elephants, and I resolved to visit the spot again. I returned to the tent at 4 p.m. satisfied that sport was to be had.

On my arrival at camp I found the natives very excited at the appearance of rain, which they firmly believed had been called specially by their chief. All were busy preparing their molotes (iron hoes), fitting new handles, and getting everything ready for the periodical sowing of their crop.

The handles of the *molotes* are extremely long, from seven to ten feet, and the instrument being shaped like a miner's spade (heart-shaped), is used like a Dutch hoe, and is an effective tool in ground that has been cleared, but is very unfitted for preparing fresh soil. Iron ore of good quality exists on the surface throughout this country.

The Latookas, like the Baris, are excellent blacksmiths, producing a result that would astonish an English workman, considering the rough nature of their tools, which are confined to a hammer, anvil, and tongs; the latter formed of a cleft-stick of green wood, while the two former are stones of various sizes. Their bellows consist of two pots about a foot deep; from the bottom of each is an earthenware pipe about two feet long, the points of which are inserted in a charcoal fire. The mouths of the pots are covered with very pliable leather, loose and well greased; in the centre of each leather covering is an upright stick about four feet long, and the bellows-blower works these rapidly with a perpendicular motion, thus producing a strong blast. The natives are exceedingly particular in the shape of their molotes, and invariably prove them by balancing them on their heads and ringing them by a blow with the finger.

The Latookas being much engaged in preparing for cultivation, I had some difficulty in arranging a hunting party; my men abhorred the idea of elephant hunting, or of anything else that required hard work and included danger. However, I succeeded in engaging Adda, the third chief of Latooka, and several natives, to act as my guides, and I made my arrangements for a stated day.

On the 17th of April I started at 5 a.m. with my three horses and two camels, the latter carrying water and food. After a march of two or three hours through the beautiful hunting-grounds formed by the valley of Latooka, with its alternate prairies and jungles, I came upon the tracks of rhinoceros, giraffes, and elephants, and shortly moved a rhinoceros, but could get no shot, owing to the thick bush in which he started and disappeared quicker than I could dismount. After a short circuit in search of the rhinoceros, we came upon a large herd of buffaloes, but at the same moment we heard elephants trumpeting at the foot of the mountains. Not wishing to fire, lest the great game should be disturbed, I contented myself with riding after the buffaloes, wonderfully followed on foot by Adda, who ran like a deer, and almost kept up with my horse, hurling his three lances successively at the buffaloes, but without success. I had left the camels in an open plain, and returning from the gallop after the buffaloes, I saw the men on the camels beckoning to me in great excitement.

Cantering towards them, they explained that a herd of bull elephants had just crossed an open space, and had passed into the jungle beyond. There was evidently abundance of game; and calling my men together, I told them to keep close to me with the spare horses and rifles, while I sent the Latookas ahead to look out for the elephants: we followed at a short distance.

In about ten minutes we saw the Latookas hurrying towards us, and almost immediately after, I saw two enormous bull elephants with splendid tusks about a hundred yards from us, apparently the leaders of an approaching herd. The ground was exceedingly favourable, being tolerably open, and yet with sufficient bush to afford a slight cover. Presently, several elephants appeared and joined the two leaders – there was evidently a considerable number in the herd, and I was on the point of dismounting to take the first shot on foot, when the Latookas, too eager, approached the herd: their red and blue helmets at once attracted the attention of the elephants, and a tremendous rush took place, the whole herd closing together and tearing off at full speed. "Follow me!" I hallooed to my men, and touching my horse with the spur, I intended to dash into the midst of the herd. Just at that instant, in his start, my horse slipped and fell suddenly upon his side, falling upon my right leg and thus pinning me to the ground. He was not up to my weight, and releasing myself, I immediately mounted my old Abyssinian hunter, Tetel, and followed the tracks of the elephants at full speed, accompanied by two of the Latookas, who ran like hounds. Galloping through the green but thornless bush, I soon came in sight of a grand bull elephant, steaming along like a locomotive engine straight before me.

Digging in the spurs, I was soon within twenty yards of him; but the ground was so unfavourable, being full of buffalo holes, that I could not pass him. In about a quarter of an hour, after a careful chase over deep ruts and gullies concealed in high grass, I arrived at a level space, and shooting ahead, I gave him a shoulder shot with the Reilly No. 10 rifle. I saw the wound in a good place, but the bull rushed along all the quicker, and again we came into bad ground that made it unwise to close. However, on the first opportunity I made a dash by him, and fired my left-hand barrel at full gallop. He slackened his speed, but I could not halt to reload, lest I should lose sight of him in the high grass and bush.

Not a man was with me to hand a spare rifle. My cowardly fellows, although light-weights and well mounted, were nowhere; the natives were outrun, as of course was Richarn, who, not being a good rider, had preferred to hunt on foot. In vain I shouted for the men; and I followed the elephant with an empty rifle for about ten minutes, until he suddenly turned round, and stood facing me in an open spot in grass about nine or ten feet high. Tetel was a grand horse for elephants, not having the slightest fear, and standing fire like a rock, never even starting under the discharge of the heaviest charge of powder. I now commenced reloading, when presently one of my men, Yaseen, came up upon Filfil. Taking a spare gun from him, I rode rapidly past the elephant, and suddenly reining up, I made a good shot exactly behind the bladebone. With a shrill scream, the elephant charged down upon me like a steam engine. In went the spurs. Tetel knew his work, and away he went over the ruts and gullies, the high dry grass whistling in my ears as we shot along at full speed, closely followed by the enraged bull for about two hundred yards.

The elephant then halted; and turning the horse's head, I again faced him and reloaded. I thought he was dying, as he stood with trunk drooping, and ears closely pressed back upon his neck. Just at this moment I heard the rush of elephants advancing through the green bush upon the rising ground above the hollow formed by the open space of high withered grass in which we were standing facing each other. My man Yaseen had bolted with his fleet horse at the first charge, and was not to be seen. Presently, the rushing sound increased, and the heads of a closely packed herd of about eighteen elephants showed above the low bushes, and they broke cover, bearing down directly upon me, both I and my horse being unobserved in the high grass. I never saw a more lovely sight; they were all bulls with immense tusks. Waiting until they were within twenty yards of me, I galloped straight at them, giving a yell that turned them. Away they rushed up the hill, but at so great a pace, that upon the rutty and broken ground I could not overtake them, and they completely distanced me. Tetel, although a wonderfully steady hunter, was an uncommonly slow horse, but upon this day he appeared to be slower than usual, and I was not at the time aware that he was seriously ill. By following three elephants separated from the herd I came up to them by a short cut, and singling out a fellow with enormous tusks, I rode straight at him. Finding himself overhauled, he charged me with such quickness and followed me up so far, that it was with the greatest difficulty that I cleared him. When he turned, I at once returned to the attack; but he entered a thick thorny jungle through which no horse could follow, and I failed to obtain a shot.

I was looking for a path through which I could penetrate the bush, when I suddenly heard natives shouting in the direction

where I had left the wounded bull. Galloping towards the spot, I
met a few scattered natives; among others, Adda. After shouting for
some time, at length Yaseen appeared upon my horse Filfil; he had
fled as usual when he saw the troop of elephants advancing, and no
one knows how far he had ridden before he thought it safe to look
behind him. With two mounted gun- bearers and five others on foot
I had been entirely deserted through the cowardice of my men. The
elephant that I had left as dying, was gone. One of the Latookas had
followed upon his tracks, and we heard this fellow shouting in the
distance. I soon overtook him, and he led rapidly upon the track
through thick bushes and high grass. In about a quarter of an hour
we came up with the elephant; he was standing in bush, facing us at
about fifty yards' distance, and immediately perceiving us, he gave
a saucy jerk with his head, and charged most determinedly. It was
exceedingly difficult to escape, owing to the bushes which impeded
the horse, while the elephant crushed them like cobwebs: however,
by turning my horse sharp round a tree, I managed to evade him
after a chase of about a hundred and fifty yards. Disappearing in the
jungle after his charge, I immediately followed him. The ground
was hard, and so trodden by elephants that it was difficult to single
out the track. There was no blood upon the ground, but only on the
trees every now and then, where he had rubbed past them in his
retreat. After nearly two hours passed in slowly following upon his
path, we suddenly broke cover and saw him travelling very quietly
through an extensive plain of high grass. The ground was gently
inclining upwards on either side the plain, but the level was a mass
of deep, hardened ruts, over which no horse could gallop. Knowing
my friend's character, I rode up the rising ground to reconnoitre: I
found it tolerably clear of holes, and far superior to the rutty bottom. My two mounted gun-bearers had now joined me, and far
from enjoying the sport, they were almost green with fright, when I
ordered them to keep close to me and to advance.

I wanted them to attract the elephant's attention, so as to enable
me to obtain a good shoulder shot. Riding along the open plain, I at
length arrived within about fifty yards of the bull, when he slowly
turned. Reining Tetel up, I immediately fired a steady shot at the
shoulder with the Reilly No. 10 – for a moment he fell upon his
knees, but, recovering with wonderful quickness, he was in full

charge upon me. Fortunately I had inspected my ground previous to the attack, and away I went up the inclination to my right, the spurs hard at work, and the elephant screaming with rage, gaining on me. My horse felt as though made of wood, and clumsily rolled along in a sort of cow-gallop; in vain I dug the spurs into his flanks, and urged him by rein and voice; not an extra stride could I get out of him, and he reeled along as though thoroughly exhausted, plunging in and out of the buffalo holes instead of jumping them. Hamed was on my horse Mouse, who went three to Tetel' one, and instead of endeavouring to divert the elephant's attention, he shot ahead, and thought of nothing but getting out of the way. Yaseen, on Filfil, had fled in another direction; thus I had the pleasure of being hunted down upon a sick and disabled horse. I kept looking round, thinking that the elephant would give in – we had been running for nearly half a mile, and the brute was overhauling me so fast that he was within ten or twelve yards of the horse's tail, with his trunk stretched out to catch him. Screaming like the whistle of an engine, he fortunately so frightened the horse that he went his best, although badly, and I turned him suddenly down the hill and doubled back like a hare. The elephant turned up the hill, and entering the jungle he relinquished the chase, when another hundred yards' run would have bagged me.

In a life's experience in elephant-hunting, I never was hunted for such a distance. Great as were Tetel's good qualities for pluck and steadiness, he had exhibited such distress and want of speed, that I was sure he failed through some sudden malady. I immediately dismounted, and the horse laid down, as I thought, to die.

Whistling loudly, I at length recalled Hamed, who had still continued his rapid flight without once looking back, although the elephant was out of sight. Yaseen was, of course, nowhere; but after a quarter of an hour's shouting and whistling, he reappeared, and I mounted Filfil, ordering Tetel to be led home.

The sun had just sunk, and the two Latookas who now joined me refused to go farther on the tracks, saying, that the elephant must die during the night, and that they would find him in the morning. We were at least ten miles from camp; I therefore fired a shot to collect my scattered men, and in about half an hour we all joined together, except the camels and their drivers, that we had left miles behind.

No one had tasted food since the previous day, nor had I drunk water, although the sun had been burning hot; I now obtained some muddy rain water from a puddle, and we went towards home, where we arrived at half-past eight, every one tired with the day's work. The camels came into camp about an hour later.

My men were all now wonderfully brave; each had some story of a narrow escape, and several declared that the elephants had run over them, but fortunately without putting their feet upon them. *big liars*

The news spread through the town that the elephant was killed; and, long before daybreak on the following morning, masses of natives had started for the jungles, where they found him lying dead. Accordingly, they stole his magnificent tusks, which they carried to the town of Wakkala, and confessed to taking all the flesh, but laid the blame of the ivory theft upon the Wakkala tribe.

There was no redress. The questions of a right of game are ever prolific of bad blood, and it was necessary in this instance to treat the matter lightly. Accordingly, the natives requested me to go out and shoot them another elephant: on the condition of obtaining the meat, they were ready to join in any hunting expedition.

The elephants in Central Africa have very superior tusks to those of Abyssinia. I had shot a considerable number in the Base country on the frontier of Abyssinia, and few tusks were above 30 lbs. weight; those in the neighbourhood of the White Nile average about 50 lbs. for each tusk of a bull elephant, while those of the females are generally about 10 lbs. I have seen monster tusks of 160 lbs., and one was in the possession of a trader, Mons. P., that weighed 172 lbs.

It is seldom that a pair of tusks is alike. As a man uses the right hand in preference to the left, so the elephant works with a particular tusk, which is termed by the traders "*el Hadam*" (the servant); this is naturally, more worn than the other, and is usually about ten pounds lighter: frequently it is broken, as the elephant uses it as a lever to uproot trees and to tear up the roots of various bushes upon which he feeds.

The African elephant is not only entirely different from the Indian species in his habits, but he also differs in form.

There are three distinguishing peculiarities. The back of the African elephant is concave, that of the Indian is convex; the ear of the African is enormous, entirely covering the shoulder when thrown back, while the ear of the Indian variety is comparatively small. The head of the African has a convex front, the top of the skull sloping back at a rapid inclination, while the head of the Indian elephant exposes a flat surface a little above the trunk.

The average size of the African elephant is larger than those of Ceylon, although I have occasionally shot monster rogues in the latter country, equal to anything that I have seen in Africa. The average height of female elephants in Ceylon is about 7 ft. 10 in. at the shoulder, and that of the males is about 9 ft.; but the usual height of the African variety I have found, by actual measurement, of females to be 9 ft., while that of the bills is 10 ft. 6 in. Thus the females of the African are equal to the males of Ceylon.

They also differ materially in their habits. In Ceylon, the elephant seeks the shade of thick forests at the rising of the sun, in which he rests until about 5 p.m., when he wanders forth upon the plains. In Africa, the country being generally more open, the elephant remains throughout the day either beneath a solitary tree, or exposed to the sun in the vast prairies, where the thick grass attains a height of from nine to twelve feet. The general food of the African elephant consists of the foliage of trees, especially of mimosas. In Ceylon, although there are many trees that serve as food, the elephant nevertheless is an extensive grass-feeder. The African variety, being almost exclusively a tree-feeder, requires his tusks to assist him in procuring food. Many of the mimosas are flat-headed, about thirty feet high, and the richer portion of the foliage confined to the crown; thus the elephant, not being able to reach to so great a height, must overturn the tree to procure the coveted food. The destruction caused by a herd of African elephants in a mimosa forest is extraordinary; and I have seen trees uprooted of so large a size, that I am convinced no single elephant could have overturned them. I have measured trees four feet six inches in circumference, and about thirty feet high, uprooted by elephants. The natives have assured me that they mutually assist each other, and that several engage together in the work of overturning a large tree. None of the mimosas have tap-roots; thus the powerful tusks of the elephants, applied as crowbars at the roots, while others pull at the branches with their trunks, will effect the destruction of a tree so large as to appear invulnerable. The Ceylon elephant rarely possessing tusks, cannot destroy a tree thicker than the thigh of an ordinary man.

In Ceylon, I have seldom met old bulls in parties – they are generally single or remain in pairs; but, in Africa, large herds are met with, consisting entirely of bulls. I have frequently seen sixteen or twenty splendid bulls together, presenting a show of ivory most exciting to a hunter. The females in Africa congregate in vast herds of many hundreds, while in Ceylon the herds seldom average more than ten.

The elephant is by far the most formidable of all animals, and the African variety is more dangerous than the Indian, as it is next to impossible to kill it by the forehead shot. The head is so peculiarly formed, that the ball either passes over the brain, or lodges in the immensely solid bones and cartilages that contain the roots of the tusks. I have measured certainly a hundred bull tusks, and I have found them buried in the head a depth of 24 inches. One large tusk, that measured 7 ft. 8 in. in length, and 22 inches in girth, was imbedded in the head a depth of 31 inches. This will convey an idea of the enormous size of the head, and of the strength of bone and cartilage required to hold in position so great a weight, and to resist the strain when the tusk is used as a lever to uproot trees.

The brain of an African elephant rests upon a plate of bone exactly above the roots of the upper grinders; it is thus wonderfully protected from a front shot, as it lies so low that the ball passes above it when the elephant raises his head, which he invariably does when in anger, until close to the object of his attack.

The character of the country naturally influences the habits of the animals: thus, Africa being more generally open than the forest-clad Ceylon, the elephant is more accustomed to activity, and is much faster than the Ceylon variety. Being an old elephant-hunter of the latter island, I was exceedingly interested in the question of variety of species, and I had always held the opinion that the African elephant might be killed with the same facility as that of Ceylon, by the forehead shot, provided that a sufficient charge of powder were used to penetrate the extra thickness of the head. I have found, by much experience, that I was entirely wrong, and that, although by chance an African elephant may be killed by the front shot, it is the exception to the rule. The danger of the sport is, accordingly, much increased, as it is next to impossible to kill the elephant when in full charge, and the only hope of safety consists in turning him by a continuous fire with heavy guns: this cannot always be effected.

I had a powerful pair of No. 10 polygroove rifles, made by Reilly of Oxford Street; they weighed fifteen pounds, and carried seven drachms of powder without a disagreeable recoil. The bullet was a blunt cone, one and a half diameter of the bore, and I used a mixture of nine-tenths lead and one-tenth quicksilver for the hardening of the projectile. This is superior to all mixtures for that purpose, as it combines hardness with extra weight; the lead must be melted in a pot by itself to a red heat, and the proportion of quicksilver must be added a ladle-full at a time, and stirred quickly with a piece of iron just in sufficient quantity to make three or four bullets. If the quicksilver is subjected to a red heat in the large lead-pot, it will evaporate. The only successful forehead shot that I made at an African elephant was shortly after my arrival in the Abyssinian territory on the Settite River; this was in thick thorny jungle, and an elephant from the herd charged with such good intention, that had she not been stopped, she must have caught one of the party. When within about five yards of the muzzle, I killed her dead by a forehead shot with a hardened bullet as described, from a Reilly No. 10 rifle, and we subsequently recovered the bullet in the vertebrae of the neck!

This extraordinary penetration led me to suppose that I should always succeed as I had done in Ceylon, and I have frequently stood the charge of an African elephant until close upon me, determined to give the forehead shot a fair trial, but I have always failed, except in the instance now mentioned; it must also be borne in mind that the elephant was a female, with a head far inferior in size and solidity to that of the male.

The temple shot, and that behind the ear, are equally fatal in Africa as in Ceylon, provided the hunter can approach within ten or twelve yards; but altogether the hunting is far more difficult, as the character of the country does not admit of an approach sufficiently close to guarantee a successful shot. In the forests of Ceylon an elephant can be stalked to within a few paces, and the shot is seldom fired at a greater distance than ten yards: thus accuracy of aim is insured; but in the open ground of Africa, an elephant can seldom be approached within fifty yards, and should he charge the hunter, escape is most difficult. I never found African elephants in good jungle, except once, and on that occasion I shot five, quite as quickly as we should kill them in Ceylon.

The character of the sport must vary according to the character of the country; thus there may be parts of Africa at variance with my description. I only relate my own experience.

Among other weapons, I had an extraordinary rifle that carried a half-pound percussion shell – this instrument of torture to the hunter was not sufficiently heavy for the weight of the projectile; it only weighed twenty pounds: thus, with a charge of ten drachms of powder, behind a half-pound shell, the recoil was so terrific, that I was spun round like a weathercock in a hurricane. I really dreaded my own rifle, although I had been accustomed to heavy charges of powder and severe recoil for many years.

None of my men could fire it, and it was looked upon with a species of awe, and was named "*Jenna el Mootfah* (child of a cannon)" by the Arabs, which being far too long a name for practice, I christened it "the Baby;" and the scream of this "Baby," loaded with a half-pound shell, was always fatal. It was far too severe, and I very seldom fired it, but it is a curious fact, that I never fired a shot with that rifle without bagging: the entire practice, during several years, was confined to about twenty shots. I was afraid to use it; but now and then it was absolutely necessary that it should be cleaned, after lying for months loaded. On such occasions my men had the gratification of firing it, and the explosion was always accompanied by two men falling on their backs (one having propped up the shooter), and "the Baby" flying some yards behind them. This rifle was made by Holland, of Bond Street, and I could highly recommend it for Goliath of Gath, but not for men of A.D. 1866.

The natives of Central Africa generally hunt the elephant for the sake of the flesh, and prior to the commencement of the White Nile trade by the Arabs, and the discovery of the Upper White Nile to the 5 degrees N. lat. by the expedition sent by Mehemet Ali

Pasha, the tusks were considered as worthless, and were treated as bones. The death of an elephant is a grand affair for the natives, as it supplies flesh for an enormous number of people, also fat, which is the great desire of all savages for internal and external purposes. There are various methods of killing them. Pitfalls are the most common, but the wary old bulls are seldom caught in this manner.

The position chosen for the pit is, almost without exception, in the vicinity of a drinking place, and the natives exhibit a great amount of cunning in felling trees across the usual run of the elephants, and sometimes cutting an open pit across the path, so as to direct the elephant by such obstacles into the path of snares. The pits are usually about twelve feet long, and three feet broad, by nine deep; these are artfully made, decreasing towards the bottom to the breadth of a foot. The general elephant route to the drinking place being blocked up, the animals are diverted by a treacherous path towards the water, the route intersected by numerous pits, all of which are carefully concealed by sticks and straw, the latter being usually strewn with elephants' dung to create a natural effect.

Should an elephant, during the night, fall through the deceitful surface, his foot becomes jammed in the bottom of the narrow grave, and he labours shoulder deep, with two feet in the pitfall so fixed that extrication is impossible. Should one animal be thus caught, a sudden panic seizes the rest of the herd, and in their hasty retreat one or more are generally victims to the numerous pits in the vicinity. The old bulls never approach a watering place rapidly, but carefully listen for danger, and then slowly advance with their warning trunks stretched to the path before them; the delicate nerves of the proboscis at once detect the hidden snare, and the victims to pitfalls are the members of large herds who, eager to push forward incautiously, put their "foot into it," like shareholders in bubble companies. Once helpless in the pit, they are easily killed with lances.

The great elephant-hunting season is in January, when the high prairies are parched and reduced to straw. At such a time, should a large herd of animals be discovered, the natives of the entire district collect together to the number of perhaps a thousand men; surrounding the elephants by embracing a considerable tract of country, they fire the grass at a given signal. In a few minutes the unconscious elephants are surrounded by a circle of fire, which, however distant, must eventually close in upon them. The men advance with the fire, which rages to the height of twenty or thirty feet. At length the elephants, alarmed by the volumes of smoke and the roaring of the flames, mingled with the shouts of the hunters, attempt an escape. They are hemmed in on every side – wherever they rush, they are met by an impassable barrier of flames and smoke, so stifling, that they are forced to retreat. Meanwhile the fatal circle is decreasing; buffaloes and antelopes, likewise doomed to a horrible fate, crowd panic stricken to the centre of the encircled ring, and the raging fire sweeps over all. Burnt and blinded by fire and smoke, the animals are now attacked by the savage crowd of hunters, excited by the helplessness of the unfortunate elephants thus miserably sacrificed, and they fall under countless spears. This destructive method of hunting ruins the game of that part of Africa, and so scarce are the antelopes, that, in a day's journey, a dozen head are seldom seen in the open prairie. *niggers didn't practice conservation*

The next method of hunting is perfectly legitimate. Should many elephants be in the neighbourhood, the natives post about a hundred men in as many large trees; these men are armed with heavy lances specially adapted to the sport, with blades about eighteen inches long and three inches broad. The elephants are driven by a great number of men towards the trees in which the spearmen are posted, and those that pass sufficiently near are speared between the shoulders. The spear being driven deep into the animal, creates a frightful wound, as the tough handle, striking against the intervening branches of trees, acts as a lever, and works the long blade of the spear within the elephant, cutting to such an extent that he soon drops from exhaustion.

The best and only really great elephant-hunters of the White Nile are the Bagara Arabs, on about the 13 degree N. lat. These men hunt on horseback, and kill the elephant in fair fight with their spears.

The lance is about fourteen feet long, of male bamboo; the blade is about fourteen inches long by nearly three inches broad; this is as sharp as a razor. Two men, thus armed and mounted, form the hunting party. Should they discover a herd, they ride up to the finest tusker and single him from the others. One man now leads the way, and the elephant, finding himself pressed, immediately charges the horse. There is much art required in leading the elephant, who follows the horse with great determination, and the rider adapts his pace so as to keep his horse so near the elephant that his attention is entirely absorbed with the hope of catching him. The other hunter should by this tine have followed close to the elephant's heels, and, dismounting when at full gallop with wonderful dexterity, he plunges his spear with both hands into the elephant about two feet below the junction of the tail, and with all his force he drives the spear about eight feet into his abdomen, and withdraws it immediately. Should he be successful in his stab, he remounts his horse and flies, or does his best to escape on foot, should he not have time to mount, as the elephant generally turns to pursue him. His comrade immediately turns his horse, and, dashing at the elephant, in his turn dismounts, and drives his lance deep into his intestines.

Generally, if the first thrust is scientifically given, the bowels protrude to such an extent that the elephant is at once disabled. Two good hunters will frequently kill several out of one herd; but in this dangerous hand-to-hand fight the hunter is often the victim. Hunting the elephant on horseback is certainly far less dangerous than on foot, but although the speed of the horse is undoubtedly superior, the chase generally takes place upon ground so disadvantageous, that he is liable to fall, in which case there is little chance for either animal or rider. So savage are the natural instincts of Africans, that they attend only to the destruction of the elephant, and never attempt its domestication.

Chapter VIII

IBRAHIM'S RETURN

Ibrahim returned from Gondokoro, bringing with him a large supply of ammunition. A wounded man of Chenooda's people also arrived, the sole relic of the fight with the Latookas; he had been left for dead, but had recovered, and for days and nights he had wandered about the country, in thirst and hunger, hiding like a wild beast from the sight of human beings, his guilty conscience marking every Latooka as an enemy. As a proof of the superiority of the natives to the Khartoumers, he had at length been met by some Latookas, and not only was well treated and fed by their women, but they had guided him to Ibrahim's camp.

The black man is a curious anomaly, the good and bad points of human nature bursting forth without any arrangement, like the flowers and thorns of his own wilderness. A creature of impulse, seldom actuated by reflection, the black man astounds by his complete obtuseness, and as suddenly confounds you by an unexpected exhibition of sympathy. From a long experience with African savages, I think it is as absurd to condemn the negro *in toto*, as it is preposterous to compare his intellectual capacity with that of the white man. It is unfortunately the fashion for one party to uphold the negro as a superior being, while the other denies him the common powers of reason. So great a difference of opinion has ever existed upon the intrinsic value of the negro, that the very perplexity of the question is a proof that he is altogether a distinct variety. So long as it is generally considered that the negro and the white man are to be governed by the same laws and guided by the same management, so long will the former remain a thorn in the side of every community to which he may unhappily belong. When the horse and the ass shall be found to match in double harness, the white man and the

African black will pull together under the same regime. It is the grand error of equalizing that which is unequal, that has lowered the negro character, and made the black man a reproach.

In his savage home, what is the African? Certainly bad, but not so bad as white men would (I believe) be under similar circumstances. He is acted upon by the bad passions inherent in human nature, but there is no exaggerated vice, such as is found in civilized countries. The strong takes from the weak, one tribe fights the other – do not perhaps we in Europe? These are the legitimate acts of independent tribes, authorized by their chiefs. They mutually enslave each other – how long is it since America and we ourselves ceased to be slaveholders? He is callous and ungrateful – in Europe is there no ingratitude?

He is cunning and a liar by nature – in Europe is all truth and sincerity? Why should the black man not be equal to the white? He is as powerful in frame, a why should he not be as exalted in mind?

In childhood I believe the negro to be in advance, in intellectual quickness, of the white child of a similar age, but the mind does not expand – it promises fruit, but does not ripen; and the negro man has grown in body, but not advanced in intellect.

The puppy of three months old is superior in intellect to a child of the same age, but the mind of the child expands, while that of the dog has arrived at its limit. The chicken of the common fowl has sufficient power and instinct to run in search of food the moment that it leaves the egg, while the young of the eagle lies helpless in its nest; but the young eagle outstrips the chicken in the course of time. The earth presents a wonderful example of variety in all classes of the human race, the animal and vegetable kingdoms. People, beasts, and plants belonging to distinct classes, exhibit special qualities and peculiarities. The existence of many hundred varieties of dogs cannot interfere with the fact that they belong to one genus: the greyhound, pug, bloodhound, pointer, poodle, mastiff, and toy terrier, are all as entirely different in their peculiar instincts as are the varieties of the human race. The different fruits and flowers continue the example; the wild grapes of the forest are grapes, but although they belong to the same class, they are distinct from the luscious Muscatel, and the wild dog-rose of the hedge, although of the same class, is inferior to the moss-rose of the garden.

From fruits and flowers we may turn to insect life, and, watch the air teeming with varieties of the same species, the thousands of butterflies and beetles, the many members of each class varying in instincts and peculiarities. Fishes, and even shellfish, all exhibit the same arrangement – that every group is divided into varieties all differing from each other, and each distinguished by some peculiar excellence or defect.

In the great system of creation that divided races and subdivided them according to mysterious laws, apportioning special qualities to each, the varieties of the human race exhibit certain characters and qualifications which adapt them for specific localities. The natural character of those races will not alter with a change of locality, but the instincts of each race will be developed in any country where they may be located. Thus, the English are as English in Australia, India, and America, as they are in England, and in every locality they exhibit the industry and energy of their native land; even so the African will remain negro in all his natural instincts, although transplanted to other soils; and those natural instincts being a love of idleness and savagedom, he will assuredly relapse into an idle and savage state, unless specially governed and forced to industry. *absolutly true!*

The history of the negro has proved the correctness of this theory. In no instance has he evinced other than a retrogression, when once freed from restraint. Like a horse without harness, he runs wild, but, if harnessed, no animal is more useful. Unfortunately, this is contrary to public opinion in England, where the vox populi assumes the right of dictation upon matters and men in which it has had no experience. The English insist upon their own weights and measures as the scales for human excellence, and it has been decreed by the multitude, inexperienced in the negro personally, that he has been a badly-treated brother; that he is a worthy member of the human family, placed in an inferior position through the prejudice and ignorance of the white man, with whom he should be upon equality.

The negro has been, and still is, thoroughly misunderstood. However severely we may condemn the horrible system of slavery, the results of emancipation have proved that the negro does not appreciate the blessings of freedom, nor does he show the slightest feeling of gratitude to the hand that broke the rivets of his fetters. His narrow mind cannot embrace that feeling of pure philanthropy that first prompted England to declare herself against slavery, and he only regards the antislavery movement as a proof of his own importance. In his limited horizon he is himself the important object, and, as a sequence to his self-conceit, he imagines that the whole world is at issue concerning the black man. The negro, therefore, being the important question, must be an important person, and he conducts himself accordingly – he is far too great a man to work. Upon this point his natural character exhibits itself most determinedly. Accordingly, he resists any attempt at coercion; being free, his first impulse is to claim an equality with those whom he lately served, and to usurp a dignity with absurd pretensions, that must inevitably insure the disgust of the white community. Ill will thus engendered, a hatred and jealousy is established between the two races, combined with the errors that in such conditions must arise upon both sides. The final question remains, Why was the negro first introduced into our colonies – and to America?

The sun is the great arbitrator between the white and the black man. There are productions necessary to civilized countries, that can alone be cultivated in tropical climates, where the white man cannot live if exposed to labour in the sun. Thus, such fertile countries as the West Indies and portions of America being without a native population, the negro was originally imported as a slave to fulfil the conditions of a labourer. In his own country he was a wild savage, and enslaved his brother man; he thus became a victim to his own system; to the institution of slavery that is indigenous to the soil of Africa, and that has not been taught to the African by the white man, as is currently reported, but that has ever been the peculiar characteristic of African tribes.

In his state of slavery the negro was compelled to work, and, through his labour, every country prospered where he had been introduced. He was suddenly freed; and from that moment he refused to work, and instead of being a useful member of society, he not only became a useless burden to the community, but a plotter and intriguer, imbued with a deadly hatred to the white man who had generously declared him free.

Now, as the negro was originally imported as a labourer, but now refuses to labour, it is self-evident that he is a lamentable failure. Either he must be compelled to work, by some stringent law against vagrancy, or those beautiful countries that prospered under the conditions of negro forced industry must yield to ruin, under negro freedom and idle independence. For an example of the results look to St. Domingo!

Under peculiar guidance, and subject to a certain restraint, the negro may be an important and most useful being; but if treated as an Englishman, he will affect the vices but none of the virtues of civilization, and his natural good qualities will be lost in his attempts to become a "white man."

Revenons a nos moutons noirs. It was amusing to watch the change that took place in a slave that had been civilized (?) by the slave-traders. Among their parties there were many blacks who had been captured, and who enjoyed the life of slave-hunting – nothing appeared so easy as to become professional in cattle *razzias* and kidnapping human beings, and the first act of the slave was to procure a slave for himself! All the best slave-hunters, and the boldest and most energetic scoundrels, were the negroes who had at one time themselves been kidnapped. These fellows aped a great and ridiculous importance. On the march they would seldom condescend to carry their own guns; a little slave boy invariably attended to his master, keeping close to his heels, and trotting along on foot during a long march, carrying a musket much longer than himself: a woman generally carried a basket with a cooking-pot, and a gourd of water and provisions, while a hired native carried the soldier's change of clothes and oxhide upon which he slept. Thus the man who had been kidnapped became the kidnapper, and the slave became the master, the only difference between him and the Arab being an absurd notion of his own dignity. It was in vain that I attempted to reason with them against the principles of slavery: they thought it wrong when they were themselves the sufferers, but were always ready to indulge in it when the preponderance of power lay upon their side.

Among Ibrahim's people, there was a black named Ibrahimawa. This fellow was a native of Bornu, and had been taken when a boy of twelve years old and sold at Constantinople; he formerly belonged to Mehemet Ali Pasha; he had been to London and Paris, and during the Crimean war he was at Kertch. Altogether he was a great traveller, and he had a natural taste for geography and botany, that marked him as a wonderful exception to the average of the party. He had run away from his master in Egypt, and had been vagabondizing about in Khartoum in handsome clothes, negro-like, persuading himself that the public admired him, and thought that he was a Bey. Having soon run through his money, he had engaged himself to Koorshid Aga to serve in his White Nile expedition.

He was an excellent example of the natural instincts of the negro remaining intact under all circumstances. Although remarkably superior to his associates, his small stock of knowledge was combined with such an exaggerated conceit, that he was to me a perpetual source of amusement, while he was positively hated by his comrades, both by Arabs and blacks, for his overbearing behaviour. Having seen many countries, he was excessively fond of recounting his adventures, all of which had so strong a colouring of the *Arabian Nights*, that he might have been the original Sinbad the Sailor. His natural talent for geography was really extraordinary; he would frequently pay me a visit, and spend hours in drawing maps with a stick upon the sand, of the countries he had visited, and especially of the Mediterranean, and the course from Egypt and Constantinople to England. Unfortunately, some long story was attached to every principal point of the voyage. The descriptions most interesting to me were those connected with the west bank of the White Nile, as he had served some years with the trading party, and had penetrated through the Makkarika, a cannibal tribe, to about two hundred miles west of Gondokoro. Both he and many of Ibrahim's party had been frequent witnesses to acts of cannibalism, during their residence among the Makkarikas. They described these cannibals as remarkably good people, but possessing a peculiar taste for dogs and human flesh. They accompanied the trading party in their *razzia*s, and invariably ate the bodies of the slain. The traders complained that they were bad associates, as they insisted upon killing and eating the children which the party wished to secure as slaves: their custom was to catch a child by its ankles, and to dash its head against the ground; thus killed, they opened the abdomen, extracted the stomach and intestines, and tying the two ankles to the neck they carried the body by slinging it over the shoulder, and thus returned to camp, where they divided it by quartering, and boiled it in a large pot. Another man in my own service had been a witness to a horrible act of cannibalism at Gondokoro.

The traders had arrived with their ivory from the West, together with a great number of slaves; the porters who carried the ivory being Makkarikas. One of the slave girls attempted to escape, and her proprietor immediately fired at her with his musket, and she fell wounded; the ball had struck her in the side. The girl was remarkably fat, and from the wound, a large lump of yellow fat exuded. No sooner had she fallen, than the Makkarikas rushed upon her in a crowd, and seizing the fat, they tore it from the wound in handfuls, the girl being still alive, while the crowd were quarrelling for the disgusting prize. Others killed her with a lance, and at once divided her by cutting off the head, and splitting the body with their lances, used as knives, cutting longitudinally from between the legs along the spine to the neck.

Many slave women and their children who witnessed this scene, rushed panic-stricken from the spot and took refuge in the trees. The Makkarikas seeing them in flight, were excited to give chase, and pulling the children from their refuge among the branches, they killed several, and in a short time a great feast was prepared for the whole party. My man, Mahommed, who was an eyewitness, declared that he could not eat his dinner for three days, so great was his disgust at this horrible feast.

Although my camp was entirely separate from that of Ibrahim, I was dreadfully pestered by his people, who, knowing that I was well supplied with many articles of which they were in need, came begging to my tent from morning till evening daily. To refuse was to insult them; and as my chance of success in the exploration unfortunately depended upon my not offending the traders I was obliged to be coldly civil, and nothing was refused them. Hardly a day passed without broken guns being brought to me for repair; and having earned an unenviable celebrity as a gunsmith, added to my possession of the requisite tools, I really had no rest, and I was kept almost constantly at work.

One day Ibrahim was seized with a dangerous fever, and was supposed to be dying. Again I was in request: and seeing that he was in a state of partial collapse, attended with the distressing symptoms of want of action of the heart, so frequently fatal at this stage of the disease, I restored him by a very powerful stimulant, and thereby gained renown as a physician, which, although useful was extremely annoying, as my tent was daily thronged with patients, all of whom expected miraculous cures for the most incurable diseases.

In this manner I gained a certain influence over the people, but I was constantly subjected to excessive annoyances and disgust, occasioned by the conduct of their party towards the Latookas. The latter were extremely unwise, being very independent and ready to take offence on the slightest pretext, and the Turks, being now 140 strong, had no fear, and there appeared every probability of hostilities. I was engaged in erecting huts, and in securing my camp; and although I offered high payment, I could not prevail on the natives to work regularly. They invariably stipulated that they were to receive their beads before they commenced work, in which case they, with few exceptions, absconded with their advanced payment.

One day a native behaved in a similar manner to the Turks; he was, accordingly, caught, and unmercifully beaten. Half an hour after, the *nogara* beat, and was answered by distant drums from the adjacent villages. In about an hour, several thousand armed men, with shields, were collected within half a mile of the Turks' camp, to avenge the insult that had been offered to one of their tribe. However, the Turks' drum beat, and their whole force drew up to their flag under arms outside their zareeba, and offered a determined front. I extract the following entry from my journal:

"These Turks are delightful neighbours; they will create a row, and I shall be dragged into it in self-defence, as the natives will distinguish no difference in a scrimmage, although they draw favourable comparisons between me and the Turks in times of peace. Not a native came to work at the huts today; I therefore sent for the two chiefs, Commoro and Moy, and had a long talk with them. They said that 'no Latooka should be beaten by common fellows like the traders' men; that I was a great chief, and that if I chose to beat them they would be content.' I gave them advice to keep quiet, and not to quarrel about trifles, as the Turks would assuredly destroy the country should a fight commence.

"At the same time, I told them that they did not treat me properly: they came to me in times of difficulty as a mediator, but although they knew I had always paid well for everything, they gave me no supplies, and I was obliged to shoot game for my daily food, although they possessed such enormous herds of cattle; neither could I procure materials or workpeople to complete my camp. The parley terminated with an understanding that they were to supply me with everything, and that they would put a stop to the intended fight. In the evening a goat was brought, and a number of men appeared with grass and wood for sale for hut-building."

The following day, some of my people went to a neighbouring village to purchase corn, but the natives insulted them, refusing to sell, saying that we should die of hunger, as no one should either give or sell us anything. This conduct must induce hostilities, as the Turks are too powerful to be insulted. I am rather anxious lest some expedition may entail the departure of the entire Turkish party, when the Latookas may seize the opportunity of attacking my innocents. The latter are now so thoroughly broken to my severe laws – "thou shalt not take slaves; neither cattle; nor fire a shot unless in self-defence" – that they are resigned to the ignoble lot of minding the donkeys, and guarding the camp.

Latooka was in a very disturbed state, and the excitement of the people was increasing daily. Two of my men went into the town to buy grass, and, without any provocation, they were surrounded by the natives, and the gun of one man was wrested from him; the other, after a tussle, in which he lost his ramrod, beat a hasty retreat. A number of the soldiers immediately collected, and I sent to the chief to demand the restoration of the gun, which was returned that evening. I could literally procure nothing without the greatest annoyance and trouble.

My men, by their mutiny and desertion at Gondokoro, had reduced a well-armed expedition to a mere remnant, dependent upon the company of a band of robbers for the means of advancing through the country. Instead of travelling as I had arranged, at the head of forty-five well-armed men, I had a miserable fifteen cowardly curs, who were employed in driving the baggage animals; thus they would be helpless in the event of an attack upon the road. I accordingly proposed to make a depot at Latooka, and to travel with only twelve donkeys and the lightest baggage. It was a continual trial of temper and wounded pride. To give up the expedition was easy, but to succeed at that period appeared hopeless; and success could only be accomplished by the greatest patience, perseverance, and most careful tact and management of all parties. It was most galling to be a hanger-on to this company of traders, who tolerated me for the sake of presents, but who hated me in their hearts.

One afternoon some natives suddenly arrived from a country named Obbo with presents from their chief for the Turks, and also for me. Ibrahim received several tusks while I received an iron hoe (*molote*), as the news had already extended to that country, that a white man was in Latooka, who wanted neither slaves nor ivory. The natives reported, that a quantity of ivory existed in their country, and Ibrahim determined to take a few men and pay it a visit, as the people were said to be extremely friendly. I requested the leader to point out the exact position of Obbo, which I found to be S.W. That was precisely the direction that I had wished to take; thus an unexpected opportunity presented itself, and I determined to start without delay. On the 2nd of May, 1863, at 9 a.m. we left Latooka, delighted to change the scene of inaction. I left five men in charge of my camp and effects, begging Commoro the chief to look after their safety, and telling him that I had no fear of trusting all to his care. Savages will seldom deceive you if thus placed upon their honour, this happy fact being one of the bright rays in their darkness, and an instance of the anomalous character of the African.

The route lay across the park-like valley of Latooka for about eighteen miles, by which time we reached the base of the mountain chain. There was no other path than the native track, which led over a low range of granite rocks, forming a ridge about four hundred feet high. It was with the greatest difficulty that the loaded donkeys could be hoisted over the numerous blocks of granite that formed an irregular flight of steps, like the ascent of the great pyramid; however, by pulling at their ears, and pushing behind, all except one succeeded in gaining the summit; he was abandoned on the pass.

We were now in the heart of the mountains, and a beautiful valley, well wooded and about six miles in width, lay before us, forming the basin of the Kanieti River that we had formerly crossed at Wakkala, between Ellyria and Latooka.

Fording this stream in a rapid current, we crossed with difficulty, the donkeys wetting all their loads. This was of no great consequence, as a violent storm suddenly overtook us and soaked everyone as thoroughly as the donkeys' packs. A few wild plantains afforded leaves which we endeavoured to use as screens, but the raindrops were far too heavy for such feeble protection. Within a mile of the river we determined to bivouac, as the evening had arrived, and in such weather an advance was out of the question. The tent having been left at Latooka, there was no help for it, and we were obliged to rest contented with our position upon about an acre of clean rock plateau upon which we lighted an enormous fire, and crouched shivering round the blaze. No grass was cut for the animals, as the men had been too busy in collecting firewood sufficient to last throughout the night. Some fowls that we had brought from Latooka had been drowned by the rain; thus my Mahommedan followers refused to eat them, as their throats had not been cut. Not being so scrupulous, and wonderfully hungry in the cold rain, Mrs. Baker and I converted them into a stew, and then took refuge, wet and miserable, under our untanned ox-hides until the following morning. Although an ox-hide is not waterproof, it will keep out a considerable amount of wet; but when thoroughly saturated, it is about as comfortable as any other wet leather, with the additional charm of an exceedingly disagreeable raw smell, very attractive to hyenas. The night being dark, several men thus lost their leather bags that they had left upon the rock.

At 6 a.m., having passed a most uncomfortable night, we started, and after a march of about two miles I was made extremely anxious for the donkeys, by being assured that it was necessary to ascend a most precipitous granite hill, at least seven hundred feet high, that rose exactly before us, and upon the very summit of which was perched a large village. There was no help by means of porters; we led our horses with difficulty up the steep face of the rock – fortunately they had never been shod, thus their firm hoofs obtained a hold where an iron shoe would have slipped; and after extreme difficulty and a most tedious struggle, we found our party all assembled on the flat summit. From this elevated point we had a superb view of the surrounding country, and I took the compass bearing of the Latooka mountain Gebel Lafeet, N. 45 degrees east. The natives of the village that we had now reached had nothing to sell but a few beans, therefore without further delay we commenced the descent upon the opposite side, and at 2:40 p.m. we reached the base, the horses and donkeys having scrambled over the large blocks of stone with the greatest labour. At the foot of the hill the country was park-like and well wooded, although there was no very large timber. Here the grass was two feet high and growing rapidly, while at Latooka all was barren. Halted at 5:20 p.m. on the banks of a small running stream, a tributary to the Kanieti. The night being fine we slept well; and the next morning at 6 a.m. we commenced the most lovely march that I have ever made in Africa. Winding through the very bosom of the mountains, well covered with forest until the bare granite peaks towered above all vegetation to the height of about 5,000 feet, we continued through narrow valleys bordered by abrupt spurs of the mountains from 1,700 to 2,000 feet high. On the peak of each was a village; evidently these impregnable positions were chosen for security. At length the great ascent was to be made, and for two hours we toiled up a steep zigzag pass. The air was most invigorating; beautiful wild flowers, some of which were highly scented, ornamented the route, and innumerable wild grape-vines hung in festoons from tree to tree. We were now in an elevated country on the range of mountains dividing the lower lands of Latooka from the high lands of Obbo. We arrived at the summit of the pass about 2,500 feet above the Latooka valley. In addition to the wild flowers were numerous fruits, all good; especially a variety of custard apple, and a full-flavoured yellow plum. The grapes were in most promising bunches, but unripe. The scenery was very fine; to the east and southeast, masses of high mountains, while to the west and south were vast tracts of park-like country of intense green. In this elevated region the season was much farther advanced than in Latooka;-this was the mountain range upon which I had formerly observed that the storms had concentrated; here the rainy season had been in full play for months, while in Latooka everything was parched. The grass on the west side of the pass was full six feet high. Although the ascent had occupied about two hours, the descent on the west side was a mere trifle, and was effected in about fifteen minutes – we were on an elevated plateau that formed the watershed between the east and west.

After a march of about twelve miles from the top of the pass, we arrived at the chief village of Obbo. The rain fell in torrents, and, soaked to the skin, we crawled into a dirty hut. This village was forty miles S.W. of Tarrangolle, my headquarters in Latooka.

The natives of Obbo are entirely different to the Latookas, both in language and appearance. They are not quite naked, except when going to war, on which occasion they are painted in stripes of red and yellow; but their usual covering is the skin of an antelope or goat, slung like a mantle across the shoulders. Their faces are well formed, with peculiarly fine-shaped noses. The headdress of the Obbo is remarkably neat, the woolly hair being matted and worked with thread into a flat form like a beaver's tail, and bound with a fine edge of raw hide to keep it in shape. This, like the headdress of Latooka, requires many years to complete.

From Obbo to the Southeast all is mountainous, the highest points of the chain rising to an elevation of four or five thousand feet above the general level of the country; to the south, although there are no actual mountains, but merely a few isolated hills, the country distinctly rises.

The entire drainage is to the west and northwest, in which direction there is a very perceptible inclination. The vegetation of Obbo, and the whole of the west side of the mountain range, is different from that upon the east side; the soil is exceedingly rich, producing an abundance of Guinea grass, with which the plains are covered. This country produces nine varieties of yams, many of which grow wild in the forests. There is one most peculiar species, called by the natives *collolollo*, that I had not met with in other countries. This variety produces several tubers at the root, and also upon the stalk; it does not spread upon the ground, like most of the vines that characterise the yams, but it climbs upon trees or upon any object that may tempt its tendrils. From every bud upon the stalk of this vine springs a bulb, somewhat kidney-shaped; this increases until, when ripe, it attains the average size of a potato.

So prolific is this plant, that one vine will produce about 150 yams: they are covered with a fine skin of a greenish brown, and are in flavour nearly equal to a potato, but rather waxy.

There are many good wild fruits, including one very similar to a walnut in its green shell; the flesh of this has a remarkably fine flavour, and the nut within exactly resembles a horse chestnut in size and fine mahogany colour. This nut is roasted, and, when ground and boiled, a species of fat or butter is skimmed from the surface of the water: this is much prized by the natives, and is used for rubbing their bodies, being considered as the best of all fats for the skin; it is also eaten.

Among the best of the wild fruits is one resembling raisins; this grows in clusters upon a large tree. Also a bright yellow fruit, as large as a Muscat grape, and several varieties of plums. None of these are produced in Latooka. Groundnuts are also in abundance in the forests; these are not like the well-known African ground-nut of the west coast, but are contained in an excessively hard shell. A fine quality of flax grows wild, but the twine generally used by the natives is made from the fibre of a species of aloe. Tobacco grows to an extraordinary size, and is prepared similarly to that of the Ellyria tribe.

When ripe, the leaves are pounded in a mortar and reduced to a pulp; the mass is then placed in a conical mould of wood, and pressed. It remains in this until dry, when it presents the shape of a loaf of sugar, and is perfectly hard. The tobacco of the Ellyria tribe is shaped into cheeses, and frequently adulterated with cowdung. I had never smoked until my arrival in Obbo, but having suffered much from fever, and the country being excessively damp, I commenced with Obbo pipes and tobacco.

Every tribe has a distinct pattern of pipe; those of the Bari have wide trumpet-shaped mouths; the Latooka are long and narrow; and the Obbo smaller and the neatest. All their pottery is badly burned, and excessively fragile if wet. The water jars are well formed, although the potter's wheel is quite unknown, and the circular form is obtained entirely by the hand. Throughout the tribes of the White Nile, the articles of pottery are limited to the tobacco-pipe and the water-jar: all other utensils are formed either of wood, or of gourd shells.

By observation, I determined the latitude of my camp at Obbo to be 4 degrees 02' N., 32 degrees 31' long. E., and the general elevation of the country 3,674 feet above the sea, the temperature about 76 degrees F. The altitude of Latooka was 2,236 feet above the sea level: thus we were, at Obbo, upon an elevated plateau, 1,438 feet above the general level of the country on the east of the mountain range. The climate would be healthy were the country sufficiently populated to war successfully against nature; but the rainfall continuing during ten months of the year, from February to the end of November, and the soil being extremely fertile, the increase of vegetation is too rapid, and the scanty population are hemmed in and overpowered by superabundant herbage. This mass of foliage, and grasses of ten feet in height interwoven with creeping plants and wild grape-vines, is perfectly impenetrable to man, and forms a vast jungle, inhabited by elephants, rhinoceros, and buffaloes, whose ponderous strength alone can overcome it. There are few antelopes, as those animals dislike the grass jungles, in which they have no protection against the lion or the leopard, as such beasts of prey can approach them unseen. In the month of January the grass is sufficiently dry to burn, but even at that period there is a quantity of fresh green grass growing between the withered stems; thus the firing of the prairies does not absolutely clear the country, but merely consumes the dry matter, and leaves a ruin of charred herbage, rendered so tough by the burning, that it is quite impossible to ride without cutting the skin from the horse's shins and shoulders. Altogether, it is a most uninteresting country, as there is no possibility of traversing it except by the narrow footpaths made by the natives.

The chief of Obbo came to meet us with several of his headmen. He was an extraordinary-looking man, about fifty-eight or sixty years of age; but, far from possessing the dignity usually belonging to a grey head, he acted the buffoon for our amusement, and might have been a clown in a pantomime.

The heavy storm having cleared, the *nogaras* beat, and our entertaining friend determined upon a grand dance; pipes and flutes were soon heard gathering from all quarters, horns brayed, and numbers of men and women began to collect in crowds, while old

Katchiba, the chief, in a state of great excitement, gave orders for the entertainment.

About a hundred men formed a circle; each man held in his left hand a small cup-shaped drum, formed of hollowed wood, one end only being perforated, and this was covered with the skin of the elephant's ear, tightly stretched. In the centre of the circle was the chief dancer, who wore, suspended from his shoulders, an immense drum, also covered with the elephant's ear. The dance commenced by all singing remarkably well a wild but agreeable tune in chorus, the big drum directing the time, and the whole of the little drums striking at certain periods with such admirable precision, that the effect was that of a single instrument. The dancing was most vigorous, and far superior to anything that I had seen among either, Arabs or savages, the figures varying continually, and ending with a *grand galop* in double circles, at a tremendous pace, the inner ring revolving in a contrary direction to the outer; the effect of this was excellent.

Although the men of Obbo wear a skin slung across their shoulders and loins, the women are almost naked, and, instead of wearing the leather apron and tail of the Latookas, they are contented with a slight fringe of leather shreds, about four inches long by two broad, suspended from a belt. The unmarried girls are entirely naked; or, if they are sufficiently rich in finery, they wear three or four strings of small white beads, about three inches in length, as a covering. The old ladies are antiquated Eves, whose dress consists of a string round the waist, in which is stuck a bunch of green leaves, the stalk uppermost. I have seen a few of the young girls that were prudes indulge in such garments; but they did not appear to be fashionable, and were adopted *faute de mieux*. One great advantage was possessed by this costume – it was always clean and fresh, and the nearest bush (if not thorny) provided a clean petticoat. When in the society of these very simple and in demeanour always modest Eves, I could not help reflecting upon the Mosaical description of our first parents, "and they sewed fig-leaves together."

Some of the Obbo women were very pretty. The caste of feature was entirely different to that of the Latookas, and a striking peculiarity was displayed in the finely arched noses of many of the natives, which strongly reminded one of the Somauli tribes. It was impossible to conjecture their origin, as they had neither traditions nor ideas of their past history.

The language is that of the Madi. There are three distinct languages – the Bari, the Latooka, and the Madi, the latter country extending south of Obbo. A few of the words, most commonly in use, will exemplify them:

English,	Obbo,	Latooka,	Bari
Water	Fee	Cari	Feeum
Fire	Mite	Nyeme	Keemang
Sun	T'sean	Narlong	Karlong
Cow	Decang	Nyeten	Kittan
Goat	Decan	Nyene	Eddeen
Milk	T'sarck	Nalle	Le
Fowl	Gweno	Nakome	Chokkore

The Obbo natives were a great and agreeable change after the Latookas, as they never asked for presents. Although the old chief, Katchiba, behaved more like a clown than a king, he was much respected by his people. He holds his authority over his subjects as general rainmaker and sorcerer. Should a subject displease him, or refuse him a gift, he curses his goats and fowls, or threatens to wither his crops, and the fear of these inflictions reduces the discontented. There are no specific taxes, but he occasionally makes a call upon the country for a certain number of goats and supplies. These are generally given, as Katchiba is a knowing old diplomatist, and he tunes his demands with great judgment. Thus, should there be a lack of rain, or too much, at the season for sowing the crops, he takes the opportunity of calling his subjects together and explaining to them how much he regrets that their conduct has compelled him to afflict them with unfavourable weather, but that it is their own fault. If they are so greedy and so stingy that they will not supply him properly, how can they expect him to think of their interests? He must have goats and corn. "No goats, no rain; that's our contract, my friends," says Katchiba. "Do as you like. I can wait; I hope you can." Should his people complain of too much rain, he threatens to pour storms and lightning upon them forever, unless they bring him so many hundred baskets of corn, etc. etc. Thus he holds his sway.

No man would think of starting upon a journey without the blessing of the old chief; and a peculiar "hocus pocus" is considered as necessary from the magic hands of Katchiba that shall charm the traveller, and preserve him from all danger of wild animals upon the road. In case of sickness he is called in, not as M.D. in our acceptation, but as "doctor of magic," and he charms both the hut and the patient against death, with the fluctuating results that must attend professionals even in sorcery. His subjects have the most thorough confidence in his power; and so great is his reputation that distant tribes frequently consult him, and beg his assistance as a magician. In this manner does old Katchiba hold his sway over his savage, but credulous people; and so long has he imposed upon the public that I believe he has at length imposed upon himself, and that he really believes he has the power of sorcery, notwithstanding repeated failures. In order to propitiate him, his people frequently present him with the prettiest of their daughters; and so constantly is he receiving additions to his domestic circle that he has been obliged to extend his establishment to prevent domestic fracas among the ladies. He has accordingly hit upon the practical expedient of keeping a certain number of wives in each of his villages: thus, when he makes a journey through his territory, he is always at home. This multiplicity of wives has been so successful that Katchiba has one hundred and sixteen children living – another proof of sorcery in the eyes of his people. One of his wives had no children, and she came to me to apply for medicine to correct some evil influence that had lowered her in her husband's estimation. The poor woman was in great distress, and complained that Katchiba was very cruel to her because she had been unable to make an addition to his family, but that she was sure I possessed some charm that would raise her to the standard of his other wives. I could not bet rid of her until I gave her the first pill that came to hand from my medicine chest, and with this she went away contented.

Katchiba was so completely established in his country, not only as a magician, but as *pere de famille*, that every one of his villages was governed by one of his sons; thus the entire government was a family affair. The sons of course believed in their father's power of sorcery, and their influence as headmen of their villages increased the prestige of the parent. Although without an idea of a Supreme Being, the whole country bowed down to sorcery. It is a curious distinction between faith and credulity; these savages, utterly devoid of belief in a Deity, and without a vestige of superstition, believed most devotedly that the general affairs of life and the control of the elements were in the hands of their old chief, and therefore they served him – not with a feeling of love, neither with a trace of religion, but with that material instinct that always influences the savage; they propitiated him for the sake of what they could obtain. It is thus almost unconquerable feeling, ever present in the savage mind, that renders his conversion difficult; he will believe in nothing, unless he can obtain some specific benefit from the object of his belief.

Savages can be ruled by two powers – force, and "humbug" – accordingly, these are the instruments made use of by those in authority: where the "force" is wanting, "humbug" is the weapon as a *pis aller.* Katchiba having no physical force, adopted cunning, and the black art controlled the savage minds of his subjects. Strange does it appear, that these uncivilized inhabitants of Central Africa should, although devoid of religion, believe implicitly in sorcery; giving a power to man superhuman, although acknowledging nothing more than human. Practical and useful magic is all that is esteemed by the savage, the higher branches would be unappreciated; and spirit-rapping and mediums are reserved for the civilized (?) of England, who would convert the black savages of Africa.

Notwithstanding his magic, Katchiba was not a bad man: he was remarkably civil, and very proud at my having paid him a visit. He gave me much information regarding the country, but assured me that I should not be able to travel south for many months, as it would be quite impossible to cross the Asua River during the rainy season; he therefore proposed that I should form a camp at Obbo, and reside there until the rains should cease. It was now May, thus I was invited to postpone my advance south until December.

I determined to make a reconnaissance south towards the dreaded Asua, or, as the Obbo people pronounced it, the Achua River, and to return to my fixed camp. Accordingly I arranged to leave Mrs. Baker at Obbo with a guard of eight men, while I should proceed south without baggage, excepting a change of clothes and a cooking pot. Katchiba promised to take the greatest care of her, and to supply her with all she might require; offering to become personally responsible for her safety; he agreed to place a spell upon the door of our hut, that nothing evil should enter it during my absence. It was a snug little dwelling, about nine feet in diameter, and perfectly round; the floor well cemented with cow-dung and clay, and the walls about four feet six inches in height, formed of mud and sticks, likewise polished off with cow-dung. The door had enlarged, and it was now a very imposing entrance of about four feet high, and a great contrast to the surrounding hut or dog-kennel with two feet height of doorway.

On the 7th of May I started with three men, and taking a course south, I rode through a most lovely country, within five miles of the base, and parallel with the chain of the Madi Mountains. There was abundance of beautiful flowers, especially of orchidaceous plants; the country was exceedingly park-like and well wooded, but generally overgrown with grass then about six feet high. After riding for about fourteen miles, one of the guides ran back, and reported elephants to be on the road a little in advance. One of my mounted men offered to accompany me should I wish to hunt them. I had no faith in my man, but I rode forward, and shortly observed a herd of ten bull elephants standing together about sixty yards from the path. The grass was high, but I rode through it to within about forty yards before I was observed; they immediately dashed away, and I followed for about a mile at a trot, the ground being so full of holes and covered with fallen trees concealed in the high grass, that I did not like to close until I should arrive in a more favourable spot. At length I shot at full gallop past an immense fellow, with tusks about five feet projecting from his jaws, and reining up, I fired with a Reilly No. 10 at the shoulder. He charged straight into me at the sound of the shot. My horse, Filfil, was utterly unfit for a hunter, as he went perfectly mad at the report of a gun fired from his back, and at the moment of the discharge he reared perpendicularly; the weight, and the recoil of the rifle, added to the sudden rearing of the horse, unseated me, and I fell, rifle in hand, backwards over his hind-quarters at the moment the elephant rushed in full charge upon the horse. Away went Filfil leaving me upon the ground in a most inglorious position; and, fortunately, the grass being high, the elephant lost sight of me and followed the horse instead of giving me his attention.

My horse was lost; my man had never even accompanied me, having lagged behind at the very commencement of the hunt. I had lost my rifle in the high grass, as I had been forced to make a short run from the spot before I knew that the elephant had followed the horse; thus I was nearly an hour before I found it, and also my azimuth compass that had fallen from my belt pouch. After much shouting and whistling, my mounted man arrived, and making him dismount, I rode my little horse Mouse, and returned to the path. My horse Filfil was lost. As a rule, hunting during the march should be avoided, and I had now paid dearly for the indiscretion.

I reached the Atabbi River about eighteen miles from Obbo. This is a fine perennial stream flowing from the Madi Mountains towards the west, forming an affluent of the Asua River. There was a good ford, with a hard gravel and rocky bottom, over which the horse partly waded and occasionally swam. There were fresh tracks of immense herds of elephants with which the country abounded, and I heard them trumpeting in the distance.

Ascending rising ground in perfectly open prairie on the opposite side of Atabbi, I saw a dense herd of about two hundred elephants – they were about a mile distant, and were moving slowly through the high grass. Just as I was riding along the path watching the immense herd, a Tetel (hartebeest) sprang from the grass in which he had been concealed, and fortunately he galloped across a small open space, where the high grass had been destroyed by the elephants. A quick shot from the little Fletcher 24 rifle doubled him up; but, recovering himself almost immediately, he was just disappearing when a shot from the left-hand barrel broke his back, to the intense delight of my people. We accordingly bivouacked for the night, and the fires were soon blazing upon a dry plateau of granite rock about seventy feet square that I had chosen for a resting-place. In the saucer-shaped hollows of the rock was good clear water from the rain of the preceding day; thus we had all the luxuries that could be desired – fire, food, and water. I seldom used a bedstead unless in camp; thus my couch was quickly and simply made upon the hard rock, softened by the addition of an armful of green boughs, upon which I laid an untanned ox-hide, and spread my Scotch plaid. My cap formed my pillow, and my handy little Fletcher rifle lay by my side beneath the plaid, together with my hunting knife; these faithful friends were never out of reach either by night or day.

The cap was a solid piece of architecture, as may be supposed from its strength to resist the weight of the head when used as a pillow. It was made by an Arab woman in Khartoum, according to my own plan; the substance was about half an inch thick of dome palm leaves very neatly twisted and sewn together. Having a flat top, and a peak both before and behind, the whole affair was covered with tanned leather, while a curtain of the same material protected the back of the neck from the sun. A strong chinstrap secured the cap upon the head, and the *tout ensemble* formed a very effective roof, completely sun-proof. Many people might have objected to the weight, but I found it no disadvantage, and the cap being tolerably waterproof, I packed my cartouche pouch and belt within it when inverted at night to form a pillow; this was an exceedingly practical arrangement, as in case of an alarm I rose from my couch armed, capped and belted, at a moment's notice.

On the following morning I started at daybreak, and after a march of about thirteen miles through the same park-like and unin-habited country as that of the preceding day, I reached the country of Farajoke, and arrived at the foot of a rocky hill, upon the summit of which was a large village. I was met by the chief and several of his people leading a goat, which was presented to me, and killed immediately as an offering, close to the feet of my horse. The chief carried a fowl, holding it by the legs, with its head downwards; he approached my horse, and stroked his fore-feet with the fowl, and then made a circle around him by dragging it upon the ground; my feet were then stroked with the fowl in the same manner as those of the horse, and I was requested to stoop, so as to enable him to wave the bird around my head; this completed, it was also waved round my horse's head, who showed his appreciation of the ceremony by rearing and lashing out behind, to the great discomfiture of the natives. The fowl did not appear to have enjoyed itself during the operation; but a knife put an end to its troubles, as, the ceremony of welcome being completed, the bird was sacrificed and handed to my headman. I was now conducted to the village. It was defended by a high bamboo fence, and was miserably dirty, forming a great contrast to the clean dwellings of the Bari and Latooka tribes. The hill upon which the village was built was about eighty feet above the general level of the country, and afforded a fine view of the surrounding landscape. On the east was the chain of Madi Mountains, the base well wooded, while to the south all was fine open pasturage of sweet herbage, about a foot high, a totally different grass to the rank vegetation we had passed through. The country was undulating, and every rise was crowned by a village. Although the name of the district is Farajoke, it is comprised in the extensive country of Sooli, together with the Shoggo and Madi tribes, all towns being under the command of petty chiefs. The general elevation of the country was 3,966 feet above the sea-level, 292 feet higher than Obbo.

The chief of Farajoke, observing me engaged in taking bearings with the compass, was anxious to know my object, which being explained, he volunteered all information respecting the country, and assured me that it would be quite impossible to cross the Asua during the rainy season, as it was a violent torrent, rushing over a rocky bed with such impetuosity, that no one would venture to swim it. There was nothing to be done at this season, and however trying to the patience, there was no alternative. Farajoke was within three days' hard marching of Faloro, the station of Debono, that had always been my projected headquarters; thus I was well advanced upon my intended route, and had the season been propitious, I could have proceeded with my baggage animals without difficulty.

The loss of my horse Filfil was a severe blow in this wild region, where beasts of burthen were unknown, and I had slight hopes of his recovery, as lions were plentiful in the country between Obbo and Farajoke; however, I offered a reward of beads and bracelets, and a number of natives were sent by the chief to scour the jungles. There was little use in remaining at Farajoke, therefore I returned to Obbo with my men and donkeys, accomplishing the whole distance (thirty miles) in one day. I was very anxious about Mrs. Baker, who had been the representative of the expedition at Obbo during my absence. Upon my approach through the forest, my well-known whistle was immediately answered by the appearance of the boy Saat, who, without any greeting, immediately rushed to the hut to give the intelligence that "Master was arrived."

I found my wife looking remarkably well, and regularly installed "at home." Several fat sheep were tied by the legs to pegs in front of the hut; a number of fowls were pecking around the entrance, and my wife awaited me on the threshold with a large pumpkin shell containing about a gallon of native beer. *Dulce domum*, although but a mud hut, the loving welcome made it happier than a palace; and that draught of beer, or fermented mud, or whatever trash it might be compared with in England, how delicious it seemed after a journey of thirty miles in the broiling sun! And the fat sheep and the fowls all looked so luxurious. Alas for destiny – my arrival cut short the existence of one being; what was joy to some was death to a sheep, and in a few moments the fattest was slain in honour of master's return, and my men were busily employed in preparing it for a general feast.

Numbers of people gathered round me: foremost among them was the old chief Katchiba, whose self-satisfied countenance exhibited an extreme purity of conscience in having adhered to his promise to act as guardian during my absence. Mrs. Baker gave him an excellent character; he had taken the greatest care of her, and had supplied all the luxuries that had so much excited my appetite on the first *coup d'oeil* [glance] of my home. He had been so mindful of his responsibility, that he had placed some of his own sons as sentries over the hut both by day and night.

I accordingly made him a present of many beads and bracelets, and a few odds and ends, that threw him into ecstacies: he had weak eyes, and the most valued present was a pair of sun-goggles, which I fitted on his head, to his intense delight, and exhibited in a looking-glass – this being likewise added to his gifts. I noticed that he was very stiff in the back, and he told me that he had had a bad fall during my absence. My wife explained the affair. He had come to her to declare his intention of procuring fowls for her from some distant village; but, said he, "My people are not very good, and perhaps they will say that they have none; but if you will lend me a horse, I will ride there, and the effect will impose upon them so much, that they will not dare to refuse me." Now, Katchiba was not a good walker, and his usual way of travelling was upon the back of a very strong subject, precisely as children are wont to ride "pic-a-back." He generally had two or three spare men, who alternately acted as guides and ponies, while one of his wives invariably accompanied him, bearing a large jar of beer, with which it was said that the old chief refreshed himself so copiously during the journey, that it sometimes became necessary for two men to carry him instead of one. This may have been merely a scandalous report in Obbo; however, it appeared that Katchiba was ready for a start, as usual accompanied by a Hebe with a jar of beer. Confident in his powers as a rider across country on a man, he considered that he could easily ride a horse. It was in vain that my wife had protested, and had prophesied a broken neck should he attempt to bestride the hitherto unknown animal: to ride he was determined.

Accordingly my horse Tetel was brought, and Katchiba was assisted upon his back. The horse recognising an awkward hand, did not move a step. "Now then," said Katchiba, "go on!" But Tetel, not understanding the Obbo language, was perfectly ignorant of his rider's wishes. "Why won't he go?" inquired Katchiba. "Touch him with your stick," cried one of my men; and acting upon the suggestion, the old sorcerer gave him a tremendous whack with his staff. This was immediately responded to by Tetel, who, quite unused to such eccentricities, gave a vigorous kick, the effect of which was to convert the sorcerer into a spread eagle, flying over his head, and landing very heavily upon the ground, amidst a roar of laughter from my men, in which I am afraid Mrs. Baker was rude enough to join. The crest-fallen Katchiba was assisted upon his legs, and feeling rather stunned, he surveyed the horse with great astonishment; but his natural instincts soon prompted him to call for the jar of beer, and after a long draught from the mighty cup, he regained his courage, and expressed an opinion that the horse was too high, as it was a long way to tumble down; he therefore requested one of the "little horses;" these were the donkeys. Accordingly he was mounted on a donkey, and held on by two men, one on either side. Thus he started most satisfactorily and exceedingly proud. On his return the following day, he said that the villagers had given him the fowls immediately, as he had told them that he had thirty Turks staying with him on a visit, and that they would burn and plunder the country unless they were immediately supplied. He considered this trifling deviation from fact as a great stroke of diplomacy in procuring the fowls.

Six days after the loss of my horse, I was delighted to see him brought back by the natives safe and well. They had hunted through an immense tract of country, and had found him grazing. He was naturally a most vicious horse, and the natives were afraid to touch him; they had accordingly driven him before them until they gained the path, which he then gladly followed. The saddle was in its place, but my sword was gone.

The rains were terrific; the mornings were invariably fine, but the clouds gathered upon the mountains soon after noon and ended daily in a perfect deluge. Not being able to proceed south, I determined to return to my headquarters at Latooka, and to wait for the dry season. I had made the reconnaissance to Farajoke, in latitude 3 degrees 32', and I saw my way clear for the future, provided my animals should remain in good condition. Accordingly, on the 21st of May, we started for Latooka in company with Ibrahim and his men, who were thoroughly sick of the Obbo climate.

Before parting, a ceremony had to be performed by Katchiba. His brother was to be our guide, and he was to receive power to control the elements as deputy-magician during the journey, lest we should be wetted by the storms, and the torrents should be so swollen as to be impassable.

With great solemnity Katchiba broke a branch from a tree, upon the leaves of which he spat in several places. This branch, thus blessed with holy water, was laid upon the ground, and a fowl was dragged around it by the chief; and our horses were then operated on precisely in the same manner as had been enacted at Farajoke. This ceremony completed, he handed the branch to his brother (our guide), who received it with much gravity, in addition to a magic whistle of antelope's horn that he suspended from his neck. All the natives wore whistles similar in appearance, being simply small horns in which they blew, the sound of which was considered either to attract or to drive away rain, at the option of the whistler. No whistle was supposed to be effective unless it had been blessed by the great magician Katchiba. The ceremony being over, all commenced whistling with all their might; and taking leave of Katchiba, with an assurance that we should again return, we started amidst a din of "toot too too-ing" upon our journey. Having an immense supply of ammunition at Latooka, I left about 200 lbs. of shot and ball with Katchiba; therefore my donkeys had but little to carry, and we travelled easily.

That night we bivouacked at the foot of the east side of the pass at about half-past five. Ibrahimawa, the Bornu man whom I have already described as the amateur botanist, had become my great ally in searching for all that was curious and interesting. Proud of his knowledge of wild plants, no sooner was the march ended than he commenced a search in the jungles for something esculent.

We were in a deep gorge on a steep knoll bounded by a ravine about sixty feet of perpendicular depth, at the bottom of which flowed a torrent. This was an excellent spot for a camp, as no guards were necessary upon the side thus protected. Bordering the ravine were a number of fine trees covered with a thorny stem creeper, with leaves much resembling those of a species of yam. These were at once pronounced by Ibrahimawa to be a perfect god-send, and after a few minutes' grubbing he produced a basketful of fine-looking yams. In an instant this display of food attracted a crowd of hungry people, including those of Ibrahim and my own men, who, not being botanists, had left the search for food to Ibrahimawa, but who determined to share the tempting results. A rush was made at his basket, which was emptied on the instant; and I am sorry to confess that the black angel Saat was one of the first to seize three or four of the largest yams, which he most unceremoniously put in a pot and deliberately cooked as though he had been the botanical discoverer. How often the original discoverer suffers, while others benefit from his labours! Ibrahimawa, the scientific botanist, was left without a yam, after all his labour of grubbing up a basketful. Pots were boiling in all directions, and a feast in store for the hungry men who had marched twenty miles without eating since the morning.

The yams were cooked; but I did not like the look of them, and seeing that the multitude was ready, I determined to reserve a few for our own eating should they be generally pronounced good. The men ate them voraciously. Hardly ten minutes had elapsed from the commencement of the feast when first one and then another disappeared, and from a distance I heard a smothered but unmistakeable sound, that reminded me of the lurching effect of a channel steamer upon a crowd of passengers. Presently the boy Saat showed symptoms of distress, and vanished from our presence; and all those that had dined off Ibrahimawa's botanical specimens were suffering from a most powerful "vomi-purgatif." The angels that watch over scientific botanists had preserved Ibrahimawa from all evil. He had discovered the yams, and the men had stolen them from him; they enjoyed the fruits, while he gained an experience invaluable at their expense. I was quite contented to have waited until others had tried them before I made the experiment. Many of the yam tribe are poisonous; there is one variety much liked at Obbo, but which is deadly in its effects should it be eaten without a certain preparation. It is first scraped, and then soaked in a running stream for a fortnight. It is then cut into thin slices, and dried in the sun until quite crisp; by this means it is rendered harmless. The dried slices are stored for use; and they are generally pounded in a mortar into flour, and used as a kind of porridge.

The sickness of the people continued for about an hour, during which time all kinds of invectives were hurled against Ibrahimawa, and his botany was termed a gigantic humbug. From that day he was very mild in his botanical conversation.

On the following morning we crossed the last range of rocky hills, and descended to the Latooka valley. Up to this point, we had seen no game; but we had now arrived in the game country, and shortly after our descent from the rocks we saw a herd of about twenty *tetel* (hartebeest). Unfortunately, just as I dismounted for the purpose of stalking them, the red flags of the Turks attracted the attention of a large party of baboons, who were sitting on the rocks, and they commenced their hoarse cry of alarm, and immediately disturbed the Tetel. One of the men, in revenge, fired a long shot at a great male, who was sitting alone upon a high rock, and by chance the ball struck him in the head. He was an immense specimen of the Cynocephalus, about as large as a mastiff, but with a long brown mane like that of the lion. This mane is much prized by the natives as an ornament. He was immediately skinned, and the hide was cut into long strips about three inches broad: the portion of mane adhering had the appearance of a fringe; each strip was worn as a scarf; thus one skin will produce about eight or ten ornaments.

I sent my men to camp, and, accompanied by Richarn, mounted on my horse Mouse, I rode through the park-like ground in quest of game. I saw varieties of antelopes, including the rare and beautiful *maharif*; but all were so wild, and the ground so open, that I could not get a shot. This was the more annoying, as the maharif was an antelope that I believed to be a new species. It had often disappointed me; for although I had frequently seen them on the southwest frontier of Abyssinia, I had never been able to procure one, owing to their extreme shyness, and to the fact of their inhabiting open plains, where stalking was impossible. I had frequently examined them with a telescope, and had thus formed an intimate acquaintance with their peculiarities. The maharif is very similar to the roan antelope of South Africa, but is mouse colour, with black and white stripes upon the face. The horns are exactly those of the roan antelope, very massive and corrugated, bending backwards to the shoulders. The withers are extremely high, which give a peculiarly heavy appearance to the shoulders, much heightened by a large and stiff black mane like that of a hog-maned horse. I have a pair of horns in my possession that I obtained through the assistance of a lion, who killed the maharif while drinking near my tent; unfortunately, the skin was torn to pieces, and the horns and skull were all that remained.

Failing, as usual, in my endeavours to obtain a shot, I made a considerable circuit, and shortly observed the tall heads of giraffes towering over the low mimosas. There is no animal in nature so picturesque in his native haunts as the giraffe. His food consists of the leaves of trees, some qualities forming special attractions, especially the varieties of the mimosa, which, being low, permit an extensive view to his telescopic eyes. He has a great objection to high forests. The immense height of the giraffe gives him a peculiar advantage, as he can command an extraordinary range of vision, and thereby be warned against the approach of his two great enemies, man and the lion. No animal is more difficult to stalk than the giraffe, and the most certain method of hunting is that pursued by the Hamran Arabs, on the frontiers of Abyssinia, who ride him down and hamstring him with the broadsword at full gallop. A good horse is required, as, although the gait of a giraffe appears excessively awkward from the fact of his moving the fore and hind legs of one side simultaneously, he attains a great pace, owing to the length of his stride, and his bounding trot is more than a match for any but a superior horse.

The hoof is as beautifully proportioned as that of the smallest gazelle, and his lengthy legs and short back give him every advantage for speed and endurance. There is a rule to be observed in hunting the giraffe on horseback: the instant he starts, he must be pressed – it is the speed that tells upon him, and the spurs must be at work at the very commencement of the hunt, and the horse pressed along at his best pace; it must be a race at top speed from the start, but, should the giraffe be allowed the slightest advantage for the first five minutes, the race will be against the horse.

I was riding Filfil, my best horse for speed, but utterly useless for the gun. I had a common regulation-sword hanging on my saddle in lieu of the long Arab broadsword that I had lost at Obbo, and starting at full gallop at the same instant as the giraffes, away we went over the beautiful park. Unfortunately Richarn was a bad rider, and I, being encumbered with a rifle, had no power to use the sword. I accordingly trusted to ride them down and to get a shot, but I felt that the unsteadiness of my horse would render it very uncertain. The wind whistled in my ears as we flew along over the open plain. The grass was not more than a foot high, and the ground hard; the giraffes about four hundred yards distant steaming along, and raising a cloud of dust from the dry earth, as on this side of the mountains there had been no rain. Filfil was a contradiction; he loved a hunt and had no fear of wild animals, but he went mad at the sound of a gun. Seeing the magnificent herd of about fifteen giraffes before him, the horse entered into the excitement and needed no spur – down a slight hollow, flying over the dry buffalo holes, now over a dry watercourse and up the incline on the other side – then again on the level, and the dust in my eyes from the cloud raised by the giraffes showed that we were gaining in the race; *misericordia*! Low jungle lay before us – the giraffes gained it, and spurring forward through a perfect cloud of dust now within a hundred yards of the game we shot through the thorny bushes. In another minute or two I was close up, and a splendid bull giraffe was crashing before me like a locomotive obelisk through the mimosas, bending the elastic boughs before him in his irresistible rush, which sprang back with a force that would have upset both horse and rider had I not carefully kept my distance. The jungle seemed alive with the crowd of orange-red, the herd was now on every side, as I pressed the great bull before me. Oh for an open plain! I was helpless to attack, and it required the greatest attention to keep up the pace through the thick mimosas without dashing against their stems and branches. The jungle became thicker, and although I was in the middle of the herd and within ten yards of several giraffes, I could do nothing. A mass of thick and tangled thorns now received them, and closed over the hardly-contested race – I was beaten.

Never mind, it was a good hunt – first-rate – but where was my camp? It was nearly dark, and I could just distinguish the pass in the distance, by which we had descended the mountain; thus I knew the direction but I had ridden about three miles, and it would be dark before I could return. However, I followed the heel tracks of the herd of giraffes. Richarn was nowhere. Although I had lost the race, and was disappointed, I now consoled myself that it was all for the best; had I killed a giraffe at that hour and distance from camp, what good would it have been? I was quite alone; thus who could have found it during the night? And before morning it would have been devoured by lions and hyenas; inoffensive and beautiful creatures, what a sin it appeared to destroy them uselessly! With these consoling and practical reflections I continued my way, until a branch of hooked thorn fixing in my nose disturbed the train of ideas and persuaded me that it was very dark, and that I had lost my way, as I could no longer distinguish either the tracks of the giraffes or the position of the mountains. Accordingly I fired my rifle as a signal, and soon after I heard a distant report in reply, and the blaze of a fire shot up suddenly in the distance on the side of the mountain. With the help of this beacon I reached the spot where our people were bivouacked; they had lighted the beacon on a rock about fifty feet above the level, as although some twenty or thirty fires were blazing, they had been obscured by the intervening jungle. I found both my wife and my men in an argumentative state as to the propriety of my remaining alone so late in the jungle; however, I also found dinner ready; the *angareps* (stretcher bedsteads) arranged by a most comfortable blazing fire, and a glance at the star-lit heavens assured me of a fine night – what more can man wish for: wife, welcome, food, fire, and fine weather?

The bivouac in the wilderness has many charms; there is a complete independence – the sentries are posted, the animals picketed and fed, and the fires arranged in a complete circle around the entire party – men, animals, and luggage all within the fiery ring; the sentries alone being on the outside. There is a species of iron-wood that is very inflammable, and being oily, it burns like a torch; this grew in great quantities, and the numerous fires fed with this vigorous fuel enlivened the bivouac with a continual blaze. My men were busy, baking their bread. On such occasions an oven is dispensed with. A prodigious fire is made while the dough is being prepared; this, when well moistened, is formed into a cake about two feet in diameter, but not thicker than two inches. The fire being in a fit state of glowing ash, a large hole is scraped in the centre, in which the flat cake is laid, and the red-hot embers are raked over it; thus buried it will bake in about twenty minutes, but the dough must be exceedingly moist or it will burn to a cinder.

On the following day we arrived at Latooka, where I found everything in good order at the depot, and the European vegetables that I had sown were all above ground. Commoro and a number of people came to meet us.

There had been but little rain at Latooka since we left, although it had been raining heavily at Obbo daily, and there was no difference in the dry sandy plain that surrounded the town, neither was there any pasturage for the animals except at a great distance.

The day after my arrival, Filfil was taken ill and died in a few hours. Tetel had been out of condition ever since the day of his failure during the elephant hunt, and he now refused his food. Sickness rapidly spread through my animals; five donkeys died within a few days, and the remainder looked poor. Two of my camels died suddenly, having eaten the poison-bush. Within a few days of this disaster my good old hunter and companion of all my former sports in the Base country, Tetel, died. These terrible blows to my expedition were most satisfactory to the Latookas, who ate the donkeys and other animals the moment they died. It was a race between the natives and the vultures as to who should be first to profit by my losses.

Not only were the animals sick, but my wife was laid up with a violent attack of gastric fever, and I was also suffering from daily attacks of ague. The smallpox broke out among the Turks. Several people died; and, to make matters worse, they insisted upon inoculating themselves and all their slaves; thus the whole camp was reeking with this horrible disease.

Fortunately my camp was separate and to windward. I strictly forbade my men to inoculate themselves, and no case of the disease occurred among my people, but it spread throughout the country. Smallpox is a scourge among the tribes of Central Africa, and it occasionally sweeps through the country and decimates the population.

Among the natives of Obbo, who had accompanied us to Latooka, was a man named Wani, who had formerly travelled far to the south, and had offered to conduct Ibrahim to a country rich in ivory that had never been visited by a trader: this man had accordingly been engaged as guide arid interpreter. In an examination of Wani I discovered that the cowrie shells were brought from a place called Magungo This name I had previously heard mentioned by the natives, but I could obtain no clue to its position. It was most important that I should discover the exact route by which the cowries arrived from the south, as it would be my guide to that direction. The information that I received from Wani at Latooka was excessively vague, and upon most slender data I founded my conclusions so carefully that my subsequent discoveries have rendered most interesting the first scent of the position which I eventually followed with success. I accordingly extract, verbatim, from my journal the note written by me at Latooka on the 26th of May, 1863, when I first received the clue to the Albert N'Yanza: "I have had a long examination of Wani, the guide and interpreter, respecting the country of Magungo. Loggo, the Bari interpreter, has always described Magungo as being on a large river, and I have concluded that it must be the Asua; but, upon cross-examination, I find he has used the word *Bahr* (in Arabic signifying river or sea) instead of

Birke (lake). This important error being discovered gives a new feature to the geography of this part."

According to his description, Magungo is situated on a lake so large that no one knows its limits. Its breadth is such that, if you journey two days east and the same distance west, there is no land visible on either quarter, while to the south its direction is utterly unknown. Large vessels arrive at Magungo from distant and unknown parts, bringing cowrie shells and beads in exchange for ivory. Upon these vessels white men have been seen. All the cowrie-shells used in Latooka and the neighbouring countries are supplied by these vessels, but none have arrived for the last two years.

"His description of distance places Magungo on about the 2 degrees N. lat. The lake can be no other than the 'N'Yanza,' which, if the position of Magungo be correct, extends much farther north than Speke had supposed. The 'white men' must be Arab traders who bring cowries from Zanzibar. I shall take the first opportunity to push for Magungo. I imagine that country belongs to Kamrasi's brother, as Wani says the king has a brother who is king of a powerful country on the west bank of the Nile but that they are ever at war with each other.

"I examined another native who had been to Magungo to purchase Simbi (the cowrie-shell); he says that a white man formerly arrived there annually, and brought a donkey with him in a boat; that he disembarked his donkey and rode about the country, dealing with the natives, and bartering cowries and brass-coil bracelets. This man had no firearms, but wore a sword. The king of Magungo was called Cherrybambi.

This information was the first clue to the facts that I subsequently established, and the account of the white men (Arabs) arriving at Magungo was confirmed by the people of that country twelve months after I obtained this vague information at Latooka.

Arabs, being simply brown, are called white men by the blacks of these countries. I was called a VERY white man as a distinction, but I have frequently been obliged to take off my shirt to exhibit the difference of colour between myself and my men, as my face was brown.

CHAPTER IX

THE TURKS ATTACK KAYALA

On the 30th May, about an hour before daybreak, I was awoke by a rattle of musketry, which continued some time in irregular volleys, and subsided into a well-sustained and steady fire in single shots. On leaving my hut, I found the camp of Koorshid's people almost empty, while my own men were climbing on the roofs of their huts to obtain a view towards the west. Nothing was in sight, although the firing still continued at a distance of about a mile, apparently on the other side of a belt of trees. I now heard that Koorshid's people had started at between three and four o'clock that morning, by Commoro's request, to attack a neighbouring town that had been somewhat rebellious. The firing continued for about two hours, when it suddenly ceased, and I shortly saw with a telescope the Turks' red ensign emerge from the forest, and we heard the roll of their drum, mingled with the lowing of oxen and the bleating of sheep. Upon nearer approach, I remarked a considerable body of men, and a large herd of cattle and sheep driven by a number of Latookas, while a knot of Turks carried something heavy in their arms.

They soon arrived, with about 2,000 head of cattle and sheep; but they had lost one of their men, killed in the fight, and his body they carried home for interment. It happened to be about the best man of the party; really a very civil fellow, and altogether rather a pleasant robber. At Commoro's instigation, the Turks had attacked the town of Kayala; but the Latookas had fought so well, that the Turks found it impossible to capture the town, which was, as usual, protected by iron-wood palisades, upon which their bullets harmlessly flattened. Not only the Latooka men had fought well, but their women broke up their grinding-stones and defended the entrance by pelting their assailants with the fragments; several of the Turks were wounded by the stones thrown with such force by these brawny Amazons that some of the gun-barrels were indented. Many of these brave women had been shot by the dastardly Turks, and one was in the act of being carried off by the "pleasant robber," when a native, running to her rescue, drove his spear through his chest and killed him on the spot. Unfortunately for the Latookas, some of their cattle had left the town to pasture just before the attack took place; these were captured by the Turks, but not one hostile foot had been able to penetrate their town. On the following day the party were busily engaged in dividing the spoil, one third belonging to the men as a bonus, while the remainder were the property of the traders' establishment, or *Meri* (government), as they term the proprietor. This portion was to be sent to Obbo as a place of security and good pasturage, and the men were to engage in other *razzia*s in Latooka, and to collect a large number of cattle to be driven south to exchange for ivory. Koorshid's camp was a scene of continual uproar, the men quarrelling over the division of the spoil.

Journal: June 2nd. – The Turks are now busy buying and selling, each man disposing of his share of the stolen cattle according to his wants: one exchanges a cow to the natives for corn and meat; another slaughters an ox, and retails small portions for *merissa*, fowls, etc., the natives flocking to the camp like vultures scenting flesh; others reserve their cattle for the purpose of purchasing the daughters of the natives for slaves under the name of wives, whom they will eventually sell in Khartoum for from twenty to thirty dollars each. My men look on in dismay at the happiness of their neighbours: like "A Peri weeping at the gate/Of Eden, stood disconsolate," so may they be seen regarding the adjoining paradise, where meat is in profusion, sweetened by being stolen. But, alas! Their cruel master does not permit them these innocent enjoyments.

Everything may be obtained for cattle as payment in this country. The natives are now hard at work making zareebas (kraals) for the cattle stolen from their own tribe and immediate neighbours, for the sake of two or three bullocks as remuneration to be divided among more than a hundred men. They are not deserving of sympathy; they are worse than vultures, being devoid of harmony even in the same tribe. The chiefs have no real control; and a small district, containing four or five towns, club together and pillage the neighbouring province. It is not surprising that the robber traders of the Nile turn this spirit of discord to their own advantage, and league themselves with one chief, to rob another, whom they eventually plunder in his turn. The natives say that sixty-five men and women were killed in the attack upon Kayala. All the Latookas consider it a great disgrace that the Turks fired upon women. Among all tribes, from Gondokoro to Obbo, a woman is respected, even in time of war. Thus, they are employed as spies, and become exceedingly dangerous; nevertheless, there is a general understanding that no woman shall be killed. The origin of this humane distinction arises, I imagine, from their scarcity. Where polygamy is in force, women should be too dear to kill; the price of a girl being from five to ten cows, her death is equal to the actual loss of that number.

Fortunately for my party, who were not cattle lifters, there was the usual abundance of game, and I could always supply myself and people with delicious wild ducks and geese. We never were tired of this light food as we varied their preparation. Sometimes I was able to procure a goat, on which occasion a grand dish was made, the paunch being arranged as a Scotch haggis of wild fowls' livers and flesh minced, with the usual additions. My garden was flourishing; we had onions, beans, melons, yams, lettuce, and radishes, which had quickly responded to several invigorating showers; the temperature was 85 degrees F in the shade during the hottest hours of the day, and 72 degrees F at night.

Salt is not procurable in Latooka; the natives seldom use it, as it is excessively difficult to make it in any quantity from the only two sources that will produce it; the best is made from goat's dung; this is reduced ashes, and saturated; the water is then strained off, and evaporated by boiling. Another quality is made of peculiar grass, with a thick fleshy stem, something like sugarcane; the ashes of this produce salt, but by no means pure. The chief of Latooka would eat a handful of salt greedily that I gave him from my large supply, and I could purchase supplies with this article better than with beads.

On the 4th of June, Ibrahim and eighty-five men started for Obbo in charge of about 400 cows and 1,000 goats. Shortly after their departure, a violent thunder-storm, attended with a deluge of rain, swept over the country, and flooded the Latooka River and the various pools that formed my game-preserves.

I looked forward to good duck-shooting on the morrow, as a heavy storm was certain to be followed by large arrivals.

On the morning of the 5th, I was out at an early hour, and in a very short time I killed eight ducks and geese. There was a certain pool surrounded by a small marsh within half a mile of my camp, that formed the greatest attraction to the wild fowl. There were two hegleek trees in this marsh; and it was merely necessary to stand beneath the shelter of either to insure good sport, as the ducks continually arrived at the pool.

I was just entering into the sport with all my heart, when I heard a shot fired in the Turks' camp, followed by loud yells, and I observed a crowd of Latookas rushing from the camp towards their town. In a few moments later, I heard the Turks' drum, and I saw people running to and fro, and the Latookas assembling from the neighbourhood with lances and shields, as though preparing for a fray. I had only two men with me, and being nearly half a mile from camp, I thought it advisable to hasten towards the spot, lest some contretemps should take place before my arrival. Accordingly I hurried over the open plain, and shortly reached my camp. I found my wife arranging the men at their posts, fearing a disturbance. They had seen me hastening towards them, and I now went to the Turks' camp, that was close by, and inquired the cause of alarm.

Never was I more disgusted. Already the vultures were swooping in circles above some object outside the camp. It appeared that a native of Kayala (the town lately attacked by the Turks) had visited Tarrangolle to inquire after a missing cow. The chiefs, Moy and Commoro, brought him to the Turks' camp, merely to prove that he had no evil intention. No sooner was it announced that he was a native of Kayala than the Turks declared he was a spy, and condemned him to be shot. The two chiefs, Moy and Commoro, feeling themselves compromised by having brought the man into such danger unwittingly, threw themselves before him, and declared that no harm should befall him, as he belonged to them. Tearing them away by the combined force of many men, the prisoner was immediately bound, and led forth by his bloodthirsty murderers to death. "Shoot the spy" was hardly pronounced, when a villain stepped forward, and placing the muzzle of his musket close to his left breast, he fired.

The man dropped dead, thus murdered in cold blood. The natives rushed in crowds from the spot, naturally supposing that a general massacre would follow so unprovoked an outrage. The body was dragged by the heels a few paces outside the camp, and the vultures were its sextons within a few minutes of the death.

It was with difficulty that I could restrain my temper under such revolting circumstances. I felt that at an unlooked-for moment I might be compromised in some serious outbreak of the natives, caused by the brutal acts of the traders. Already it was declared unsafe to venture out shooting without ten or twelve armed men as escort.

A mixture of cowardice and brutality, the traders' party became exceedingly timid, as a report was current that the inhabitants of Kayala intended to ally themselves to those of Tarrangolle, and to attack the Turks in their camp. I accordingly strengthened my position by building a tower of palisades, that entirely commanded all approaches to my *zareeba*.

Latooka was already spoiled by the Turks: it was now difficult to procure flour and milk for beads, as the traders' people, since the attack on Kayala, had commenced the system of purchasing all supplies with either goats or beef, which having been stolen, was their cheapest medium of exchange. Although rich in beads and copper, I was actually poor, as I could not obtain supplies. Accordingly I allowanced my men two pounds of beads monthly, and they went to distant villages and purchased their own provisions independently of me.

On the 11th June, at 7:20 a.m., there was a curious phenomenon; the sky was perfectly clear, but we were startled by a noise like the sudden explosion of a mine, or the roar of heavy cannon, almost immediately repeated. It appeared to have originated among the mountains, about sixteen miles distant due south of my camp. I could only account for this occurrence by the supposition that an immense mass of the granite rock might have detached itself from a high mountain, and, in falling to the valley, it might have bounded from a projection on the mountain's side, and thus have caused a double report.

June 13. – I shot ten ducks and geese before breakfast, including one of the large black and white geese with the crimson head and neck. On my return to camp I weighed this – exactly eleven pounds; this goose has on either pinion-joint a sharp, horny spur, an inch in length. During my morning stroll I met hundreds of natives running excitedly with shields and spears towards Adda's village: they were going to steal the cattle from a village about four miles distant; thus there will be a fight in the course of the day. The Latooka stream is now full, and has the appearance of a permanent river carrying a considerable body of water to the Sobat.

I met with two thieves while duck-shooting this morning – the one an eagle, and the other a native. The beautiful white-throated fish-eagle may generally be seen perched upon a bough overhanging the stream, ready for any prey that may offer. This morning I shot two ducks right and left as they flew down the course of the river – -one fell dead in the water, but the other, badly hit, fluttered along the surface for some distance, and was immediately chased and seized by a fish-eagle which, quite reckless of the gun, had been watching the sport from a high tree, and evinced a desire to share the results. My men, not to be done out of their breakfast, gave chase, shouting and yelling to frighten the eagle, and one of them having a gun loaded with buckshot, fired, and the whirr-r of the charge induced the eagle to drop the duck, which was triumphantly seized by the man.

The other thief was a native. I fired a long shot at a drake; the bird flew a considerable distance and towered, falling about a quarter of a mile distant. A Latooka was hoeing close to where it fell, and we distinctly saw him pick up the bird and run to a bush, in which he hid it: upon our arrival he continued his work as though nothing had happened, and denied all knowledge of it: he was accordingly led by the ear to the bush, where we found the duck carefully secreted.

June 14. – The natives lost one man killed in the fight yesterday, therefore the night was passed in singing and dancing.

The country is drying up; although the stream is full there is no rain in Latooka, the water in the river being the eastern drainage of the Obbo Mountains, where it rains daily.

Ibrahimawa, the Bornu man, alias "Sinbad the Sailor," the great traveller, amuses and bores me daily with his long and wonderful stories of his travels. The style of his narratives may be conjectured from the following extracts: "There was a country adjoining Bornu, where the king was so fat and heavy that he could not walk, until the doctors opened his belly and cut the fat out, which operation was repeated annually."

He described another country as a perfect Paradise, where no one ever drank anything so inferior as water. This country was so wealthy that the poorest man could drink *merissa*. He illustrated the general intoxication by saying, that after 3 p.m. no one was sober, throughout the country, and from that hour the cows, goats, and fowls were all drunk, as they drank the *merissa* left in the jars by their owners, who were all asleep.

He knew all about England, having been a servant, on a Turkish frigate that was sent to Gravesend. He described an evening entertainment most vividly. He had been to a ball at an English pasha's in Blackwall, and had succeeded wonderfully with some charming English ladies excessively *decollete*, upon whom he felt sure he had left a lasting impression, as several had fallen in love with him on the spot, supposing him to be a pasha.

Such were instances of life and recollections of Ibrahimawa, the Bornu.

On June 16, Koorshid's people returned from Obbo. Ibrahim and a few men had remained there, and distrusting the warlike spirit of the Latookas, he now recalled the entire establishment from Tarrangolle, intending to make a station at the more peaceful country of Obbo. An extract from my journal on that day explains my feelings: "This is most annoying; I had arranged my camp and garden, etc. for the wet season, and I must now leave everything, as it is impossible to remain in this country with my small force alone; the natives have become so bad (since the cattle *razzia*) that a considerable armed party is obliged to go to the stream for water. It is remarkably pleasant travelling in the vicinity of the traders; they convert every country into a wasp's nest; they have neither plan of action nor determination, and I, being unfortunately dependent upon their movements, am more like a donkey than an explorer, that is saddled and ridden away at a moment's notice. About sixty natives of Obbo accompanied the men sent by Ibrahim to carry the effects; I require at least fifty, as so many of my transport animals are dead." Nothing can exceed the laziness and dogged indolence of my men; I have only four who are worth having – Richarn, Hamed, Sali, and Taher.

All the men in either camp were discontented at the order to move, as they had made themselves comfortable, expecting to remain in Latooka during the wet season. The two chiefs, Moy and Commoro, found themselves in a dilemma, as they had allied themselves with the Turks in the attack upon the neighbouring town, depending upon them for future support; they were now left in the lurch, and felt themselves hardly a match for their enemies. A few extracts from my journal will close our sojourn at Latooka:

"June 18th. – The white ants are a curse upon the country; although the hut is swept daily and their galleries destroyed, they rebuild everything during the night, scaling the supports to the roof and entering the thatch. Articles of leather or wood are the first devoured. The rapidity with which they repair their galleries is wonderful; all their work is carried on with cement; the earth is contained in their stomachs, and this being mixed with some glutinous matter they deposit it as bees do their wax. Although the earth of this country if tempered for housebuilding will crumble in the rain, the hills of the white ants remain solid and waterproof, owing to the glue in the cement. I have seen three varieties of white ants – the largest about the size of a small wasp: this does not attack dwellings, but subsists upon fallen trees. The second variety is not so large; this species seldom enters buildings. The third is the greatest pest: this is the smallest, but thick and juicy; the earth is literally alive with them, nor is there one square foot of ground free from them in Latooka.

"June 19th. – Had a bad attack of fever yesterday that has been hanging about me for some days. Weighed all the luggage and packed the stores in loads of fifty pounds each for the natives to carry.

"June 20th. – Busy making new ropes from the bark of a mimosa; all hands at work, as we start the day after to-morrow. My loss in animals makes a difference of twenty-three porters' loads. I shall take forty natives as the bad roads will necessitate light loads for the donkeys. I have now only fourteen donkeys; these are in good condition, and would thrive, were not the birds so destructive by pecking sores upon their backs. These sores would heal quickly by the application of gunpowder, but the birds irritate and enlarge them until the animal is rendered useless. I have lost two donkeys simply from the attacks of these birds; the only remaining camel and some of the donkeys I have covered with jackets made of tent-cloth.

"June 21st. – Nil.

"June 22d. – We were awoken last night by a report from the sentry that natives were prowling around the camp; I accordingly posted three additional guards. At a little after 2 a.m. a shot was fired, followed by two others in quick succession, and a sound as of many feet running quickly was heard passing the entrance of the camp. I was up in a moment, and my men were quickly under arms: the Turks' drum beat, and their camp (that was contiguous to mine) was alive with men, but all was darkness. I lighted my policeman's lantern, that was always kept ready trimmed, and I soon arrived at the spot where the shot had been fired. The natives had been endeavouring to steal the cattle from the Turks' *kraal*, and favoured by the darkness they had commenced burrowing with the intention of removing the thorn bushes that formed the fence. Unfortunately for the thieves, they were unaware that there were watchers in the kraal among the cattle: it was a pitch dark night, and nothing could be distinguished; but the attention of one of the sentries was attracted by the snorting and stamping of the goats, that evidently denoted the presence of something uncommon. He then perceived close to him, on the other side the hedge, a dark object crouching, and others standing, and he heard the bushes moving as though some one was at work to remove them. He immediately fired; and the sound of a rush of men in retreat induced both him and the other sentry to repeat the shot. By the light of the lantern we now searched the place, and discovered the body of a native lying close to the fence just above a considerable hole that he had scraped beneath the thorns, in order to extract the stems that were buried in the ground, and thus by drawing away the bushes he would have effected an entrance. He had commenced operations exactly oppo-site the sentry, and the musket being loaded with mould-shot, he had received the contents at close quarters. Although he had tempted fate and met with deserved misfortune, it was most disgusting to witness the brutality of the Turks, who, tying ropes to the ankles, dragged the body to the entrance of the camp, and wished for amusement to drive their bayonets through the chest.

"Although dying, the man was not dead: a shot had entered one eye, knocking it out; several had entered the face, chest, and thighs, as he was in a stooping position when the gun was fired. I would not allow him to be mutilated, and after groaning in agony for some time, he died. The traders' people immediately amputated the hands at the wrists, to detach the copper bracelets, while others cut off his helmet of beads, and the body was very considerately dragged close to the entrance of my camp.

"June 22nd. – Finding that the disgusting Turks had deposited the dead body almost at my door, I had it removed a couple of hundred yards to leeward. The various birds of prey immediately collected – buzzards, vultures, crows, and the great Marabou stork. I observed a great bare-necked vulture almost succeed in turning the body over by pulling at the flesh of the arm at the opposite side to that where it stood. I have noticed that birds of prey invariably commence their attack upon the eyes, inner portions of the thighs, and beneath the arms, before they devour the coarser portions. In a few hours a well-picked skeleton was all that was left of the Latooka."

We were to start on the following day. My wife was dangerously ill with bilious fever, and was unable to stand, and I endeavoured to persuade the traders' party to postpone their departure for a few days. They would not hear of such a proposal; they had so irritated the Latookas that they feared an attack, and their captain, or *vakeel*, Ibrahim, had ordered them immediately to vacate the country. This was a most awkward position for me. The traders had induced the hostility of the country, and I should bear the brunt of it should I remain behind alone. Without their presence I should be unable to procure porters, as the natives would not accompany my feeble party, especially as I could offer them no other payment but beads or copper. The rains had commenced within the last few days at Latooka, and on the route towards Obbo we should encounter continual storms. We were to march by a long and circuitous route to avoid the rocky passes that would be dangerous in the present spirit of the country, especially as the traders possessed large herds that must accompany the party. They allowed five days' march for the distance to Obbo by the intended route. This was not an alluring programme for the week's entertainment, with my wife almost in a dying state! However, I set to work, and fitted an *angarep* with arched hoops from end to end, so as to form a frame like the cap of a wagon. This I covered with two waterproof Abyssinian tanned hides securely strapped; and lashing two long poles parallel to the sides of the *angarep*, I formed an excellent palanquin. In this she was assisted, and we started on 23d June.

Our joint parties consisted of about three hundred men. On arrival at the base of the mountains, instead of crossing them as before, we skirted the chain to the northwest, and then rounding through a natural gap, we ascended gradually towards the south.

On the fifth day we were, at 5 a.m., within twelve miles of Obbo, and we bivouacked on a huge mass of granite on the side of a hill, forming an inclining plateau of about an acre. The natives who accompanied us were immediately ordered to clear the grass from the insterstices of the rocks, and hardly had they commenced when a slight disturbance, among some loose stones that were being removed, showed that something was wrong. In an instant lances and stones were hurled at some object by the crowd, and upon my arrival I saw the most horrid monster that I have ever experienced. I immediately pinned his head to the ground and severed it at one blow with my hunting-knife, damaging the keen edge of my favourite weapon upon the hard rock. It was a puff adder of the most extraordinary dimensions. I then fetched my measuring-tape from the game-bag, in which it was always at hand. Although the snake was only 5 ft. 4 in. in length it was slightly above 15 inches in girth. The tail was, as usual in poisonous snakes, extremely blunt, and the head perfectly fiat, and about 2 1/2 inches broad, but unfortunately during my short absence to fetch the measure the natives had crushed it with a rock. They had thus destroyed it as a specimen, and had broken three of the teeth, but I counted eight, and secured five poison-fangs, the two most prominent being nearly an inch in length. The poison-fangs of snakes are artfully contrived by some diabolical freak of nature as pointed tubes, through which the poison is injected into the base of the wound inflicted. The extreme point of the fang is solid, and is so finely sharpened that beneath a powerful microscope it is perfectly smooth, although the point of the finest needle is rough. A short distance above the solid point of the fang the surface of the tube appears as though cut away, like the first cut of a quill in forming a pen: through this aperture the poison is injected.

Hardly had I secured the fangs, when a tremendous clap of thunder shook the earth and echoed from rock to rock among the high mountains that rose abruptly on our left within a mile. Again the lightning flashed, and almost simultaneously, a deafening peal roared from the black cloud above us, just as I was kneeling over the archenemy to skin him. He looked so Satanic with his flat head, and minute cold grey eye, and scaly hide, with the lightning flashing and the thunder roaring around him; I felt like St. Dunstan with the devil, and skinned him. The natives and also my men were horrified, as they would not touch any portion of such a snake with their hands: even its skin was supposed by these people to be noxious. Down came the rain; I believe it could not have rained harder. Mrs. Baker in the palanquin was fortunately like a snail in her shell; but I had nothing for protection except an oxhide: throwing myself upon my *angarep* I drew it over me. The natives had already lighted prodigious fires, and all crowded around the blaze; but what would have been the Great Fire of London in that storm?

In half an hour the fire was out; such a deluge fell that the ravine that was dry when we first bivouacked, was now an impassable torrent. My oxhide had become tripe, and my *angarep*, being covered with a mat, was some inches deep in water. Throwing away the mat, the pond escaped through the sieve-like network, but left me drenched. Throughout the night it poured. We had been wet through every day during the journey from Latooka, but the nights had been fine; this was superlative misery to all. At length it ceased – morning dawned; we could not procure fire, as everything was saturated, and we started on our march through forest and high reeking grass. By this circuitous route from Latooka we avoided all difficult passes, as the ground on the west side of the chain of mountains ascended rapidly but regularly to Obbo. On arrival at my former hut I found a great change; the grass was at least ten feet high, and my little camp was concealed in the rank vegetation. Old Katchiba came to meet us, but brought nothing, as he said the Turks had eaten up the country. An extract from my journal, dated July 1, explains the misery of our position:

"This Obbo country is now a land of starvation. The natives refuse to supply provision for beads; nor will they barter anything unless in exchange for flesh. This is the curse that the Turks have brought upon the country by stealing cattle and throwing them away wholesale. We have literally nothing to eat except tullaboon, a small bitter grain used in lieu of corn by the natives: there is no game; if it existed, shooting would be impossible, as the grass is impenetrable. I hear that the Turks intend to make a *razzia* on the Shoggo country near Farajoke; thus they will stir up a wasp's nest for me wherever I go, and render it impossible for my small party to proceed alone, or even to remain in peace. I shall be truly thankful to quit this abominable land; in my experience I never saw such scoundrels as Africa produces – the natives of the Soudan being worse than all. It is impossible to make a servant of any of these people; the apathy, indolence, dishonesty combined with dirtiness, are beyond description; and their abhorrence of anything like order increases their natural dislike to Europeans. I have not one man even approaching to a servant; the animals are neglected, therefore they die. And were I to die they would rejoice, as they would immediately join Koorshid's people in cattle stealing and slave hunting; charming followers in the time of danger! Such men destroy all pleasure, and render exploration a mere toil. No one can imagine the hardships and annoyances to which we are subject, with the additional disgust of being somewhat dependent upon the traders' band of robbers. For this miserable situation my *vakeel* is entirely responsible; had my original escort been faithful, I should have been entirely independent, and could with my transport animals have penetrated far south before the commencement of the rainy season. Altogether I am thoroughly sick of this expedition, but I shall plod onwards with dogged obstinacy; God only knows the end. I shall be grateful should the day ever arrive once more to see Old England."

Both my wife and I were excessively ill with bilious fever, and neither could assist the other. The old chief, Katchiba, hearing that we were dying, came to charm us with some magic spell. He found us lying helpless, and he immediately procured a small branch of a tree, and filling his mouth with water, he squirted it over the leaves and about the floor of the hut; he then waved the branch around my wife's head, also around mine, and completed the ceremony by sticking it in the thatch above the doorway; he told us we should now get better, and perfectly: satisfied, he took his leave. The hut was swarming with rats and white ants, the former racing over our bodies during the night, and burrowing through the floor, filling our only room with mounds like molehills. As fast as we stopped the holes, others were made with determined perseverance. Having a supply of arsenic, I gave them an entertainment, the effect being disagreeable to all parties, as the rats died in their holes, and created a horrible effluvium, while fresh hosts took the place of the departed. Now and then a snake would be seen gliding within the thatch, having taken shelter from the pouring rain. The smallpox was raging throughout the country, and the natives were dying like flies in winter. The country was extremely unhealthy, owing to the constant rain and the rank herbage, which prevented a free circulation of air, and from the extreme damp induced fevers. The temperature was 65 degrees Fahr. at night, and 72 degrees during the day; dense clouds obscured the sun for many days, and the air was reeking with moisture. In the evening it was always necessary to keep a blazing fire within the hut, as the floor and walls were wet and chilly.

The wet herbage disagreed with my baggage animals.

Innumerable flies appeared, including the Tsetse, and in a few weeks the donkeys had no hair left, either on their ears or legs; they drooped and died one by one. It was in vain that I erected sheds, and lighted fires; nothing would protect them from the flies. The moment the fires were lit, the animals would rush wildly into the smoke, from which nothing would drive them, and in the clouds of imaginary protection they would remain all day, refusing food. On the 16th of July my last horse, Mouse, died; he had a very long tail, for which I obtained a cow in exchange. Nothing was prized so highly as horse's tails, the hairs being used for stringing beads, and also for making tufts as ornaments, to be suspended from the elbows. It was highly fashionable in Obbo for the men to wear such tufts, formed of the bushy ends of cow's-tails. It was also "the thing" to wear six or eight polished rings of iron, fastened so tightly round the throat as to almost choke the wearer, somewhat resembling dog-collars.

On 18th July, the natives held a great consultation, and ended with a war-dance; they were all painted in various patterns, with red ochre and white pipe-clay; their heads adorned with very tasteful ornaments of cowrie-shells, surmounted by plumes of ostrich-feathers, which drooped over the back of the neck. After the dance, the old chief addressed them in a long and vehement speech; he was followed by several other speakers, all of whom were remarkably fluent, and the resolution of the meeting was declared that the *nogara*s were to be beaten, and men collected to accompany the Turks on a *razzia* in the Madi country.

Ibrahim started with 120 armed men and a mass of Obbo people on the marauding expedition.

On the following day Katchiba came to see us, bringing a present of flour. I gave him a tin plate, a wooden spoon, the last of the teacups, and a tinsel paper of mother-of-pearl shirt buttons, which took his fancy so immensely, that my wife was begged to suspend it from his neck like a medal. He was really a very good old fellow – by far the best I have seen in Africa. He was very suspicious of the Turks, who, he said, would ultimately ruin him, as, by attacking the Madi tribe, they would become his enemies, and invade Obbo when the Turks should leave. Cattle were of very little use in his country, as the flies would kill them; he had tried all his magic art, but it was of no avail against the flies; my donkeys would all assuredly die. He said that the losses inflicted upon the various tribes by the Turks were ruinous, as their chief means of subsistence was destroyed; without cattle they could procure no wives; milk, their principle diet, was denied them, and they were driven to despair; thus they would fight for their cattle, although they would allow their families to be carried off without resistance; cattle would procure another family, but if the animals were stolen, there would be no remedy.

Flies by day, rats and innumerable bugs by night, heavy dew, daily rain, and impenetrable reeking grass rendered Obbo a prison about as disagreeable as could exist.

The many months of tiresome inaction that I was forced to remain in this position, I will not venture to inflict upon the reader, but I will content myself with extracts from my journal from time to time, that will exhibit the general character of the situation.

"Aug. 2d. – Several of my men have fever; the boy, Saat, upon receiving a dose of calomel, asked, 'whether he was to swallow the paper in which it was wrapped?' This is not the first time that I have been asked the same question by my men. Saat feels the ennui of Obbo, and finds it difficult to amuse himself; he has accordingly become so far scientific, that he has investigated the machinery of two of my watches, both of which he has destroyed. I am now reduced to one watch, the solitary survivor of four that formed my original family of timekeepers. Having commenced as a drummer, Saat feels the loss of his drum that was smashed by the camel; he accordingly keeps his hand in by practising upon anything that he can adapt to that purpose, the sacred kettle inverted, and a tin cup, having been drummed until the one became leaky, and the bottom of the other disappeared.

"Saat and the black woman are, unfortunately, enemies, and the monotony of the establishment is sometimes broken by a stand-up fight between him and his vicious antagonist, Gaddum Her. The latter has received a practical proof that the boy is growing strong, as I found him the other day improving her style of beauty by sitting astride upon her stomach, and punching her eyes with his fists, as she lay upon the ground furrowing Saat's fat cheeks with her very dirty nails. It is only fair to the boy to say that Gaddum Her is always the aggressor.

"It is absurd to see the self-importance of the miserable cut-throats belonging to Koorshid's party, who, far too great to act as common soldiers, swagger about with little slave-boys in attendance, who carry their muskets. I often compare the hard lot of our honest poor in England with that of these scoundrels, whose courage consists in plundering and murdering defenceless natives, while the robbers fatten on the spoil. I am most anxious to see whether the English government will take active notice of the White Nile trade, or whether diplomacy will confine them to simple protest and correspondence, to be silenced by a promise from the Egyptian government to put a stop to the present atrocities. The

Egyptian government will of course promise, and, as usual with Turks, will never perform. On the other hand, the savages are themselves bad; one tribe welcomes the Turks as allies against their neighbours, and sees no crime in murder, provided the result be 'cattle.' This, of course, produces general confusion.

"Aug. 6th. – The difficulties of procuring provisions are most serious: the only method of purchasing flour is as follows. The natives will not sell it for anything but flesh; to purchase an ox, I require molotes (hoes): to obtain molotes I must sell my clothes and shoes to the traders' men. The ox is then driven to a distant village, and is there slaughtered, and the flesh being divided into about a hundred small portions, my men sit upon the ground with three large baskets, into which are emptied minute baskets of flour as the natives produce them, one in exchange for each parcel of meat. This tedious process is a specimen of Central African difficulties in the simple act of purchasing flour. The Obbo natives are similar to the Bari in some of their habits. I have had great difficulty in breaking my cowkeeper of his disgusting custom of washing the milk bowl with cow's urine, and even mixing some with the milk; he declares that unless he washes his hands with such water before milking, the cow will lose her milk. This filthy custom is unaccountable. The Obbo natives wash out their mouths with their own urine. This habit may have originated in the total absence of salt in their country. The Latookas, on the contrary, are very clean, and milk could be purchased in their own vessels without fear.

"Aug. 8th – Having killed a fat ox, the men are busily engaged in boiling down the fat. Care should be taken to sprinkle a few drops of water in the pot when the fat is supposed to be sufficiently boiled; should it hiss, as though poured upon melted lead, it is ready; but if it be silent, the fat is not sufficiently boiled, and it will not keep.

"Three runaway female slaves were captured by Koorshid's people this morning, two of whom were brutally treated. On the whole the female slaves are well kept when very young, but well thrashed when the black bloom of youth has passed.

"Aug. 11th. – At this season immense beetles are at work in vast numbers, walking off with every species of dung, by forming it into balls as large as small apples, and rolling them away with their hind legs, while they walk backwards by means of the forelegs. Should a ball of dung roll into a deep rut, I have frequently seen another beetle come to the assistance of the proprietor of the ball, and quarrel for its possession after their joint labours have raised it to the level.

"This species was the holy scarabaeus of the ancient Egyptians; it appears shortly after the commencement of the wet season, its labours continuing until the cessation of the rains, at which time it disappears. Was it not worshipped by the ancients as the harbinger of the high Nile? The existence of Lower Egypt depending upon the annual inundation, the rise of the river was observed with general anxiety. The beetle appears at the commencement of the rise in the river level, and from its great size and extraordinary activity in clearing the earth from all kinds of ordure, its presence is remarkable. Appearing at the season of the flood, may not the ancients have imagined some connexion between the beetle and the river, and have considered it sacred as the harbinger of the inundation?

"There is a wild bean in this country, the blossom of which has a delicious perfume of violets. I regret that I have not a supply of paper for botanical specimens, as many beautiful flowers appeared at the commencement of the rains. Few thorns and no gums form a strong contrast to the Soudan, where nearly every tree and shrub is armed.

"Aug. 13th. – I had a long examination of a slave woman, Bacheeta, belonging to one of Koorshid's men. She had been sent two years ago by the king, Kamrasi, from Unyoro, as a spy among the traders, with orders to attract them to the country if appearances were favourable, but to return with a report should they be dangerous people.

"On her arrival at Faloro, Debono's people captured her, and she was eventually sold to her present owner. She speaks Arabic, having learnt it from the traders' people. She declares that Magungo, the place of which I have heard so much, is only four days' hard marching for a native, direct from Faloro, but eight days' for the Turks; and that it is equi-distant from Faloro and from Kamrasi's capital in Unyoro. She had heard of the Luta N'Zige, as reported to Speke, but she knew it only by the name of 'Kara-Wootan-N'Zige.'

"She corroborated the accounts I had formerly received, of large boats arriving with Arabs at Magungo, and she described the lake as a 'white sheet as far as the eye could reach.' She particularized it as a peculiar water, that was unlike other waters, as it would 'come up to a water-jar, if put upon the shore, and carry it away and break it.' By this description I understood 'waves.' She also described the 'Gondokoro River,' or White Nile, as flowing into and out of the lake, and she spoke of a 'great roar of water that fell from the sky.'

"I trust I may succeed in reaching this lake: if not, my entire time, labour, and expenditure will have been wasted, as I throw sport entirely aside for the sake of this exploration. Were I to think of shooting in preference to exploring, I could have excellent sport on the Atabbi River during the dry season, as also on the Kanieti, in the vicinity of Wakkala; but I must neglect all but the great object, and push on to Kamrasi's capital, and from thence to the lake. My great anxiety lies in the conduct of Koorshid's party; should they make *razzias* south, I shall be ruined, as my men will be afraid to advance through a disturbed country. I must keep on good terms with the chief of the party, as I depend upon him for an interpreter and porters.

"My plan is to prevail on Ibrahim to commence an ivory trade in Kamrasi's country that might be legitimately conducted, instead of the present atrocious system of robbery and murder. I like Koorshid, as he is a bold-spoken robber instead of acting the hypocrite like the other traders of Khartoum; thus, as he was the only man that was civil to me, I would do him a good turn could I establish an honest trade between Kamrasi and himself; at the same time, I should have the advantage of his party as escort to the desired country. The case commercially lies as follows:

"Kamrasi's country, Unyoro, is a virgin land, where beads are hardly known, and where the king is the despotic ruler, whose word is law. All trade would be conducted through him alone, in the shape of presents, he giving elephants' tusks, while, in return, Koorshid would send him beads and various articles annually. Koorshid would thus be the sole trader with Kamrasi according to White Nile rules, and the abominable system of cattle robbery would be avoided.

"The great difficulty attending trade in a distant country is the want of means of transport, one tribe, being generally hostile to the adjoining, fears to afford porters beyond the frontier. If I can prove that the Lake Luta N'Zige is one source of the Nile with a navigable junction, I can at once do away with the great difficulty, and open up a direct trade for Koorshid. The Lake is in Kamrasi's own dominions: thus he will have no fear in supplying porters to deliver the ivory at a depot that might be established, either on the lake or at its junction with the Nile. A vessel should be built upon the lake, to trade with the surrounding coasts, and to receive the ivory from the depot. This vessel would then descend from the lake to the While Nile, to the head of the cataracts, where a camp should be formed, from which, in a few days' march, the ivory would reach Gondokoro.

"A large trade might thus be established, as not only Unyoro would supply ivory, but the lake would open the navigation to the very heart of Africa. The advantage of dealing with Kamrasi direct would be great, as he is not a mere savage, demanding beads and bracelets; but he would receive printed cottons, and goods of various kinds, by which means the ivory would be obtained at a merely nominal rate. The depot on the Luta N'Zige should be a general store, at which the vessel ascending from the station above the cataracts would deliver the various goods from Gondokoro, and from this store the goods would be disseminated throughout the countries bordering the lake by means of vessels.

"The only drawback to this honest trade would be the general hatred of anything honest by the Khartoumers; the charms of cattle razzias and slave-hunting, with the attendant murders, attract these villanous cut-throats to the White Nile expeditions, and I fear it would be difficult to raise the number of armed men required for safety, were legitimate trade the sole object of the ivory hunter.

"Even in Obbo, I believe that printed calicoes, red woollen shirts, blankets, etc. would purchase ivory. The elevation of this country being upwards of 3,600 feet, the nights are cold, and even the day is cold during the wet season; thus clothing is required; this we see in the first rudiments of covering, the skins of beasts used by the natives; the Obbo people being the first tribe that adopts a particle of clothing from the Shillook country (lat. 10 degrees) throughout the entire course of the White Nile to this latitude (4 degrees 02 minutes). Kamrasi's tribe are well covered, and farther south, towards Zanzibar, all tribes are clothed more or less; thus Obbo is the clothing frontier, where the climate has first prompted the savage to cover himself, while in the hot lowlands he remains in a state of nakedness. Where clothing is required, English manufacturers would find a market in exchange for ivory; thus from this point a fair trade might be commenced.

"From Farajoke, in the Sooli country, lat. 3 degrees 33 minutes, up to this date the most southern limit of my explorations, the lake is about nine or ten days' march in a direct course; but such a route is impossible, owing to Debono's establishment occupying the intervening country, and the rules of the traders forbid a trespass upon their assumed territory. Koorshid's men would refuse to advance by that route; my men, if alone, will be afraid to travel, and will find some excuse for not proceeding; from the very outset they have been an absolute burthen upon me, receiving a monthly allowance of two pounds of beads per head for doing literally nothing, after having ruined the independence of my expedition by their mutiny at Gondokoro.

"Aug. 23d. – My last camel died to-day; thus all my horses and camels are dead, and only eight donkeys remain out of twenty-one; most of these will die, if not all. There can be no doubt that the excessive wet in all the food, owing to the constant rain and dew, is the principal cause of disease. The camels, horses, and donkeys of the Soudan, all thrive in the hot dry air of that country, and are unsuited for this damp climate.

"Had I been without transport animals, my expedition could not have left Gondokoro, as there was no possibility of procuring porters. I had always expected that my animals would die, but I had hoped they would have carried me to the equator: this they would have accomplished during the two months of comparative dry weather following my arrival at Gondokoro, had not the mutiny thwarted all my plans, and thrown me into the wet season. My animals have delivered me at Obbo, and have died in inaction, instead of wearing out upon the road. Had I been able to start direct from Gondokoro, as I had intended, my animals would have delivered me in Kamrasi's country before the arrival of the heavy rains.

"There is an excellent species of gourd in Obbo; it is pear-shaped, about ten inches long, and seven in diameter, with a white skin, and warts upon the surface; this is the most delicate and the best-flavoured that I have ever eaten.

"There are two varieties of castor-oil plant in this country – one with a purple stem and bright red veins in the leaves, that is remarkably handsome. Also a wild plantain, with a crimson stem to the leaf; this does not grow to the height of the common plantain, but is simply a plume of leaves springing from the ground without a parent stem.

"Aug. 30th. – Mrs. Baker and I made a morning call for the first time upon old Katchiba by his express desire. His courtyard was cemented and clean, about a hundred feet in diameter, surrounded by palisades, which were overgrown with gourds and the climbing yam, Collolollo. There were several large huts in the inclosure, belonging to his wives; he received us very politely, and begged us to enter his principal residence; it was simply arranged, being the usual circular hut, but about twenty-five feet in diameter.

"Creeping on all fours through the narrow doorway, we found ourselves in the presence of one of his wives, who was preparing *merissa*. The furniture of the apartment was practical, and quite in accordance with the taste of the old chief, as the whole establishment appeared to be devoted to brewing *merissa*. There were several immense jars capable of holding about thirty gallons: some of these were devoted to beer, while one was reserved to contain little presents that he had received from ourselves and the Turks, including a much-esteemed red flannel shirt: these recherche objects were packed in the jar, and covered by a smaller vessel inverted on the mouth to protect them from rats and white ants. Two or three well-prepared ox-hides were spread upon the ground; and he requested Mrs. Baker to sit on his right hand, while I sat upon the left. Thus satisfactorily arranged, he called for some *merissa*, which his wife immediately brought in an immense gourd-shell, and both my wife and I having drunk, he took a long draught, and finished the gourd.

"The delightful old sorcerer, determined to entertain us, called for his rababa: a species of harp was handed to him; this was formed of a hollow base and an upright piece of wood, from which descended eight strings. Some time was expended in carefully tuning his instrument, which, being completed, he asked, 'if he should sing?' Fully prepared for something comic, we begged him to begin. He sang a most plaintive and remarkably wild, but pleasing air, accompanying himself perfectly on his harp, producing the best music that I had ever heard among savages. In fact, music and dancing were old Katchiba's delight, especially if combined with deep potations.

"His song over, he rose from his seat and departed, but presently reappeared leading a sheep by a string, which he begged us to accept. I thanked him for his attention, but I assured him that we had not paid him a visit with the expectation of receiving a present, and that we could not think of accepting it, as we had simply called upon him as friends; he accordingly handed the sheep to his wife, and shortly after we rose to depart. Having effected an exit by creeping through the doorway, he led us both by the hand in a most friendly way for about a hundred yards on our path, and took leave most gracefully, expressing a hope that we should frequently come to see him.

"On our return home we found the sheep waiting for us; determined not to be refused, he had sent it on before us. I accordingly returned him a most gorgeous necklace of the most valuable beads, and gave the native who had brought the sheep a present for himself and wife; thus all parties were satisfied, and the sheep was immediately killed for dinner.

"The following morning Katchiba appeared at my door with a large red flag made of a piece of cotton cloth that the Turks had given him; he was accompanied by two men beating large drums, and a third playing a kind of clarionet: this playing at soldiers was an imitation of the Turks. He was in great spirits, being perfectly delighted with the necklace I had sent him.

"Oct. 6th. – I have examined my only remaining donkey: he is a picture of misery – eyes and nose running, coat staring, and he is about to start to join his departed comrades; he has packed up for his last journey. With his loose skin hanging to his withered frame he looked like the British lion on the shield over the door of the Khartoum consulate. In that artistic effort the lion was equally lean and ragged, having perhaps been thus represented by the artist as a pictorial allusion to the smallness of the Consul's pay; the illustration over the shabby gateway utters, 'Behold my leanness! 150l per annum!'

"I feel a touch of the poetic stealing over me when I look at my departing donkey. 'I never loved a dear gazelle,' etc.: but the practical question, 'Who is to carry the portmanteau?' remains unanswered. I do not believe the Turks have any intention of going to Kamrasi's country; they are afraid, as they have heard that he is a powerful king, and they fear the restrictions that power will place upon their felonious propensities. In that case I shall go on without them; but they have deceived me, by borrowing 165 lbs. of beads which they cannot repay; this puts me to much inconvenience. The Asua River is still impassable, according to native reports; this will, prevent a general advance south. Should the rains cease, the river will fall rapidly, and I shall make a forward move and escape this prison of high grass and inaction.

"Oct. 11th. – Lions roaring every night, but not visible. I set my men to work to construct a fortified camp, a simple oblong of palisades with two flanking projections at opposite angles to command all approaches; the lazy scoundrels are sulky in consequence. Their daily occupation is drinking *merissa*, sleeping, and strumming on the rababa, while that of the black women is quarrelling – one ebony sister insulting the other by telling her that she is as 'black as the kettle,' and recommending her, 'to eat poison.'

"Oct. 17th. – I expect an attack of fever tomorrow or next day, as I understand from constant and painful experiences every step of this insidious disease. For some days one feels a certain uneasiness of spirits difficult to explain; no peculiar symptom is observed until a day or two before the attack, when great lassitude is felt, with a desire to sleep. Rheumatic pains in the loins, back, and joints of the limbs are accompanied by a sense of great weakness. A cold fit comes on very quickly; this is so severe that it almost immediately affects the stomach, producing painful vomiting with severe retching. The eyes are heavy and painful, the head hot and aching, the extremities pale and cold, pulse very weak, and about fifty-six beats per minute; the action of the heart distressingly weak, with total prostration of strength. This shivering and vomiting continues for about two hours, attended with great difficulty of breathing. The hot stage then comes on, the retching still continuing, with the difficulty of breathing, intense weakness and restlessness for about an hour and a half, which, should the remedies be successful, terminate in profuse perspiration and sleep. The attack ends, leaving the stomach in a dreadful state of weakness. The fever is remittent, the attack returning almost at the same hour every two days, and reducing the patient rapidly to a mere skeleton; the stomach refuses to act, and death ensues. Any severe action of the mind, such as grief or anger, is almost certain to be succeeded by fever in this country. My stock of quinine is reduced to a few grains, and my work lies before me; my cattle are all dead. We are both weakened by repeated fever, and travelling must be on foot."

Chapter X

LIFE AT OBBO

For months we dragged on a miserable existence at Obbo, wrecked by fever; the quinine exhausted; thus the disease worried me almost to death, returning at intervals of a few days. Fortunately my wife did not suffer so much as I did. I had nevertheless prepared for the journey south; and as travelling on foot would have been impossible in our weak state, I had purchased and trained three oxen in lieu of horses. They were named Beef, Steaks, and Suet. Beef was a magnificent animal, but having been bitten by the flies, he so lost his condition that I changed his name to Bones. We were ready to start, and the natives reported that early in 'January the Asua would be fordable. I had arranged with Ibrahim that he should supply me with porters for payment in copper bracelets, and that he should accompany me with one hundred men to Kamrasi's country (Unyoro), on condition that he would restrain his people from all misdemeanours, and that they should be entirely subservient to me. It was the month of December, and during the nine months that I had been in correspondence with his party I had succeeded in acquiring an extraordinary influence. Although my camp was nearly three-quarters of a mile from their zareeba, I had been besieged daily for many months for everything that was wanted; my camp was a kind of general store that appeared to be inexhaustible. I gave all that I had with a good grace, and thereby gained the goodwill of the robbers, especially as my large medicine chest contained a supply of drugs that rendered me in their eyes a physician of the first importance. I had been very successful with my patients; and the medicines that I generally used being those which produced a very decided effect, both the Turks and natives considered them with perfect faith. There was seldom any difficulty in prognosticating the effect of tartar emetic, and this became the favourite drug that was applied for almost daily; a dose of three grains enchanting the patient, who always advertised my fame by saying, "He told me I should be sick, and, by Allah, there was no mistake about it." Accordingly there was a great run upon the tartar emetic. Many people in Debono's camp had died, including several of my deserters who had joined them. News was brought that, in three separate fights with the natives, my deserters had been killed on every occasion, and my men and those of Ibrahim unhesitatingly declared it was the hand of God. None of Ibrahim's men had died since we left Latooka. One man, who had been badly wounded by a lance thrust through his abdomen, I successfully treated; the trading party, who would at one time gladly have exterminated me, now exclaimed, "What shall we do when the Sowar (traveller) leaves the country?" Mrs. Baker had been exceedingly kind to the women and children of both the traders and natives, and together we had created so favourable an impression that we were always referred to as umpires in every dispute. My own men, although indolent, were so completely disciplined that they would not have dared to disobey an order, and they looked back upon their former mutinous conduct with surprise at their own audacity, and declared that they feared to return to Khartoum, as they were sure that I should not forgive them.

I had promised Ibrahim that I would use my influence with the King of Unyoro to procure him the ivory of that country; I had a good supply of beads, while Ibrahim had none; thus he was dependent upon me for opening the road. Everything looked fair, and had I been strong and well I should have enjoyed the future prospect; but I was weak and almost useless, and weighed down with anxiety lest I might die and my wife would be left alone.

The rains had ceased, and the wild grapes were ripe the natives brought them in great quantities in exchange for a few beads. They were in extremely large bunches, invariably black, and of a good size, but not juicy – the flavour was good, and they were most refreshing, and certainly benefited my health. I pressed about two hundred pounds of grapes in the large sponging bath, but procured so little juice, and that so thick, that winemaking proved a failure; it fermented, and we drank it, but it was not wine. One day, hearing a great noise of voices and blowing of horns in the direction of Katchiba's residence, I sent to inquire the cause. The old chief himself appeared very angry and excited. He said, that his people were very bad, that they had been making a great noise and finding fault with him because he had not supplied them with a few showers, as they wanted to sow their crop of tullaboon. There had been no rain for about a fortnight.

"Well," I replied, "you are the rainmaker; why don't you give your people rain?" "Give my people rain!" said Katchiba. "I give them rain if they don't give me goats? You don't know my people; if I am fool enough to give them rain before they give me the goats, they would let me starve! No, no! Let them wait – if they don't bring me supplies of corn, goats, fowls, yams, *merissa*, and all that I require, not one drop of rain shall ever fall again in Obbo! Impudent brutes are my people! Do you know, they have positively threatened to kill me unless I bring the rain? They shan't have a drop; I will wither the crops, and bring a plague upon their flocks. I'll teach these rascals to insult me!"

With all this bluster, I saw that old Katchiba was in a great dilemma, and that he would give anything for a shower, but that he did not know how to get out of the scrape. It was a common freak of the tribes to sacrifice the rainmaker, should he be unsuccessful. He suddenly altered his tone, and asked, "Have you any rain in your country?" I replied that we had, every now and then. "How do you bring it? Are you a rainmaker?" I told him that no one believed in rainmakers in our country, but that we understood how to bottle lightning (meaning electricity). "I don't keep mine in bottles, but I have a houseful of thunder and lightning," he most coolly replied; "but if you can bottle lightning you must understand rainmaking.

"What do you think of the weather today?" I immediately saw the drift of the cunning old Katchiba; he wanted professional advice. I replied, that he must know all about it, as he was a regular rainmaker. "Of course I do," he answered, "but I want to know what YOU think of it." "Well," I said, "I don't think we shall have any steady rain, but I think we may have a heavy shower in about four days." (I said this as I had observed fleecy clouds gathering daily in the afternoon). "Just my opinion!" said Katchiba, delighted. "In four or perhaps in five days I intend to give them one shower; just one shower; yes, I'll just step down to them now, and tell the rascals, that if they will bring me some goats by this evening, and some corn tomorrow morning, I will give them in four or five days just one shower." To give effect to his declaration he gave several toots upon his magic whistle. "Do you use whistles in your country?" inquired Katchiba. I only replied by giving so shrill and deafening a whistle on my fingers that Katchiba stopped his ears; and relapsing into a smile of admiration he took a glance at the sky from the doorway to see if any sudden effect bad been produced. "Whistle again," he said; and once more I performed like the whistle of a locomotive. "That will do, we shall have it," said the cunning old rainmaker; and proud of having so knowingly obtained "counsel's opinion" on his case, he toddled off to his impatient subjects.

In a few days a sudden storm of rain and violent thunder added to Katchiba's renown, and after the shower, horns were blowing and *nogara*s were beating in honour of their chief. *Entre nous*, my whistle was considered infallible.

The natives were busy sowing the new crop just as the last crop was ripening. It did not appear likely that they would reap much for their labour, as the elephants, having an accurate knowledge of the season, visited their fields nightly, and devoured and trampled the greater portion. I had been too ill to think of shooting, as there was no other method than to watch in the tullaboon fields at night; the high grass in which the elephants harboured being impenetrable. Feeling a little better I took my men to the field about a mile from the village, and dug a hole, in which I intended to watch. That night I took Richarn, and we sat together in our narrow grave. There was no sound throughout the night. I was well wrapped up in a Scotch plaid, but an attack of ague came on, and I shivered as though in Lapland. I had several rifles in the grave; among others "the Baby," that carried a half-pound explosive shell. At about 4 a.m. I heard the distant trumpet of an elephant, and I immediately ordered Richarn to watch, and to report to me their arrival. It was extremely dark, but Richarn presently sank slowly down, and whispered, "Here they are!"

Taking "the Baby," I quietly rose, and listening attentively, I could distinctly hear the elephants tearing off the heads of the tullaboon, and crunching the crisp grain. I could distinguish the dark forms of the herd about thirty paces from me, but much too indistinct for a shot. I stood with my elbows resting on the edge of the hole, and the heavy rifle balanced, waiting for an opportunity. I had a papersight arranged for night shooting, and I several times tried to get the line of an elephant's shoulder, but to no purpose; I could distinguish the sight clearly, but not the elephant. As I was watching the herd I suddenly heard a trumpet close to my left, and I perceived an elephant quickly walking exactly towards my grave. I waited with the rifle at my shoulder until he was within about twelve paces; I then whistled, and he stopped, and turned quickly, exposing his side. Taking the line of the foreleg, I fired at the shoulder. The tremendous flash and smoke of ten drachms of powder completely blinded me, and the sudden reaction of darkness increased the obscurity. I could distinguish nothing; but I heard a heavy fall, and a few moments after I could hear a rustling in the grass as the herd of elephants retreated into the grass jungles. Richarn declared that the elephant had fallen; but I again heard a rustling in the high grass jungle within eighty yards of me, and this sound continued in the same place. I accordingly concluded that the elephant was very badly wounded, and that he could not move from the spot. Nothing could be seen.

At length the birds began to chirp, and the "blacksmith" (as I named one of the first to wake, whose two sharp ringing notes exactly resemble the blows of a hammer upon an anvil) told me that it was nearly daybreak. The grey of morning had just appeared when I heard voices, and I saw Mrs. Baker coming along the field with a party of men, whom she had brought down from the village with knives and axes. She had heard the roar of the heavy rifle, and knowing "the Baby's" scream, and the usual fatal effects, she had considered the elephant as bagged. The natives had also heard the report, and people began to accumulate from all quarters for the sake of the flesh. The elephant was not dead, but was standing about ten yards within the grass jungle; however, in a short time a heavy fall sounded his knell, and the crowd rushed in. He was a fine bull, and before I allowed him to be cut up, I sent for the measuring tape; the result being as follows:

From tip of trunk to fleshy end of tail 26 ft. 0.5 in.

Height from shoulder to forefoot in a perpendicular line 10 ft. 6.5 in.

Girth of forefoot 4 ft. 10.25 in.

Length of one tusk in the curve 6 ft. 6 in. *76 inches*

Ditto of fellow tusk (el Hadam, the servant) 5 ft. 11 in.

Weight of tusks 80 lbs. + 69 lbs. = 149 lbs.

The ridiculous accounts that I have read, stating that the height of elephants attains fifteen feet, is simply laughable ignorance. A difference of a foot in an elephant's height is enormous; he appears a giant among his lesser comrades. Observe the difference between a horse sixteen hands high and a pony of thirteen hands, and the difference of a foot in the height of a quadruped is exemplified. The word being given, the crowd rushed upon the elephant, and about three hundred people were attacking the carcase with knives and lances. About a dozen men were working inside as though in a tunnel; they had chosen this locality as being near to the fat, which was greatly coveted.

A few days later I attempted to set fire to the grass jungle, but it would not burn thoroughly, leaving scorched stems that were rendered still tougher by the fire. On the following evening I took a stroll over the burnt ground to look for game. No elephants had visited the spot; but as I was walking along expecting nothing, up jumped a wild boar and sow from the entrance of a large hole of the Manis, or great scaled anteater. Being thus taken by surprise, the boar very imprudently charged me, and was immediately knocked over dead by a shot through the spine from the little Fletcher rifle, while the left-hand barrel rolled over his companion, who almost immediately recovered and disappeared in the grass jungle; however, there was pork for those who liked it, and I went to the camp and sent a number of natives to bring it home. The Obbo people were delighted, as it was their favourite game, but none of my people would touch the unclean animal. The wild pigs of this country live underground; they take possession of the holes made by the Manis: these they enlarge and form cool and secure retreats.

A bad attack of fever laid me up until the 31st of December. On the first day of January, 1864, I was hardly able to stand, and was nearly worn out at the very time that I required my strength, as we were to start south in a few days.

Although my quinine had been long since exhausted, I had reserved ten grains to enable me to start in case the fever should attack me at the time of departure. I now swallowed my last dose, and on 3d January, I find the following note in my journal: "All ready for a start tomorrow. I trust the year 1864 will bring better luck than the past, that having been the most annoying that I have ever experienced, and full of fever. I hope now to reach Kamrasi's country in a fortnight, and to obtain guides from him direct to the lake. My Latooka, to whom I have been very kind, has absconded: there is no difference in any of these savages; if hungry, they will fawn upon you, and when filled, they will desert. I believe that ten years' residence in the Soudan and this country would spoil an angel, and would turn the best heart to stone."

It was difficult to procure porters, therefore I left all my effects at my camp in charge of two of my men, and I determined to travel light, without the tent, and to take little beyond ammunition and cooking utensils. Ibrahim left forty-five men in his zareeba, and on the 5th of January we started. Mrs. Baker rode her ox, but my animal being very shy, I ordered him to be driven for about a mile with the others to accustom him to the crowd: not approving of the expedition, he bolted into the high grass with my English saddle, and I never saw him again. In my weak state I had to walk. We had not gone far when a large fly fastened upon Mrs. Baker's ox, just by his tail, the effect of which was to produce so sudden a kick and plunge, that he threw her to the ground and hurt her considerably: she accordingly changed the animal, and rode a splendid ox that Ibrahim very civilly offered. I had to walk to the Atabbi, about eighteen miles, which, although a pleasant stroll when in good health, I found rather fatiguing. We bivouacked on the south bank of the Atabbi.

The next morning, after a walk of about eight miles, I purchased of one of the Turks the best ox that I have ever ridden, at the price of a double-barrelled gun – it was a great relief to be well mounted, as I was quite unfit for a journey on foot.

At 4:30 p.m. we arrived at one of the villages of Farajoke. The character of the country had entirely changed; instead of the rank and superabundant vegetation of Obbo, we were in a beautiful open country, naturally drained by its undulating character, and abounding in most beautiful low pasturage. Vast herds of cattle belonged to the different villages, but these had all been driven to conceal-ment, as the report had been received that the Turks were approach-ing. The country was thickly populated, but the natives appeared very mistrustful; the Turks immediately entered the villages, and ransacked the granaries for corn, digging up the yams, and helping themselves to everything as though quite at home. I was on a beau-tiful grass sward on the gentle slope of a hill: here I arranged to biv-ouac for the night.

In three days' march from this point through beautiful park-like country, we arrived at the Asua River. The entire route from Fara-joke had been a gentle descent, and I found this point of the Asua in lat N. 3 degrees 12 minutes to be 2,875 feet above the sea level, 1,091 feet lower than Farajoke. The river was a hundred and twenty paces broad, and from the bed to the top of the perpendicular banks was about fifteen feet. At this season it was almost dry, and a nar-row channel of about six inches deep flowed through the centre of the otherwise exhausted river. The bed was much obstructed by rocks, and the inclination was so rapid that I could readily conceive the impossibility of crossing it during the rains. It formed the great drain of the country, all its waters flowing to the Nile, but during the dry months it was most insignificant. The country between Farajoke and the Asua, although lovely, was very thinly populated, and the only villages that I saw were built upon low hills of bare granite, which lay in huge piles of disjointed fragments.

On arrival at the river, while the men were washing in the clear stream, I took a rifle and strolled along the margin; I shortly observed a herd of the beautiful Mehedehet antelopes feeding upon the rich but low grass of a sandbank in the very centre of the river. Stalking them to within a hundred and twenty paces they obtained my wind, and, ceasing to graze, they gazed intently at me. I was on the high bank among the bushes, and I immediately picked out the biggest, and fired, missing my mark. All dashed away except the animal at which I fired, who stood in uncertainty for a few moments, when the second barrel of the Fletcher 24 rifle knocked him over, striking him through the neck. Hearing the quick double shot, my people came running to the spot, accompanied by a num-ber of the native porters, and were rejoiced to find a good supply of meat; the antelope weighed about five hundred pounds, and was sufficient to afford a good dinner for the whole party.

The Mehedehet is about 13 hands high, with rough, brown hair like the Samber deer of India. Our resting-place was on the dry, rocky bed of the river, close to the edge of the shallow but clear stream that rippled over the uneven surface. Some beautiful tamarind trees afforded a most agreeable shade, and altogether it was a charming place to bivouac. Although at Obbo the grass was not sufficiently dry to burn, in this country it was reduced to a crisp straw, and I immediately set fire to the prairies; the wind was strong, and we had a grand blaze, the flames crackling and leaping about thirty feet high, and sweeping along with so mad a fury that within an hour the entire country was a continuous line of fire. Not a trace of vegetation remained behind; the country appeared as though covered with a pall of black velvet. Returning from my work, I found my camping place well arranged – beds prepared, and a good dinner ready of antelope soup and cutlets. On waking the next morning, I found that the Turks had all disappeared during the night, and that I was alone with my people. It was shortly explained that they had departed to attack some village, to which they were guided by some natives who had accompanied them from Farajoke.

I accordingly took my rifle and strolled along the margin of the river to look for game, accompanied by two of my porters. Although it was a most likely country, being a natural park well timbered, with a river flowing through the midst, there was a great scarcity of wild animals. At length, in crossing a ravine that had stopped the progress of the fire, an antelope (water buck) jumped out of a hollow, and, rushing through the high grass, he exposed himself for an instant in crossing the summit of a bare knoll, and received a ball from the little Fletcher in the hindquarters. Although badly wounded, he was too nimble for my natives, who chased him with their spears for about a quarter of a mile. These fellows tracked him beautifully, and we at length found him hiding in a deep pool in the river, and he was immediately dispatched.

After a long walk, during which I did not obtain another shot, I returned to my resting-place, and, refreshed by a bathe in the cool river, I slept as sound as though in the most luxurious bed in

England. On the following morning I went out early, and shot a small species of antelope; and shortly after my return to breakfast, the Turks' party arrived, bringing with them about three hundred head of cattle that they had captured from the Madi tribe. They did not seem at all in good spirits, and I shortly heard that they had lost their standard-bearer, killed in the fight, and that the flag had been in great peril, and had been saved by the courage of a young Bari slave. The ensign was separated from the main party, and was attacked by four natives, who killed the bearer, and snatched away the flag: this would inevitably have been lost, had not the Bari boy of about fifteen shot the foremost native dead with a pistol, and, snatching the flag from his hands, ran with it towards the Turks, some of whom coming up at that instant, the natives did not think it wise to pursue their advantage. A number of slaves had been captured; among others, several young children, one of whom was an infant. These unfortunate women and children, excepting the infant, were all tied by the neck with a long leathern thong, so as to form a living chain, and guards were set over them to prevent escape.

The Bari natives would make good soldiers, as they are far more courageous than most of the savage tribes. The best men among the party of Ibrahim are Baris; among them is a boy named Arnout; he is the drummer, and he once saved his master in a fight by suddenly presenting his drumstick like a pistol at several natives, who had attacked him while unloaded. The natives, seeing the determined attitude of the boy, and thinking that the drumstick was a firearm, ran off. We started at daybreak on 13th January, and, ascending the whole way, we reached Shooa, in latitude 3 degrees 4 minutes. The route throughout had been of the same parklike character, interspersed with occasional hills of fine granite, piled in the enormous blocks so characteristic of that stone.

Shooa was a lovely place. A fine granite mountain ascended in one block in a sheer precipice for about 800 feet from its base, perfectly abrupt on the eastern side, while the other portions of the mountain were covered with fine forest trees, and picturesquely dotted over with villages. This country formed a natural park, remarkably well watered by numerous rivulets, ornamented with fine timber, and interspersed with numerous high rocks of granite, which from a distance produced the effect of ruined castles.

The pasturage was of a superior quality, and of the same description as that of Farajoke. The country being undulating, there was a small brook in every valley that formed a natural drain. Accordingly, the more elevated land was remarkably dry and healthy. On arrival at the foot of the abrupt mountain, we camped beneath an immense india-rubber tree, that afforded a delightful shade, from which elevated spot we had a superb view of the surrounding country, and could see the position of Debono's camp, about twenty-five miles to the west by north, at the foot of the Faloro hills.

By Casella's thermometer, I determined the altitude of Shooa to be 3,877 feet – 1,002 feet above the Asua River, and 89 feet lower than Farajoke. These observations of the thermometer agreed with the natural appearance of the country, the Asua River forming the main drain in a deep valley, into which innumerable rivulets convey the drainage from both north and south. Accordingly, the Asua, receiving the Atabbi River, which is the main drain of the western face of the Madi mountains, and the entire drainage of the Madi and Shooa countries, together with that of extensive countries to the east of Shooa, including the rivers Chombi and Udat, from Lira and Umiro, it becomes a tremendous torrent so long as the rains continue, and conveys a grand volume of water to the Nile; but the inclination of all these countries tending rapidly to the northwest, the bed of the Asua River partakes of the general incline, and so quickly empties after the cessation of the rains that it becomes nil as a river. By the mean of several observations I determined the latitude of Shooa 3 degrees 04 minutes, longitude 32 degrees 04 minutes E.

We were now about twelve miles south of Debono's outpost, Faloro. The whole of the Shooa country was assumed to belong to Mahommed Wat-el-Mek, the *vakeel* of Debono, and we had passed the ashes of several villages that had been burnt and plundered by these people between Farajoke and this point; the entire country had been laid waste.

There was no great chief at Shooa; each village had a separate headman; formerly the population had occupied the lower ground, but since the Turks had been established at Faloro and had plundered the neighbouring tribes, the natives had forsaken their villages and had located themselves among the mountains for security. It was the intention of Ibrahim to break through the rules accepted by the White Nile traders, and to establish himself at Shooa, which, although claimed by Debono's people, would form an excellent point d'appui for operations towards the unknown south.

Shooa was "flowing with milk and honey;" fowls, butter, goats, were in abundance and ridiculously cheap; beads were of great value, as few had ever reached that country. The women flocked to see Mrs. Baker, bringing presents of milk and flour, and receiving beads and bracelets in return. The people were precisely the same as those of Obbo and Farajoke in language and appearance, exceedingly mild in their manner, and anxious to be on good terms.

The cultivation in this country was superior to anything that I had seen farther north; large quantities of sesame were grown and carefully harvested, the crop being gathered and arranged in oblong frames about twenty feet long by twelve high. These were inclined at an angle of about sixty – the pods of the sesame plants on one face, so that the frames resembled enormous brushes. In this manner the crop was dried previous to being stored in the granaries. Of the latter there were two kinds – the wicker-work smeared with cow dung, supported on four posts, with a thatched roof; and a simple contrivance by fixing a stout pole about twenty feet long perpendicularly in the earth. About four feet from the ground a bundle of strong and long reeds are tied tightly round the pole; hoops of wicker-work are then bound round them at intervals until they assume the form of an inverted umbrella half expanded; this being filled with grain, fresh reeds are added, until the work has extended to within a few feet of the top of the pole; the whole is then capped with reeds securely strapped: the entire granary has the appearance of a cigar, but thicker in proportion about the middle.

Two days after our arrival at Shooa, the whole of our Obbo porters absconded: they had heard that we were bound for Kamrasi's country, and having received exaggerated accounts of his power from the Shooa people, they had determined upon retreat: thus we were at once unable to proceed, unless we could procure porters from Shooa. This was exceedingly difficult, as Kamrasi was well known here, and was not loved. His country was known as Quanda, and I at once recognised the corruption of Speke's Uganda. The slave woman, Bacheeta, who had formerly given me in Obbo so much information concerning Kamrasi's country, was to be our interpreter; but we also had the luck to discover a lad who had formerly been employed by Mahommed in Faloro, who also spoke the language of Quanda, and had learnt a little Arabic. I now discovered that the slave woman Bacheeta had formerly been in the service of a chief named Sali, who had been killed by Kamrasi. Sali was a friend of Rionga (Kamrasi's greatest enemy), and I had been warned by Speke not to set foot upon Rionga's territory, or all travelling in Unyoro would be cut off. I plainly saw that Bacheeta was in favour of Rionga, as a friend of the murdered Sali, by whom she had had two children, and that she would most likely tamper with the guide, and that we should be led to Rionga instead of to Kamrasi. There were "wheels within wheels." It was now reported that in the past year, immediately after the departure of Speke and Grant from Gondokoro, when Debono's people had left me in the manner already described, they had marched direct to Rionga, allied themselves to him, crossed the Nile with his people, and had attacked Kamrasi's country, killing about three hundred of his men, and capturing many slaves. I now understood why they had deceived me at Gondokoro; they had obtained information of the country from Speke's people, and had made use of it by immediately attacking Kamrasi in conjunction with Rionga.

This would be a pleasant introduction for me on entering Unyoro, as almost immediately after the departure of Speke and Grant, Kamrasi had been invaded by the very people into whose hands his messengers had delivered them, when they were guided from Unyoro to the Turks' station at Faloro; he would naturally have considered that the Turks had been sent by Speke to attack him; thus the road appeared closed to all exploration, through the atrocities of Debono's people.

Many of Ibrahim's men, at hearing this intelligence, refused to proceed to Unyoro. Fortunately for me, Ibrahim had been extremely unlucky in procuring ivory; the year had almost passed away, and he had a mere nothing with which to return to Gondokoro. I impressed upon him how enraged Koorshid would be should he return with such a trifle; already his own men declared that he was neglecting *razzias*, because he was to receive a present from me if we reached Unyoro; this they would report to his master (Koorshid), and it would be believed should he fail in securing ivory. I guaranteed him 100 cantars (10,000 lbs.) if he would push on at all hazards with me to Kamrasi, and secure me porters from Shooa. Ibrahim behaved remarkably well. For some time past I had acquired a great influence over him, and he depended so thoroughly upon my opinion that he declared himself ready to do all that I suggested. Accordingly I desired him to call his men together, and to leave in Shooa all those who were disinclined to follow us.

At once I arranged for a start, lest some fresh idea should enter the ever-suspicious brains of our followers, and mar the expedition.

It was difficult to procure porters, and I abandoned all that was not indispensable – our last few pounds of rice and coffee, and even the great sponging-bath, that emblem of civilization that had been clung to even when the tent had been left behind.

On the 18th January, 1864, we left Shooa. The pure air of that country had invigorated us, and I was so improved in strength, that I enjoyed the excitement of the launch into unknown lands. The Turks knew nothing of the route south, and I accordingly took the lead of the entire party. I had come to a distinct understanding with Ibrahim that Kamrasi's country should belong to me; not an act of felony would be permitted; all were to be under my government, and I would insure him at least 100 cantars of tusks.

Eight miles of agreeable march through the usual parklike country brought us to the village of Fatiko, situated upon a splendid plateau of rock upon elevated ground with beautiful granite cliffs, bordering a level tableland of fine grass that would have formed a racecourse. The high rocks were covered with natives, perched upon the outline like a flock of ravens.

We halted to rest under some fine trees growing among large isolated blocks of granite and gneiss. In a short time the natives assembled around us: they were wonderfully friendly, and insisted upon a personal introduction to both myself and Mrs. Baker. We were thus compelled to hold a levee; not the passive and cold ceremony of Europe, but a most active undertaking, as each native that was introduced performed the salaam of his country, by seizing both my hands and raising my arms three times to their full stretch above my head. After about one hundred Fatikos had been thus gratified by our submission to this infliction, and our arms had been subjected to at least three hundred stretches each, I gave the order to saddle the oxen immediately, and we escaped a further proof of Fatiko affection that was already preparing, as masses of natives were streaming down the rocks hurrying to be introduced. Notwithstanding the fatigue of the ceremony, I took a great fancy to these poor people: they had prepared a quantity of *merissa* and a sheep for our lunch, which they begged us to remain and enjoy before we started; but the pumping action of half a village not yet gratified by a presentation was too much; and, mounting our oxen, with aching shoulders we bade adieu to Fatiko.

Descending the picturesque rocky hill of Fatiko, we entered upon a totally distinct country. We had now before us an interminable sea of prairies, covering to the horizon a series of gentle undulations inclining from east to west. There were no trees except the dolape palms; these were scattered at long intervals in the bright yellow surface of high grass. The path was narrow, but good, and after an hour's march we halted for the night on the banks of a deep and clear stream, the Un-y-ame; this stream is perennial, and receiving many rivulets from Shooa, it forms a considerable torrent during the rainy season, and joins the Nile in N. lat. 3 degrees 32 minutes at the limit reached by Signor Miani, 1859, the first traveller who ever attained a point so far south in Nile explorations from Egypt. There was no wood for fires, neither dung of animals; thus without fuel we went supperless to bed. Although the sun was painfully hot during the day, the nights were so cold (about 55 degrees F.) that we could hardly sleep.

For two days we marched through high dry grass, (about ten feet), when a clear night allowed an observation, and the meridian altitude of Capella gave latitude 2 degrees 45 minutes 37 seconds. In this interminable sea of prairie it was interesting to watch our progress south. On the following day our guide lost the road; a large herd of elephants had obscured it by trampling hundreds of paths in all directions. The wind was strong from the north, and I proposed to clear the country to the south by firing the prairies.

There were numerous deep swamps in the bottoms between the undulations, and upon arrival at one of these green dells we fired the grass on the opposite side. In a few minutes it roared before us, and we enjoyed the grand sight of the boundless prairies blazing like infernal regions, and rapidly clearing a path south. Flocks of buzzards and the beautiful varieties of flycatchers thronged to the dense smoke to prey upon the innumerable insects that endeavoured to escape from the approaching fire.

In about an hour we marched over the black and smoking ground, every now and then meeting dead stumps of palm trees blazing; until we at length reached another swamp. There the fire had terminated in its course south, being stopped by the high green reeds, and it was raging to the east and west. Again the tedious operation had to be performed, and the grass was fired in many places on the opposite side of the swamp, while we waited until the cleared way was sufficiently cool to allow the march. We were perfectly black, as the wind brought showers of ashes that fell like snow, but turned us into Ethiopians. I had led the way on foot from the hour we left Fatiko, as, the country being uninhabited for five days' march between that place and Kamrasi's, the men had more faith in my steering by the compass than they had in the native guide. I felt sure that we were being deceived, and that the woman Bacheeta had directed the guide to take us to Rionga's. Accordingly that night, when Canopus was in the meridian, I asked our conductor to point by a star the direction of Karuma Falls. He immediately pointed to Canopus, which I knew by Speke's map should be the direction of Rionga's islands, and I charged him with the deceit. He appeared very much astonished, and asked me why I wanted a guide if I knew the way, confessing that Karuma Falls were "a little to the east of the star." I thanked Speke and Grant at that moment, and upon many other occasions, for the map they had so generously given me! It has been my greatest satisfaction to have completed their great discovery, and to bear testimony to the correctness of their map and general observations.

The march was exceedingly fatiguing: there was a swamp at least every half hour during the day, at each of which we had the greatest difficulty in driving the oxen, who were above the girths in mud. One swamp was so deep that we had to carry the luggage piecemeal on an *angarep* by about twelve men, and my wife being subjected to the same operation was too heavy, and the people returned with her as impracticable. I accordingly volunteered for service, and carried her on my back; but when in the middle of the swamp, the tenacious bottom gave way, and I sank, and remained immoveably fixed, while she floundered froglike in the muddy water. I was extricated by the united efforts of several men, and she was landed by being dragged through the swamp. We marched for upwards of ten hours per day, so great were the delays in crossing the morasses and in clearing off the grass jungle by burning.

On the fourth day we left the prairies, and entered a noble forest; this was also so choked with high grass that it was impossible to proceed without burning the country in advance. There had been no semblance of a path for some time; and the only signs of game that we had seen were the tracks of elephants and a large herd of buffaloes, the fire having scared all wild animals from the neighbourhood. An attack of fever seized me suddenly, and I was obliged to lie down for four or five hours under a tree until the fit had passed away, when, weak and good for nothing, I again mounted my ox and rode on. On the 22d January, from an elevated position in the forest at sunrise, we saw a cloud of fog hanging in a distant valley, which betokened the presence of the Somerset River. The guide assured us that we should reach the river that day. I extract the note from my journal on that occasion:

"Marched, 6h. 20m., reaching the Somerset River, or Victoria White Nile. I never made so tedious a journey, owing to the delays of grass, streams, and deep swamps, but since we gained the forest these obstacles were not so numerous. Many tracks of elephants, rhinoceros, and buffaloes; but we saw nothing. Halted about eighty feet above the river; altitude above sea level, by observation, 3,864 ft. I went to the river to see if the other side was inhabited; saw two villages on an island; the natives came across in a canoe, bringing the brother of Rionga with them; the guide, as I had feared during the journey, has deceived us, and taken us direct to Rionga's country. On the north side the river all is uninhabited forest, full of buffalo and elephant pitfalls, into which three of our cattle have already fallen, including my beautiful riding ox, which is thus so sprained as to be rendered useless. The natives at first supposed we were Mahommed Wat-el-Mek's people, but finding their mistake they would give no information, merely saying that the lake was not far from here. They said 'they were friends of Mahommed's people who attacked Kamrasi, and Rionga being his enemy became their ally.' I must now be very careful, lest the news should reach Kamrasi that I am in Rionga's country, which would cut off all chance of travelling in Unyoro. The slave woman, Bacheeta, secretly instructed the guide to lead us to Rionga instead of to Kamrasi, precisely as I had suspected. The Karuma Falls are a day's march east of this, at which point we must cross the river. Obtained a clear observation of Capella, meridian altitude showing latitude 2 degrees 18 minutes N."

We could get no supplies from Rionga's people, who returned to their island after their conference with Bacheeta, promising to send us some plantains and a basket of flour; but upon gaining their secure retreat they shouted, that we might go to Kamrasi if we liked, but that we should receive no assistance from them. Early in the morning we started for Karuma. This part of the forest was perfectly open, as the grass had been burnt by the natives about three weeks ago, and the young shoots of the vines were appearing from the scorched roots; among other plants was an abundance of the prickly asparagus, of which I collected a basketful. Nothing could exceed the beauty of the march. Our course through the noble forest was parallel with the river, that roared beneath us on our right in a succession of rapids and falls between high cliffs covered with groves of bananas and varieties of palms, including the graceful wild date – the certain sign of either marsh or river. The Victoria Nile or Somerset River was about 150 yards wide; the cliffs on the south side were higher than those upon the north, being about 150 feet above the river. These heights were thronged with natives, who had collected from the numerous villages that ornamented the cliffs situated among groves of plantains; they were armed with spears and shields; the population ran parallel to our line of march, shouting and gesticulating as though daring us to cross the river.

After a most enjoyable march through the exciting scene of the glorious river crashing over innumerable falls – and in many places ornamented with rocky islands, upon which were villages and plantain groves – we at length approached the Karuma Falls, close to the village of Atada above the ferry. The heights were crowded with natives, and a canoe was sent across to within parleying distance of our side, as the roar of the rapids prevented our voices from being heard except at a short distance. Bacheeta now explained, that Speke's brother had arrived from his country to pay Kamrasi a visit, and had brought him valuable presents.

"Why has he brought so many men with him?" inquired the people from the canoe.

"There are so many presents for the *M'Kamma* (King) that he has many men to carry them," shouted Bacheeta.

"Let us look at him!" cried the headman in the boat – having prepared for the introduction by changing my clothes in a grove of plantains for my dressing room, and altering my costume to a tweed suit, something similar to that worn by Speke, I climbed up a high and almost perpendicular rock that formed a natural pinnacle on the face of the cliff, and, waving my cap to the crowd on the opposite side, I looked almost as imposing as Nelson in Trafalgar Square.

I instructed Bacheeta, who climbed up the giddy height after me, to shout to the people that an English lady, my wife, had also arrived, and that we wished immediately to be presented to the king and his family, as we had come to thank him for his kind treatment of Speke and Grant, who had arrived safe in their own county. Upon this being explained and repeated several times, the canoe approached the shore.

I ordered all our people to retire, and to conceal themselves among the plantains, that the natives might not be startled by so imposing a force, while Mrs. Baker and I advanced alone to meet Kamrasi's people, who were men of some importance. Upon landing through the high reeds, they immediately recognized the similarity of my beard and general complexion to that of Speke; and their welcome was at once displayed by the most extravagant dancing and gesticulating with lances and shields, as though intending to attack, rushing at me with the points of their lances thrust close to my face, and shouting and singing in great excitement.

I made each of them a present of a bead necklace, and explained to them my wish that there should be no delay in my presentation to Kamrasi, as Speke had complained that he bad been kept waiting fifteen days before the king had condescended to see him; that, if this occurred, no Englishman would ever visit him, as such a reception would be considered an insult. The headman replied that he felt sure I was not an impostor; but that very shortly after the departure of Speke and Grant in the previous year, a number of people had arrived in their name, introducing themselves as their greatest friends: they had been ferried across the river, and well received by Kamrasi's orders, and had been presented with ivory, slaves, and leopard skins, as tokens of friendship; but they had departed, and suddenly returned with Rionga's people, and had attacked the village in which they had been so well received; and upon the country being assembled to resist them, about three hundred of Kamrasi's men had been killed in the fight. The king had therefore given orders that, upon pain of death, no stranger should cross the river. He continued: that when they saw our people marching along the bank of the river, they imagined them to be the same party that had attacked them formerly, and they were prepared to resist them, and had sent on a messenger to Kamrasi, who was three days' march from Karuma, at his capital M'Rooli; until they received a reply, it would be impossible to allow us to enter the country. He promised to despatch another messenger immediately to inform the king who we were, but that we must certainly wait until his return. I explained that we had nothing to eat, and that it would be very inconvenient to remain in such a spot; that I considered the suspicion displayed was exceedingly unfair, as they must see that my wife and I were white people like Speke and Grant, whereas those who had deceived them were of a totally different race, all being either black or brown.

I told him that it did not much matter; that I had very beautiful presents intended for Kamrasi; but that another great king would be only too glad to accept them, without throwing obstacles in my way. I should accordingly return with my presents.

At the same time I ordered a handsome Persian carpet, about fifteen feet square, to be displayed as one of the presents intended for the king. The gorgeous colours, as the carpet was unfolded, produced a general exclamation before the effect of astonishment wore off, I had a basket unpacked, and displayed upon a cloth a heap of superb necklaces, that we had prepared while at Obbo, of the choicest beads, many as large as marbles, and glittering with every colour of the rainbow. The garden of jewels of Aladdin's wonderful lamp could not have produced more enticing fruit. Beads were extremely rare in Kamrasi's land; the few that existed had arrived from Zanzibar, and all that I exhibited were entirely new varieties. I explained that I had many other presents, but that it was not necessary to unpack them, as we were about to return with them to visit another king, who lived some days' journey distant. "Don't go; don't go away," said the headman and his companions. "Kamrasi will..."

Here an unmistakeable pantomimic action explained their meaning better than words; throwing their heads well back, they sawed across their throats with their forefingers, making horrible grimaces, indicative of the cutting of throats. I could not resist laughing at the terror that my threat of returning with the presents had created, they explained, that Kamrasi would not only kill them, but would destroy the entire village of Atada should we return without visiting him, but that he would perhaps punish them in precisely the same manner should they ferry us across without special orders. "Please yourselves," I replied; "if my party is not ferried across by the time the sum reaches that spot on the heavens (pointing to the position it would occupy at about 3 p.m.), I shall return." In a state of great excitement they promised to hold a conference on the other side, and to see what arrangements could be made. They returned to Atada, leaving the whole party, including Ibrahim, exceedingly disconcerted – having nothing to eat, an impassable river before them, and five days' march of uninhabited wilderness in their rear.

Karuma Falls were about three hundred yards to our left as we faced Atada; they were very insignificant, not exceeding five feet in height, but curiously regular, as a ridge of rock over which they fell extended like a wall across the river. The falls were exactly at the bend of the river, which, from that point, turned suddenly to the west. The whole day passed in shouting and gesticulating our peaceful intentions to the crowd assembled on the heights on the opposite side of the river, but the boat did not return until long after the time appointed; even then the natives would only approach sufficiently near to be heard, but nothing would induce them to land.

They explained, that there was a division of opinion among the people on the other side; some were in favour of receiving us, but the greater number were of opinion that we intended hostilities; therefore we must wait until orders could be sent from the king.

To assure the people of our peaceful intentions, I begged them to take Mrs. Baker and myself aalone, and to leave the armed party on this side of the river until a reply should be received from Kamrasi. At this suggestion the boat immediately returned to the other side.

The day passed away, and as the sun set we perceived the canoe again paddling across the river; this time it approached direct, and the same people landed that had received the necklaces in the morning. They said that they had held a conference with the headman, and that they had agreed to receive my wife and myself, but no other person. I replied, that my servants must accompany us, as we were quite as great personages as Kamrasi, and could not possibly travel without attendants. To this they demurred; therefore I dropped the subject, and proposed to load the canoe with all the presents intended for Kamrasi. There was no objection to this, and I ordered Richarn, Saat, and Ibrahim to get into the canoe to stow away the luggage as it should be handed to them, but on no account to leave the boat. I had already prepared everything in readiness; and a bundle of rifles tied up in a large blanket, and 500 rounds of ball cartridge, were unconsciously received on board as presents. I had instructed Ibrahim to accompany us as my servant, as he was better than most of the men in the event of a row; and I had given orders, that in case of a preconcerted signal being given, the whole force should swim the river, supporting themselves and guns upon bundles of papyrus rush.

The men thought us perfectly mad, and declared that we should be murdered immediately when on the other side; however, they prepared for crossing the river in case of treachery.

At the last moment, when the boat was about to leave the shore, two of the best men jumped in with their guns; however, the natives positively refused to start; therefore, to avoid suspicion, I ordered them to retire, but I left word that on the morrow I would send the canoe across with supplies, and that one or two men should endeavour to accompany the boat to our side on every trip.

It was quite dark when we started. The canoe was formed of a large hollow tree, capable of holding twenty people, and the natives paddled us across the rapid current just below the falls. A large fire was blazing upon the opposite shore, on a level with the river, to guide us to the landing place. Gliding through a narrow passage in the reeds, we touched the shore and landed upon a slippery rock, close to the fire, amidst a crowd of people, who immediately struck up a deafening welcome with horns and flageolets, and marched us up the steep face of the rocky cliff through a dark grove of bananas. Torches led the way, followed by a long file of spearmen; then came the noisy band and ourselves – I towing my wife up the precipitous path, while my few attendants followed behind with a number of natives who had volunteered to carry the luggage.

On arrival at the top of the cliff, we were about 180 feet above the river, and after a walk of about a quarter of a mile, we were triumphantly led into the heart of the village, and halted in a small courtyard in front of the headman's residence.

Keedja waited to receive us by a blazing fire. Not having had anything to eat, we were uncommonly hungry, and to our great delight a basketful of ripe plantains was presented to us; these were the first that I had seen for many years. A gourd bottle of plantain wine was offered, and immediately emptied; it resembled extremely poor cider. We were now surrounded by a mass of natives, no longer the naked savages to whom we had been accustomed, but well-dressed men, wearing robes of bark cloth, arranged in various fashions, generally like the Arab *tope* or the Roman toga. Several of the headmen now explained to us the atrocious treachery of Debono's men, who had been welcomed as friends of Speke and Grant, but who had repaid the hospitality by plundering and massacreing their hosts. I assured them that no one would be more wroth than Speke when I should make him aware of the manner in which his name had been used, and that I should make a point of reporting the circumstance to the British government. At the same time I advised them not to trust any but white people, should others arrive in my name, or in those of Speke and Grant. I upheld their character as that of Englishmen, and I begged them to state "if ever they had deceived them?" They replied that "there could not be better men." I answered, "You must trust me, as I trust entirely in you, and have placed myself in your hands; but if you have ever had cause to mistrust a white man, kill me at once! Either kill me, or trust in me; but let there be no suspicions."

They seemed much pleased with the conversation, and a man stepped forward and showed me a small string of blue beads that Speke had given him for ferrying him across the river. This little souvenir of my old friend was most interesting; after a year's wandering and many difficulties, this was the first time that I had actually come upon his track. Many people told me that they had known Speke and Grant; the former bore the name of "Mollegge ("the bearded one"), while Grant had been named Masanga ("the elephant's tusk"), owing to his height. The latter had been wounded at Lucknow during the Indian mutiny, and I spoke to the people of the loss of his finger; this crowned my success, as they knew without doubt that I had seen him. It was late, therefore I begged the crowd to depart, but to send a messenger the first thing in the morning to inform Kamrasi who we were, and to beg him to permit us to visit him without loss of time.

A bundle of straw was laid on the ground for Mrs. Baker and myself, and, in lieu of other beds, the ground was our resting place. It was bitterly cold that night, as the guns were packed up in the large blanket, and, not wishing to expose them, we were contented with a Scotch plaid each. Ibrahim, Saat, and Richarn watched by turns. On the following morning an immense crowd of native thronged to see us. There was a very beautiful tree about a hundred yards from the village, capable of shading upwards of a thousand men, and I proposed that we should sit beneath this protection and hold a conference. The headman of the village gave us a large hut with a grand doorway of about seven feet high, of which my wife took possession, while I joined the crowd at the tree. There were about six hundred men seated respectfully on the ground around me, while I sat with my back to the huge knotty trunk, with Ibrahim and Richarn at a few paces distant.

The subject of conversation was merely a repetition that of the preceding night, with the simple addition some questions respecting the lake. Not a man would give the slightest information; the only reply, upon my forcing the question, was the pantomime already described, by passing the forefinger across the throat, and exclaiming "Kamrasi!" The entire population was tongue-locked.

I tried the children; to no purpose, they were all dumb. White-headed old men I questioned as to the distance of the lake from this point: they replied, "We are children, ask the old people who know the country." Never was freemasonry more secret than the land of Unyoro. It was useless to persevere. I therefore changed the subject by saying that our people were starving on the other side, and that provisions must be sent immediately. In all savage countries the most trifling demand requires much talking. They said that provisions were scarce, and that until Kamrasi should give the order, they could give no supplies. Understanding most thoroughly the natural instincts of the natives, I told them that I must send the canoe across to fetch three oxen that I wished to slaughter. The bait took at once, and several men ran for the canoe, and we sent one of our black women across with a message to the people that three men, with their guns and ammunition, were to accompany the canoe and guide three oxen across by swimming them with ropes tied to their horns. These were the riding oxen of some of the men that it was necessary to slaughter, to exchange the flesh for flour and other supplies.

Hardly had the few boatmen departed, than some one shouted suddenly, and the entire crowd sprang to their feet and rushed towards the hut where I had left Mrs. Baker. For the moment I thought that the hut was on fire, and I joined the crowd and arrived at the doorway, where I found a tremendous press to see some extraordinary sight. Everyone was squeezing for the best place; and, driving them on one side, I found the wonder that had excited their curiosity. The hut being very dark, my wife had employed her solitude during my conference with the natives in dressing her hair at the doorway, which, being very long and blonde, was suddenly noticed by some natives – a shout was given, the rush described had taken place, and the hut was literally mobbed by the crowd of savages eager to see the extraordinary novelty. The gorilla would not make a greater stir in London streets than we appeared to create at Atada.

The oxen shortly arrived; one was immediately killed, and the flesh divided into numerous small portions arranged upon the hide.

Blonde hair and white people immediately lost their attractions, and the crowd turned their attention to beef – we gave them to understand that we required flour, beans, and sweet potatoes in exchange.

The market soon went briskly, and whole rows of girls and women arrived, bringing baskets filled with the desired provisions. The women were neatly dressed in short petticoats with a double skirt – many exposed the bosom, while others wore a piece of bark cloth arranged as a plaid across the chest and shoulders. This cloth is the produce of a species of fig tree, the bark of which is stripped off in large pieces and then soaked in water and beaten with a mallet: in appearance it much resembles corduroy, and is the colour of tanned leather; the finer qualities are peculiarly soft to the touch, as though of woven cotton. Every garden is full of this species of tree, as their cultivation is necessary for the supply of clothing; when a man takes a wife he plants a certain number of trees, that are to be the tailors of the expected family.

The market being closed, the canoe was laden with provisions, and sent across to our hungry people on the other side the river.

The difference between the Unyoro people and the tribes we had hitherto seen was most striking. On the north side of the river the natives were either stark naked, or wore a mere apology for clothing in the shape of a skin slung across their shoulders: the river appeared to be the limit of utter savagedom, and the people of Unyoro considered the indecency of nakedness precisely in the same light as among Europeans.

The northern district of Unyoro at Karuma is called Chopi, the language being the same as the Madi, and different to the southern and central portions of the kingdom. The people are distinct in their type, but they have the woolly hair of negroes, like all other tribes of the White Nile.

By astronomical observation I determined the latitude of Atada at Karuma Falls, 2 degrees 15 minutes; and by Casella's thermometer, the altitude of the river level above the sea 3,996 feet.

After the disgusting naked tribes that we had been travelling amongst for more than twelve months, it was a delightful change to find ourselves in comparative civilization: this was evinced not only in the decency of clothing, but also in the manufactures of the country. The blacksmiths were exceedingly clever, and used iron hammers instead of stone; they drew fine wire from the thick copper and brass wire that they received from Zanzibar; their bellows were the same as those used by the more savage tribes – but the greatest proof of their superior civilization was exhibited in their pottery.

Nearly all savages have some idea of earthenware; but the scale of advancement of a country between savagedom and civilization may generally be determined by the example of its pottery. The Chinese, who were as civilized as they are at the present day at a period when the English were barbarians, were ever celebrated for the manufacture of porcelain, and the difference between savages and civilized countries is always thus exemplified; the savage makes earthenware, but the civilized make porcelain – thus the gradations from the rudest earthenware will mark the improvement in the scale of civilization. The prime utensil of the African savage is the gourd; the shell of which is the bowl presented to him by nature as the first idea from which he is to model. Nature, adapting herself to the requirements of animals and man, appears in these savage countries to yield abundantly much that savage man can want. Gourds with exceedingly strong shells not only grow wild, which if divided in halves afford bowls, but great and quaint varieties form natural bottles of all sizes, from the tiny phial to the demijohn containing five gallons. The most savage tribes content themselves with the productions of nature, confining their manufacture to a coarse and half-baked jar for carrying water; but the semi-savage, like those of Unyoro, affords an example of the first step towards manufacturing art, by the fact of copying from nature: the utter savage makes use of nature – the gourd is his utensil; and the more advanced natives of Unyoro adopt it as the model for their pottery. They make a fine quality of jet black earthenware, producing excellent tobacco-pipes most finely worked in imitation of the small egg-shaped gourd; of the same earthenware they make extremely pretty bowls, and also bottles copied from the varieties of the bottle gourds: thus, in this humble art, we see the first effort of the human mind in manufactures, in taking nature for a model; precisely as the beautiful Corinthian capital originated in a design from a basket of flowers.

A few extracts from my journal will describe the delay at Atada:

"Jan. 26th, 1864. – The huts are very large, about 20 feet in diameter, made entirely of reeds and straw, and very lofty, looking in the interior like huge inverted baskets, beehive shaped, very different to the dog-kennels of the more northern tribes. We received a message today that we were not to expect Kamrasi, as 'great men were never in a hurry to pay visits.' None of the principal chiefs have yet appeared. Kidgwiga is expected today; but people are flocking in from the country to see the white lady. It is very trying to the patience to wait here until it pleases these almighty niggers to permit our people to cross the river.

"Jan. 27th. – Time passing fruitlessly while every day is valuable. The rains will, I fear, commence before my work is completed; and the Asua River, if flooded, will cut off my return to Gondokoro. In this district there is a large population and extensive cultivation. There are many trees resembling the Vacoua of Mauritius, but the leaves are of a different texture, producing a species of flax. Every day there is a report that the headman, sent by Kamrasi, is on the road; but I see no signs of him.

"Jan. 28th. – Reports brought that Kamrasi has sent his headman with a large force, including some of Speke's deserters. They are to inspect me, and report whether I am really a white man and an Englishman. If so, I believe we are to proceed; if not, I suppose we are to be exterminated. Lest there should be any mistake I have taken all necessary precautions; but, having only eight men on this side the river, I shall be certain to lose my baggage in the event of a disturbance, as no one could transport it to the canoe.

"Jan. 29th. – Plantains, sweet potatoes, and eggs supplied in great quantities. The natives are much amused at our trying the eggs in water before purchase. Plantains, three for one small bead. The headman is expected today. A polite message arrived last night from Kamrasi inviting us to his capital, and apologizing for being unable to come in person. This morning the force, sent by Kamrasi, is reported to be within an hour's march of Atada. In midday the headman arrived with a great number of men, accompanied by three of Speke's deserters, one of whom has been created a chief by Kamrasi, and presented with two wives.

"I received them standing; and after thorough inspection I was pronounced to be 'Speke's own brother,' and all were satisfied. However, the business was not yet over: plenty of talk, and another delay of four days, was declared necessary until the king should reply to the satisfactory message about to be sent. Losing all patience, I stormed, declaring Kamrasi to be mere dust; while a white man was a king in comparison. I ordered all my luggage to be conveyed immediately to the canoe, and declared that I would return immediately to my own country; that I did not wish to see any one so utterly devoid of manners as Kamrasi, and that no other white man would ever visit his kingdom.

"The effect was magical! I rose hastily to depart. The chiefs implored, declaring that Kamrasi would kill them all if I retreated: to prevent which misfortune they secretly instructed the canoe to be removed. I was in a great rage; and about 400 natives, who were present, scattered in all quarters, thinking that there would be a serious quarrel. I told the chiefs that nothing should stop me, and that I would seize the canoe by force unless my whole party should be brought over from the opposite side that instant. This was agreed upon. One of Ibrahim's men exchanged and drank blood from the arm of Speke's deserter, who was Kamrasi's representative; and peace thus firmly established, several canoes were at once employed, and sixty of our men were brought across the river before sunset. The natives had nevertheless taken the precaution to send all their women away from the village.

"Jan. 30th. – This morning all remaining men and baggage were brought across the river, and supplies were brought in large quantities for sale. We are to march tomorrow direct to Kamrasi's capital; they say he will give me a guide to the lake.

"The natives of this country are particularly neat in all they do; they never bring anything to sell unless carefully packed in the neatest parcels, generally formed of the bark of the plantain, and sometimes of the inner portions of reeds stripped into snow-white stalks, which are bound round the parcels with the utmost care. Should the plantain cider, 'maroua,' be brought in a jar, the mouth is neatly covered with a fringe-like mat of these clean white rushes split into shreds. Not even tobacco is brought for sale unless most carefully packed. During a journey, a pretty, bottle-shaped, long-necked gourd is carried with a store of plantain cider: the mouth of the bottle is stopped with a bundle of the white rush shreds, through which a reed is inserted that reaches to the bottom: thus the drink can be sucked up during the march without the necessity of halting; nor is it possible to spill it by the movement of walking.

"The natives prepare the skins of goats very beautifully, making them as soft as chamois leather; these they cut into squares, and sew together as neatly as would be effected by a European tailor, converting them into mantles which are prized far more highly than bark cloth, on account of their durability: they manufacture their own needles, not by boring the eye, but by sharpening the end into a fine point and turning it over, the extremity being hammered into a small cut in the body of the needle to prevent it from catching.

"Clothes of all kinds are in great demand here, and would be accepted to any amount in exchange for ivory. Beads are extremely valuable, and would purchase ivory in large quantities, but the country would, in a few years, become overstocked. Clothes being perishable articles would always be in demand to supply those worn out; but beads, being imperishable, very soon glut the market. Here is, as I had always anticipated, an opportunity for commencing legitimate trade.

"Jan. 31st. – Throngs of natives arrived to carry our luggage *gratis* by the king's orders. Started at 7 a.m. and marched ten miles and a half parallel with the Nile, south; the country thickly populated, and much cultivated with sesame, sweet potatoes, beans, tullaboon, dhurra, Indian corn, and plantains.

"The native porters relieved each other at every village, fresh men being always in readiness on the road. The river is here on a level with the country, having no high banks; thus there is a great fall from Karuma towards the west. Halted in a grove of plantains near a village. The plantains of this country are much higher than those of Ceylon, and the stems are black, rising to 25 or 30 feet. The chief of the district came to meet us, and insisted upon our remaining at his village today and tomorrow to 'eat and drink,' or Kamrasi would kill him; thus we are delayed when time is precious. The chief's name is 'Matta-Goomi.' There is now no secret about the lake. Both he and all the natives say that the Luta N'Zige Lake is larger than the Victoria N'Yanza, and that both lakes are fed by rivers from the great mountain Bartooma. Is that mountain the M'fumbiro of Speke (the difference of name being local)? According to the position of the mountain pointed out by the chief, it bears from this spot S. 45 degrees W. Latitude of this place by meridian altitude of Capella, 2 degrees 5 minutes 32 seconds.

"F. (my wife) taken seriously ill with bilious fever.

"Feb. 1st. – F. dreadfully ill; all the natives have turned out of their villages, leaving their huts and gardens at our disposal. This is the custom of the country should the king give orders that a visitor is to be conducted through his dominions.

"The natives of Unyoro have a very superior implement to the molote used among the northern tribes; it is an extremely powerful hoe, fitted upon a handle, similar to those used on the sugar estates in the West Indies, but the blade is heart-shaped: with these they cultivate the ground very deep for their beds of sweet potatoes. The temperature during the day ranges from 80 degrees to 84 degrees, and at night it is cold, 56 degrees to 58 degrees Fahr. It is very unhealthy, owing to the proximity of the river.

"Feb. 2d. – Marched five miles. F. carried in a litter, very ill. I fell ill likewise. Halted.

"Feb. 3d. – F. very ill. Carried her four miles and halted.

"Feb. 4th. – F. most seriously ill. Started at 7:30 a.m., she being carried in a litter; but I also fell ill upon the road, and having been held on my ox by two men for some time, I at length fell in their arms, and was laid under a tree for about five hours; getting better, I rode for two hours, course south. Mountains in view to south and southeast, about ten miles distant. The country, forest interspersed with villages: the Somerset generally parallel to the route. There are no tamarinds in this neighbourhood, nor any other acid fruit; thus one is sorely pressed in the hours of fever. One of the black women servants, Fadeela, is dying of fever.

"Feb. 5th. – F. (Mrs. Baker) so ill, that even the litter is too much for her. Heaven help us in this country! The altitude of the river level above the sea at this point is 4,056 feet.

"Feb. 6th. – F. slightly better. Started at 7 a.m. The country the same as usual. Halted at a village after a short march of three miles and a half. Here we are detained for a day while a message is sent to Kamrasi. Tomorrow, I believe, we are to arrive at the capital of

the tyrant. He sent me a message today, that the houses he had prepared for me had been destroyed by fire, and to beg me to wait until
he should have completed others. The truth is, he is afraid of our
large party, and he delays us in every manner possible, in order to
receive daily reports of our behaviour on the road. Latitude by
observation at this point, 1 degree 50 minutes 47 seconds N.

"Feb. 7th. – Detained here for a day. I never saw natives so
filthy in their dwellings as the people of Unyoro. Goats and fowls
share the but with the owner, which, being littered down with
straw, is a mere cattle-shed, redolent of man and beast. The natives
sleep upon a mass of straw, upon a raised platform, this at night
being covered with a dressed skin. Yesterday the natives brought
coffee in small quantities to sell. They have no idea of using it as a
drink, but simply chew it raw as a stimulant. It is a small and finely
shaped grain, with a good flavour. It is brought from the country of
Utumbi, about a degree south of this spot.

"Feb. 8th. – Marched eight miles due south. The river makes a
long bend to E.N.E., and this morning's march formed the chord of
the arc. Halted; again delayed for the day, as we are not far from the
capital, and a messenger must be sent to the king for instructions
before we proceed. I never saw such abject cowardice as the
redoubted Kamrasi exhibits. Debono's *vakeel* having made a *razzia*
upon his frontier has so cowed him, that he has now left his residence, and retreated to the other side of a river, from which point he
sends false messages to delay our advance as much as possible.
There is a total absence of dignity in his behaviour; no great man is
sent to parley, but the king receives contradictory reports from the
many-tongued natives that have utterly perplexed him. He is told
by some that we are the same people that came with Ras-Galla
(Debono's captain), and he has neither the courage to repel or to
receive us. Our force of 112 armed men could eat the country in the
event of a fight, provided that a large supply of ammunition were at
hand. The present store is sixty rounds for each man, which would
not be sufficient.

"Feb. 9th. – After endless discussions and repeated messages
exchanged with the king, he at length sent word that I was to come
alone. To this I objected; and, upon my starting with my men, the
guide refused to proceed. I at once turned back, and told the chief

(our guide) that I no longer wished to see Kamrasi, who must be a mere fool, and I should return to my country. This created a great stir, and messengers were at once despatched to the king, who returned an answer that I might bring all my men, but that only five of the Turks could be allowed with Ibrahim. The woman Bacheeta had told the natives that we were separate parties.

"A severe attack of fever prevented me from starting. This terrible complaint worries me sadly, as I have no quinine.

"Feb. 10th. – The woman Fadeela died of fever. I am rather better, and the chief is already here to escort us to Kamrasi. After a quick march of three hours through immense woods, we reached the capital – a large village of grass huts, situated on a barren slope. We were ferried across a river in large canoes, capable of carrying fifty men, but formed of a single tree upwards of four feet wide. Kamrasi was reported to be in his residence on the opposite side; but, upon our arrival at the south bank, we found ourselves thoroughly deceived. We were upon a miserable flat, level with the river, and in the wet season forming a marsh at the junction with the Kafoor River with the Somerset. The latter river bounded the flat on the east, very wide and sluggish, and much overgrown with papyrus and lotus. The river we had just crossed was the Kafoor; it was perfectly dead water, and about eighty yards wide, including the beds of papyrus on either side. We were shown some filthy huts that were to form our camp. The spot was swarming with mosquitoes, and we had nothing to eat except a few fowls that I had brought with me. Kamrasi was on the other side of the river: they had cunningly separated us from him, and had returned with the canoes. Thus we were prisoners upon the swamp. This was our welcome from the King of Unyoro! I now heard that Speke and Grant had been lodged in this same spot.

"Feb. 10th. – Ibrahim was extremely nervous, as were also my men; they declared that treachery was intended, as the boats had been withdrawn, and they proposed that we should swim the river and march back to our main party, who had been left three hours in the rear. I was ill with fever, also my wife, and the unwholesome air of the marsh aggravated the disease. Our luggage had been left at our last station, as this was a condition stipulated by Kamrasi: thus we had to sleep upon the damp ground of the marsh in the filthy hut, as the heavy dew at night necessitated shelter. With great difficulty I accompanied Ibrahim and a few men to the bank of the river where we had landed yesterday, and, climbing upon a white ant hill to obtain a view over the high reeds, I scanned the village with a telescope. The scene was rather exciting; crowds of people were rushing about in all directions, and gathering from all quarters towards the river: the slope from the river to the town M'Rooli was black with natives, and I saw about a dozen large canoes preparing to transport them to our side. I returned from my elevated observatory to Ibrahim, who, on the low ground only a few yards distant, could not see the opposite side of the river owing to the high grass and reeds. Without saying more, I merely begged him to mount upon the anthill and look towards M'Rooli. Hardly had he cast a glance at the scene described, than he jumped down from his stand, and cried, 'They are going to attack us!' 'Let us retreat to the camp and prepare for a fight!' 'Let us fire at them from here as they cross in the canoes,' cried others; 'the buckshot will clear them off when packed in the boats.' This my panic-stricken followers would have done, had I not been present.

"'Fools!' I said, 'do you not see that the natives have no shields with them, but merely lances? Would they commence an attack without their shields? Kamrasi is coming in state to visit us.' This idea was by no means accepted by my people, and we reached our little camp, and for the sake of precaution we stationed the men in positions behind a hedge of thorns. Ibrahim had managed to bring twelve picked men instead of five as stipulated; thus we were a party of twenty-four. I was of very little use, as the fever was so strong upon me that I lay helpless on the ground."

In a short time the canoes arrived, and for about an hour they were employed in crossing and recrossing, and landing great numbers of men, until they at length advanced and took possession of some huts about 200 yards from our camp. They now hallooed out that Kamrasi had arrived, and seeing some oxen with the party, I felt sure they had no evil intentions. I ordered my men to carry me in their arms to the king, and to accompany me with the presents, as I was determined to have a personal interview, although only fit for a hospital.

Upon my approach, the crowd gave way, and I was shortly laid on a mat at the king's feet. He was a fine-looking man, but with a peculiar expression of countenance, owing to his extremely prominent eyes; he was about six feet high, beautifully clean, and was dressed in a long robe of bark-cloth most gracefully folded. The nails of his hands and feet were carefully attended, and his complexion was about as dark a brown as that of an Abyssinian. He sat upon a copper stool placed upon a carpet of leopard skins, and he was surrounded by about ten of his principal chiefs.

Our interpreter, Bacheeta, now informed him who I was, and what were my intentions. He said that he was sorry I had been so long on the road, but that he had been obliged to be cautious, having been deceived by Debono's people. I replied, that I was an Englishman, a friend of Speke and Grant – that they had described the reception they had met with from him, and that I had come to thank him, and to offer him a few presents in return for his kindness, and to request him to give me a guide to the Lake Luta N'Zige. He laughed at the name and repeated it several times with his chiefs, – he then said, it was not Luta, but M'Wootan N'Zige – but that it was six months' journey from M'Rooli, and that in my weak condition I could not possibly reach it; that I should die upon the road, and that the king of my country would perhaps imagine that I had been murdered, and might invade his territory. I replied, that I was weak with the toil of years in the hot countries of Africa, but that I was in search of the great lake, and should not return until I had succeeded; that I had no king, but a powerful Queen who watched over all her subjects, and that no Englishman could be murdered with impunity; therefore he should send me to the lake without delay, and there would be the lesser chance of my dying in his country.

I explained that the river Nile flowed for a distance of two years' journey through wonderful countries, and reached the sea, from which many valuable articles would be sent to him in exchange for ivory, could I only discover the great lake. As a proof of this, I had brought him a few curiosities that I trusted he would accept, and I regretted that the impossibility of procuring porters had necessitated the abandonment of others that had been intended for him.

I ordered the men to unpack the Persian carpet, which was spread upon the ground before him. I then gave him an *Abbia* (large white Cashmere mantle), a red silk netted sash, a pair of scarlet Turkish shoes, several pairs of socks, a double-barrelled gun and ammunition, and a great heap of first-class beads made up into gorgeous necklaces and girdles. He took very little notice of the presents, but requested that the gun might be fired off. This was done, to the utter confusion of the crowd, who rushed away in such haste, that they tumbled over each other like so many rabbits; this delighted the king, who, although himself startled, now roared with laughter. He told me that I must be hungry and thirsty, therefore he hoped I would accept something to eat and drink: accordingly he presented me with seventeen cows, twenty pots of sour plantain cider and many loads of unripe plantains. I inquired whether Speke had left a medicine chest with him. He replied that it was a very feverish country, and that he and his people had used all the medicine. Thus my last hope of quinine was cut off. I had always trusted to obtain a supply from the king, as Speke had told me that he had left a bottle with him. It was quite impossible to obtain any information from him, and I was carried back to my hut, where I found Mrs. Baker lying down with fever, and neither could render assistance to the other.

On the following morning the king again appeared. I was better, and I had a long interview. He did not appear to heed my questions, but he at once requested that I would ally myself with him, and attack his enemy, Rionga. I told him that I could not embroil myself in such quarrels, but that I had only one object, which was the lake. I requested that he would give Ibrahim a large quantity of ivory, and that on his return from Gondokoro he would bring him most valuable articles in exchange. He said that he was not sure whether my belly was black or white – by this he intended to express "evil or good intentions" – but that if it were white I should of course have no objection to exchange blood with him, as a proof of friendship and sincerity. This was rather too strong a dose! I replied that it would be impossible, as in my country the shedding of blood was considered a proof of hostility; therefore he must accept Ibrahim as my substitute. Accordingly the arms were bared and pricked; as the blood flowed, it was licked by either party; and an alliance was concluded. Ibrahim agreed to act with him against all his enemies. It was arranged that Ibrahim now belonged to Kamrasi, and that henceforth our parties should be entirely separate.

"It rained in torrents, and our hut became so damp from the absorption of the marsh soil, that my feet sank in the muddy floor. I had fever daily at about 3 p.m. and lay perfectly helpless for five or six hours, until the attack passed off; this reduced me to extreme weakness. My wife suffered quite as acutely. It was a position of abject misery, which will be better explained by a few rough extracts from my journal:

"Feb. 16th. – All my porters have deserted, having heard that the lake is so far distant; I have not one man left to carry my luggage. Should we not be able to cross the Asua River before the flood, we shall be nailed for another year to this abominable country, ill with fever, and without medicine, clothes, or supplies.

"Feb. 17th. – Fever last night; rain, as usual, with mud accompaniment. One of Kamrasi's headmen, whose tongue I have loosened by presents, tells me that he has been to the lake in ten days to purchase salt, and that a man loaded with salt can return in fifteen days. God knows the truth! And I am pressed for time, while Kamrasi delays me in the most annoying manner.

"Kamrasi came today; as usual, he wanted all that I had, and insisted upon a present of my sword, watch, and compass, all of which I positively refused. I told him that he had deceived me by saying that the lake was so distant as six months' journey, as I knew that it was only ten days. He rudely answered, 'Go, if you like; but don't blame me if you can't get back: it is twenty days' march; you may believe it or not, as you choose.' To my question as to the means of procuring porters, he gave no reply, except by asking for my sword, and for my beautiful little Fletcher rifle.

"I retired to my hut in disgust. This afternoon a messenger arrived from the king with twenty-four small pieces of straw, cut into lengths of about four inches. These he laid carefully in a row, and explained that Speke had given that number of presents, whereas I had only given ten, the latter figure being carefully exemplified by ten pieces of straw; he wished to know 'why I did not give him the same number as he had received from Speke?' This miserable, grasping, lying coward is nevertheless a king, and the success of my expedition depends upon him.

"Feb. 20th. – Cloudy, as usual; neither sun, moon, nor stars will show themselves. Fortunately, milk can be procured here. I live upon buttermilk. Kamrasi came, and gave twenty elephants' tusks as a present to Ibrahim. There is a report that Debono's people, under the command of Ras-Galla, are once more at Rionga's; this has frightened him awfully.

"Feb. 21st. – This morning Kamrasi was civil enough to allow us to quit the marsh, the mosquito-nest and fever-bed where we had been in durance, and we crossed to the other side of the Kafoor River, and quartered in M'Rooli. I went to see him, and, after a long consultation, he promised to send me to the lake tomorrow. I immediately took off my sword and belt, and presented them to him, explaining that, as I was now convinced of his friendship, I had a pleasure in offering my sword as a proof of my amicable feeling, as I thus placed the weapon of self-defence in his hand, and I should trust to his protection. As a proof of the temper of the blade, I offered to cut through the strongest shield he could produce. This delighted him amazingly. I now trust to be able to reach the junction of the Somerset with the M'Wootan N'Zige at Magungo, and from thence to overtake Ibrahim at Shooa, and to hurry on to Gondokoro, where a boat will be waiting for me from Khartoum.

"Ibrahim and his men marched this morning, on their return to Karuma, leaving me here with my little party of thirteen men.

"Should I succeed in discovering the lake I shall thank God most sincerely. The toil, anxiety, the biting annoyances I have daily been obliged to put up with in my association with the Turks, added to our now constant ill-health, are enough to break down the constitution of an elephant. Every day I must give – to the Turks, give – to the natives, give! If I lend anything to the Turks, it is an insult should I ask for its return. One hasty word might have upset my boat; and now, for twelve months, I have had to talk, to explain, to manage, and to lead the brutes in this direction, like a coachman driving jibbing horses. Hosts of presents to Ibrahim, combined with a vivid description of the advantages that he would secure by opening a trade with Kamrasi, at length led him to this country, which I could not have reached without his aid, as it would have been impossible for me to have procured porters without cattle. The porters I have always received from him as far as Karuma for a payment of six copper rings per head for every journey. I have now arranged that he shall leave for me thirty head of cattle at Shooa; thus, should he have started for Gondokoro before my arrival at Shooa, I shall be able to procure porters, and arrive in time for the expected boat.

"Up to this day astronomical observations have been impossible, a thick coat of slate colour obscuring the heavens. Tonight I obtained a good observation of Canopus, giving latitude 1 degree 38 minutes N. By Casella's thermometer I made the altitude of the Somerset at M'Rooli 4,061 feet above the sea, showing a fall of 65 feet between this point and below the falls at Karuma in a distance of 37 miles of latitude.

"Just as Ibrahim was leaving this morning I was obliged to secure the slave Bacheeta as interpreter, at the price of three double-barrelled guns to purchase her freedom. I explained to her that she was now free, and that I wished her to act as interpreter during my stay in Unyoro; and that I would then leave her in her own country, Chopi, on my return from the lake. Far from being pleased at the change, she regretted the loss of the Turks, and became excessively sulky, although my wife decked her out with beads, and gave her a new petticoat to put her in a good humour.

"Feb. 22d. – Kamrasi promised to send me porters, and that we should start for the lake today, but there is no sign of preparation; thus am I delayed when every day is so precious. Added to this trouble, the woman that I have as an interpreter wall not speak, being the most sulky individual I ever encountered. In the evening Kamrasi sent to say he would give a guide and porters tomorrow morning. It is impossible to depend upon him."

After some delay we were at length honoured by a visit from Kamrasi, accompanied by a number of his people, and he promised that we should start on the following day. He pointed out a chief and a guide who were to have us in their charge, and who were to see that we obtained all that we should require. He concluded, as usual, by asking for my watch and for a number of beads; the latter I gave him, together with a quantity of ammunition for his guns. He showed me a beautiful double-barrelled rifle by Blissett, that Speke had given him. I wished to secure this, to give to Speke on my return to England, as he had told me, when at Gondokoro, how he had been obliged to part with that and many other articles sorely against his will. I therefore offered to give him three common double-barrelled guns in exchange for the rifle. This he declined, as he was quite aware of the difference in quality. He then produced a large silver chronometer that he had received from Speke. "It was dead," he said, "and he wished me to repair it." This I declared to be impossible. He then confessed to having explained its construction, and the cause of the ticking, to his people, by the aid of a needle, and that it had never ticked since that occasion. I regretted to see such "pearls cast before swine," as the rifle and chronometer in the hands of Kamrasi. Thus he had plundered Speke and Grant of all they possessed before he would allow them to proceed.

It is the rapacity of the chiefs of the various tribes that renders African exploration so difficult. Each tribe wishes to monopolize your entire stock of valuables, without which the traveller would be utterly helpless. The difficulty of procuring porters limits the amount of baggage thus a given supply must carry you through a certain period of time; if your supply should fail, the expedition terminates with your power of giving. It is thus extremely difficult to arrange the expenditure so as to satisfy all parties, and still to retain a sufficient balance. Being utterly cut off from all communication with the world, there is no possibility of receiving assistance. The traveller depends entirely upon himself, under Providence, and must. adapt himself and his means to circumstances.

Chapter XI

THE START FOR THE LAKE

The day of starting at length arrived; the chief and guide appeared, and we were led to the Kafoor River, where canoes were in readiness to transport us to the south side. This was to our old quarters on the marsh. The direct course to the lake was west, and I fully expected some deception, as it was impossible to trust Kamrasi. I complained to the guide, and insisted upon his pointing out the direction of the lake, which he did, in its real position, west; but he explained that we must follow the south bank of the Kafoor River for some days, as there was an impassable morass that precluded a direct course. This did not appear satisfactory, and the whole affair looked suspicious, as we had formerly been deceived by being led across the river in the same spot, and not allowed to return. We were now led along the banks of the Kafoor for about a mile, until we arrived at a cluster of huts; here we were to wait for Kamrasi, who had promised to take leave of us. The sun was overpowering, and we dismounted from our oxen, and took shelter in a blacksmith's shed. In about an hour Kamrasi arrived, attended by a considerable number of men, and took his seat in our shed. I felt convinced that his visit was simply intended to peel the last skin from the onion. I had already given him nearly all that I had, but he hoped to extract the whole before I should depart.

He almost immediately commenced the conversation by asking for a pretty yellow muslin Turkish handkerchief fringed with silver drops that Mrs. Baker wore upon her head: one of these had already been given to him, and I explained that this was the last remaining, and that she required it. He "must" have it...It was given.

He then demanded other handkerchiefs. We had literally nothing but a few most ragged towels; he would accept no excuse, and insisted upon a portmanteau being unpacked, that he might satisfy himself by actual inspection. The luggage, all ready for the journey, had to be unstrapped and examined, and the rags were displayed in succession; but so wretched and uninviting was the exhibition of the family linen, that he simply returned them, and said they did not suit him. Beads he must have, or I was his enemy. A selection of the best opal beads was immediately given him. I rose from the stone upon which I was sitting, and declared that we must start immediately. "Don't be in a hurry," he replied; "you have plenty of time; but you have not given me that watch you promised me." This was my only watch that he had begged for, and had been refused every day during my stay at M'Rooli. So pertinacious a beggar I had never seen. I explained to him that, without the watch, my, journey would be useless, but that I would give him all that I had except the watch when the exploration should be completed, as I should require nothing on my direct return to Gondokoro. At the same time, I repeated to him the arrangement for the journey that he had promised, begging him not to deceive me, as my wife and I should both die if we were compelled to remain another year in this country by losing the annual boats in Gondokoro. The understanding was this: he was to give me porters to the lake, where I was to be furnished with canoes to take me to Magungo, which was situated at the junction of the Somerset. From Magungo he told me that I should see the Nile issuing from the lake close to the spot where the Somerset entered, and that the canoes should take me down the river, and porters should carry my effects from the nearest point to Shooa, and deliver me at my old station without delay. Should he be faithful to this engagement, I trusted to procure porters from Shooa, and to reach Gondokoro in time for the annual boats. I had arranged that a boat should be sent from Khartoum to await me at Gondokoro early in this year, 1864; but I felt sure that should I be long delayed, the boat would return without me, as the people would be afraid to remain alone at Gondokoro after the other boats had quitted.

In our present weak state another year of Central Africa without quinine appeared to warrant death; it was a race against time, all was untrodden ground before us, and the distance quite uncertain. I trembled for my wife, and weighed the risk of another year in

this horrible country should we lose the boats. With the self-sacri-
ficing devotion that she had shown in every trial, she implored me
not to think of any risks on her account, but to push forward and
discover the lake – -that she had determined not to return until she
had herself reached the M'Wootan N'Zige.

I now requested Kamrasi to allow us to take leave, as we had
not an hour to lose. In the coolest manner he replied, "I will send
you to the lake and to Shooa, as I have promised; but, YOU MUST
LEAVE YOUR WIFE WITH ME!" At that moment we were surrounded by a great number of natives, and my suspicions of treachery at having been led across the Kafoor River appeared confirmed
by this insolent demand. If this were to be the end of the expedition
I resolved that it should also be the end of Kamrasi, and, drawing
my revolver quietly, I held it within two feet of his chest, and looking at him with undisguised contempt, I told him that if I touched
the trigger, not all his men could save him: and that if he dared to
repeat the insult I would shoot him on the spot. At the same time I
explained to him that in my country such insolence would entail
bloodshed, and that I looked upon him as an ignorant ox who knew
no better, and that this excuse alone could save him. My wife, naturally indignant, had risen from her seat, and, maddened with the
excitement of the moment, she made him a little speech in Arabic
(not a word of which he understood), with a countenance almost as
amiable as the head of Medusa. Altogether the *mise en scene*
utterly astonished him; the woman Bacheeta, although savage, had
appropriated the insult to her mistress, and she also fearlessly let fly
at Kamrasi, translating as nearly as she could the complimentary
address that Medusa had just delivered.

Whether this little *coup de theatre* had so impressed Kamrasi
with British female independence that he wished to be off his bar-
gain, I cannot say, but with an air of complete astonishment, he
said, "Don't be angry! I had no intention of offending you by asking
for your wife; I will give you a wife, if you want one, and I thought
you might have no objection to give me yours; it is my custom to
give my visitors pretty wives, and I thought you might exchange.
Don't make a fuss about it; if you don't like it, there's an end of it; I
will never mention it again." This very practical apology I received
very sternly, and merely insisted upon starting. He seemed rather

confused at having committed himself, and to make amends he called his people and ordered them to carry our loads.

His men ordered a number of women, who had assembled out of curiosity, to shoulder the luggage and carry it to the next village, where they would be relieved. I assisted my wife upon her ox, and with a very cold *adieu* to Kamrasi, I turned my back most gladly on M'Rooli.

The country was a vast flat of grassland interspersed with small villages and patches of sweet potatoes; these were very inferior, owing to the want of drainage. For about two miles we continued on the banks of the Kafoor River; the women who carried the luggage were straggling in disorder, and my few men were much scattered in their endeavours to collect them. We approached a considerable village; but just as we were nearing it, out rushed about six hundred men with lances and shields, screaming and yelling like so many demons. For the moment, I thought it was an attack, but almost immediately I noticed that women and children were mingled with the men.

My men had not taken so cool a view of the excited throng that was now approaching us at full speed, brandishing their spears, and engaging with each other in mock combat. "There's a fight! There's a fight!" my men exclaimed; "we are attacked! Fire at them, *Hawaga.*" However, in a few seconds I persuaded them that it was a mere parade, and that there was no danger. With a rush, like a cloud of locusts, the natives closed around us, dancing, gesticulating, and yelling before my ox, feigning to attack us with spears and shields, then engaging in sham fights with each other, and behaving like so many madmen. A very tall chief accompanied them; and one of their men was suddenly knocked down, and attacked by the crowd with sticks and lances, and lay on the ground covered with blood: what his offence had been I did not hear. The entire crowd were most grotesquely got up, being dressed in either leopard or white monkey skins, with cows' tails strapped on behind, and antelopes' horns fitted upon their heads, while their chins were ornamented with false beards, made of the bushy ends of cows' tails sewed together. Altogether, I never saw a more unearthly set of creatures; they were perfect illustrations of my childish ideas of devils – horns, tails, and all, excepting the hoofs; they were our escort, furnished by Kamrasi to accompany us to the lake. Fortunately for all parties the Turks were not with us on that occasion, or the satanic escort would certainly have been received with a volley when they so rashly advanced to compliment us by their absurd performances.

We marched till 7 p.m. over flat, uninteresting country, and then halted at a miserable village which the people had deserted, as they expected our arrival. The following morning I found much difficulty in getting our escort together, as they had been foraging throughout the neighbourhood; these "devil's own" were a portion of Kamrasi's troops, who considered themselves entitled to plunder *ad libitum* throughout the march; however, after some delay, they collected, and their tall chief approached me, and begged that a gun might be fired as a curiosity. The escort had crowded around us, and as the boy Saat was close to me, I ordered him to fire his gun. This was Saat's greatest delight, and bang went one barrel unexpectedly, close to the tall chief's ear. The effect was charming. The tall chief, thinking himself injured, clasped his head with both hands, and bolted through the crowd, which, struck with a sudden panic, rushed away in all directions, the "devil's own" tumbling over each other, and utterly scattered by the second barrel which Saat exultingly fired in derision as Kamrasi's warlike regiment dissolved before a sound. I felt quite sure, that in the event of a fight, one scream from "the Baby," with its charge of forty small bullets, would win the battle, if well delivered into a crowd of Kamrasi's troops.

That afternoon, after a march through a most beautiful forest of large mimosas in full blossom, we arrived at the morass that had necessitated this great detour from our direct course to the lake. It was nearly three-quarters of a mile broad, and so deep, that in many places the oxen were obliged to swim; both Mrs. Baker and I were carried across on our *angareps* by twelve men with the greatest difficulty; the guide, who waded before us to show the way, suddenly disappeared in a deep hole, and his bundle that he had carried on his head, being of light substance, was seen floating like a buoy upon the surface; after a thorough sousing, the guide reappeared, and scrambled out, and we made a circuit, the men toiling frequently up to their necks through mud and water. On arrival at the opposite side we continued through the same beautiful forest, and slept that night at a deserted village, M'Baze. I obtained two observations; one of Capella, giving lat. 1 degrees 24 minutes 47 seconds N., and of Canopus 1 degree 23 minutes 29 seconds.

The next day we were much annoyed by our native escort; instead of attending to us, they employed their time in capering and dancing about, screaming and gesticulating, and suddenly rushing off in advance whenever we approached a village, which they plundered before we could arrive. In this manner every place was stripped; nor could we procure anything to eat unless by purchasing it for beads from the native escort. We slept at Karche, lat. 1 degree 19 minutes 31 seconds N.

We were both ill, but were obliged to ride through the hottest hours of the sun, as our followers were never ready to start at an early hour in the morning. The native escort were perfectly independent, and so utterly wild and savage in their manner, that they appeared more dangerous than the general inhabitants of the country.

My wife was extremely anxious, since the occasion of Kamrasi's "proposal," as she was suspicious that so large an escort as three hundred men had been given for some treacherous purpose, and that I should perhaps be waylaid to enable them to steal her for the king. I had not the slightest fear of such an occurrence, as sentries were always on guard during the night, and I was well prepared during the day.

On the following morning we had the usual difficulty in collecting porters, those of the preceding day having absconded, and others were recruited from distant villages by the native escort, who enjoyed the excuse of hunting for porters, as it gave them an opportunity of foraging throughout the neighbourhood. During this time we had to wait until the sun was high; we thus lost the cool hours of morning, and it increased our fatigue. Having at length started, we arrived in the afternoon at the Kafoor River, at a bend from the south where it was necessary to cross over in our westerly course. The stream was in the centre of a marsh, and although deep, it was so covered with thickly matted water-grass and other aquatic plants, that a natural floating bridge was established by a carpet of weeds about two feet thick: upon this waving and unsteady surface the men ran quickly across, sinking merely to the ankles, although beneath the tough vegetation there was deep water. It was equally impossible to ride or to be carried over this treacherous surface; thus I led the way, and begged Mrs. Baker to follow me on foot as quickly as possible, precisely in my track. The river was about eighty yards wide, and I had scarcely completed a fourth of the distance and looked back to see if my wife followed close to me, when I was horrified to see her standing in one spot, and sinking gradually through the weeds, while her face was distorted and perfectly purple. Almost as soon as I perceived her, she fell, as though shot dead.

In an instant I was by her side; and with the assistance of eight or ten of my men, who were fortunately close to me, I dragged her like a corpse through the yielding vegetation, and up to our waists we scrambled across to the other side, just keeping her head above the water: to have carried her would have been impossible, as we should all have sunk together through the weeds. I laid her under a tree, and bathed her head and face with water, as for the moment I thought she had fainted; but she lay perfectly insensible, as though dead, with teeth and hands firmly clenched, and her eyes open, but fixed. It was a *coup de soleil* [sunstroke].

Many of the porters had gone on ahead with the baggage; and I started off a man in haste to recall an *angarep* upon which to carry her, and also for a bag with a change of clothes, as we had dragged her through the river. It was in vain that I rubbed her heart, and the black women rubbed her feet, to endeavour to restore animation. At length the litter came, and after changing her clothes, she was carried mournfully forward as a corpse. Constantly we had to halt and support her head, as a painful rattling in the throat betokened suffocation.

At length we reached a village, and halted for the night. I laid her carefully in a miserable hut, and watched beside her. I opened her clenched teeth with a small wooden wedge, and inserted a wet rag, upon which I dropped water to moisten her tongue, which was dry as fur. The unfeeling brutes that composed the native escort were yelling and dancing as though all were well; and I ordered their chief at once to return with them to Kamrasi, as I would travel with them no longer. At first they refused to return; until at length I vowed that I would fire into them should they accompany us on the following morning. Day broke and it was a relief to have got rid of the brutal escort. They had departed, and I had now my own men, and the guides supplied by Kamrasi.

There was nothing to eat in this spot. My wife had never stirred since she fell by the *coup de soleil*, and merely respired about five times in a minute. It was impossible to remain; the people would have starved. She was laid gently upon her litter, and we started forward on our funeral course. I was ill and broken-hearted, and I followed by her side through the long day's march over wild park-lands and streams, with thick forest and deep marshy bottoms; over undulating hills, and through valleys of tall papyrus rushes, which, as we brushed through them on our melancholy way, waved over the litter like the black plumes of a hearse. We halted at a village, and again the night was passed in watching. I was wet, and coated with mud from the swampy marsh, and shivered with ague; but the cold within was greater than all. No change had taken place; she had never moved. I had plenty of fat, and I made four balls of about half a pound, each of which would burn for three hours. A piece of a broken water-jar formed a lamp, several pieces of rag serving for wicks. So in solitude the still calm night passed away as I sat by her side and watched. In the drawn and distorted features that lay before me I could hardly trace the same face that for years had been my comfort through all the difficulties and dangers of my path. Was she to die? Was so terrible a sacrifice to be the result of my selfish exile?

Again the night passed away. Once more the march. Though weak and ill, and for two nights without a moment's sleep, I felt no fatigue, but mechanically followed by the side of the litter as though in a dream. The same wild country diversified with marsh and forest. Again we halted. The night came, and I sat by her side in a miserable hut, with the feeble lamp flickering while she lay as in death. She had never moved a muscle since she fell. My people slept. I was alone, and no sound broke the stillness of the night. The ears ached at the utter silence, till the sudden wild cry of a hyena made me shudder as the horrible thought rushed through my brain, that, should she be buried in this lonely spot, the hyena would disturb her rest.

The morning was not far distant; it was past four o'clock. I had passed the night in replacing wet cloths upon her head and moistening her lips, as she lay apparently lifeless on her litter. I could do nothing more; in solitude and abject misery in that dark hour, in a country of savage heathens, thousand of miles away from a Christian land, I beseeched an aid above all human, trusting alone to Him.

The morning broke; my lamp had just burnt out, and, cramped with the night's watching, I rose from my low seat, and seeing that she lay in the same unaltered state, I went to the door of the hut to breathe one gasp of the fresh morning air. I was watching the first red streak that heralded the rising sun, when I was startled by the words, "Thank God," faintly uttered behind me. Suddenly she had awoke from her torpor, and with a heart overflowing I went to her bedside. Her eyes were full of madness! She spoke; but the brain was gone!

I will not inflict a description of the terrible trial of seven days of brain fever, with its attendant horrors. The rain poured in torrents, and day after day we were forced to travel, for want of provisions, not being able to remain in one position. Every now and then we shot a few guinea fowl, but rarely; there was no game, although the country was most favourable. In the forests we procured wild honey, but the deserted villages contained no supplies, as we were on the frontier of Uganda, and M'tese's people had plundered the district. For seven nights I had not slept, and although as weak as a reed, I had marched by the side of her litter. Nature could resist no longer. We reached a village one evening; she had been in violent convulsions successively – it was all but over. I laid her down on her litter within a hut; covered her with a Scotch plaid; and I fell upon my mat insensible, worn out with sorrow and fatigue. My men put a new handle to the pickaxe that evening, and sought for a dry spot to dig her grave!

Chapter XII

RECOVERED

The sun had risen when I woke. I had slept, and, horrified as the idea flashed upon me that she must be dead, and that I had not been with her, I started up. She lay upon her bed, pale as marble, and with that calm serenity that the features assume when the cares of life no longer act upon the mind, and the body rests in death. The dreadful thought bowed me down; but as I gazed upon her in fear, her chest gently heaved, not with the convulsive throbs of fever, but naturally. She was asleep; and when at a sudden noise she opened her eyes, they were calm and clear. She was saved! When not a ray of hope remained, God alone knows what helped us. The gratitude of that moment I will not attempt to describe.

Fortunately there were many fowls in this village; we found several nests of fresh eggs in the straw which littered the hut; these were most acceptable after our hard fare, and produced a good supply of soup.

Having rested for two days, we again moved forward, Mrs. Baker being carried on a litter. We now continued on elevated ground, on the north side of a valley running from west to east, about sixteen miles broad, and exceedingly swampy. The rocks composing the ridge upon which we travelled due west were all gneiss and quartz, with occasional breaks, forming narrow valleys, all of which were swamps choked with immense papyrus rushes, that made the march very fatiguing. In one of these muddy bottoms one of my riding oxen that was ill, stuck fast, and we were obliged to abandon it, intending to send a number of natives to drag it out with ropes.

On arrival at a village, our guide started about fifty men for this purpose, while we continued our journey. That evening we reached a village belonging to a headman, and very superior to most that we had passed on the route from M'Rooli: large sugarcanes of the blue variety were growing in the fields, and I had seen coffee growing wild in the forest in the vicinity. I was sitting at the door of the hut about two hours after sunset, smoking a pipe of excellent tobacco, when I suddenly heard a great singing in chorus advancing rapidly from a distance towards the entrance of the courtyard. At first I imagined that the natives intended dancing, which was an infliction that I wished to avoid, as I was tired and feverish; but in a few minutes the boy Saat introduced a headman, who told me that the riding ox had died in the swamp where he had stuck fast in the morning, and that the natives had brought his body to me. "What!" I replied, "brought his body, the entire ox, to me?" "The entire ox as he died is delivered at your door," answered the headman; "I could not allow any of your property to be lost upon the road. Had the body of the ox not been delivered to you, we might have been suspected of having stolen it." I went to the entrance of the courtyard, and amidst a crowd of natives I found the entire ox exactly as he had died. They had carried him about eight miles on a litter, which they had constructed of two immensely long posts with cross-pieces of bamboo, upon which they had laid the body. They would not eat the flesh, and seemed quite disgusted at the idea, as they replied that it had died.

It is a curious distinction of the Unyoro people, that they are peculiarly clean feeders, and will not touch either the flesh of animals that have died, neither of those that are sick; nor will they eat the crocodile. They asked for no remuneration for bringing their heavy load so great a distance; and they departed in good humour as a matter of course.

Never were such contradictory people as these creatures; they had troubled us dreadfully during the journey, as they would suddenly exclaim against the weight of their loads, and throw them down, and bolt into the high grass; yet now they had of their own free will delivered to me a whole dead ox from a distance of eight miles, precisely as though it had been an object of the greatest value.

The name of this village was Parkani. For several days past our guides had told us that we were very near to the lake, and we were now assured that we should reach it on the morrow. I had noticed a lofty range of mountains at an immense distance west, and I had imagined that the lake lay on the other side of this chain; but I was now informed that those mountains formed the western frontier of the M'Wootan N'Zige, and that the lake was actually within a march of Parkani. I could not believe it possible that we were so near the object of our search. The guide Rabonga now appeared, and declared that if we started early on the following morning we should be able to wash in the lake by noon!

That night I hardly slept. For years I had striven to reach the sources of the Nile. In my nightly dreams during that arduous voyage I had always failed, but after so much hard work and perseverance the cup was at my very lips, and I was to drink at the mysterious fountain before another sun should set – at that great reservoir of Nature that ever since creation had baffled all discovery. I had hoped, and prayed, and striven through all kinds of difficulties, in sickness, starvation, and fatigue, to reach that hidden source; and when it had appeared impossible, we had both determined to die upon the road rather than return defeated. Was it possible that it was so near, and that tomorrow we could say, "the work is accomplished?"

March 14th. – The sun had not risen when I was spurring my ox after the guide, who, having been promised a double handful of beads on arrival at the lake, had caught the enthusiasm of the moment. The day broke beautifully clear, and having crossed a deep valley between the hills, we toiled up the opposite slope. I hurried to the summit. The glory of our prize burst suddenly upon me! There, like a sea of quicksilver, lay far beneath the grand expanse of water, – a boundless sea horizon on the south and southwest, glittering in the noonday sun; and on the west, at fifty or sixty miles' distance, blue mountains rose from the bosom of the lake to a height of about 7,000 feet above its level.

It is impossible to describe the triumph of that moment; here was the reward for all our labour – for the years of tenacity with which we had toiled through Africa. England had won the sources of the Nile! Long before I reached this spot, I had arranged to give three cheers with all our men in English style in honour of the discovery, but now that I looked down upon the great inland sea lying nestled in the very heart of Africa, and thought how vainly mankind had sought these sources throughout so many ages, and reflected that I had been the humble instrument permitted to unravel this portion of the great mystery when so many greater than I had failed, I felt too serious to vent my feelings in vain cheers for victory, and I sincerely thanked God for having guided and supported us through all dangers to the good end. I was about 1,500 feet above the lake, and I looked down from the steep granite cliff upon those welcome waters – upon that vast reservoir which nourished Egypt and brought fertility where all was wilderness – upon that great source so long hidden from mankind; that source of bounty and of blessings to millions of human beings; and as one of the greatest objects in nature, I determined to honour it with a great name. As an imperishable memorial of one loved and mourned by our gracious Queen and deplored by every Englishman, I called this great lake the Albert N'Yanza. The Victoria and the Albert Lakes are the two sources of the Nile.

The zigzag path to descend to the lake was so steep and dangerous that we were forced to leave our oxen with a guide, who was to take them to Magungo and wait for our arrival. We commenced the descent of the steep pass on foot. I led the way, grasping a stout bamboo. My wife in extreme weakness tottered down the pass, supporting herself upon my shoulder, and stopping to rest every twenty paces. After a toilsome descent of about two hours, weak with years of fever, but for the moment strengthened by success, we gained the level plain below the cliff. A walk of about a mile through flat sandy meadows of fine turf interspersed with trees and bush, brought us to the water's edge. The waves were rolling upon a white pebbly beach: I rushed into the lake, and thirsty with heat and fatigue, with a heart full of gratitude, I drank deeply from the sources of the Nile. Within a quarter of a mile of the lake was a fishing village named Vacovia, in which we now established ourselves. Everything smelt of fish – and everything looked like fishing; not the "gentle art" of England with rod and fly, but harpoons were leaning against the huts, and lines almost as thick as the little finger were hanging up to dry, to which were attached iron hooks of a size that said much for the monsters of the Albert Lake. On entering the hut I found a prodigious quantity of tackle; the lines were beautifully made of the fibre of the plantain stem, and were exceedingly elastic, and well adapted to withstand the first rush of a heavy fish; the hooks were very coarse, but well barbed, and varied in size from two to six inches. A number of harpoons and floats for hippopotami were arranged in good order, and the tout ensemble of the hut showed that the owner was a sportsman.

The harpoons for hippopotami were precisely the same pattern as those used by the Hamran Arabs on the Taka frontier of Abyssinia, having a narrow blade of three-quarters of an inch in width, with only one barb. The rope fitted to the harpoon was beautifully made of plantain fibre, and the float was a huge piece of ambatch-wood about fifteen inches in diameter. They speared the hippopotamus from canoes, and these large floats were necessary to be easily distinguished in the rough waters of the lake.

My men were perfectly astounded at the appearance of the lake. The journey had been so long, and hope deferred had so completely sickened their hearts, that they had long since disbelieved in the existence of the lake, and they were persuaded that I was leading them to the sea. They now looked at the lake with amazement – two of them had already seen the sea at Alexandria, and they unhesitatingly declared that this was the sea, but that it was not salt.

Vacovia was a miserable place, and the soil was so impregnated with salt, that no cultivation was possible. Salt was the natural product of the country; and the population were employed in its manufacture, which constituted the business of the lake shores – being exchanged for supplies from the interior. I went to examine the pits: these were about six feet deep, from which was dug a black sandy mud that was placed in large earthenware jars; these were supported upon frames, and mixed with water, which filtering rapidly through small holes in the bottom, was received in jars beneath: this water was again used with fresh mud until it became a strong brine, when it was boiled and evaporated. The salt was white, but very bitter. I imagine that it has been formed by the decay of aquatic plants that have been washed ashore by the waves; decomposing, they have formed a mud deposit, and much potash is combined with the salt. The flat sandy meadow that extends from the lake for about a mile to the foot of the precipitous cliffs of 1,500 feet, appears to have formed at one period the bottom of the lake –

in fact, the flat land of Vacovia looks like a bay, as the mountain cliffs about five miles south and north descend abruptly to the water, and the flat is the bottom of a horseshoe formed by the cliffs. Were the level of the lake fifteen feet higher, this flat would be flooded to the base of the hills.

I procured a couple of kids from the chief of the village for some blue beads, and having received an ox as a present from the headman of Parkani in return for a number of beads and bracelets, I gave my men a grand feast in honour of the discovery; I made them an address, explaining to them how much trouble we should have been saved had my whole party behaved well from the first commencement and trusted to my guidance, as we should have arrived here twelve mouths ago; at the same time I told them, that it was a greater honour to have achieved the task with so small a force as thirteen men, and that as the lake was thus happily reached, and Mrs. Baker was restored to health after so terrible a danger, I should forgive them past offences and wipe out all that had been noted against them in my journal. This delighted my people, who ejaculated "*El hamd el Illah* (thank God)!" and fell to immediately at their beef.

At sunrise on the following morning I took the compass, and accompanied by the chief of the village, my guide Rabonga, and the woman Bacheeta, I went to the borders of the lake to survey the country. It was beautifully clear, and with a powerful telescope I could distinguish two large waterfalls that cleft the sides of the mountains on the opposite shore. Although the outline of the mountains was distinct upon the bright blue sky, and the dark shades upon their sides denoted deep gorges, I could not distinguish other features than the two great falls, which looked like threads of silver on the dark face of the mountains. No base had been visible, even from an elevation of 1,500 feet above the water level, on my first view of the lake, but the chain of lofty mountains on the west appeared to rise suddenly from the water. This appearance must have been due to the great distance, the base being below the horizon, as dense columns of smoke were ascending apparently from the surface of the water: this must have been produced by the burning of prairies at the foot of the mountains. The chief assured me that large canoes had been known to cross over from the other side, but that it required four days and nights of hard rowing to accomplish the voyage, and that many boats had been lost in the attempt. The canoes of Unyoro were not adapted for so dangerous a journey, but the western shore of the lake was comprised in the great kingdom of Malegga, governed by King Kajoro, who possessed large canoes, and traded with Kamrasi from a point opposite to Magungo, where the lake was contracted to the width of one day's voyage. He described Malegga as a very powerful country, and of greater extent than either Unyora or Uganda. South of Malegga was a country named Tori, governed by a king of the same name; beyond that country to the south on the western shore, no intelligence could be obtained from any one.

The lake was known to extend as far south as Karagwe; and the old story was repeated, that Rumanika, the king of that country, was in the habit of sending ivory-hunting parties to the lake at Utumbi, and that formerly they had navigated the lake to Magungo. This was a curious confirmation of the report given me by Speke at Gondokoro, who wrote: "Rumanika is constantly in the habit of sending ivory-hunting parties to Utumbi."

The eastern shores of the lake were, from north to south, occupied by Chopi, Unyoro, Uganda, Utumbi, and Karagwe: from the last point, which could not be less than about two degrees south latitude, the lake was reported to turn suddenly to the west, and to continue in that direction for an unknown distance. North of Malegga, on the west of the lake, was a small country called M'Caroli; then Koshi, on the west side of the Nile at its exit from the lake; and on the east side of the Nile was the Madi, opposite to Koshi. Both the guide and the chief of Vacovia informed me that we should be taken by canoes to Magungo, to the point at which the Somerset that we had left at Karuma joined the lake; but that we could not ascend it, as it was a succession of cataracts the whole way from Karuma until within a short distance of Magungo. The exit of the Nile from the lake at Koshi was navigable for a considerable distance, and canoes could descend the river as far as the Madi.

They both agreed that the level of the lake was never lower than at present, and that it never rose higher than a mark upon the beach that accounted for an increase of about four feet. The beach was perfectly clean sand, upon which the waves rolled like those of the sea, throwing up weeds precisely as seaweed may be seen upon the English shore. It was a grand sight to look upon this vast reser- voir of the mighty Nile, and to watch the heavy swell tumbling upon the beach, while far to the southwest the eye searched as vainly for a bound as though upon the Atlantic. It was with extreme emotion that I enjoyed this glorious scene. My wife, who had followed me so devotedly, stood by my side pale and exhausted – a wreck upon the shores of the great Albert Lake that we had so long striven to reach. No European foot had ever trod upon its sand, nor had the eyes of a white man ever scanned its vast expanse of water. We were the first; and this was the key to the great secret that even Julius Caesar yearned to unravel, but in vain. Here was the great basin of the Nile that received every drop of water, even from the passing shower to the roaring mountain torrent that drained from Central Africa towards the north. This was the great reservoir of the Nile!

The first *coup d'oeil* from the summit of the cliff 1,500 feet above the level had suggested what a closer examination confirmed. The lake was a vast depression far below the general level of the country, surrounded by precipitous cliffs, and bounded on the west and southwest by great ranges of mountains from five to seven thousand feet above the level of its waters – thus it was the one great reservoir into which everything must drain; and from this vast rocky cistern the Nile made its exit, a giant in its birth. It was a grand arrangement of Nature for the birth of so mighty and important a stream as the river Nile. The Victoria N'Yanza of Speke formed a reservoir at a high altitude, receiving a drainage from the west by the Kitangule River, and Speke had seen the M'fumbiro Mountain at a great distance as a peak among other mountains from which the streams descended, which by uniting formed the main river Kitangule, the principal feeder of the Victoria lake from the west, in about the 2 degrees S. latitude: thus the same chain of mountains that fed the Victoria on the east must have a watershed to the west and north that would flow into the Albert Lake. The general drainage of the Nile basin tending from south to north, and the Albert Lake extending much farther north than the Victoria, it receives the river from the latter lake, and thus monopolizes the entire headwaters of the Nile. The Albert is the grand reservoir, while the Victoria is the eastern source, the parent streams that form these lakes are from the same origin, and the Kitangule sheds its waters to the Victoria to be received eventually by the Albert, precisely as the highlands of M'fumbiro and the Blue Mountains pour their northern drainage direct into the Albert Lake. The entire Nile system, from the first Abyssinian tributary the Atbara in N. latitude 17 deg. 37 min. even to the equator, exhibits a uniform drainage from S.E. to N.W., every tributary flowing in that direction to the main stream of the Nile; this system is persisted in by the Victoria Nile, which having continued a northerly course from its exit from the Victoria lake to Karuma in lat. 2 degrees 16' N. turns suddenly to the west and meets the Albert Lake at Magungo; thus, a line drawn from Magungo to the Ripon Falls from the Victoria lake will prove the general slope of the country to be the same as exemplified throughout the entire system of the eastern basin of the Nile, tending from S.E. to N.W.

That many considerable affluents flow into the Albert Lake there is no doubt. The two waterfalls seen by telescope upon the western shore descending from the Blue Mountains must be most important streams, or they could not have been distinguished at so great a distance as fifty or sixty miles; the natives assured me that very many streams, varying in size, descended the mountains upon all sides into the general reservoir.

I returned to my hut: the flat turf in the vicinity of the village was strewn with the bones of immense fish, hippopotami, and crocodiles; but the latter reptiles were merely caught in revenge for any outrage committed by them, as their flesh was looked upon with disgust by the natives of Unyoro. They were so numerous and voracious in the lake, that the natives cautioned us not to allow the women to venture into the water even to the knees when filling their water jars.

It was most important that we should hurry forward on our journey, as our return to England depended entirely upon the possibility of reaching Gondokoro before the end of April, otherwise the boats would have departed. I impressed upon our guide and the chief that we must be furnished with large canoes immediately, as we had no time to spare, and I started off Rabonga to Magungo, where he was to meet us with our riding oxen. The animals would be taken by a path upon the high ground; there was no possibility of travelling near the lake, as the cliffs in many places descended abruptly into deep water. I made him a present of a large quantity of beads that I had promised to give him upon reaching the lake; he took his departure, agreeing to meet us at Magungo with our oxen, and to have porters in readiness to convey us direct to Shooa.

On the following morning not one of our party could rise from the ground. Thirteen men, the boy Saat, four women, and we ourselves, were all down with fever. The air was hot and close, and the country frightfully unhealthy. The natives assured us that all strangers suffered in a similar manner, and that no one could live at Vacovia without repeated attacks of fever.

The delay in supplying the boats was most annoying; every hour was precious; and the lying natives deceived us in every manner possible, delaying us purposely in the hope of extorting beads.

The latitude of Vacovia was 1 degree 15 min. N.; longitude 30 degrees 50 min. E. My farthest southern point on the road from M'Rooli was latitude 1 degree 13 minutes. We were now to turn our faces towards the north, and every day's journey would bring us nearer home. But where was home? As I looked at the map of the world, and at the little red spot that represented old England far, far away, and then gazed on the wasted form and haggard face of my wife and at my own attenuated frame, I hardly dared hope for home again. We had now been three years ever toiling onwards, and having completed the exploration of all the Abyssinian affluents of the Nile, in itself an arduous undertaking, we were now actually at the Nile head. We had neither health nor supplies, and the great journey lay all before us.

Notwithstanding my daily entreaties that boats might be supplied without delay, eight days were passed at Vacovia, during which time the whole party suffered more or less from fever. At length canoes were reported to have arrived, and I was requested to inspect them. They were merely single trees neatly hollowed out, but very inferior in size to the large canoes on the Nile at M'Rooli. The largest boat was thirty-two feet long, but I selected for ourselves one of twenty-six feet, but wider and deeper.

Fortunately I had purchased at Khartoum an English screw auger 1 1/4 inch in diameter, and this tool I had brought with me, foreseeing some difficulties in boating arrangements. I now bored holes two feet apart in the gunwale of the canoe, and having prepared long elastic wands, I spanned them in arches across the boat and lashed them to the auger holes. This completed, I secured them by diagonal pieces, and concluded by thatching the framework with a thin coating of reeds to protect us from the sun; over the thatch I stretched ox-hides well drawn and lashed, so as to render our roof waterproof. This arrangement formed a tortoise-like protection that would be proof against sun and rain. I then arranged some logs of exceedingly light wood along the bottom of the canoe, and covered them with a thick bed of grass; this was covered with an Abyssinian tanned ox-hide, and arranged with Scotch plaids. The arrangements completed, afforded a cabin, perhaps not as luxurious as those of the Peninsular and Oriental Company's vessels, but both rain- and sun-proof, which was the great *desideratum*. In this rough vessel we embarked on a calm morning, when hardly a ripple moved the even surface of the lake. Each canoe had four rowers, two at either end. Their paddles were beautifully shaped, hewn from one piece of wood, the blade being rather wider than that of an ordinary spade, but concave in the inner side, so as to give the rower a great hold upon the water. Having purchased with some difficulty a few fowls and dried fish, I put the greater number of my men in the larger canoe; and with Richarn, Saat, and the women, including the interpreter Bacheeta, we led the way, and started from Vacovia on the broad surface of the Albert N'Yanza. The rowers paddled bravely; and the canoe, although heavily laden, went along at about four miles an hour. There was no excitement in Vacovia, and the chief and two or three attendants were all who came to see us off; they had a suspicion that bystanders might be invited to assist as rowers, therefore the entire population of the village had deserted.

At leaving the shore, the chief had asked for a few beads, which, on receiving, he threw into the lake to propitiate the inhabitants of the deep, that no hippopotami should upset the canoe.

Our first day's voyage was delightful. The lake was calm, the sky cloudy, and the scenery most lovely. At times the mountains on the west coast were not discernible, and the lake appeared of indefinite width. We coasted within a hundred yards of the east shore; sometimes we passed flats of sand and bush of perhaps a mile in width from the water to the base of the mountain cliffs; at other times we passed directly underneath stupendous heights of about 1,500 feet, which ascended abruptly from the deep, so that we fended the canoes off the sides, and assisted our progress by pushing against the rock with bamboos. These precipitous rocks were all primitive, frequently of granite and gneiss, and mixed in many places with red porphyry. In the clefts were beautiful evergreens of every tint, including giant euphorbias; and wherever a rivulet or spring glittered through the dark foliage of a ravine, it was shaded by the graceful and feathery wild date.

Great numbers of hippopotami were sporting in the water, but I refused to fire at them, as the death of such a monster would be certain to delay us for at least a day, as the boatmen would not forsake the flesh. Crocodiles were exceedingly numerous both in and out of the water; wherever a sandy beach invited them to bask, several monsters were to be seen, like trunks of trees, lying in the sun. On the edge of the beach above high-water mark were low bushes, and from this cover the crocodiles came scuttling down into the water, frightened at the approach of the canoe. There were neither ducks nor geese, as there were no feeding-grounds: deep water was close to the shore.

Our boatmen worked well, and long after dark we continued our voyage, until the canoe was suddenly steered to the shore, and we grounded upon a steep beach of perfectly clean sand. We were informed that we were near a village, and the boatmen proposed to leave us here for the night, while they should proceed in search of provisions. Seeing that they intended to take the paddles with them, I ordered these important implements to be returned to the boats, and a guard set over them, while several of my men should accompany the boatmen to the reported village. In the meantime, we arranged our *angareps* upon the beach, lighted a fire with some driftwood, and prepared for the night. The men shortly returned, accompanied by several natives, with two fowls and one small kid. The latter was immediately consigned to the large copper pot, and I paid about three times its value to the natives, to encourage them to bring supplies on the following morning.

While dinner was preparing, I took an observation, and found our latitude was 1 degree 33 minutes N. We had travelled well, having made 16 minutes direct northwards.

On the first crowing of our solitary cock, we prepared to start; the boatmen were gone!

As soon as it was light, I took two men and went to the village, supposing they were sleeping in their huts. Within three hundred paces of the boats, upon a fine turfy sward, on rising ground, were three miserable fishing huts. These constituted the village. Upon arrival, no one was to be found: the natives had deserted. A fine tract of broken grassland formed a kind of amphitheatre beneath the range of cliffs. These I scanned with the telescope, but I could trace no signs of man. We were evidently deserted by our boatmen, and the natives had accompanied them to avoid being pressed into our service.

On my return to the canoes with this intelligence, my men were quite in despair: they could not believe that the boatmen had really absconded, and they begged me to allow them to search the country in the hope of finding another village. Strictly forbidding any man to absent himself from the boats, I congratulated ourselves on having well guarded the paddles, which there was no doubt would have been stolen by the boatmen had I allowed them to remain in their possession. I agreed to wait until 3 p.m. Should the boatmen not return by that hour, I intended to proceed without them. There was no dependence to be placed upon these contradictory natives. Kindness was entirely thrown away upon them. We had Kamrasi's orders for boats and men, but in this distant frontier the natives did not appear to attach much importance to their king: nevertheless, we were dependent upon them. Every hour was valuable, as our only chance of reaching Gondokoro in time for the boats depended upon rapidity of travelling. At the moment when I wished to press forward, delays occurred that were most trying.

Three p.m. arrived, but no signs of natives. "Jump into the boats, my lads!" I cried to my men; "I know the route." The canoes were pushed from the shore, and my people manned the paddles. Five of my men were professional boatmen, but no one understood the management of paddles except myself. It was in vain that I attempted to instruct my crew. Pull they certainly did; but – ye gods who watch over boats – round and round we pirouetted, the two canoes waltzing and polking together in their great ball-room, the Albert N'Yanza. The voyage would have lasted *ad infinitum*. After three hours' exertion, we reached a point of rock that stretched as a promontory into the lake. This bluff point was covered with thick jungle to the summit, and at the base was a small plot of sandy beach, from which there was no exit except by water, as the cliff descended sheer to the lake upon either side. It poured with rain, and with much difficulty we lighted a fire. Mosquitoes were in clouds, and the night was so warm that it was impossible to sleep beneath the blankets. Arranging the *angareps* upon the sand, with the raw oxhides as coverlets, we lay down in the rain. It was too hot to sleep in the boat, especially as the temporary cabin was a perfect mosquito nest. That night I considered the best plan to be adopted, and resolved to adapt a paddle as a rudder on the following morning. It rained without ceasing the whole night; and, at break of day, the scene was sufficiently miserable. The men lay on the wet sand, covered up with their raw hides, soaked completely through, but still fast asleep, from which nothing would arouse them. My wife was also wet and wretched. It still rained. I was soon at work.

Cutting a thwart in the stern of the canoe with my hunting-knife, I bored a hole beneath it with the large auger, and securely lashed a paddle with a thong of rawhide that I cut off my well-saturated coverlet. I made a most effective rudder. None of my men had assisted me; they had remained beneath their soaked skins, smoking their short pipes, while I was hard at work. They were perfectly apathetic with despair, as their ridiculous efforts at paddling on the previous evening had completely extinguished all hope within them. They were quite resigned to their destiny, and considered themselves as sacrificed to geography.

I threw them the auger, and explained that I was ready to start, and should wait for no one; and, cutting two bamboos, I arranged a mast and yard, upon which I fitted a large Scotch plaid for a sail. We shoved off the boat; fortunately we had two or three spare paddles, therefore the rudder paddle was not missed. I took the helm, and instructed my men to think of nothing but pulling hard. Away we went as straight as an arrow, to the intense delight of my people.

There was very little wind, but a light air filled the plaid and eased us gently forward.

Upon rounding the promontory we found ourselves in a large bay, the opposite headland being visible at about eight or ten miles' distance. Should we coast the bay it would occupy two days. There was another small promontory farther in shore; I therefore resolved to steer direct for that point before venturing in a straight line from one headland to the other.

Upon looking behind me, I observed our canoe consort about a mile astern, amusing herself with pointing to all parts of the compass – the lazy men not having taken the trouble to adapt the rudder as I had ordered them.

We travelled at about four miles an hour, and my people were so elated that they declared themselves ready to row, without assistance, to the Nile junction. The water was perfectly calm, and upon rounding the next promontory I was rejoiced to see a village in a snug little bay, and a great number of canoes drawn up on the sandy beach, and others engaged in fishing. A number of natives were standing on the sand close to the water's edge, about half a mile from us, and I steered directly towards them. Upon our close approach, they immediately sat down, and held up their paddles above their heads; this was an unmistakeable sign that they intended to volunteer as boatmen, and I steered the boat upon the beach. No sooner had we grounded, than they rushed into the water and boarded us, most good-humouredly pulling down our mast and sail, which appeared to them highly absurd (as they never use sails); and they explained that they had seen on the other side the headland that we were strangers, and their chief had ordered them to assist us. I now begged them to send six men to the assistance of the lagging canoe; this they promised to do, and, after waiting for some time, we started at a rattling pace to pull across the wide bay from point to point.

When in the centre of the bay we were about four miles from land. At this time a swell set in from the southwest. While at Vacovia I had observed, that although the mornings were calm, a strong wind generally arose at 1 p.m. from S.W. that brought a heavy sea upon the beach. I was now afraid that we should be subject to a gale before we could reach the opposite headland, as the rising swell betokened wind from the old quarter, especially as dark thunderclouds were gathering on the western shore.

I told Bacheeta to urge the rowers forward, as our heavy canoe would certainly be swamped in the event of a gale. I looked at my watch: it was past noon, and I felt sure that we should catch a southwester by about one o'clock. My men looked rather green at the ominous black clouds and the increasing swell, but exclaimed, "*Inshallah*, there will be no wind." With due deference to their faith in predestination, I insisted upon their working the spare paddles, as our safety depended upon reaching the shore before the approaching storm. They had learnt to believe in my opinion, and they exerted themselves to their utmost. The old boat rushed through the water, but the surface of the lake was rapidly changing; the western shore was no longer visible, the water was dark, and innumerable white crests tipped the waves. The canoe laboured heavily, and occasionally shipped water, which was immediately baled out with gourd shells by my men, who now exclaimed, "*Wah Illahi el kalam betar el Hawaga sahhe* (By Allah, what the *Hawaga* says is true)!" We were within about a mile and a half of the point for which we had been steering, when we could no longer keep our course; we had shipped several heavy seas, and had we not been well supplied with utensils for baling, we should have been swamped. Several bursts of thunder and vivid lightning were followed by a tremendous gale from about the W.S.W. before which we were obliged to run for the shore.

In a short space of time a most dangerous sea arose, and on several occasions the waves broke against the arched covering of the canoe, which happily protected her in a slight degree, although we were drenched with water.

Every one was at work baling with all their might; I had no idea that the canoe could live. Down came the rain in torrents, swept along with a terrific wind; nothing was discernible except the high cliffs looming through the storm, and I only trusted that we might arrive upon a sandy beach, and not upon bluff rocks. We went along at a grand rate, as the arched cover of the canoe acted somewhat as a sail; and it was an exciting moment when we at length neared the shore, and approached the foaming breakers that were rolling wildly upon (happily) a sandy beach beneath the cliffs. I told my men to be ready to jump out the moment that we should touch the sand, and to secure the canoe by hauling the head up the beach. All were ready, and we rushed through the surf, the native boatmen paddling like steam engines. "Here comes a wave; look out!" And just as we almost touched the beach, a heavy breaker broke over the black women who were sitting in the stern, and swamped the boat. My men jumped into the water like ducks, and the next moment we were all rolled in confusion on the sandy shore. The men stuck well to the boat, and hauled her firmly on the sand, while my wife crawled out of her primitive cabin like a caddis worm from its nest, half drowned, and jumped upon the shore. "*El hamd el Illah* (thank God)!" we all exclaimed; "now for a pull – all together!" And having so far secured the boat that she could not be washed away, I ordered the men to discharge the cargo, and then to pull her out of the lake. Everything was destroyed except the gunpowder; that was all in canisters. But where was the other canoe? I made up my mind that it must be lost, for although much longer than our boat, it was lower in the water. After some time and much anxiety, we perceived it running for the shore about half a mile in our rear; it was in the midst of the breakers, and several times I lost sight of it; but the old tree behaved well, and brought the crew safe to the shore.

Fortunately there was a village not far from the spot where we landed, and we took possession of a hut, lighted a good fire, and wrapped ourselves in Scotch plaids and blankets wrung out, while our clothes were being dried, as there was not a dry rag in our possession.

We could procure nothing to eat, except a few dried fish that, not having been salted, were rather high flavoured. Our fowls, and also two pet quails, were drowned in the boat during the storm; however, the drowned fowls were made into a stew, and with a blazing fire, and clean straw to sleep upon, the night's rest was perhaps as perfect as in the luxury of home.

On the following morning we were detained by bad weather, as a heavy sea was still running, and we were determined not to risk our canoes in another gale. It was a beautiful neighbourhood, enlivened by a magnificent waterfall that fell about a thousand feet from the mountains, as the Kaiigiri River emptied itself into the lake in a splendid volume of water. This river rises in the great marsh that we had crossed on our way from M'Rooli to Vacovia. In this neighbourhood we gathered some mushrooms – the true *Agaricus campestras* of Europe – which were a great luxury.

In the afternoon the sea subsided, and we again started. We had not proceeded above three miles from the village, when I observed an elephant bathing in the lake; he was in water so deep, that he stood with only the top of his head and trunk above the surface. As we approached, he sunk entirely, only the tip of his trunk remaining above the water. I ordered the boatmen to put the canoe as close to him as possible, and we passed within thirty yards, just as he raised his head from his luxurious bath.

I was sorely tempted to fire, but remembering my resolve, refrained from disturbing him, and he slowly quitted the lake, and entered the thick jungle. A short distance beyond this spot two large crocodiles were lying upon the beach asleep; but upon the approach of the canoe they plunged into the water, and raised their heads above the surface at about twenty-five paces. I was uncertain about my Fletcher rifle, as it had been exposed to so much wet; therefore, to discharge it, I took a shot at the nearest crocodile just behind the eye. The little rifle was in perfect order – thanks to Eley's "double waterproof central firecaps," which will resist all weathers – and the bullet striking the exact spot, the great reptile gave a convulsive lash with his tail, and turning on his back, with his paws above the water, he gradually sunk. The native boatmen were dreadfully frightened at the report of the rifle, to the great amusement of their countrywoman, Bacheeta, and it was with difficulty that I persuaded them to direct the canoe to the exact spot. Being close to the shore, the water was not more than eight feet deep, and so beautifully clear, that I could, when just above the crocodile, perceive it lying at the bottom on its belly, and distinguish the bloody head that had been shattered by the bullet. While one of my men prepared a slip-knot, I took a long lance that belonged to a boatman, and drove it deep through the tough scales into the back of the neck; hauling gently, upon the lance I raised the head near to the surface, and slipping the noose over it, the crocodile was secured. It appeared to be quite dead, and the flesh would be a *bonne-bouche* for my men; therefore we towed it to the shore.

It was a fine monster, about sixteen feet long; and although it had appeared dead, it bit furiously at a thick male bamboo which I ran into its mouth to prevent it from snapping during the process of decapitation. The natives regarded my men with disgust as they cut huge lumps of the choicest morsels and stowed them in the canoes; this did not occupy more than a quarter of an hour, and hurrying on board, we continued our voyage, well provided with meat – for all who liked it. To my taste nothing can be more disgusting than crocodile flesh. I have eaten almost everything; but although I have tasted crocodile, I could never succeed in swallowing it; the combined flavour of bad fish, rotten flesh, and musk, is the *carte de diner* [menu] offered to the epicure.

That evening we saw an elephant with an enormous pair of tusks; he was standing on a hill about a quarter of a mile from the boats as we halted. I was aided to resist this temptation by an attack of fever: it rained as usual, and no village being in the neighbourhood, we bivouacked in the rain on the beach in clouds of mosquitoes.

The discomforts of this lake voyage were great; in the day we were cramped in our small cabin like two tortoises in one shell, and at night it almost invariably rained. We were accustomed to the wet, but no acclimatisation can render the European body mosquito-proof; thus we had little rest. It was hard work for me, but for my unfortunate wife, who had hardly recovered from her attack of *coup de soleil*, such hardships were most distressing.

On the following morning the lake was calm, and we started early. The monotony of the voyage was broken by the presence of several fine herds of elephants, consisting entirely of bulls. I counted fourteen of these grand animals, all with large tusks, bathing together in a small shallow lake beneath the mountains, having a communication with the main lake through a sandy beach; these elephants were only knee deep, and having been bathing they were perfectly clean, and their colossal black forms and large white tusks formed a beautiful picture in the calm lake beneath the lofty cliffs. It was a scene in harmony with the solitude of the Nile Sources – the wilderness of rocks and forest, the Blue Mountains in the distance, and the great fountain of nature adorned with the mighty beasts of Africa; the elephants in undisturbed grandeur, and hippopotami disporting their huge forms in the great parent of the Egyptian river.

I ordered the boatmen to run the canoe ashore, that we might land and enjoy the scene. We then discovered seven elephants on the shore within about two hundred yards of us in high grass, while the main herd of fourteen splendid bulls bathed majestically in the placid lake, showering cold streams from their trunks over their backs and shoulders. There was no time to lose, as every hour was important: quitting the shore, we once more paddled along the coast.

Day after day passed, the time occupied in travelling from sunrise to midday, at which hour a strong gale with rain and thunder occurred regularly, and obliged us to haul our canoes ashore. The country was very thinly inhabited, and the villages were poor and wretched; the people most inhospitable. At length we arrived at a considerable town situated in a beautiful bay beneath precipitous cliffs, the grassy sides of which were covered with flocks of goats; this was Eppigoya, and the boatmen that we had procured from the last village were to deliver us in this spot. The delays in procuring boatmen were most annoying: it appeared that the king had sent orders that each village was to supply the necessary rowers; thus we were paddled from place to place, at each of which the men were changed, and no amount of payment would induce them to continue with us to the end of our voyage.

Landing at Eppigoya, we were at once met by the headman, and I proposed that he should sell us a few kids, as the idea of a mutton chop was most appetizing. Far from supplying us with this luxury, the natives immediately drove their flocks away, and after receiving a large present of beads, the headman brought us a present of a sick lamb almost at the point of natural death, and merely skin and bone. Fortunately there were fowls in thousands, as the natives did not use them for food; these we purchased for one blue bead (*monjoor*) each, which in current value was equal to 250 fowls for a shilling. Eggs were brought in baskets containing several hundreds, but they were all poultry.

At Eppigoya the best salt was produced, and we purchased a good supply – also some dried fish; thus provisioned, we procured boatmen, and again started on our voyage.

Hardly had we proceeded two hundred yards, when we were steered direct to the shore below the town, and our boatmen coolly laid down their paddles and told us that they had performed their share, and that as Eppigoya was divided into four parts under separate headmen, each portion would supply rowers!

Ridiculous as this appeared, there was no contesting their decision; and thus we were handed over from one to the other, and delayed for about three hours in changing boatmen four times within a distance of less than a mile! The perfect absurdity of such a regulation, combined with the delay when time was most precious, was trying to the temper. At every change, the headman accompanied the boatmen to our canoe, and presented us with three fowls at parting; thus our canoes formed a floating poultry show as we had already purchased large supplies. Our livestock bothered us dreadfully; being without baskets, the fowls were determined upon suicide, and many jumped deliberately overboard, while others that were tied by the legs were drowned in the bottom of the leaky canoe.

After the tenth day from our departure from Vacovia the scenery increased in beauty. The lake had contracted to about thirty miles in width, and was decreasing rapidly northward; the trees upon the mountains upon the western shore could be distinguished. Continuing our voyage north, the western shore projected suddenly, and diminished the width of the lake to about twenty miles. It was no longer the great inland sea that at Vacovia had so impressed me, with the clean pebbly beach that had hitherto formed the shore, but vast banks of reeds growing upon floating vegetation prevented the canoes from landing. These banks were most peculiar, as they appeared to have been formed of decayed vegetation, from which the papyrus rushes took root; the thickness of the floating mass was about three feet, and so tough and firm that a man could walk upon it, merely sinking above his ankles in the soft ooze. Beneath this raft of vegetation was extremely deep water, and the shore for a width of about half a mile was entirely protected by this extraordinary formation. One day a tremendous gale of wind and heavy sea broke off large portions, and the wind acting upon the rushes like sails, carried floating islands of some acres about the lake to be deposited wherever they might chance to hitch.

On the thirteenth day we found ourselves at the end of our lake voyage. The lake at this point was between fifteen and twenty miles across, and the appearance of the country to the north was that of a delta. The shores upon either side were choked with vast banks of reeds, and as the canoe skirted the edge of that upon the east coast, we could find no bottom with a bamboo of twenty-five feet in length, although the floating mass appeared like terra forma. We were in a perfect wilderness of vegetation: On the west were mountains of about 4,000 feet above the lake level, a continuation of the chain that formed the western shore from the south: these mountains decreased in height towards the north, in which direction the lake terminated in a broad valley of reeds.

We were told that we had arrived at Magungo, and that this was the spot where the boats invariably crossed from Malegga on the western shore to Kamrasi's country. The boatmen proposed that we should land upon the floating vegetation, as that would be a short cut to the village or town of Magungo; but as the swell of the water against the abrupt raft of reeds threatened to swamp the canoe, I preferred coasting until we should discover a good landing place. After skirting the floating reeds for about a mile, we turned sharp to the east, and entered a broad channel of water bounded on either side by the everlasting reeds. This we were informed was the embouchure of the Somerset River from the Victoria N'Yanza. The same river that we had crossed at Karuma, boiling and tearing along its rocky course, now entered the Albert N'Yanza as dead water! I could not understand this; there was not the slightest current; the channel was about half a mile wide, and I could hardly convince myself that this was not an arm of the lake branching to the east. After searching for some time for a landing place among the wonderful banks of reeds, we discovered a passage that had evidently been used as an approach by canoes, but so narrow that our large canoe could with difficulty be dragged through – all the men walking through the mud and reeds, and towing with their utmost strength. Several hundred paces of this tedious work brought us through the rushes into open water, about eight feet deep, opposite to a clean rocky shore. We had heard voices for some time while obscured on the other side of the rushes, and we now found a number of natives, who had arrived to meet us, with the chief of

Magungo and our guide Rabonga, whom we had sent in advance with the riding oxen from Vacovia. The water was extremely shallow near the shore, and the natives rushed in and dragged the canoes by sheer force over the mud to the land. We had been so entirely hidden while on the lake on the other side of the reed bank that we had been unable to see the eastern, or Magungo shore; we now found ourselves in a delightful spot beneath the shade of several enormous trees on firm sandy and rocky ground, while the country rose in a rapid incline to the town of Magungo, about a mile distant, on an elevated ridge.

My first question was concerning the riding oxen. They were reported in good order. We were invited to wait under a tree until the presents from the headmen should be delivered. Accordingly, while my wife sat under the shade, I went to the waterside to examine the fishing arrangements of the natives, that were on an extensive scale. For many hundred feet, the edges of the floating reeds were arranged to prevent the possibility of a large fish entering the open water adjoining the shore without being trapped. A regular system of baskets was fixed at intervals, with guiding fences to their mouths. Each basket was about six feet in diameter, and the mouth about eighteen inches; thus the arrangements were for the monsters of the lake, the large bones of which, strewed about the vicinity, were a witness of their size. My men had just secured the half of a splendid fish, known in the Nile as the *baggera*. They had found it in the water, the other portion having been bitten off by a crocodile. The piece in their possession weighed about fifty pounds. This is one of the best fish in the lake. It is shaped like the perch, but is coloured externally like the salmon. I also obtained from the natives an exceedingly good fish, of a peculiar form, having four long feelers at the positions that would be occupied by the limbs of reptiles; these looked like rudiments of legs. It had somewhat the appearance of an eel; but, being oviparous, it can have no connexion with that genus. The natives had a most killing way of fishing with the hook and line for heavy fish. They arranged rows of tall bamboos, the ends stuck firmly in the bottom, in a depth of about six feet of water, and about five or ten yards apart. On the top of each was a lump of ambatch-wood about ten inches in diameter. Around this was wound a powerful line, and, a small hole being made in this float, it was lightly fixed upon the point of the bamboo, or fishing rod. The line was securely attached to the bamboo, then wound round the large float, while the hook, baited with a live fish, was thrown to some distance beyond. Long rows of these fixed rods were set every morning by natives in canoes, and watchers attended them during the day, while they took their chance by night. When a large fish took the bait, his first rush unhitched the ambatch-float from the point of the bamboo, which, revolving upon the water, paid out line as required. When entirely run out, the great size and buoyancy of the float served to check and to exhaust the fish. There are several varieties of fish that exceed 200 lbs. weight.

A number of people now arrived from the village, bringing a goat, fowls, eggs, and sour milk, and, beyond all luxuries, fresh butter. I delighted the chief, in return for his civility, by giving him a quantity of beads, and we were led up the hill towards Magungo.

The day was beautifully clear. The soil was sandy and poor, therefore the road was clean and hard; and, after the many days' boating, we enjoyed the walk, and the splendid view that lay before us when we arrived at Magungo, and looked back upon the lake. We were about 250 feet above the water level. There were no longer the abrupt cliffs, descending to the lake, that we had seen in the south, but the general level of the country appeared to be about 500 feet above the water, at a distance of five or six miles, from which point the ground descended in undulations, Magungo being situated on the summit of the nearest incline. The mountains on the Malegga side, with the lake in the foreground, were the most prominent objects, forming the western boundary. A few miles north there appeared to be a gap in the range, and the lake continued to the west, but much contracted, while the mountain range on the northern side of the gap continued to the northeast. Due north and northeast the country was a dead flat, and far as the eye could reach was an extent of bright green reeds, marking the course of the Nile as it made its exit from the lake. The sheet of water at Magungo being about seventeen miles in width, ended in a long strip or tail to the north, until it was lost in the flat valley of green rushes. This valley may have been from four to six miles wide, and was bounded upon its west bank by the continuation of the chain of mountains that had formed the western boundary of the lake. The natives told me that canoes could navigate the Nile in its course from the lake to the Madi country, as there were no cataracts for a great distance, but that both the Madi and the Koshi were hostile, and that the current of the river was so strong, that should the canoe descend from the lake, it could not return without many rowers. They pointed out the country of Koshi on the west bank of the Nile, at its exit from the lake, which included the mountains that bordered the river. The small country, M'Caroli, joined Malegga, and continued to the west, towards the Makkarika. The natives most positively refused to take me down the Nile from the lake into the Madi, as they said that they would be killed by the people, who were their enemies, as I should not be with them on their return up the river.

The exit of the Nile from the lake was plain enough, and if the broad channel of dead water were indeed the entrance of the Victoria Nile (Somerset), the information obtained by Speke would be remarkably confirmed. Up to the present time all the information that I had received from Kamrasi and his people had been correct. He had told me that I should be about twenty days from M'Rooli to the lake; I had been eighteen. He had also told me that the Somerset flowed from Karuma direct to the lake, and that, having joined it, the great Nile issued from the lake almost immediately, and flowed through the Koshi and Madi tribes. I now saw the river issuing from the lake within eighteen miles of Magungo, and the Koshi and the Madi countries appeared close to me, bordering it on the west and east. Kamrasi being the king, it was natural that he should know his own frontier most intimately; but, although the chief of Magungo and all the natives assured me that the broad channel of dead water at my feet was positively the brawling river that I had crossed below the Karuma Falls, I could not understand how so fine a body of water as that had appeared could possibly enter the Albert Lake as dead water. The guide and natives laughed at my unbelief, and declared that it was dead water for a considerable distance from the junction with the lake, but that a great waterfall rushed down from a mountain, and that beyond that fall the river was merely a succession of cataracts throughout the entire distance of about six days' march to Karuma Falls. My real wish was to descend the Nile in canoes from its exit from the lake with my own men as boatmen, and thus in a short time to reach the cataracts in the Madi country; there to forsake the canoes and all my baggage, and to march direct to Gondokoro with only our guns and ammunition. I knew from native report that the Nile was navigable as far as the Madi country to about Miani's tree, which Speke had laid down by astronomical observation in lat. 3 degrees 34 minutes; this would be only seven days' march from Gondokoro, and by such a direct course I should be sure to arrive in time for the boats to Khartoum. I had promised Speke that I would explore most thoroughly the doubtful portion of the river that he had been forced to neglect from Karuma Falls to the lake. I was myself confused at the dead water junction; and, although I knew that the natives must be right – as it was their own river, and they had no inducement to mislead me – I was determined to sacrifice every other wish in order to fulfil my promise, and thus to settle the Nile question most absolutely. That the Nile flowed out of the lake I had heard, and I had also confirmed by actual inspection; from Magungo I looked upon the two countries, Koshi and Madi, through which it flowed, and these countries I must actually pass through and again meet the Nile before I could reach Gondokoro. Thus the only point necessary to swear to, was the river between the lake and the Karuma Falls.

I had a bad attack of fever that evening, and missed my star for the latitude; but on the following morning before daybreak I obtained a good observation of Vega, and determined the latitude of Magungo 2 degrees 16 minutes due west from Atada or Karuma Falls. This was a strong confirmation that the river beneath my feet was the Somerset that I had crossed in the same latitude at Atada, where the river was running due west, and where the natives had pointed in that direction as its course to the lake. Nevertheless, I was determined to verify it, although by this circuitous route I might lose the boats from Gondokoro and become a prisoner in Central Africa, ill, and without quinine, for another year. I proposed it to my wife, who not only voted in her state of abject weakness to complete the river to Karuma, but wished, if possible, to return and follow the Nile from the lake down to Gondokoro! This latter resolve, based upon the simple principle of "seeing is believing," was a sacrifice most nobly proposed, but simply impossible and unnecessary.

We saw from our point at Magungo the Koshi and Madi countries, and the Nile flowing out of the lake through them. We must of necessity pass through those countries on our road to Gondokoro direct from Karuma via Shooa, and should we not meet the river in the Madi and Koshi country, the Nile that we now saw would not be the Nile of Gondokoro. We knew, however, that it was so, as Speke and Grant had gone by that route, and had met the Nile near Miani's tree in lat. 3 degrees 34 min. in the Madi country, the Koshi being on its western bank; thus, as we were now at the Nile head and saw it passing through the Madi and Koshi, any argument against the river would be the argumentum ad absurdum. I ordered the boats to be got ready to start immediately.

The chief gave me much information, confirming the accounts that I had heard a year previous in the Latooka countries, that formerly cowrie shells were brought in boats from the south, and that these shells and brass coil brackets came by the lake from Karagwe. He called also several of the natives of Malegga, who had arrived with beautifully prepared mantles of antelope and goatskins, to exchange for bracelets and glass beads. The Malegga people were in appearance the same as those of Unyoro, but they spoke a different language.

The boats being ready, we took leave of the chief, leaving him an acceptable present of beads, and we descended the hill to the river, thankful at having so far successfully terminated the expedition as to have traced the lake to that important point Magungo, which had been our clue to the discovery even so far away in time and place as the distant country of Latooka. We were both very weak and ill, and my knees trembled beneath me as we walked down the easy descent. I, in my enervated state, endeavouring to assist my wife, we were the "blind leading the blind;" but had life closed on that day we could have died most happily, for the hard fight through sickness and misery had ended in victory; and, although I looked to home as a paradise never to be regained, I could have lain down to sleep in contentment on this spot, with the consolation that, if the body had been vanquished, we died with the prize in our grasp. On arrival at the canoes we found everything in readiness, and the boatmen already in their places. A crowd of natives pushed us over the shallows, and once in deep water we passed through a broad canal which led us into the open channel without the labour of towing through the narrow inlet by which we had arrived. Once in the broad channel of dead water we steered due east, and made rapid way until the evening. The river as it now appeared, although devoid of current, was an average of about 500 yards in width. Before we halted for the night I was subjected to a most severe attack of fever, and upon the boat reaching a certain spot I was carried on a litter, perfectly unconscious, to a village, attended carefully by my poor sick wife, who, herself half dead, followed me on foot through the marshes in pitch darkness, and watched over me until the morning. At daybreak I was too weak to stand, and we were both carried down to the canoes, and, crawling helplessly within our grass awning, we lay down like logs while the canoes continued their voyage. Many of our men were also suffering from fever. The malaria of the dense masses of floating vegetation was most poisonous; and upon looking back to the canoe that followed in our wake, I observed all my men sitting crouched together sick and dispirited, looking like departed spirits being ferried across the melancholy Styx. The river now contracted rapidly to about 250 yards in width about ten miles from Magungo. We had left the vast flats of rush banks, and entered a channel between high ground, forming steep forest-covered hills, about 200 feet on either side, north and south: nevertheless there was no perceptible stream, although there was no doubt that we were actually in the channel of a river. The water was clear and exceedingly deep. In the evening we halted, and slept on a mud bank close to the water. The grass in the forest was very high and rank; thus we were glad to find an open space for a bivouac, although a nest of mosquitoes and malaria.

On waking the next morning, I observed that a thick fog covered the surface of the river; and as I lay upon my back, on my *angarep*, I amused myself before I woke my men by watching the fog slowly lifting from the river. While thus employed I was struck by the fact, that the little green water-plants, like floating cabbages (*Pistia Stratiotes*, L.), were certainly, although very slowly, moving to the west. I immediately jumped up, and watched them most attentively; there was no doubt about it; they were travelling towards the Albert Lake. We were now about eighteen miles in a direct line from Magungo, and there was a current in the river, which, however slight, was nevertheless perceptible.

Our toilette did not take long to arrange, as we had thrown ourselves down at night with our clothes on; accordingly we entered the canoe at once, and gave the order to start.

The woman Bacheeta knew the country, as she had formerly been to Magungo when in the service of Sali, who had been subsequently murdered by Kamrasi; she now informed me that we should terminate our canoe voyage on that day, as we should arrive at the great waterfall of which she had often spoken. As we proceeded the river gradually narrowed to about 180 yards, and when the paddles ceased working we could distinctly hear the roar of water. I had heard this on waking in the morning, but at the time I had imagined it to proceed from distant thunder. By ten o'clock the current had so increased as we proceeded, that it was distinctly perceptible, although weak. The roar of the waterfall was extremely loud, and after sharp pulling for a couple of hours, during which time the stream increased, we arrived at a few deserted fishing huts, at a point where the river made a slight turn. I never saw such an extraordinary show of crocodiles as were exposed on every sandbank on the sides of the river; they lay like logs of timber close together, and upon one bank we counted twenty-seven, of large size; every basking place was crowded in a similar manner. From the time we had fairly entered the river, it had been confined by heights somewhat precipitous on either side, rising to about 180 feet. At this point the cliffs were still higher, and exceedingly abrupt. From the roar of the water, I was sure that the fall would be in sight if we turned the corner at the bend of the river; accordingly I ordered the boatmen to row as far as they could: to this they at first objected, as they wished to stop at the deserted fishing village, which they explained was to be the limit of the journey, farther progress being impossible.

However, I explained that I merely wished to see the fall, and they rowed immediately up the stream, which was now strong against us. Upon rounding the corner, a magnificent sight burst suddenly upon us. On either side the river were beautifully wooded cliffs rising abruptly to a height of about 300 feet; rocks were jutting out from the intensely green foliage; and rushing through a gap that cleft the rock exactly before us, the river, contracted from a grand stream, was pent up in a narrow gorge of scarcely fifty yards in width; roaring furiously through the rock-bound pass, it plunged in one leap of about 120 feet perpendicular into a dark abyss below.

The fall of water was snow white, which had a superb effect as it contrasted with the dark cliffs that walled the river, while the graceful palms of the tropics and wild plantains perfected the beauty of the view. This was the greatest waterfall of the Nile, and, in honour of the distinguished President of the Royal Geographical Society, I named it the Murchison Falls, as the most important object throughout the entire course of the river.

The boatmen, having been promised a present of beads to induce them to approach the fall as close as possible, succeeded in bringing the canoe within about 300 yards of the base, but the power of the current and the whirlpools in the river rendered it impossible to proceed farther. There was a sandbank on our left which was literally covered with crocodiles lying parallel to each other like trunks of trees prepared for shipment; they had no fear of the canoe until we approached within about twenty yards of them, when they slowly crept into the water; all excepting one, an immense fellow who lazily lagged behind, and immediately dropped dead as a bullet from the little Fletcher No. 24 struck him in the brain. So alarmed were the boatmen at the unexpected report of the rifle that they immediately dropped into the body of the canoe, one of them losing his paddle. Nothing would induce them to attend to the boat, as I had fired a second shot at the crocodile as a *quietus*, and the natives did not know how often the alarming noise would be repeated. Accordingly we were at the mercy of the powerful stream, and the canoe was whisked round by the eddy and carried against a thick bank of high reeds; hardly had we touched this obstruction when a tremendous commotion took place in the rushes, and in an instant a great bull hippopotamus charged the canoe, and with a severe shock striking the bottom he lifted us half out of the water. The natives who were in the bottom of the boat positively yelled with terror, not knowing whether the shock was in any way connected with the dreaded report of the rifle; the black women screamed; and the boy Saat handing me a spare rifle, and

Richarn being ready likewise, we looked out for a shot should the angry hippo again attack us.

A few kicks bestowed by my angry men upon the recumbent boatmen restored them to the perpendicular. The first thing necessary was to hunt for the lost paddle that was floating down the rapid current. The hippopotamus, proud of having disturbed us, but doubtless thinking us rather hard of texture, raised his head to take a last view of his enemy, but sank too rapidly to permit a shot. Crocodile heads of enormous size were on all sides, appearing and vanishing rapidly as they rose to survey us; at one time we counted eighteen upon the surface. Fine fun it would have been for these monsters had the bull hippo been successful in his attempt to capsize us; the fat black woman, Karka, would have been a dainty morsel. Having recovered the lost paddle, I prevailed upon the boatmen to keep the canoe steady while I made a sketch of the Murchison Falls, which being completed, we drifted rapidly down to the landing place at the deserted fishing village, and bade adieu to the navigation of the lake and river of Central Africa.

The few huts that existed in this spot were mere ruins. Clouds had portended rain, and down it came, as it usually did once in every twenty-four hours. However, that passed away by the next morning, and the day broke discovering us about as wet and wretched as we were accustomed to be. I now started off four of my men with the boatmen and the interpreter Bacheeta to the nearest village, to inquire whether our guide Rabonga had arrived with our riding oxen, as our future travelling was to be on land, and the limit of our navigation must have been well known to him. After some hours the people returned, minus the boatmen, with a message from the headman of a village they had visited, that the oxen were there, but not the guide Rabonga, who had remained at Magungo, but that the animals should be brought to us that evening, together with porters to convey the luggage. In the evening a number of people arrived, bringing some plantain cider and plantains as a present from the headman; and promising that, upon the following morning, we should be conducted to his village.

The next day we started, but not until the afternoon, as we had to await the arrival of the headman, who was to escort us. Our oxen were brought, and if we looked wretched, the animals were a match. They had been bitten by the fly, thousands of which were at this spot. Their coats were staring, ears drooping, noses running, and heads hanging down; all the symptoms of fly-bite, together with extreme looseness of the bowels. I saw that it was all up with our animals. Weak as I was myself, I was obliged to walk, as my ox could not carry me up the steep inclination, and I toiled languidly to the summit of the cliff. It poured with rain. Upon arrival at the summit we were in precisely the same parklike land that characterises Chopi and Unyoro, but the grass was about seven feet high; and from the constant rain, and the extreme fertility of the soil, the country was choked with vegetation. We were now above the Murchison Falls, and we heard the roaring of the water beneath us to our left. We continued our route parallel to the river above the Falls, steering east; and a little before evening we arrived at a small village belonging to the headman who accompanied us. I was chilled and wet; my wife had fortunately been carried on her litter, which was protected by a hide roofing. Feverish and exhausted, I procured from the natives some good acid plums, and refreshed by these I was able to boil my thermometer and take the altitude.

On the following morning we started, the route as before parallel to the river, and so close that the roar of the rapids was extremely loud. The river flowed in a deep ravine upon our left. We continued for a day's march along the Somerset, crossing many ravines and torrents, until we turned suddenly down to the left, and arriving at the bank we were to be transported to an island called Patooan, that was the residence of a chief. It was about an hour after sunset, and being dark, my riding ox, who was being driven as too weak to carry me, fell into an elephant pitfall. After much hallooing, a canoe was brought from the island, which was not more than fifty yards from the mainland, and we were ferried across. We were both very ill with a sudden attack of fever; and my wife, not being able to stand, was, on arrival at the island, carried on a litter I knew not whither, escorted by some of my men, while I lay down on the wet ground quite exhausted with the annihilating disease. At length the remainder of my men crossed over, and those who had carried my wife to the village returning with firebrands, I managed to creep after them with the aid of a long stick, upon which I rested with both hands. After a walk, through a forest of high trees, for about a quarter of a mile, I arrived at a village where I was shown a wretched hut, the stars being visible through the roof. In this my wife lay dreadfully ill upon her *angarep*, and I fell down upon some straw. About an hour later, a violent thunderstorm broke over us, and our hut was perfectly flooded; we, being far too ill and helpless to move from our positions, remained dripping wet and shivering with fever until the morning. Our servants and people had, like all natives, made themselves much more comfortable than their employers; nor did they attempt to interfere with our misery in any way until summoned to appear at sunrise.

The island of Patooan was about half a mile long by 150 yards wide, and was one of the numerous masses of rocks that choke the river between Karuma Falls and the great Murchison cataract. The rock was entirely of grey granite, from the clefts of which beautiful forest trees grew so thickly that the entire island was in shade. In the middle of this secluded spot was a considerable village, thickly inhabited, as the population of the mainland had fled from their dwellings and had taken refuge upon the numerous river islands, as the war was raging between Rionga and Kamrasi. A succession of islands from the east of Patooan continued to within a march of Karuma Falls. These were in the possession of Rionga, and a still more powerful chief and ally, Fowooka, who were the deadly enemies of Kamrasi.

It now appeared that after my departure from M'Rooli to search for the lake, Ibrahim had been instructed by Kamrasi to accompany his army, and attack Fowooka. This had been effected, but the attack had been confined to a bombardment by musketry from the high cliffs of the river upon the people confined upon one of the islands. A number of men had been killed, and Ibrahim had returned to Gondokoro with a quantity of ivory and porters supplied by Kamrasi; but he had left ten of his armed men as hostages with the king, to act as his guard until he should return on the following year to Unyoro. Ibrahim and his strong party having quitted the country, Fowooka had invaded the mainland of Chopi, and had burnt and destroyed all the villages, and killed many people, including a powerful chief of Kamrasi's, the father of the headman of the island of Patooan where we were now staying. Accordingly the fugitives from the destroyed villages had taken refuge upon the island of Patooan, and others of the same character. The headman informed us that it would be impossible to proceed along the bank of the river to Karuma, as that entire line of country was in possession of the enemy. This was sufficient to assure me that I should not procure porters.

There was no end to the difficulties and trouble in this horrible country. My exploration was completed, as it was by no means necessary to continue the route from Patooan to Karuma. I had followed the Somerset from its junction with the lake at Magungo to this point; here it was a beautiful river, precisely similar in character to the point at which I had left it at Karuma: we were now within thirty miles of that place, and about eighteen miles from the point opposite Rionga's island, where we had first hit upon the river on our arrival from the north. The direction was perfectly in accordance with my observations at Karuma, and at Magungo, the Somerset running from east to west. The river was about 180 to 200 yards in width, but much obstructed with rocks and islands; the stream ran at about four miles per hour, and the rapids and falls were so numerous that the roar of water had been continuous throughout our march from Murchison Falls. By observations of Casella's thermometer I made the altitude of the river level at the island of Patooan 3,195 feet; thus from this point to the level of the Albert Lake at Magungo there was a fall of 475 feet – this difference being included between Patooan and the foot of Murchison Falls: the latter, being at the lowest estimate 120 feet, left 355 feet to be accounted for between Patooan and the top of the falls. As the ledges of rock throughout the course of the river formed a series of steps, this was a natural difference in altitude that suggested the correctness of the observations.

At the river level below Karuma Falls I had measured the altitude at 3,996 feet above the sea level. Thus, there was a fall from that point to Patooan of 801 feet, and a total of 1,276 feet in the descent of the river from Karuma to the Albert N'Yanza. These measurements, most carefully taken, corroborated the opinion suggested by the natural appearance of the river, which was a mere succession of cataracts throughout its westerly course from Karuma.

To me these observations were more than usually interesting, as when I had met my friend Speke at Gondokoro he was much perplexed concerning the extraordinary difference in his observation between the altitude of the river level at Karuma Falls, lat. 2 degrees 15', and at Gebel Kookoo in the Madi country, lat. 3 degrees 34', the point at which he subsequently met the river. He knew that both rivers were the Nile, as he bad been told this by the natives; the one, before it had joined the Albert Lake – the other, after its exit; but he had been told that the river was navigable from Gebel Kookoo, lat. 3 degrees 34', straight up to the junction of the lake; thus, there could be no great difference in altitude between the lake and the Nile where he met it, in lat. 3 degrees 34'. Nevertheless, he found so enormous a difference in his observations between the river at Karuma and at Gebel Kookoo, that he concluded there must be a fall between Karuma and the Albert Lake of at least 1,000 feet; by careful measurements I proved the closeness of his reasoning and observation, by finding a fall of only 275 feet more than he had anticipated. From Karuma to the Albert Lake (although unvisited by Speke), he had marked upon his map, "river falls 1,000 feet;" by actual measurement I proved it to be 1,275 feet.

The altitudes measured by me have been examined, and the thermometer that I used had been tested at Kew, and its errors corrected since my return to England; thus all altitudes observed with that thermometer should be correct, as the results, after correction by Mr. Dunkin, of the Greenwich Royal Observatory, are those now quoted. It will therefore be interesting to compare the observations taken at the various points on the Nile and Albert Lake in the countries of Unyoro and Chopi – the correctness of which relatively will be seen by comparison:

1861
Jan. 22. Rionga's island, 80 feet above the Nile 3,864 Ft.
Jan. 25. Karuma, below the falls, river level Atadaj 3,996 Ft.
Jan. 31. So. of Karuma, river level on road to M'Rooli 4,056 Ft.
1864
Feb. 21. M'Rooli lat. 1 degree 38' river level 4,061 Ft.
Mar. 14. Albert N'Yanza, lake level 2,720 Ft.
April 7. Island of Patooan (Shooa Moru) river level 3,195 Ft.

By these observations it will be seen that from M'Rooli, in lat. 1 degree 38' to Karuma in lat. 2 degree 15', there is a fall of sixty-five feet; say minus five feet, for the Karuma Falls equals sixty feet fall in 37' of latitude; or allowing for the great bend of the river, twenty miles of extra course, it will be equal to about sixty statute miles of actual river from M'Rooli to Atada or Karuma Falls, showing a fall or one foot per mile. From M'Rooli to the head of the Karuma Falls the river is navigable; thus the observations of altitudes showing a fall of one foot per mile must be extremely accurate.

The next observations to be compared are those from Karuma Falls throughout the westerly course of the river to the Albert Lake:

River level below Karuma Falls 3,996 Ft.
Rionga's island 3,864 – 80 Ft. cliff
3,784 Ft. – 212 fall to the west
River level at island of Patooan (Shooa Moru)
3,195 Ft.– 589 fall from Rionga's island
Level of Albert Lake 2,720 Ft. – 475 fall from Patooan to lake
From Karuma 1,276 Ft. fall

These observations were extremely satisfactory, and showed that the thermometer (Casella's) behaved well at every boiling, as there was no confusion of altitudes, but each observation corroborated the preceding. The latitude of the island of Patooan by observation was 2 degrees 16': we were thus due west of Magungo, and east of Karuma Falls.

Chapter XIII

TREACHEROUS DESIGNS OF THE NATIVES

We were prisoners on the island of Patooan, as we could not procure porters at any price to remove our effects. We had lost all our riding oxen within a few days; they had succumbed to the flies, and the only animal alive was already half dead; this was the little bull that had always carried the boy Saat. It was the 8th April, and within a few days the boats upon which we depended for our return to civilization would assuredly quit Gondokoro. I offered the natives all the beads that I had (about 50 lbs.) and the whole of my baggage, if they would carry us to Shooa direct from this spot. We were in perfect despair, as we were both completely worn out with fever and fatigue, and certain death seemed to stare us in the face should we remain in this unhealthy spot; worse than death was the idea of losing the boats and becoming prisoners for another year in this dreadful land; which must inevitably happen should we not hurry direct to Gondokoro without delay. The natives, with their usual cunning, at length offered to convey us to Shooa, provided that I paid them the beads in advance; the boats were prepared to ferry us across the river, but I fortunately discovered through the woman Bacheeta their treacherous intention of placing us on the uninhabited wilderness on the north side, and leaving us to die of hunger. They had conspired together to land us, but to immediately return with the boats after having thus got rid of the incubus of their guests.

We were in a great dilemma – had we been in good health, I would have forsaken everything but the guns and ammunition, and have marched direct to Gondokoro on foot: but this was utterly impossible; neither my wife nor I could walk a quarter of a mile without fainting – there was no guide – and the country was now overgrown with impenetrable grass and tangled vegetation eight feet high; we were in the midst of the rainy season – not a day passed without a few hours of deluge; altogether it was a most heartbreaking position. Added to the distress of mind at being thus thwarted, there was also a great scarcity of provision. Many of my men were weak, the whole party having suffered much from fever – in fact, we were completely helpless.

Our guide Rabonga, who had accompanied us from M'Rooli, had absconded, and we were left to shift for ourselves. I was determined not to remain on the island, as I suspected that the boats might be taken away, and that we should be kept prisoners; I therefore ordered my men to take the canoes, and to ferry us to the mainland, from whence we had come. The headman, upon hearing this order, offered to carry us to a village, and then to await orders from Kamrasi as to whether we were to be forwarded to Shooa or not. The district in which the island of Patooan was situated was called Shooa Moru, although having no connexion with the Shooa in the Madi country to which we were bound.

We were ferried across to the main shore, and both in our respective *angareps* were carried by the natives for about three miles: arriving at a deserted village, half of which was in ashes, having been burnt and plundered by the enemy, we were deposited on the ground in front of an old hut in the pouring rain, and were informed that we should remain there that night, but that on the following morning we should proceed to our destination.

Not trusting the natives, I ordered my men to disarm them, and to retain their spears and shields as security for their appearance on the following day. This effected, we were carried into a filthy hut about six inches deep in mud, as the roof was much out of repair, and the heavy rain had flooded it daily for some weeks. I had a canal cut through the muddy floor, and in misery and low spirits we took possession.

On the following morning not a native was present! We had been entirely deserted; although I held the spears and shields, every man had absconded – there were neither inhabitants nor provisions – the whole country was a wilderness of rank grass that hemmed us in on all sides; not an animal, nor even a bird, was to be seen; it was a miserable, damp, lifeless country. We were on elevated ground, and the valley of the Somerset was about two miles to our north, the river roaring sullenly in its obstructed passage, its course marked by the double belt of huge dark trees that grew upon its banks.

My men were naturally outrageous, and they proposed that we should return to Patooan, seize the canoes, and take provisions by force, as we had been disgracefully deceived. The natives had merely deposited us here to get us out of the way, and in this spot we might starve. Of course I would not countenance the proposal of seizing provisions, but I directed my men to search among the ruined villages for buried corn, in company with the woman Bacheeta, who, being a native of this country, would be up to the ways of the people, and might assist in the discovery.

After some hours passed in rambling over the black ashes of several villages that had been burnt, they discovered a hollow place, by sounding the earth with a stick, and, upon digging, they arrived at a granary of the seed known as *tullaboon*; this was a great prize, as, although mouldy and bitter, it would keep us from starving. The women of the party were soon hard at work grinding, as many of the necessary stones had been found among the ruins.

Fortunately there were three varieties of plants growing wild in great profusion, that, when boiled, were a good substitute for spinach; thus we were rich in vegetables, although without a morsel of fat or animal food. Our dinner consisted daily of a mess of black porridge of bitter mouldy flour, that no English pig would condescend to notice, and a large dish of spinach. "Better a dinner of herbs where love is, etc." often occurred to me; but I am not sure that I was quite of that opinion after a fortnight's grazing upon spinach.

Tea and coffee were things of the past, the very idea of which made our mouths water; but I found a species of wild thyme growing in the jungles, and this, when boiled, formed a tolerable substitute for tea; sometimes our men procured a little wild honey, which, added to the thyme tea, we considered a great luxury.

This wretched fare, in our exhausted state from fever and general effects of climate, so completely disabled us that for nearly two months my wife lay helpless on one *angarep*, and I upon the other;

neither of us could walk. The hut was like all in Kamrasi's country, a perfect forest of thick poles to support the roof (I counted thirty-two); thus, although it was tolerably large, there was but little accommodation. These poles we now found very convenient, as we were so weak, that we could not rise from bed without hauling by one of the supports.

We were very nearly dead, and our amusement was a childish conversation about the good things in England, and my idea of perfect happiness was an English beefsteak and a bottle of pale ale; for such a luxury I would most willingly have sold my birthright at that hungry moment. We were perfect skeletons; and it was annoying to see how we suffered upon the bad fare, while our men apparently throve. There were plenty of wild red peppers, and the men seemed to enjoy a mixture of porridge and legumes *a la sauce piquante.* They were astonished at my falling away on this food, but they yielded to my argument when I suggested that "a lion would starve where a donkey grew fat." I must confess that this state of existence did not improve my temper, which, I fear, became nearly as bitter as the porridge. My people had a windfall of luck, as Saat's ox, that had lingered for a long time, lay down to die, and stretching himself out, commenced kicking his last kick; the men immediately assisted him by cutting his throat, and this supply of beef was a luxury which, even in my hungry state, was not the English beefsteak for which I sighed; and I declined the diseased bull.

The men made several long excursions through the country to endeavour to purchase provisions, but in two months they procured only two kids; the entire country was deserted, owing to the war between Kamrasi and Fowooka. Every day the boy Saat and the woman Bacheeta sallied out and conversed with the inhabitants of the different islands on the river; sometimes, but very rarely, they returned with a fowl; such an event caused great rejoicing.

We had now given up all hope of Gondokoro, and were perfectly resigned to our fate; this, we felt sure, was to be buried in Chopi. I wrote instructions in my journal, in case of death, and told my headman to be sure to deliver my maps, observations, and papers to the English Consul at Khartoum; this was my only care, as I feared that all my labour might be lost should I die. I had no fear for my wife, as she was quite as bad as I, and if one should die, the other would certainly follow; in fact, this had been agreed upon, lest she should fall into the hands of Kamrasi at my death. We had struggled to win, and I thanked God that we had won; if death were to be the price, at all events we were at the goal, and we both looked upon death rather as a pleasure, as affording rest; there would be no more suffering; no fever; no long journey before us, that in our weak state was an infliction; the only wish was to lay down the burden.

Curious is the warfare between the animal instincts and the mind! Death would have been a release that I would have courted, but I should have liked that one English beefsteak and pale ale before I died! During our misery of constant fever and starvation at Shooa Moru, insult had been added to injury. There was no doubt that we had been thus deserted by Kamrasi's orders, as every seven or eight days one of his chiefs arrived, and told me that the king was with his army only four days' march from me, and that he was preparing to attack Fowooka, but that he wished me to join him, as with my fourteen guns we should win a great victory. This treacherous conduct, after his promise to forward me without delay to Shooa, enraged me exceedingly. We had lost the boats at Gondokoro, and we were now nailed to the country for another year, should we live, which was not likely; not only had the brutal king thus deceived us, but he was deliberately starving us into conditions, his aim being that my men should assist him against his enemy. At one time the old enemy tempted me sorely to join Fowooka against Kamrasi; but, discarding the idea, generated in a moment of passion, I determined to resist his proposals to the last. It was perfectly true that the king was within thirty miles of us, that he was aware of our misery; and he made use of our extremity to force us to become his allies.

After more than two months passed in this distress it became evident that something must be done; I sent my headman, or *vakeel*, and one man, with a native as a guide (that Saat and Bacheeta had procured from an island), with instructions to go direct to Kamrasi, to abuse him thoroughly in my name for having thus treated us, and tell him that I was much insulted at his treating with me through a third party in proposing an alliance. My *vakeel* was to explain that I was a much more powerful chief than Kamrasi, and that if he required my alliance, he must treat with me in person, and immediately send fifty men to transport my wife, myself, and effects to his camp, where we might, in a personal interview, come to terms. I told my *vakeel* to return to me with the fifty men, and to be sure to bring from Kamrasi some token by which I should know that he had actually seen him. The *vakeel* and Yaseen started.

After some days, the absconded guide, Rabonga, appeared with a number of men, but without either my *vakeel* or Yaseen. He carried with him a small gourd bottle, carefully stopped; this he broke, and extracted from the inside two pieces of printed paper, that Kamrasi had sent to me in reply.

On examining the papers, I found them to be portions of the English Church Service translated into (I think) the Kiswahili language, by Dr. Krapf! There were many notes in pencil on the margin, written in English, as translations of words in the text. It quickly occurred to me that Speke must have given this book to Kamrasi on his arrival from Zanzibar, and that he now extracted the leaves, and sent them to me as the token I had demanded to show that my message had been delivered to him. Rabonga made a lame excuse for his previous desertion; he delivered a thin ox that Kamrasi had sent me, and he declared that his orders were, that he should take my whole party immediately to Kamrasi, as he was anxious that we should attack Fowooka without loss of time; we were positively to start on the following morning! My bait had taken, and we should escape from this frightful spot, Shooa Moru.

On the following morning we were carried in our litters by a number of men. The ox had been killed, the whole party had revelled in good food, and a supply sufficient for the journey was taken by my men.

Without inflicting the tedium of the journey upon the reader, it will be sufficient to say that the country was the same as usual, being a vast park overgrown with immense grass. Every day the porters bolted, and we were left deserted at the charred ruins of various villages that had been plundered by Fowooka's people. It poured with rain; there was no cover, as all the huts had been burnt, and we were stricken with severe fever daily. However, after five days of absurdly slow marching, the roar of the rapids being distinctly audible at night, we arrived one morning at a deserted camp of about 3,000 huts, which were just being ignited by several natives. This had been Kamrasi's headquarters, which he had quitted, and according to native custom it was to be destroyed by fire. It was reported that the king had removed to another position within an hour's march, and that he had constructed a new camp. Although throughout the journey from Shooa Moru the country had been excessively wild and uncultivated, this neighbourhood was a mass of extensive plantain groves and burnt villages, but every plantain tree had been cut through the middle and recklessly destroyed. This destruction had been perpetrated by Fowooka's people, who had invaded the country, but had retreated on the advance of Kamrasi's army.

After winding through dense jungles of bamboos and interminable groves of destroyed plantains, we perceived the tops of a number of grass huts appearing among the trees. My men now begged to be allowed to fire a salute, as it was reported that the ten men of Ibrahim's party who had been left as hostages were quartered at this village with Kamrasi. Hardly had the firing commenced, when it was immediately replied to by the Turks from their camp, who, upon our approach, came out to meet us with great manifestations of delight and wonder at our having accomplished our long and difficult voyage.

My *vakeel* and Yaseen were the first to meet us, with an apology that severe fever had compelled them to remain in camp instead of returning to Shooa Moru according to my orders, but they had delivered my message to Kamrasi, who had, as I had supposed, sent two leaves out of a book Speke had given him, as a reply. An immense amount of news had to be exchanged between my men and those of Ibrahim; they had quite given us up for lost, until they heard that we were at Shooa Moru. A report had reached them that my wife was dead, and that I had died a few days later. A great amount of kissing and embracing took place, Arab fashion, between the two parties; and they all came to kiss my hand and that of my wife, with the exclamation, that "By Allah, no woman in the world had a heart so tough as to dare to face what she had gone through. *El hamd el Illah! El hamd el Illah bel salaam* (Thank God – be grateful to God)!" was exclaimed on all sides by the swarthy throng of brigands who pressed round us, really glad to welcome us back again; and I could not help thinking of the difference in their manner now and fourteen months ago, when they had attempted to drive us back from Gondokoro.

On entering the village I found a hut prepared for me by the orders of my *vakeel*: it was very small, and I immediately ordered a fence and courtyard to be constructed. There were great numbers of natives, and a crowd of noisy fellows pressed around us that were only dispersed by a liberal allowance of the stick, well laid on by the Turks, who were not quite so mild in their ways as my people. A fat ox was immediately slaughtered by the *vakeel* commanding the Turks' party, and a great feast was soon in preparation, as our people were determined to fraternize.

Hardly were we seated in our hut, when my *vakeel* announced that Kamrasi had arrived to pay me a visit. In a few minutes he was ushered into the hut. Far from being abashed, he entered with a loud laugh totally different to his former dignified manner." Well, here you are at last!" he exclaimed. Apparently highly amused with our wretched appearance, he continued, "So you have been to the M'Wootan N'Zige! Well, you don't look much the better for it; why, I should not have known you! Ha, ha, ha!" I was not in a humour to enjoy his attempts at facetiousness; I therefore told him, that he had behaved disgracefully and meanly, and that I should publish his character among the adjoining tribes as below that of the most petty chief that I had ever seen. "Never mind," he replied, "it's all over now; you really are thin, both of you; it was your own fault; why did you not agree to fight Fowooka? You should have been supplied with fat cows and milk and butter, had you behaved well. I will have my men ready to attack Fowooka tomorrow; the Turks have ten men; you have thirteen; thirteen and ten make twenty-three; you shall be carried if you can't walk, and we will give Fowooka no chance – he must be killed – only kill him, and MY BROTHER will give you half of his kingdom." He continued, "You shall have supplies tomorrow; I will go to my brother, who is the great M'Kammaa Kamrasi, and he will send you all you require. I am a little man, he is a big one; I have nothing; he has everything, and he longs to see you; you must go to him directly, he lives close by." I hardly knew whether he was drunk or sober. "My brother the great M'Kamma Kamrasi!" I felt bewildered with astonishment:

then, "If you are not Kamrasi, pray who are you?" I asked. "Who am I?" he replied, "ha, ha, ha! That's very good; who am I? Why, I am M'Gambi, the brother of Kamrasi; I am the younger brother, but he is the king."

The deceit of this country was incredible – I had positively never seen the real Kamrasi up to this moment, and this man M'Gambi now confessed to having impersonated the king his brother, as Kamrasi was afraid that I might be in league with Debono's people to murder him, and therefore he had ordered his brother M'Gambi to act the king.

I now remembered, that the woman Bacheeta had on several occasions during the journey told us that the Kamrasi we had seen was not the true M'Kamma Kamrasi; but at the time I had paid little attention to her, as she was constantly grumbling, and I imagined that this was merely said in ill temper, referring to her murdered master Sali as the rightful king.

I called the *vakeel* of the Turks, Eddrees: he said, that he also had heard long since that M'Gambi was not Kamrasi as we had all supposed, but that he had never seen the great king, as M'Gambi had always acted as viceroy; he confirmed the accounts I had just received, that the real Kamrasi was not far from this village, the name of which was Kisoona. I told M'Gambi that I did not wish to see his brother the king, as I should perhaps be again deceived and be introduced to some impostor like himself; and that as I did not choose to be made a fool of, I should decline the introduction. This distressed him exceedingly; he said, that the king was really so great a man that he, his own brother, dared not sit on a stool in his presence, and that he had only kept in retirement as a matter of precaution, as Debono's people had allied themselves with his enemy Rionga in the preceding year, and he dreaded treachery. I laughed contemptuously at M'Gambi, telling him that if a woman like my wife dared to trust herself far from her own country among such savages as Kamrasi's people, their king must be weaker than a woman if he dare not show himself in his own territory. I concluded by saying, that I should not go to see Kamrasi, but that he should come to visit me. M'Gambi promised to send a good cow on the following morning, as we had not tasted milk for some months, and we were in great want of strengthening food. He took his leave, having received a small present of minute beads of various colours.

I could not help wondering at the curious combination of pride and abject cowardice that had been displayed by the redoubted Kamrasi ever since our first entrance to his territory. Speke when at Gondokoro had told me how he had been kept waiting for fifteen days before the king had condescended to see him. I now understood that this delay had been occasioned more by fear than pride, and that, in his cowardice, the king fell back upon his dignity as an excuse for absenting himself.

With the addition of the Turks' party we were now twenty-four armed men. Although they had not seen the real king Kamrasi, they had been well treated since Ibrahim's departure, having received each a present of a young slave girl as a wife, while, as a distinguishing mark of royal favour, the *vakeel* Eddrees had received two wives instead of one; they had also received regular supplies of flour and beef – the latter in the shape of a fat ox presented every seventh day, together with a liberal supply of plantain cider.

On the following morning after my arrival at Kisoona, M'Gambi appeared, beseeching me to go and visit the king. I replied that I was hungry and weak from want of food, and that I wanted to see meat, and not the man who had starved me. In the afternoon a beautiful cow appeared with her young calf, also a fat sheep, and two pots of plantain cider, as a present from Kamrasi. That evening we revelled in milk, a luxury that we had not tasted for some months. The cow gave such a quantity that we looked forward to the establishment of a dairy and already contemplated cheesemaking. I sent the king a present of a pound of powder in canister, a box of caps and a variety of trifles, explaining that I was quite out of stores and presents, as I had been kept so long in his country that I was reduced to beggary, as I had expected to have returned to my own country long before this.

In the evening, M'Gambi appeared with a message from the king, saying that I was his greatest friend, and that he would not think of taking anything from me, as he was sure that I must be hard up; that he desired nothing, but would be much obliged if I would give him the little double rifle that I always carried, and my watch and compass! He wanted "nothing," only my Fletcher rifle, that I would as soon have parted with as the bone of my arm: and these three articles were the same for which I had been so pertinaciously bored before my departure from M'Rooli. It was of no use to be wroth; I therefore quietly replied that I should not give them, as Kamrasi had failed in his promise to forward me to Shooa; but that I required no presents from him, as he always expected a thousandfold in return. M'Gambi said that all would be right if I would only agree to pay the king a visit. I objected to this, as I told him the king, his brother, did not want to see me, but only to observe what I had, in order to beg for all that he saw. He appeared much hurt, and assured me that he would be himself responsible that nothing of the kind should happen, and that he merely begged as a favour that I would visit the king on the following morning, and that people should be ready to carry me if I were unable to walk. Accordingly I arranged to be carried to Kamrasi's camp at about 8 a.m.

At the hour appointed M'Gambi appeared, with a great crowd of natives. My clothes were in rags – and as personal appearance has a certain effect, even in Central Africa, I determined to present myself to the king in as favourable a light as possible. I happened to possess a full-dress Highland suit that I had worn when I lived in Perthshire many years ago; this I had treasured as serviceable upon an occasion like the present; accordingly I was quickly attired in kilt, sporran, and Glengarry bonnet, and to the utter amazement of the crowd, the ragged-looking object that had arrived in Kisoona now issued from the obscure hut, with plaid and kilt of Athole tartan. A general shout of exclamation arose from the assembled crowd; and taking my seat upon an *angarep*, I was immediately shouldered by a number of men, and attended by ten of my people as escorts, I was carried towards the camp of the great Kamrasi.

In about half an hour we arrived. The camp, composed of grass huts, extended over a large extent of ground, and the approach was perfectly black with the throng that crowded to meet me. Women, children, dogs, and men all thronged at the entrance of the street that led to Kamrasi's residence. Pushing our way through this inquisitive multitude, we continued through the camp until at length we reached the dwelling of the king. Halting for the moment, a message was immediately received that we should proceed; we accordingly entered through a narrow passage between high reed fences, and I found myself in the presence of the actual king of Unyoro, Kamrasi. He was sitting in a kind of porch in front of a hut, and upon seeing me he hardly condescended to look at me for more than a moment; he then turned to his attendants and made some remark that appeared to amuse them, as they all grinned as little men are wont to do when a great man makes a bad joke.

I had ordered one of my men to carry my stool; I was determined not to sit upon the earth, as the king would glory in my humiliation. M'Gambi, his brother, who had formerly played the part of king, now sat upon the ground a few feet from Kamrasi, who was seated upon the same stool of copper that M'Gambi had used when I first saw him at M'Rooli. Several of his chiefs also sat upon the straw with which the porch was littered. I made a *salaam* and took my seat upon my stool. Not a word passed between us for about five minutes, during which time the king eyed me most attentively, and made various remarks to the chiefs who were present; at length he asked me why I had not been to see him before. I replied, "Because I had been starved in his country, and I was too weak to walk." He said I should soon be strong, as he would now give me a good supply of food, but that he could not send provisions to Shooa Moru, as Fowooka held that country. Without replying to this wretched excuse for his neglect, I merely told him that I was happy to have seen him before my departure, as I was not aware until recently that I had been duped by M'Gambi. He answered me very coolly, saying that although I had not seen him he had nevertheless seen me, as he was among the crowd of native escort on the day that we left M'Rooli. Thus he had watched our start at the very place where his brother M'Gambi had impersonated the king.

Kamrasi was a remarkably fine man, tall and well proportioned, with a handsome face of a dark brown colour, but a peculiarly sinister expression; he was beautifully clean, and instead of wearing the bark cloth common among the people, he was dressed in a fine mantle of black and white goatskins, as soft as chamois leather. His people sat on the ground at some distance from his throne; when they approached to address him on any subject they crawled upon their hands and knees to his feet, and touched the ground with their foreheads.

True to his natural instincts, the king commenced begging, and being much struck with the Highland costume, he demanded it as a proof of friendship, saying, that if I refused I could not be his friend. The watch, compass, and double Fletcher rifle were asked for in their turn, all of which I refused to give him. He appeared much annoyed, therefore I presented him with a pound canister of powder, a box of caps, and a few bullets. He replied, "What's the use of the ammunition if you won't give me your rifle?" I explained that I had already given him a gun, and that he had a rifle of Speke's. Disgusted with his importunity I rose to depart, telling him that "I should not return to visit him, as I did not believe he was the real Kamrasi. I had heard that Kamrasi was a great king, but that he was a mere beggar, and was doubtless an impostor, like M'Gambi." At this he seemed highly amused, and begged me not to leave so suddenly, as he could not permit me to depart empty handed. He then gave certain orders to his people, and after a little delay, two loads of flour arrived, together with a goat and two jars of sour plantain cider. These presents he ordered to be forwarded to Kisoona. I rose to take leave, but the crowd, eager to see what was going forward, pressed closely upon the entrance of the approach; seeing which, the king gave certain orders, and immediately four or five men with long heavy bludgeons rushed at the mob and belaboured them right and left, putting the mass to flight pell-mell through the narrow lanes of the camp.

I was then carried back to my camp at Kisoona, where I was received by a great crowd of people.

Chapter XIV

AT HOME IN KISOONA

IT appeared that Kisoona was to be headquarters until I should have an opportunity of quitting the country for Shooa. Therefore I constructed a comfortable little hut surrounded by a courtyard strongly fenced, in which I arranged a Rakooba, or open shed, in which to sit during the hottest hours of the day.

My cow that I had received from Kamrasi gave plenty of milk, and every second day we were enabled to make a small cheese about the size of a six-pound cannon-shot. The abundance of milk made a rapid change in our appearance; and Kisoona, although a place of complete *ennui*, was a delightful change after the privations of the last four months. Every week the king sent me an ox and a quantity of flour for myself and people, and the whole party grew fat. We used the milk native fashion, never drinking it until curdled; taken in this form it will agree with the most delicate stomach, but if used fresh in large quantities it induces biliousness. The young girls of thirteen and fourteen that are the wives of the king are not appreciated unless extremely fat – they are subjected to a regular system of fattening in order to increase their charms; thus at an early age they are compelled to drink daily about a gallon of curded milk, the swallowing of which is frequently enforced by the whip; the result is extreme obesity. In hot climates milk will curdle in two or three hours if placed in a vessel that has previously contained sour milk. When curdled it should be well beaten together until it assumes the appearance of cream; in this state, if seasoned with a little salt, it is most nourishing and easy of digestion. The Arabs invariably use it in this manner, and improve it by the addition of red pepper. The natives of Unyoro will not eat red pepper, as they believe that men and women become barren by its use.

Although the fever had so completely taken possession of me that I was subject to an attack almost daily, the milk fattened me extremely, and kept up my strength, which otherwise must have failed. The change from starvation to good food produced a marvellous effect. Curious as it may appear, although we were in a land of plantains, the ripe fruit was in the greatest scarcity. The natives invariably eat them unripe, the green fruit when boiled being a fair substitute for potatoes – the ripe plantains were used for brewing plantain cider, but they were never eaten. The method of cider-making was simple. The fruit was buried in a deep hole and covered with straw and earth; at the expiration of about eight days the green plantains thus interred had become ripe; they were then peeled and pulped within a large wooden trough resembling a canoe; this was filled with water, and the pulp being well mashed and stirred, it was left to ferment for two days, after which time it was fit to drink.

Throughout the country of Unyoro, plantains in various forms were the staple article of food, upon which the inhabitants placed more dependence than upon all other crops. The green plantains were not only used as potatoes, but when peeled they were cut in thin slices and dried in the sun until crisp; in this state they were stored in the granaries, and when required for use they were boiled into a pulp and made into a most palatable soup or stew. Flour of plantains was remarkably good; this was made by grinding the fruit when dried as described; it was then, as usual with all other articles in that country, most beautifully packed in long narrow parcels, either formed of plantain bark or of the white interior of rushes worked into mats. This bark served as brown paper, but had the advantage of being waterproof. The fibre of the plantain formed both thread and cord, thus the principal requirements of the natives were supplied by this most useful tree. The natives were exceedingly clever in working braid from the plantain fibre, which was of so fine a texture that it had the appearance of a hair chain; nor could the difference be detected without a close examination. Small bags netted with the same twine were most delicate, and in all that was produced in Unyoro there was a remarkably good taste displayed in the manufacture.

The beads most valued were the white opal, the red porcelain, and the minute varieties generally used for working on screens in England; these small beads (These were given to me by Speke at Gondokoro) of various colours were much esteemed, and were worked into pretty ornaments, about the shape of a walnut, to be worn suspended from the neck. I had a small quantity of the latter variety that I presented to Kamrasi, who prized them as we should value precious stones.

Not only were the natives clever generally in their ideas, but they were exceedingly cunning in their bargains. Every morning, shortly after sunrise, men might be heard crying their wares throughout the camp – such as, "Tobacco, tobacco; two packets going for either beads or *simbis* (cowrie shells)!" "Milk to sell for beads or salt!" "Salt to exchange for lance-heads!" "Coffee, coffee, going cheap for red beads!" "Butter for five *jenettos* (red beads – these were given to me by Speke at Gondokoro) a lump!"

The butter was invariably packed in a plantain leaf, but frequently the package was plastered with cow dung and clay, which, when dry, formed a hard coating, and protected it from the air; this gave it a bad flavour, and we returned it to the dealer as useless. A short time after, he returned with fresh butter in a perfectly new green leaf, and we were requested to taste it. Being about the size and shape of a cocoanut, and wrapped carefully in a leaf with only the point exposed, I of course tasted from that portion, and approving the flavour, the purchase was completed. We were fairly cheated, as the butter dealer had packed the old rejected butter in a fresh leaf, and had placed a small piece of sweet butter on the top as a tasting point. They constantly attempted this trick.

As retailers they took extraordinary pains to divide everything into minimum packets, which they sold for a few beads, always declaring that they had only one packet to dispose of, but immediately producing another when that was sold. This method of dealing was exceedingly troublesome, as it was difficult to obtain supplies in any quantity. My only resource was to send Saat to market daily to purchase all he could find, and he usually returned after some hours' absence with a basket containing coffee, tobacco, and butter.

We were comfortably settled at Kisoona, and the luxury of coffee after so long an abstinence was a perfect blessing. Nevertheless, in spite of good food, I was a martyr to fever, which attacked me daily at about 2 p.m. and continued until sunset. Being without quinine I tried vapour baths, and by the recommendation of one of the Turks I pounded and boiled a quantity of the leaves of the castor-oil plant in a large pot containing about four gallons: this plant was in great abundance. Every morning I arranged a bath by sitting in a blanket, thus forming a kind of tent, with the pot of boiling water beneath my stool. Half an hour passed in this intense heat produced a most profuse perspiration, and from the commencement of the vapour system the attacks of fever moderated both in violence and frequency. In about a fortnight, the complaint had so much abated that my spirits rose in equal proportion, and, although weak, I had no mortal fear of my old enemy.

The king, Kamrasi, had supplied me with provisions, but I was troubled daily by messengers who requested me to appear before him to make arrangements for the proposed attack upon Rionga and Fowooka. My excuse for non-attendance was my weak state; but Kamrasi determined not to be evaded, and one day his headman Quonga announced that the king would pay me a visit on the following morning. Although I had but little remaining from my stock of baggage except the guns, ammunition, and astronomical instruments, I was obliged to hide everything underneath the beds, lest the avaricious eyes of Kamrasi should detect a "want." True to his appointment, he appeared with numerous attendants, and was ushered into my little hut. I had a very rude but serviceable armchair that one of my men had constructed; in this the king was invited to sit. Hardly was he seated, when he leant back, stretched out his legs, and making some remark to his attendants concerning his personal comfort, he asked for the chair as a present. I promised to have one made for him immediately. This being arranged, he surveyed the barren little hut, vainly endeavouring to fix his eyes upon something that he could demand; but so fruitless was his search, that he laughingly turned to his people and said, "How was it that they wanted so many porters, if they had nothing to carry?" My interpreter explained, that many things had been spoiled during the storms on the lake, and had been left behind; that our provisions had long since been consumed, and that our clothes were worn out – thus we had nothing left but a few beads. "New varieties, no doubt," he replied; "give me all that you have of the small blue and the large red!" We had carefully hidden the main stock, and a few had been arranged in bags to be produced as the occasion might require; these were now unpacked by the boy Saat and laid before the king. I told him to make his choice, which he did precisely as I had anticipated, by making presents to his surrounding friends out of my stock, and monopolizing the remainder for his share: the division of the portions among his people was a modest way of taking the whole, as he would immediately demand their return upon quitting my hut. No sooner were the beads secured than he repeated the original demand for my watch and the No. 24 double rifle; these I resolutely refused. He then requested permission to see the contents of a few of the baskets and bags that formed our worn-out luggage. There was nothing that took his fancy except needles, thread, lancets, medicines, and a small tooth-comb; the latter interested him exceedingly, as I explained that the object of the Turks in collecting ivory was to sell it to Europeans who manufactured it into many articles, among which were small tooth-combs such as he then examined. He could not understand how the teeth could be so finely cut. Upon the use of the comb being explained, he immediately attempted to practise upon his woolly head; failing in the operation, he adapted the instrument to a different purpose, and commenced scratching beneath the wool most vigorously: the effect being satisfactory, he at once demanded the comb, which was handed to each of the surrounding chiefs, all of whom had a trial of its properties, and, every head having been scratched, it was returned to the king, who handed it to Quonga, the headman that received his presents. So complete was the success of the comb that he proposed to send me one of the largest elephant's tusks, which I was to take to England and cut into as many small tooth-combs as it would produce for himself and his chiefs.

The lancets were next admired, and were declared to be admirably adapted for paring his nails – they were therefore presented to him. Then came the investigation of the medicine chest, and every bottle was applied to his nose, and a small quantity of the contents was requested. On the properties of tartar-emetic being explained, he proposed to swallow a dose immediately, as he had been suffering from headache, but as he was some distance from home I advised him to postpone the dose until his return; I accordingly made up about a dozen powders, one of which (three grains) he was to take that evening.

The concave mirror, our last looking-glass, was then discovered; the distortion of face it produced was a great amusement, and after it had been repeatedly handed round, it was added to his presents. More gunpowder was demanded, and a pound canister and a box of caps were presented to him, but I positively refused the desired bullets.

To change the conversation, I inquired whether he or any of his people knew from whence their race originated, as their language and appearance were totally different to the tribes that I had visited front the north. He told me that he knew his grandfather, whose name was Cherrybambi, but that he knew nothing of the history of the country, except that it had formerly been a very extensive kingdom, and that Uganda and Utumbi had been comprised in the country of Kitwara with Unyoro and Chopi.

The kingdom of Kitwara extended from the frontier of Karagwe to the Victoria Nile at Magungo, and Karuma, bounded on all sides but the south by that river and the Victoria and the Albert Lakes; the latter lake forming the western frontier. During the reign of Cherrybambi, the province of Utumbi revolted, and not only became independent, but drove Cherrybambi from Uganda across the Kafoor river to Unyoro. This revolt continued until Cherrybambi's death, when the father of M'tese (the present king of Uganda), who was a native of Utumbi, attacked and conquered Uganda and became king. From that time there has been continual war between Uganda and Unyoro; or, as Kamrasi calls his kingdom, Kitwara, that being the ancient name: to the present day, M'tese, the king of Uganda, is one of his greatest enemies. It was in vain that I attempted to trace his descent from the Gallas; both upon this and other occasions he and his people denied all knowledge of their ancient history.

He informed me that Chopi had also revolted after the death of Cherrybambi, and that he had reconquered it only ten or twelve years ago, but that even now the natives were not to be trusted, as many had leagued with Fowooka and Rionga, whose desire was to annex Chopi and to form a separate kingdom: these chiefs had possession of the river islands, which strongholds it was impossible to attack without guns, as the rapids were so dangerous that canoes could only approach by a certain passage.

Kamrasi expressed his determination to kill both of the refractory chiefs, as he would have no rest during their lives; he disclaimed all relationship with Rionga, who had been represented to Speke as his brother, and he concluded by requesting me to assist him in an attack upon the river islands, promising that if I should kill Fowooka and Rionga he would give me a large portion of his territory.

He suggested that I should stand upon a high cliff that commanded Fowooka's island; from that point I could pick off not only the chief, but all his people, by firing steadily with the little double 24 rifle; he continued even farther, that if I were too ill to go myself, I should "lend" him my little Fletcher 24 rifle, give him my men to assist his army, and he would pick off Rionga himself from the cliff above the river: this was his mild way of securing the rifle which he had coveted ever since my arrival in his country. I told him plainly that I could not mix myself up with his quarrels; that I travelled with only one object, of doing good, and that I would harm no one unless in self-defence, therefore I could not be the aggressor; but that should Fowooka and Rionga attack his position I should be most happy to lend him my aid to repel them. Far from appreciating my ideas of fair play, he immediately rose from his chair, and without taking leave he walked out of the hut, attended by his people.

The next morning I heard that he had considered himself poisoned by the tarter-emetic but that he was now well.

From that day I received no supplies for myself or my people, as the king was affronted. A week passed away, and I was obliged to purchase meat and flour from Eddrees, the lieutenant who commanded the Turks' party of nine men. I gave this man a double-barrelled gun, and he behaved well.

One day I was lying upon my bed with a fit of ague, when it was reported that four men had arrived from M'tese, the king of Uganda, who wished to see me. Unfortunately my *vakeel* delayed the men for so long that they departed, promising to return again, having obtained from my people all information concerning me: these were spies from the king of Uganda, whose object at that time was unknown to us.

The weeks passed slowly at Kisoona, as there was a tedious monotony in the lack of incident; every day was a repetition of the preceding. My time was passed in keeping a regular journal; mapping; and in writing letters to friends in England, although there was no communication. This task afforded the greatest pleasure, as I could thus converse in imagination with those far away. The thought frequently occurred to me that they might no longer exist, and that the separation of years might be the parting forever; nevertheless there was a melancholy satisfaction at thus blankly corresponding with those whom I had loved in former years. Thus the time slowly ebbed away; the maps were perfected; information that I had received was confirmed by the repeated examination of natives; and a few little black children who were allowed to run about our courtyard like so many puppies afforded a study of the African savage in embryo. This monotony was shortly disturbed.

At about 9 p.m. one night we were suddenly disturbed by a tremendous din – hundreds of *nogara*s were beating, horns blowing, and natives screaming in all directions. I immediately jumped out of bed, and buckling on my belt I took my rifle and left the hut. The village was alive with people all dressed for war, and bearded with cows' tails, dancing and rushing about with shields and spears, attacking imaginary enemies. Bacheeta informed me that Fowooka's people had crossed the Nile and were within three hours' march of Kisoona, accompanied by a hundred and fifty of Debono's trading party, the same that had formerly attacked Kamrasi in the preceding year in company with Rionga's people. It was reported, that having crossed the Nile they were marching direct on Kisoona, with the intention of attacking the country and of killing Kamrasi. M'Gambi, the brother of Kamrasi, whose hut was only twenty yards distant, immediately came to me with the news: he was in a state of great alarm, and was determined to run off to the king immediately to recommend his flight. After some time I succeeded in convincing him that this was unnecessary, and that I might be of great service in this dilemma if Kamrasi would come personally to me early on the following morning.

The sun had just risen, when the king unceremoniously marched into my hut; he was no longer the dignified monarch of Kitwara clothed in a beautiful mantle of fine skins, but he wore nothing but a short kilt of blue baize that Speke had given him, and a scarf thrown across his shoulders. He was dreadfully alarmed, and could hardly be persuaded to leave his weapons outside the door, according to the custom of the country – these were three lances and a double-barrelled rifle that had been given him by Speke. I was much amused at his trepidation, and observing the curious change in his costume, I complimented him upon the practical cut of his dress, that was better adapted for fighting than the long and cumbrous mantle. "Fighting!" he exclaimed, with the horror of Bob Acres, "I am not going to fight! I have dressed lightly to be able to run quickly. I mean to run away! Who can fight against guns? Those people have one hundred and fifty guns; you must run with me; we can do nothing against them; you have only thirteen men; Eddrees has only ten; what can twenty-three do against a hundred and fifty? Pack up your things and run; we must be off into the high grass and hide at once; the enemy is expected every moment!"

I never saw a man in such a deplorable state of abject fright, and I could not help laughing aloud at the miserable coward who represented a kingdom. Calling my headman, I ordered him to hoist the English ensign on my tall flagstaff in the courtyard. In a few moments the old flag was waving in a brisk breeze and floating over my little hut. There is something that warms the heart in the sight of the Union Jack when thousands of miles away from the old country. I now explained to Kamrasi that both he and his country were under the protection of that flag, which was the emblem of England; and that so long as he trusted to me, although I had refused to join him in attacking Fowooka, he should see that I was his true ally, as I would defend him against all attacks. I told him to send a large quantity of supplies into my camp, and to procure guides immediately, as I should send some of my men without delay to the enemy's camp with a message to the *vakeel* of Deb-ono's party. Slightly reassured by this arrangement, he called Quonga, and ordered him to procure two of his chiefs to accompany my men. The best of his men, Cassave, appeared immediately; this was a famous fellow, who had always been civil and anxious to do his duty both to his master and to me. I summoned Eddrees, and ordered him to send four of his men with an equal number of mine to the camp of Fowooka to make a report of the invading force, and to see whether it was true that Debono's people were arrived as invaders. In half an hour from the receipt of my order, the party started; eight well-armed men accompanied by about twenty natives of Kamrasi's with two days' provisions. Kisoona was about ten miles from the Victoria Nile.

At about 5 p.m. on the following day my men returned, accompanied by ten men and a *choush*, or sergeant, of Debono's party; they had determined to prove whether I was actually in the country, as they had received a report some months ago that both my wife and I were dead; they imagined that the men that I had sent to their camp were those of the rival party belonging to Ibrahim, who had wished to drive them out of Kamrasi's country by using my name. However, they were now undeceived, as the first object that met their view was the English flag on the high flagstaff, and they were shortly led into my courtyard, where they were introduced to me in person. They sat in a half-circle around me.

Assuming great authority, I asked them how they could presume to attack a country under the protection of the British flag? I informed them that Unyoro belonged to me by right of discovery, and that I had given Ibrahim the exclusive right to the produce of that country, on the condition that he should do nothing contrary to the will of the reigning king, Kamrasi; that Ibrahim had behaved well; that I had been guided to the lake and had returned, and that we were now actually fed by the king; and we were suddenly invaded by Turkish subjects in connexion with a hostile tribe, who thus insulted the English flag. I explained to them that I should not only resist any attack that might be made upon Kamrasi, but that I should report the whole affair to the Turkish authorities upon my return to Khartoum; and that, should a shot be fired or a slave be stolen in Kamrasi's country, the leader of their party, Mahommed Wat-el-Mek, would be hanged.

They replied that they were not aware that I was in the country; that they were allies of Fowooka, Rionga, and Owine, the three hostile chiefs; that they had received both ivory and slaves from them on condition that they should kill Kamrasi; and that, according to the custom of the White Nile trade, they had agreed to these conditions. They complained that it was very hard upon them to march six days through an uninhabited wilderness between their station at Faloro and Fowooka's islands and to return empty handed. In reply I told them, that they should carry a letter from me to their *vakeel* Mahommed, in which I should give him twelve hours from the receipt of my order to recross the river with his entire party and their allies and quit Kamrasi's country.

They demurred to this alternative: but I shortly settled their objections, by ordering my *vakeel* to write the necessary letter, and desiring them to start before sunrise on the following morning. Kamrasi had been suspicious that I had sent for Mahommed's party to invade him because he had kept me starving at Shooa Moru instead of forwarding me to Shooa as he had promised. This suspicion placed me in an awkward position; I therefore called M'Gambi (his brother) in presence of the Turks, and explained the whole affair face to face, desiring Mahommed's people themselves to explain to him that they would retire from the country simply because I commanded them to do so, but that, had I not been there, they would have attacked him. This they repeated with a very bad grace, boasting, at the completion, that, were it not for me, they would shoot M'Gambi where he stood at that moment. The latter, fully aware of their good intentions, suddenly disappeared. My letter to Mahommed was delivered to Suleiman *Choush*, the leader of his party, and I ordered a sheep to be killed for their supper. At sunrise on the following morning they all departed, accompanied by six of my men, who were to bring a reply to my letter. These people had two donkeys, and just as they were starting, a crowd of natives made a rush to gather a heap of dung that lay beneath the animals; a great fight and tussle took place for the possession of this valuable medicine, in the midst of which the donkey lifted up his voice and brayed so lustily that the crowd rushed away with more eagerness than they had exhibited on arriving, alarmed at the savage voice of the unknown animal. It appeared that the dung of the donkey rubbed upon the skin was supposed to be a cure for rheumatism, and that this rare specific was brought from a distant country in the East where such animals existed.

Chapter XV

Kamrasi Begs For The British Flag

Kamrasi, thus freed from his invaders, was almost stupefied with astonishment. He immediately paid me a visit, and as he entered the courtyard he stopped to look at the flag that was gaily fluttering above him, as though it were a talisman. He inquired why the Turks were awed by an apparent trifle. I explained that the flag was well known, and might be seen in every part of the world; wherever it was hoisted it was respected, as he had just witnessed, even at so great a distance from home and unsupported, as in Unyoro.

Seizing the opportunity, he demanded it, saying, "What shall I do when you leave my country and take that with you? These Turks will surely return. Give me the flag, and they will be afraid to attack me!" I was obliged to explain to him that "the respect for the British ensign had not been gained by running away on the approach of danger, as he had proposed on the arrival of the enemy, and that its honour could not be confided to any stranger." True to his uncontrollable instinct of begging, he replied, "If you cannot give me the flag, give me at least that little double-barrelled rifle that you do not require, as you are going home; then I can defend myself should the Turks attack me."

I was excessively disgusted; he had just been saved by my intervention, and his manner of thanking me was by begging most pertinaciously for the rifle that I had refused him on more than twenty occasions. I requested him never to mention the subject again, as I would not part with it under any circumstances. Just at this moment I heard an uproar outside my gate, and loud screams, attended with heavy blows. A man was dragged past the entrance of the courtyard bound hand and foot, and was immediately cudgelled to death by a crowd of natives. This operation continued for some minutes, until his bones had been thoroughly broken up by the repeated blows of clubs. The body was dragged to a grove of plantains, and was there left for the vultures, who in a few minutes congregated around it.

It appeared that the offence thus summarily punished was the simple act of conversing with some of the natives who had attended Mahommed's men from Fowooka's island to Kisoona: a conversation with one of the enemy was considered high treason, and was punished with immediate death. In such cases, where either Kamrasi or his brother M'Gambi determined upon the sudden execution of a criminal, the signal was given by touching the condemned with the point of a lance: this sign was the order that was immediately obeyed by the guards who were in attendance, and the culprit was beaten to death upon the spot. Sometimes the condemned was touched by a stick instead of a lance point; this was a signal that he should be killed by the lance, and the sentence was carried out by thrusting him through the body with numerous spears – thus the instrument used to slay the criminal was always contrary to the sign.

On the day following this event, drums were beating, horns blowing, and crowds of natives were singing and dancing in all directions; pots of plantain cider were distributed, and general festivities proclaimed the joy of the people at the news that Mahommed's party had retreated across the river, according to their agreement with me. My men had returned with a letter from Mahommed, stating that he was neither afraid of Ibrahim's people nor of Kamrasi, but that as I claimed the country, he must retire. Not only had he retired with his thwarted allies, but, disgusted at the failure of his expedition, he had quarrelled with Fowooka, and had plundered him of all his cattle, together with a number of slaves: this termination of the affair had so delighted Kamrasi that he had ordered general rejoicings: he killed a number of oxen, and distributed them among his people, and intoxicated half the country with presents of maroua, or the plantain cider.

Altogether Mahommed, the *vakeel* of Debono, had behaved well to me in this affair, although rather shabbily to his allies: he sent me six pieces of soap, and a few strings of blue beads and jenettos (red glass beads) as a proof that he parted with no ill feeling. Hardly were the Turks in retreat when Kamrasi determined to give the finishing stroke to his enemies. He sent great quantities of ivory to the camp, and one evening his people laid about twenty tusks at my door, begging me to count them. I told him to give the ivory to Ibrahim's men, as I required nothing; but that should Ibrahim find a large quantity ready for him on his return to the country, he would do anything that he might desire.

A few days later, whole lines of porters arrived, carrying enormous elephants' tusks to Eddrees, the *vakeel*. Early the next morning, Kamrasi's entire army arrived laden with provisions, each man carrying about 40 lbs. of flour in a package upon his head. The Turks' party of ten men joined them, and I heard that an attack was meditated upon Fowooka.

A few days after the expedition had started, the Turks and about 1,000 natives returned. Kamrasi was overjoyed; they had gained a complete victory, having entirely routed Fowooka, and not only captured the islands and massacred the greater number of the inhabitants, but they had captured all the wives of the rebel chiefs, together with a number of inferior slaves, and a herd of goats that had fortunately escaped the search of Mahommed's retreating party. Fowooka and Owine had escaped by crossing to the northern shore, but their power was irretrievably ruined, their villages plundered and burned, and their women and children captured.

A number of old women had been taken in the general *razzia*; these could not walk sufficiently fast to keep up with their victors during the return march, they had accordingly all been killed on the road as being cumbersome: in every case they were killed by being beaten on the back of the neck with a club. Such were the brutalities indulged in.

On the following morning I went to visit the captives; the women were sitting in an open shed, apparently much dejected. I examined the hands of about fourteen, all of which were well shaped and beautifully soft, proving that they were women of high degree who never worked laboriously: they were for the most part remarkably good looking, of soft and pleasing expression, dark brown complexion, fine noses, woolly hair, and good figures, precisely similar to the general style of women in Chopi and Unyoro.

Among the captives was a woman with a most beautiful child, a boy about twelve months old; all these were slaves, and the greater number were in a most pitiable state, being perfectly unfit for labour, having been accustomed to luxury as the women of chiefs of high position. Curiously enough, the woman Bacheeta, who had accompanied us to visit these unfortunate captives, now recognised her former mistress, who was the wife of the murdered Sali; she had been captured with the wives and daughters of Rionga. Bacheeta immediately fell on her knees and crept towards her on all fours, precisely as the subjects of Kamrasi were accustomed to approach his throne. Sali had held as high a position as Fowooka, and had been treacherously killed by Kamrasi at M'Rooli in the presence of Bacheeta. At that time peace had been established between Kamrasi and the three great chiefs, who were invited to a conference at M'Rooli with a treacherous design on the part of the king. Hardly had they arrived, when Rionga was seized by Kamrasi's orders, and confined in a circular but with high mud walls and no doorway; the prisoner was hoisted up and lowered down through an aperture in the roof. He was condemned to be burnt alive on the following morning for some imaginary offence, while Sali and Fowooka were to be either pardoned or murdered, as circumstances might dictate. Sali was a great friend of Rionga, and determined to rescue him; accordingly he plied the guards with drink, and engaged them in singing throughout the night on one side of the prison, while his men burrowed like rabbits beneath the wall on the opposite side, and rescued Rionga, who escaped.

Sali showed extreme folly in remaining at M'Rooli, and Kamrasi, suspicious of his complicity, immediately ordered him to be seized and cut to pieces; he was accordingly tied to a stake, and tortured by having his limbs cut off piecemeal – the hands being first severed at the wrists, and the arms at the elbow joints. Bacheeta was an eyewitness of this horrible act, and testified to the courage of Sali, who, while under the torture, cried out to his friends in the crowd, warning them to fly and save themselves, as he was a dead man, and they would share his fate should they remain. Some escaped, including Fowooka, but many were massacred on the spot, and the woman Bacheeta was captured by Kamrasi and subsequently sent by him to the Turks' camp at Faloro, as already described. From that day unremitting warfare was carried on between Kamrasi and the island chiefs; the climax was their defeat, and the capture of their women, through the assistance of the Turks.

Kamrasi's delight at the victory knew no bounds; ivory poured into the camp, and a hut was actually filled with elephants' tusks of the largest size. Eddrees, the leader of the Turks' party, knowing that the victory was gained by the aid of his guns, refused to give up the captives on the demand of the king, claiming them as prisoners belonging to Ibrahim, and declining any arguments upon the matter until his master should arrive in the country. Kamrasi urged that, although the guns had been of great service, no prisoners could have been captured without the aid of his canoes, that had been brought by land, dragged all the way from Karuma by hundreds of his people in readiness for the attack upon the islands.

As usual in all cases of dispute, I was to be referee. Kamrasi sent his factotum Cassave in the night to my hut to confer with me without the Turks' knowledge; then came his brother, M'Gambi, and at length, after being pestered daily by messengers, the great king arrived in person. He said that Eddrees was excessively insolent, and had threatened to shoot him; that he had insulted him when on his throne surrounded by his chiefs, and that, had he not been introduced into the country by me, he would have killed him and his men on the spot.

I advised Kamrasi not to talk too big, as he had lately seen what only ten guns had effected in the fight with Fowooka, and he might imagine the results that would occur should he even hint at hostility, as the large parties of Ibrahim and the men of Mahommed Wat-el-Mek would immediately unite and destroy both him and his country, and place his now beaten enemy Fowooka upon his throne should a hair of a Turk's head be missing. The gallant Kamrasi turned almost green at the bare suggestion of this possibility. I advised him not to quarrel about straws, assuring him, that as I had become responsible for the behaviour of the Turks while in his country, he need have no fear; but that, on the other hand, he must be both just and generous. If he would give them a supply of ivory, he might always reckon upon them as valuable allies; but if he attempted to quarrel, they would assuredly destroy his country after my departure. Of course he requested me never to think of leaving him, but to take up my abode for life in Kitwara, promising me all that I should require in addition to a large territory. I replied that the climate did not agree with me, and that nothing would induce me to remain, but that, as the boats would not arrive at Gondokoro for six months (until February), I might as well reside with him as anywhere else. At the same time, I assured him that his professed friendship for me was a delusion, as he only regarded me as a shield between him and danger. After a long conversation, I succeeded in persuading him not to interfere in matters regarding prisoners of war, and to look upon Eddrees only as a *vakeel* until Ibrahim should arrive. He left my hut promising not to mention the affair again; but the next, day he sent Cassave to Eddrees, demanding two of the prettiest women who were captives. In reply, Eddrees, who was an extremely hotheaded fellow, went straight to Kamrasi, and spoke to him in a most insulting manner, refusing his request. The king immediately rose from his seat and turned his back upon the offender. Off rushed Eddrees, boiling with passion, to his camp, summoned his men well armed, and marched straight towards the residence of Kamrasi to demand satisfaction for the affront.

Fortunately, my *vakeel* brought me the intelligence, and I sent after him, ordering his immediate return, and declaring that no one should break the peace so long as I was in the country. In about ten minutes, both he and his men slunk back ashamed, mutually accusing each other, as is usual in cases of failure. This was an instance of the madness of these Turks in assuming the offensive, when, in the event of a fight, defeat must have been certain. They were positively without ammunition, having fired away all their cartridges except about five rounds for each man in the attack upon Fowooka. Fortunately, this was unknown to Kamrasi. I had a large supply, as my men were never permitted to fire a shot without my special permission.

The party of Turks were now completely in my power. I sent for Eddrees, and also for the king: the latter had already heard from the natives of the approach of the armed Turks, and of my interference. He refused to appear in person, but sent his brother M'Gambi, who was, as usual, the cat's-paw. M'Gambi was highly offended, and declared that Kamrasi had forbidden Eddrees ever to appear again in his presence. I insisted upon Eddrees apologizing, and it was resolved that all future negotiations should be carried on through me alone.

I suggested that it would be advisable for all parties that a message should be sent without delay to Ibrahim at Shooa, as it was highly necessary that he should be present, as I should not continue responsible for the conduct of the Turks. When I arrived in Unyoro it was with the intention of visiting the lake, and returning immediately. I had been delayed entirely through Kamrasi's orders, and I could not be held responsible for Eddrees; my agreement had been to guarantee the conduct of the Turks under Ibrahim, who was the commander of the party. Eddrees, who, being without ammunition, was now excessively humble and wished for reinforcements, offered to send five men to Shooa, provided that Kamrasi would allow some natives to accompany them. This did not suit the ideas of the suspicious M'Gambi, who suspected that he intended to misrepresent Kamrasi's conduct to prejudice Ibrahim against him. Accordingly, he declined his offer, but agreed to give porters and guides, should I wish to send any of my men with a letter. This suited my views exactly; I longed to quit Kamrasi's country, as Kisoona was a prison of high grass and inaction, and could I only return to Shooa, I could pass my time pleasantly in a fine open country and healthy climate, with the advantage of being five days' march nearer home than Unyoro. Accordingly, I instructed my *vakeel* to write a letter to Ibrahim, calling him immediately to Kisoona, informing him that a large quantity of ivory was collected, which, should Eddrees create a disturbance, would be lost. On the following morning, four of my men started for Shooa, accompanied by a number of natives.

Kisoona relapsed into its former monotony-the war with Fowooka being over, the natives, free from care, passed their time in singing and drinking; it was next to impossible to sleep at night, as crowds of people all drunk were yelling in chorus, blowing horns and beating drums from sunset until morning. The women took no part in this amusement, as it was the custom in Unyoro for the men to enjoy themselves in laziness, while the women performed all the labour of the fields. Thus they were fatigued, and glad to rest, while the men passed the night in uproarious merriment. The usual style of singing was a rapid chant delivered as a solo, while at intervals the crowd burst out in a deafening chorus together with the drums and horns; the latter were formed of immense gourds which, growing in a peculiar shape, with long bottle necks, were easily converted into musical (?) instruments. Every now and then a cry of fire in the middle of the night enlivened the ennui of our existence; the huts were littered deep with straw, and the inmates, intoxicated, frequently fell asleep with their huge pipes alight, which, falling in the dry straw, at once occasioned a conflagration. In such cases the flames spread from hut to hut with immense rapidity, and frequently four or five hundred huts in Kamrasi's large camp were destroyed by fire, and rebuilt in a few days. I was anxious concerning my powder, as, in the event of fire, the blaze of the straw hut was so instantaneous that nothing could be saved: should my powder explode, I should be entirely defenceless. Accordingly, after a conflagration in my neighbourhood, I insisted upon removing all huts within a circuit of thirty yards of my dwelling: the natives demurring, I at once ordered my men to pull down the houses, and thereby relieved myself from drunken and dangerous neighbours.

Although we had been regularly supplied with beef by the king, we now found it most difficult to procure fowls; the war with Fowooka had occasioned the destruction of nearly all the poultry in the neighbourhood of Kisoona, as Kamrasi and his kojoors (magicians) were occupied with daily sacrifices, deducing prognostications of coming events from the appearances of the entrails of the birds slain. The king was surrounded by sorcerers, both men and women; these people were distinguished from others by witch-like chaplets of various dried roots worn upon the head; some of them had dried lizards, crocodiles' teeth, lions' claws, minute tortoiseshells, etc. added to their collection of charms. They could have subscribed to the witches' cauldron of Macbeth:

> *"Eye of newt and toe of frog,*
> *Wool of bat and tongue of dog,*
> *Adder's fork and blindworm's sting,*
> *Lizard's leg and owlet's wing,*
> *For a charm of powerful trouble,*
> *Like a hell-broth boil and bubble."*

On the first appearance of these women, many of whom were old and haggard, I felt inclined to repeat Banquo's question: "What are these, so withered and so wild in their attire, that look not like the inhabitants o' the earth, and yet aren't? Live you? Or are you aught that man may question?"

In such witches and wizards Kamrasi and his people believed implicitly. Bacheeta, and also my men, told me that when my wife was expected to die during the attack of *coup de soleil*, the guide had procured a witch, who had killed a fowl to question it whether she would recover and reach the lake. The fowl in its dying struggle protruded its tongue, which sign is considered affirmative; after this reply the natives had no doubt of the result. These people, although far superior to the tribes on the north of the Nile in general intelligence, had no idea of a Supreme Being, nor any object of worship, their faith resting upon a simple belief in magic like that of the natives of Madi and Obbo.

Some weeks passed without a reply from Shooa to the letter I had forwarded by my men, neither had any news been received of their arrival; we had relapsed into the usual monotony of existence. This was happily broken by a most important event.

On the 6th September, M'Gambi came to my hut in a state of great excitement, with the intelligence that the M'was, the natives of Uganda, had invaded Kamrasi's country with a large army; that they had already crossed the Kafoor River and had captured M'Rooli, and that they were marching through the country direct to Kisoona, with the intention of killing Kamrasi and of attacking us, and annexing the country of Unyoro to M'tese's dominions. My force was reduced by four men that I had sent to Shooa – thus we were a party of twenty guns, including the Turks, who unfortunately had no ammunition.

There was no doubt about the truth of the intelligence; the natives seemed in great consternation, as the M'was were far more powerful than Kamrasi's people, and every invasion from that country had been attended with the total rout of the Unyoro forces. I told M'Gambi that messengers must be sent off at once to Shooa with a letter that I would write to Ibrahim, summoning him immediately to Karuma with a force of 100 men; at the same time I suggested that we should leave Kisoona and march with Kamrasi's army direct to Karuma, there to establish a fortified camp to command the passage of the river, and to secure a number of canoes to provide a passage for Ibrahim's people whenever they could effect a junction – otherwise, the M'was might destroy the boats and cut off the Turks on their arrival at the ferry. Kisoona was an exceedingly disadvantageous situation, as it was a mere forest of trees and tangled herbage ten or twelve feet high, in which the enemy could approach us unperceived, secure from our guns. M'Gambi quite approved of my advice, and hurried off to the king, who, as usual in cases of necessity, came to me without delay. He was very excited, and said that messengers arrived four or five times a day, bringing reports of every movement of the enemy, who were advancing rapidly in three divisions, one by the route direct from M'Rooli to Karuma that I had followed on my arrival at Atada, another direct to Kisoona, and a third between these two parallels, so as to cut off his retreat to an island in the Nile, where he had formerly taken refuge when his country was invaded by the same people. I begged him not to think of retiring to the island, but to take my advice and fight it out, in which case I should be happy to assist him, as I was his guest, and I had a perfect right to repel any aggression.

Accordingly I drew a plan of operations, showing how a camp could be formed on the cliff above Karuma Falls, having two sides protected by the river, while a kraal could be formed in the vicinity completely commanded by our guns, where his cattle would remain in perfect security. He listened with wandering eyes to all military arrangements, and concluded by abandoning all idea of resistance, but resolutely adhering to his plan of flight to the island that had protected him on a former occasion.

We could only agree upon two points, the evacuation of Kisoona as untenable, and the necessity of despatching a summons to Ibrahim immediately. The latter decision was acted upon that instant, and runners were despatched with a letter to Shooa. Kamrasi decided to wait until the next morning for reports from expected messengers on the movements of the enemy, otherwise he might run into the very jaws of the danger he wished to avoid; and he promised to send porters to carry us and our effects, should it be necessary to march to Karuma: with this understanding, he departed. Bacheeta now assured me that the M'was were so dreaded by the Unyoro people that nothing would induce them to fight; therefore I must not depend upon Kamrasi in any way, but must make independent arrangements: she informed me, that the invasion was caused by accounts given to M'tese by Goobo Goolah, one of Speke's deserters, who had run away from Kamrasi shortly after our arrival in the country, and had reported to M'tese, the king of Uganda, that we were on our way to pay him a visit with many valuable presents, but that Kamrasi had prevented us from proceeding, in order to monopolise the merchandise. Enraged at this act of his great enemy Kamrasi, he had sent spies to corroborate the testimony of Goobo Goolah (these were the four men who had appeared some weeks ago), which being confirmed, he had sent an army to destroy both Kamrasi and his country, and to capture us and lead us to his capital. This was the explanation of the affair given by Bacheeta, who, with a woman's curiosity and tact, picked up information in the camps almost as correctly as a Times correspondent.

This was very enjoyable – the monotony of our existence had been unbearable, and here was an invigorating little difficulty with just sufficient piquancy to excite our spirits. My men were so thoroughly drilled and accustomed to complete obedience and dependence upon my guidance, that they had quite changed their characters. I called Eddrees, gave him ten rounds of ball cartridge for each of his men, and told him to keep with my party should we be obliged to march: he immediately called a number of natives and concealed all his ivory in the jungle. At about 9 p.m. the camp was in an uproar; suddenly drums beat in all quarters, in reply to *nogaras* that sounded the alarm in Kamrasi's camp; horns bellowed; men and women yelled; huts were set on fire; and in the blaze of light hundreds of natives, all armed and dressed for war, rushed frantically about, as usual upon such occasions, gesticulating, and engaging in mock fight with each other, as though full of valour and boiling over with a desire to meet the enemy. Bacheeta, who was a sworn enemy to Kamrasi, was delighted at his approaching discomfiture. As some of the most desperate looking warriors, dressed with horns upon their heads, rushed up to us brandishing their spears, she shouted in derision, "Dance away, my boys! Now's your time when the enemy is far away; but if you see a M'was as big as the boy Saat, you will run as fast as your legs can carry you."

The M'Was were reported to be so close to Kisoona that their *nogara*s had been heard from Kamrasi's position, therefore we were to be ready to march for Atada before daybreak on the following morning. There was little sleep that night, as all the luggage had to be packed in readiness for the early start. Cassave, who could always be depended upon, arrived at my hut, and told me that messengers had reported that the M'was had swept everything before them, having captured all the women and cattle of the country and killed a great number of people; that they had seen the light of burning villages from Kamrasi's camp, and that it was doubtful whether the route was open to Atada. I suggested that men should be sent on in advance, to report if the path were occupied: this was immediately done.

Before daybreak on the following morning an immense volume of light with dense clouds of smoke in the direction of Kamrasi's position showed that his camp had been fired, according to custom, and that his retreat had commenced; thousands of grass huts were in flames, and I could not help being annoyed at the folly of these natives at thus giving the enemy notice of their retreat, by a signal that could be seen at many miles' distance, when success depended upon rapid and secret movements.

Shortly after these signs of the march, crowds of women, men, cows, goats, and luggage appeared, advancing in single file through a grove of plantains and passing within twenty yards of us in an endless string. It was pouring with rain, and women carrying their children were slipping along the muddy path, while throngs of armed men and porters pushed rudely by, until at last the gallant Kamrasi himself appeared with a great number of women (his wives), several of whom were carried on litters, being too fat to walk. He took no notice of me as he passed by. M'Gambi was standing by me, and he explained that we were to close the rear, Kamrasi having concluded that it was advisable to have the guns between him and the enemy.

For upwards of an hour the crowd of thousands of people and cattle filed past; at length the last straggler closed the line of march. But where were our promised porters? Not a man was forthcoming, and we were now the sole occupants of the deserted village, excepting M'Gambi and Cassave. These men declared that the people were so frightened that no one would remain to carry us and ours effects, but that they would go to a neighbouring villa and bring porters to convey us to Foweera tomorrow, as that was the spot where Kamrasi wished us to camp; at Foweera there was no high grass, and the country was perfectly open, so that the rifles could command an extensive range. The cunning and duplicity of Kamrasi were extraordinary – he promised, only to deceive; his object in leaving us here was premeditated, as he knew that the M'was, should they pursue him, must fight us before they could follow on his path; we were therefore to be left to defend his rear. The order to camp at Foweera had a similar motive. I knew the country, as we had passed it on our march from Atada to M'Rooli; it was about three miles from Karuma Falls, and would form a position in Kamrasi's rear when he should locate, himself upon the island. Foweera was an excellent military point, as it was equidistant from the Nile north and east at the angle where the river turned to the west from Atada.

I was so annoyed at the deception practised by Kamrasi that I determined to fraternise with the M'was, should they appear at Kisoona; and I made up my mind not to fire a shot except in absolute necessity for so faithless an ally as the king. This I explained to M'Gambi, and threatened that if porters were not supplied I would wait at Kisoona, join the M'was on their arrival, and with them as allies I would attack the island which Kamrasi boasted was his stronghold. This idea frightened M'Gambi, and both he and Cassave started to procure porters, promising most faithfully to appear that evening, and to start together to Foweera on the following morning. We were a party of twenty guns; there was no fear in the event of an attack. I ordered all the huts of the village to be burned except those belonging to our men; thus we had a clear space for the guns in case of necessity. In the evening, true to his promise, M'Gambi appeared with a number of natives, but Cassave had followed Kamrasi.

At sunrise on the following day we started, my wife in a litter, and I in a chair. The road was extremely bad, excessively muddy from the rain of yesterday, trodden deeply by the hoofs of herds of cattle, and by the feet of the thousands that had formed Kamrasi's army and camp followers. There was no variety in the country, it was the same undulating land overgrown with impenetrable grass, and wooded with mimosas; every swamp being shaded by clumps of the graceful wild date. After a march of about eight miles we found the route dry and dusty, the rain on the preceding day having been partial. There was no water on the road and we were all thirsty, having calculated on a supply from the heavy rain. Although many thousands of people had travelled on the path so recently as the previous day, it was nevertheless narrow and hemmed in by the high grass, as the crowd had marched in single file and had therefore not widened the route. This caused great delay to the porters who carried the litter, as they marched two deep; thus one man had to struggle through the high grass. M'Gambi started off in advance of the party with several natives at a rapid pace, while the Turks and some of my men guarded the ammunition, and I remained in company with the litter and five of my men to bring up the rear. The progress of the litter was so slow that, after travelling all day until sunset, we were outmarched, and just as it was getting dark, we arrived at a spot where a path branched to the south, while the main path that we had been follow-ing continued E.N.E. At this point a native was waiting, having been stationed there by the Turks to direct us to the south; he explained that the people had halted at a village close by. Pushing our way through the narrow path we shortly arrived at the village of Deang. This consisted of a few deserted huts scattered among extensive groves of plantains. Here we found Eddrees and the Turks, with their captives from the attack on Fowooka; passing their huts, we took possession of two clean and new huts in the midst of a well-cultivated field of beans that were about six inches above the ground, the cleared field forming an oasis in the middle of the surrounding grass jungle There was no water; it was already dark, and, although we had travelled through the heat of the day, no one had drunk since the morning. We were intensely thirsty, and the men searched in vain among the deserted huts in the hope of finding a supply in the water jars they were all empty. Fortunately we had a little sour milk in a jar that we had carried with us, barely sufficient for two persons. There was nothing to eat except unripe plantains: these we boiled as a substitute for potatoes. I disarmed all the porters, placing their lances and shields under my bedstead in the hut, lest their owners should abscond during the night. It now appeared that our party had scattered most disgracefully; those in advance with the ammunition who bad been ordered not to quit their charge for an instant, had outmarched the main body, leaving Eddrees and a few men with the captive women, who could not walk fast, and my small guard who had attended the litter.

No one ate much that night, as all were too thirsty. On the following morning I found to my dismay that all of our porters had absconded, except two men who had slept in the same hut with my people; we were for about the hundredth time deserted in this detestable country. I ordered Eddrees to push on to Foweera, and to desire my men with the ammunition to wait there until I should arrive, and to request Kamrasi to send porters immediately to assist us. Foweera was about thirteen miles from Deang, our present position. Eddrees and his party started, and I immediately sent my men with empty jars to search in all directions for water; they returned in about an hour, having been unsuccessful. I again ordered them to search in another direction, and should they find a native, to force him to be their guide to a drinking place. In about three hours they returned, accompanied by two old men, and laden with three large jars of good water; they had found the old people in a deserted village, and they had guided them to a spring about three miles distant. Our chief want being supplied, we had no fear of starving, as there was abundance of plantains, and we had about a dozen cheeses that we had manufactured while at Kisoona, in addition to a large supply of flour. A slight touch of fever attacked me, and I at length fell asleep.

I was awakened by the voices of my men, who were standing at the door of my hut with most doleful countenances. They explained that Richarn was missing, and was supposed to have been killed by the natives. My *vakeel* held a broken ramrod in his hand: this suspicious witness was covered with blood. It appeared that while I was asleep, Richarn and one of my men named Mahommed had taken their guns, and without orders had rambled through the country in search of a village, with the intention of procuring porters, if possible, to carry us to Foweera.

They had arrived at a nest of small villages, and had succeeded in engaging four men; these Richarn left in charge of Mahommed while he proceeded alone to a neighbouring village. Shortly after his departure Mahommed heard the report of a gun in that direction about half a mile distant, and leaving his charge, he ran towards the spot. On arrival, he found the village deserted, and on searching the neighbourhood, and vainly calling Richarn, he came upon a large pool of blood opposite several huts; lying upon the blood was the broken ramrod of Richarn's gun. After searching without success, he had returned with the melancholy report of this disaster. I was very fond of Richarn; he had followed me faithfully for years, and with fewer faults than most of his race, he had exhibited many sterling qualities. I waited for two days in this spot, searching for him in all directions. On one occasion my men saw a number of men and women howling in a village not far from the place where the accident had happened; on the approach of my people they fled into the jungles: thus, there was no doubt that Richarn must have shot a man before he had been killed, as the natives were mourning for the dead.

I was much distressed at this calamity; my faithful Richarn was dead, and the double-barrelled Purdey that he carried was lost; this belonged to my friend Oswell, of South African and Lake Ngami celebrity; it was a much-prized weapon, with which he had hunted for five years all the heavy game of Africa with such untiring zeal that much of the wood of the stock was eaten away by the "wait a bit" thorns in his passage on horseback at full speed through the jungles. He had very kindly lent me this old companion of his sports, and I had entrusted it to Richarn as my most careful man: both man and gun were now lost.

Having vainly searched for two days, and my men having seen several village dogs with their mouths and feet covered with blood, we came to the conclusion that his body had been dragged into the grass jungle by the natives, and there, concealed, it had been discovered and devoured by the dogs.

No porters had arrived from Kamrasi, neither had any reply been sent to the message I had forwarded by Eddrees; the evening arrived, and, much dispirited at the loss of my old servant, I lay down on my *angarep* for the night. At about eight o'clock, in the stillness of our solitude, my men asleep, with the exception of the sentry, we were startled by the sound of a *nogara* at no great distance to the south of our huts. The two natives who had remained with us immediately woke the men, and declared that the drums we heard were those of the M'was, who were evidently approaching our village; the natives knew the peculiar sound of the *nogara*s of the enemy, which were different to those of Kamrasi. This was rather awkward – our ammunition was at Foweera, and we had no more than the supply in our cartouche boxes, my men thirty rounds each, while I carried in my pouch twenty-one. Our position was untenable, as the drinking place was three miles distant. Again the *nogara* sounded, and the native guides declared that they could not remain where we then were, but they would conceal themselves in the high grass. My wife proposed that we should forsake our luggage, and march at once for Foweera and effect a junction with our men and ammunition before daybreak. I was sure that it could not be less than twelve or thirteen miles, and in her weak state it would be impossible for her to accomplish the distance, through high grass, in darkness, over a rough path, with the chance of the route being already occupied by the enemy. However, she was determined to risk the march. I accordingly prepared to start at 9 p.m., as at that time the moon would be about 30 degrees above the horizon and would afford us a good light. I piled all the luggage within the hut, packed our blankets in a canvas bag, to be carried by one of the natives, and ordered one of our black women to carry a jar of water. Thus provided, and forsaking all other effects, we started at exactly nine o'clock, following our two natives as guides.

Our course was about E.N.E. The moon was bright, but the great height of the grass shadowed the narrow path so that neither ruts nor stones were visible. The dew was exceedingly heavy, and in brushing through the rank vegetation we were soon wet to the skin. This was our first attempt at walking a distance since many months, and being dreadfully out of condition, I much feared that one of us might be attacked by fever before we should have accomplished the march; at all events, there was no alternative but to push ahead until we should reach Foweera, however distant. We walked for about three hours along a narrow but unmistakeable path, well trodden by the cattle and people that had accompanied Kamrasi.

Suddenly we arrived at a place where a path diverged to the right, while another led to the left: the former was much trodden by cattle, and the guides declared this to be the right direction. Perfectly certain of their mistake, as Foweera lay to the east, while such a course would lead us due south, I refused to follow, and ordered the party to halt while I made a survey of the neighbourhood. I shortly discovered in the bright moonlight that the larger path to the south had been caused by the cattle that had been driven in that direction, but had again returned by the same route. It was evident that some village lay to the south, at which Kamrasi and his army had slept, and that they had returned by the same path to the Foweera main route on the following morning. I soon discovered cattle tracks on the smaller path to the east: this I determined to follow. My guides were of little use, and they confessed that they had only once visited the Foweera country. We were bound for the principal village that belonged to the chief Kalloe, an excellent man, who had frequently visited us at Kisoona.

Not far from the branch roads we came suddenly upon a few huts, the inmates of which were awake. They gave us the unpleasant intelligence that the M'was occupied the country in advance, and that we should not be able to pass them on our present route, as they were close to that spot. It was now past midnight, the country was perfectly still, and having no confidence in the guides I led the way.

About a mile from the huts that we had passed we suddenly observed the light of numerous fires, and a great number of temporary huts formed of green grass and plantain leaves: this was the camp of the M'was. I did not observe any people, nor did we wait long in our present position, but taking a path that led to the north, we quietly and stealthily continued our march through walls of high grass, until in about an hour we arrived in a totally different country. There was no longer the dismal grass jungle in which a man was as much lost as a rabbit in a field of corn, but beautiful park-like glades of rich and tender grass, like an English meadow, stretched before us in the pale moonlight, darkened in many places by the shadows of isolated trees and clumps of forest. Continuing along this agreeable route, we suddenly arrived at a spot where numerous well-beaten paths branched into all directions. This was extreme confusion. We had left the direct route to Foweera when we had made the detour to avoid the M'was' camp. I knew that, as we had then turned to the north, our course should now be due east. There was a path leading in that direction; but just as we were quietly deliberating upon the most advisable course, we heard distant voices. Any voice in this neighbourhood I concluded must be that of an enemy, therefore I ordered my people to sit down, while two men concealed themselves on the borders of a jungle, about a hundred yards distant, as sentries.

I then sent Bacheeta and one of the guides towards the spot from which the sound of voices had proceeded, to listen to their language, and to report whether they were M'was, or people of Foweera. The spies started cautiously on their errand.

About five minutes passed in utter silence; the voices that we had heard had ceased. We were very cold, being wet through with the dew. My wife was much fatigued, and now rested by sitting on the bag of blankets. I was afraid of remaining long in inaction, lest she should become stiff and be unable to march.

We had been thus waiting for about ten minutes, when we were suddenly startled by the most fearful and piercing yell I ever heard. This proceeded from the jungle where one of my men was on guard, about a hundred yards distant.

For the moment I thought he had been caught by a lion, and cocking my rifle, I ran towards the spot. Before I reached the jungle I saw one of the sentries running in the same direction, and two other figures approaching, one being dragged along by the throat by my man Moosa. He had a prisoner. It appeared, that while he was crouching beneath the bushes at the entrance of the main path that led through the jungle, he suddenly observed a man quietly stealing along the forest close to him. He waited, unobserved, until the figure had passed him, when he quickly sprang upon him from behind, seizing his spear with his left hand and grasping his throat with his right.

This sudden and unexpected attack from an unseen enemy had so terrified the native that he had uttered the extraordinary yell that had startled our party. He was now triumphantly led by his captor, but he was so prostrated by fear that he trembled as though in an ague fit. I endeavoured to reassure him, and Bacheeta shortly returning with the guide, we discovered the value of our prize.

Far from being an enemy, he was one of Kalloe's men, who had been sent to spy the M'was from Foweera: thus we had a dependable guide. This little incident was as refreshing as a glass of sherry during the night's march, and we enjoyed a hearty laugh. Bacheeta had been unsuccessful in finding the origin of the voices, as they had ceased shortly after she had left us. It appeared that our captive had also heard the voices, and he was stealthily endeavouring to ascertain the cause when he was so roughly seized by Moosa. We now explained to him our route, and he at once led the way, relieving the native who had hitherto carried the bag of blankets. We had made a considerable circuit by turning from the direct path, but we now had the advantage of seeing the open country before us, and marching upon a good and even path. We walked for about three hours from this spot at a brisk pace, my wife falling three times from sheer fatigue, which induced stumbling over the slightest inequalities in the road. At length we descended a valley, and crossing a slight hollow, we commenced the ascent of a gentle inclination upon a beautiful grassy undulation crowned by a clump of large trees. In the stillness of the night wherever we had halted we had distinctly heard the distant roar of the river; but the sound had so much increased within the last hour that I felt convinced we must be near Foweera at the bend of the Victoria Nile. My wife was so exhausted with the long march, rendered doubly fatiguing by the dew that had added additional weight to her clothes, that she could hardly ascend the hill we had just commenced. For the last hour our guide had declared that Foweera was close to us; but experienced in natives' descriptions of distance, we were quite uncertain as to the hour at which we should arrive. We were already at the top of the hill, and within about two hundred yards of the dense clump of trees my wife was obliged to confess that she could go no farther. Just at that moment a cock crowed; another replied immediately from the clump of trees close to us, and the guide, little appreciating the blessing of his announcement, told us that we had arrived at Kalloe's village, for which we were bound.

It was nearly 5 a.m., and we had marched from Deang at 9 p.m. There was some caution required in approaching the village, as, should one of the Turks' sentries be on guard, he would in all probability fire at the first object he might see, without a challenge. I therefore ordered my men to shout, while I gave my well-known whistle that would be a signal of our arrival. For some time we exerted our lungs in this manner before we received a reply, and I began to fear that our people were not at this village: at length a well-known voice replied in Arabic. The sentries and the whole party were positively asleep, although close to an enemy's country. They were soon awake when it was reported that we had arrived, and upon our entering the village they crowded around us with the usual welcome. A large fire was lighted in a spacious hut, and fortunately, the portmanteau having preceded us together with the ammunition, we were provided with a change of clothes.

I slept for a couple of hours, and then sent for the chief of Foweera, Kalloe. Both he and his son appeared; they said that their spies had reported that the M'was would attack this village on the following day; that they had devastated the entire country and occupied the whole of Unyoro and Chopi; that they had cut off a large herd of cattle belonging to Kamrasi, and he had only just reached the island in time for security, as the enemy had arrived at the spot and killed a number of people who were too late to embark. Kalloe reported that Kamrasi had fired at the M'was from the island, but having no bullets his rifle was useless. The M'was had returned the fire, being provided with four guns that they had procured from Speke's deserters; they were in the same condition as Kamrasi, having no bullets; thus a harmless fusilade had been carried on by both parties. The M'was had retired from their position on the bank of the river by Kamrasi's island, and had proceeded to Atada, which they had destroyed.

They were now within three miles of us; nevertheless the foolish Kalloe expressed his determination of driving his cattle to Kamrasi's island for security, about two miles distant. I endeavoured to persuade him that they would be perfectly safe if under our protection, but his only reply was to order his son to drive them off immediately.

That day, Kalloe and all the natives quitted the village and fled to an island for security, leaving us masters of the position. I served out a quantity of ammunition to the Turks, and we were perfectly prepared. The drums of the M'was were heard in all directions both day and night; but we were perfectly comfortable, as the granaries were well filled, and innumerable fowls stored both this and the closely adjoining deserted villages.

On the following day M'Gambi appeared with a message from Kamrasi, begging us to come and form a camp on the bank of the river opposite to his island to protect him from the M'was, who would assuredly return and attack him in canoes. I told him plainly that I should not interfere to assist him, as he had left me on the road at Deang; that Richarn had been killed by his people, and that one of my guns was still in their possession, added to which I had been obliged to forsake all my baggage, owing to the desertion of the porters; for all these errors I should hold Kamrasi responsible. He replied that he did not think Richarn was killed, but that he had shot the chief of a village dead, having got into some quarrel with the natives.

The conversation ended by my adhering to my intention of remaining independent at Foweera. M'Gambi said they were very miserable on the island, that no one could rest day or night for the mosquitoes, and that they were suffering from famine; he had several men with him, who at once set to work to thrash out corn from the well-filled granaries of the village, and they departed heavily laden. During the day a few natives of the district found their way into the village for a similar purpose. I had previously heard that the inhabitants of Foweera were disaffected, and that many were in correspondence with the enemy. I accordingly instructed Bacheeta to converse with the people, and to endeavour through them to get into communication with the M'was, assuring them that I should remain neutral, unless attacked, but if their intentions were hostile I was quite ready to fight. At the same time I instructed her to explain that I should be sorry to fire at the servants of M'tese, as he had behaved well to my friends Speke and Grant, but that the best way to avoid a collision would be for the M'was to keep at a distance from my camp. Bacheeta told me that this assurance would be certain to reach the chief of the M'was, as many of the natives of Chopi were in league with them against Kamrasi.

In the afternoon of that day I strolled outside the village with some of my men to accompany the party to the drinking place from which we procured our water; it was about a quarter of a mile from the camp, and it was considered dangerous for any one to venture so far without the protection of an armed party.

We had just returned, and were standing in the cool of the evening on the lawn opposite the entrance of the camp, when one of my men came rushing towards us, shouting, "Richarn! Richarn's come back!" In another moment I saw with extreme delight the jet black Richarn, whom I had mourned as lost, quietly marching towards us. The meeting was almost pathetic. I took him warmly by the hand and gave him a few words of welcome, but my *vakeel*, who had never cared for him before, threw himself upon his neck and burst out crying like a child. How long this sobbing would have continued I know not, as several of my Arabs caught the infection and began to be lachrymose, while Richarn, embraced on all sides, stood the ordeal most stoically, looking extremely bewildered, but totally unconscious of the cause of so much weeping. To change the current of feeling, I told the boy Saat to fetch a large gourd-shell of *merissa*, of which I had received a good supply from Kalloe. This soon arrived, and was by far the most acceptable welcome to Richarn, who drank like a whale. So large was the gourd, that even after the mighty draught enough remained for the rest of the party to sip. Refreshed by the much-loved drink, Richarn now told us his story. When separated from Mahommed at the village he had found a great number of people, some of whom were our runaway porters; on his attempting to persuade them to return, a quarrel had taken place, and the chief of the village heading his men had advanced on Richarn and seized his gun; at the same time the chief called to his men to kill him. Richarn drew his knife to release his gun; seeing which, the chief relaxed his hold, and stepping a pace back he raised his lance to strike; at the same moment Richarn pulled the trigger and shot him dead. The natives, panic-stricken at the sudden effect of the shot, rushed away, and Richarn, profiting by the opportunity, disappeared in the high grass, and fled. Once in the interminable sea of grass that was almost impenetrable, he wandered for two days without water: hearing the distant roar of the Nile, he at length reached it when nearly exhausted with thirst and fatigue; he then followed up the stream to Karuma, avoided the M'was – and knowing the road thence to M'Rooli that we had formerly travelled, he arrived at Foweera. His ramrod had been broken in the struggle when the chief seized his gun, and to his great aston- ishment I now showed him the piece that we had picked up on the pool of blood. He had made an excellent loading-rod with his hunt- ing knife by shaping a sapling of hard wood, and had reloaded his gun; thus with a good supply of ammunition he had not much fear of the natives. Kamrasi had evidently heard the true account of the affair.

Late in the evening we heard from a native that the whole of Kalloe's cattle that he had driven from Foweera had been captured by the enemy on their way to the river island, and that one of his sons and several natives who had driven them were killed; this was the result of his precipitate flight.

The M'was followed up their advantages with uninterrupted success, overrunning the entire country even to the shores of the Albert Lake, and driving off the cattle, together with all the women that had not taken refuge upon the numerous islands of the Victoria Nile. During this time, Kamrasi and his wives, together with his principal chiefs, resided in the misery of mosquitoes and malaria on the river; great numbers of people died of disease and starvation.

M'Gambi appeared frequently at our camp in order to procure corn, and from him we received reports of the distress of the peo- ple; his appearance had much changed; he looked half starved, and complained that he had nothing to drink but Nile water, as they had neither corn, nor pots in which they could make *merissa*, and the M'was had destroyed all the plantains, therefore they could not pre- pare cider.

Among other losses my two cows were reported by M'Gambi to have been stolen by the M'was, in company with the cattle of Kamrasi, with which they had been driven from Kisoona. I did not believe it, as he also told me that all the luggage that I had left at Deang had like wise been stolen by the enemy. But I had heard from Bacheeta that the natives of that neighbourhood had carried it (about six loads) direct to Kamrasi's island; thus it was in his pos- session at the same time that he declared it to have been stolen by the M'was. I told him, that I should hold him responsible, and that he should pay me the value of the lost effects in a certain number of cows.

A few days after this conversation, my cows and the whole of my luggage were delivered to me in safety. Kamrasi had evidently intended to appropriate them, but being pressed by the M'was and his old enemies on the east bank of the Nile (the Langgos), who had made common cause with the invaders, the time was not favourable for a quarrel with either me or the Turks.

On the evening of the 19th September, a few days after this occurrence, intelligence was brought into camp that Ibrahim and a hundred men had arrived at Karuma Falls at the ferry by which we had formerly crossed the river to Atada. I immediately despatched ten men to investigate the truth of the report. In about two hours they returned in high spirits, having exchanged greeting with Ibrahim and his party across the river. Kamrasi had despatched boats to another ferry above the Falls to facilitate the passage of the entire party on the following morning, as he wished them to attack the M'was immediately.

Not being desirous of such an encounter, the M'was, who had witnessed the arrival of this powerful reinforcement, immediately retreated, and by sunrise they had fallen back about twenty miles on the road to M'Rooli.

On the morning of the 20th Ibrahim arrived, bringing with him the Post from England; that being addressed to the consul at Khartoum had been forwarded to Gondokoro by the annual boats, and taken charge of by Ibrahim on his arrival at that station last April with ivory from the interior. My letters were of very old dates, none under two years, with the exception of one from Speke, who had sent me the Illustrated London News, containing his portrait and that of Grant; also Punch, with an illustration of Punch's discovery of the Nile sources. For a whole day I revelled in the luxury of letters and newspapers.

Ibrahim had very kindly thought of our necessities when at Gondokoro, and had brought me a piece of coarse cotton cloth of Arab manufacture (darmoor) for clothes for myself, and a piece of cotton print for a dress for Mrs. Baker, in addition to a large jar of honey, and some rice and coffee – the latter being the balance of my old stock that I bad been obliged to forsake for want of porters at Shooa. He told me that all my effects that I had left at Obbo had been returned to Gondokoro, and that my two men, whom I had left in charge, had returned with them to Khartoum, on board the vessel that had been sent for me from that place, but which had joined the traders' boats on their return voyage. Ibrahim had assured the captain that it was impossible that we could arrive during that year. It was thus fortunate that we had not pushed on for Gondokoro after April in expectation of finding the boat awaiting us. However, "all's well that ends well," and Ibrahim was astounded at our success, but rather shocked at our personal appearance, as we were thin and haggard, and our clothes had been so frequently repaired that they would hardly hold together.

On the 23d September we moved our camp, and took possession of a village within half a mile of the Victoria Nile. Kamrasi was now very valorous, and returned from his island to a large village on the banks of the river. He sent Ibrahim an immense quantity of ivory, in addition to the store that had been concealed by Eddrees on our departure from Kisoona; this was sent for, and in a few days it was safely deposited in the general camp. Ibrahim was amazed at the fortune that awaited him. I congratulated him most heartily on the success of the two expeditions – the geographical, and the ivory trade; the latter having far more than fulfilled my promise.

Kamrasi determined to invade the Langgo country immediately, as they had received Fowooka after his defeat, and he was now residing with the chief. Accordingly, eighty of Ibrahim's men were despatched across the river, and in three days they destroyed a number of villages, and captured about 200 head of cattle, together with a number of prisoners, including many women. Great rejoicings took place on their return; Ibrahim presented Kamrasi with a hundred cows, and in return for this generosity the king sent thirty immense tusks, and promised a hundred more within a few days.

Another expedition was demanded, and was quickly undertaken with similar success; this time Fowooka narrowly escaped, as a Turk fired at him, but missed and killed a native who stood by him. On the return of the party, Kamrasi received another present of cattle, and again the ivory flowed into the camp.

In the meantime, I had made myself excessively comfortable; we were in a beautiful and highly cultivated district, in the midst of immense fields of sweet potatoes. The idea struck me that I could manufacture spirit from this source, as they were so excessively sweet as to be disagreeable as a vegetable. Accordingly I collected a great number of large jars that were used by the natives for brewing *merissa*; in these I boiled several hundredweight of potatoes to a pulp. There were jars containing about twenty gallons; these I filled with the pulp mashed with water, to which I added yeast from a brewing of *merissa*. While this mixture was fermenting I constructed my still, by fixing a jar of about twelve gallons on a neat furnace of clay, and inserting the mouth of a smaller jar upon the top; the smaller jar thus inverted became the dome of the still. In the top of this I bored a hole, in which I fitted a long reed of about an inch in diameter, which descended to my condenser; the latter was the kettle, sunk by a weight in a large pan of cold water.

My still worked beautifully, and produced four or five bottles of good spirit daily; this I stored in large bottle gourds, containing about four gallons each. My men were excessively fond of attending to the distillery, especially Richarn, who took a deep interest in the operation, but who was frequently found dead asleep on his back; the fire out; and the still at a standstill. Of course he could not be suspected of having tried the produce of his manufactory! I found an extraordinary change in my health from the time that I commenced drinking the potato whisky. Every day I drank hot toddy. I became strong, and from that time to the present day my fever left me, occurring only once or twice during the first six months, and then quitting me entirely. Not having tasted either wine or spirits for nearly two years, the sudden change from total abstinence to a moderate allowance of stimulant produced a marvellous effect. Ibrahim and some of his men established stills; several became intoxicated, which so delighted M'Gambi, who happened to be present, that he begged a bottle of spirit from Ibrahim as a sample for Kamrasi. It appears that the king got drunk so quickly upon the potent spirit, that he had an especial desire to repeat the dose – he called it the *maroua* (cider) of our country, and pronounced it so far superior to his own that he determined to establish a factory. When I explained to him that it was the produce of sweet potatoes, he expressed his great regret that he had never sufficiently appreciated their value, and he expressed a determination to cultivate whole districts. Ibrahim was requested to leave one of his men who understood the management of a still, to establish and undertake the direction of King Kamrasi's Central African Unyoro Potato-Whisky Company, Unlimited.

Ibrahim had brought a variety of presents for Kamrasi: fifty pounds of beads, a revolver pistol, cotton cloths, blue glass tumblers, looking-glasses, etc. These donations, added to the pleasure afforded by the defeat of his enemies, put his majesty into excellent humour, sad he frequently came to visit us. On one occasion I gave him the portraits of Speke and Grant: the latter he recognised immediately; he could not understand the pictures in Punch, declaring that he (Punch) was not an Englishman, as he neither resembled me nor Speke; but he was exceedingly pleased with the Paris fashions in the Illustrated London News, which we cut out with a pair of scissors, and gave him as specimens of English ladies in full dress.

The war being concluded by the total discomfiture of his enemies, Kamrasi was determined to destroy all those inhabitants of Foweera who had in any way connived as the attack of the M'was. Daily executions took place in the summary manner already described, the victims being captured, led before the king, and butchered in his presence without a trial.

Among others suspected as favourable to revolution was Kalloe, the chief of Foweera; next to Kamrasi and M'Gambi he was the principal man in the kingdom; he was much beloved by the entire population of Chopi and Foweera, and I had always found him most intelligent and friendly. One night, at about eight o'clock, Ibrahim came to my hut looking very mysterious, and after assuring himself that no one was present, he confided to me that he had received orders from Kamrasi to attack Kalloe's village before daybreak on the following morning, to surround his dwelling, and to shoot him as he attempted to escape; Ibrahim was further instructed to capture the women and children of the village as his perquisites. At the very moment that thus treacherous compact had been entered into with Ibrahim, Kamrasi had pretended to be upon the most friendly terms with Kalloe, who was then in his camp; but he did not lay violent hands upon him, as, many of the natives being in his favour, the consequences might have been disagreeable: thus he had secretly ordered his destruction. I at once desired Ibrahim at all hazards to renounce so horrible a design. Never did I feel so full of revolution as at that moment; my first impulse was to assist Kalloe to dethrone Kamrasi, and to usurp the kingdom. Ibrahim had an eye to business; he knew, that should he offend Kamrasi there would be an end to the ivory trade for the present. The country was so rich in ivory that it was a perfect bank upon which he could draw without limit, provided that he remained an ally of the king; but no trade could be carried on with the natives, all business being prohibited by Kamrasi, who himself monopolised the profits. In the event of war, not a tusk would be obtained, as the ivory in possession of the natives was never stored in their huts, but was concealed in the earth. The Turks were now mercenaries employed by the king to do any bloody work that he might require.

Ibrahim was in a dilemma. I offered to take the entire onus upon myself. That Kalloe should not be murdered I was determined; the old man had on several occasions been very obliging to me and to my people, and I resolved to save him at any risk. His son, perfectly unsuspicious of evil, was at that moment in our camp, having fraternized with some of my men. I sent for him immediately and explained the entire plot, concluding by telling him to run that instant at full speed to his father (about two miles distant), and to send away all the women and children from the village, but to bring Kalloe to my hut; that I would hoist the British flag, as I had done at Kisoona, and this should protect him from the bloodthirsty Kamrasi, who would not dare to seize him. Should he refuse to trust me, he must fly immediately, as the Turks would attack the village before daybreak. Away started the astonished son in the dark night at full speed along the well-known path, to give the warning.

I now arranged with Ibrahim that to avoid offending Kamrasi he should make a false attack upon the village at the time appointed; he would find it deserted, and there would be an end of the matter should Kalloe prefer flight to trusting in my protection, which I felt sure he would. Midnight arrived, and no signs of Kalloe had appeared; I went to sleep, satisfied that he was safe. Before daybreak eighty men of the Turks' party started upon their feigned expedition; in about two hours they returned, having found the village deserted; the bird had flown. I was delighted at the success of this ruse, but I should have been more satisfied had Kalloe placed himself in my hands: this I had felt sure he would decline, as the character of the natives is generally so false and mistrustful that he would suspect a snare.

At about noon we heard yells; drums were beating and horns blowing in all directions. For the moment I thought that Kalloe had raised the country against Kamrasi, as I observed many hundred men dressed for war, scouring the beautiful open park, like hounds upon a scent. The Turks beat their drum and called their men under arms beneath the ensign planted outside the village – not knowing the intention of the unusual gathering. It shortly transpired that Kamrasi had heard of the escape of Kalloe, and, enraged at the loss of his prey, he had immediately started about a thousand men in pursuit.

In the evening I heard that he had been captured. I sent to Kamrasi directly, to beg him to postpone his execution, as I wished to speak with him on the following morning.

At sunrise I started, and found the king sitting in his but, while Kalloe was lying under a plantain tree perfectly resigned, with his leg in the Kamrasi shoe – a block of wood of about four feet long and ten inches thick (the rough trunk of a tree); his left foot had been thrust through a small hole in the log, while a peg driven through at right angles just above the instep effectually secured the prisoner. This was a favourite punishment of the king; the prisoner might thus languish until released by death; it was impossible to sit up, and difficult to lie down, the log having to be adjusted by an attendant according to the movement of the body. I told Kamrasi that as I had saved him from the attack of the Turks at Kisoona I must grant me a favour, and spare Kalloe's life: this request, to my astonishment, he at once granted (a few days afterwards he shot Kalloe with his own hands) and added, that he should only keep him in the "shoe" for a few days, until his people should bring him a hundred cows as a fine, in which case he should release him. I had no faith in his promise, as I had before heard that it was his practice to put the shoe upon any rich man in order to extract a fine, upon the payment of which the unfortunate prisoner was on some occasions killed instead of liberated. However, I had done all in my power; and had Kalloe been a man of determination, he could have saved himself by trusting implicitly to me. As I returned to the camp, I could not help reflecting on the ingratitude I had experienced among all the natives; on many occasions I had exerted myself to benefit others in whom I had no personal interest, but in no single instance had I ever received even a look of gratitude.

Two days after this occurrence I ordered the boy Saat to go as usual in search of supplies to the neighbouring villages; but as he was starting, Ibrahim advised him to wait a little, as something was wrong, and it would be dangerous to go alone. A few minutes later, I heard three shots fired in rapid succession at about three-quarters of a mile distant. The Turks and my men immediately thronged outside the village, which position being on a hill, we had a panoramic view of the surrounding country.

We shortly perceived a number of men, including a few of the Turks' party, approaching from an opposite hill, carrying something heavy in their arms. With the telescope I distinguished a mat on which some object of weight was laboriously supported, the bearers grasping the corners in their hands. "One of our people is killed!" murmured one Turk. "Perhaps it's only a native," said another. "Who would trouble himself to carry a black fellow home!" exclaimed a third. The mystery was soon cleared by the arrival of the party with the dead body of one of Kamrasi's headmen; one ball had struck him through the chest, another through the right arm, and the third had passed through the body from side to side. He had been shot by some Bari slaves who acted as soldiers belonging to the Turks' party. It appeared that the deceased had formerly sent seventy elephants' tusks to the people of Mahommed Wat-el-Mek against the orders of Kamrasi, who had prohibited the export of ivory from his kingdom, as he had agreed to deal exclusively with Ibrahim. The culprit was therefore condemned to death, but having some powerful adherents in his village, Kamrasi had thought it advisable to employ the Turks to shoot him; this task they gladly accepted, as they were minus seventy tusks through his conduct. Without my knowledge, a small party had started in open daylight to his village close to our camp, and on attempting to enter the fence, several lances were thrown at the Turks; the deceased rushed from the hut attempting to escape, and was immediately shot dead by three of the Bari soldiers. The hands were then (as usual in all these countries) amputated at the wrists, in order to detach the copper bracelets; the body being dragged about two hundred paces from the village, was suspended by the neck to a branch of the tamarind tree. All the slave women (about seventy) and children were then driven down to the spot by the Turks to view the body as it swung from the branch; when thoroughly horrified by the sight, they were threatened to be served precisely in a similar manner should they ever attempt to escape.

Superlatively brutal as this appeared, I could not help reflecting that our public executions in England convey a similar moral; the only difference being in the conduct of the women; the savages having to be driven to the sight as witnesses, while European females throng curiously to such disgusting exhibitions. A few minutes after the departure of the crowd, the tree was covered with vultures, all watching the prospective feast. (The woman Bacheeta ran away, and we never saw her again. Some time after, we heard that she had escaped to Fowooka's people, fearing to be left by us, as we had promised, in Chopi.)

In the evening Kamrasi sent a number of women and children as presents to Ibrahim: altogether he had given him seventy-two slaves in addition to those captured in the various wars. There never was a more supreme despot than the king Kamrasi – not only the property, but the families of his subjects were at his disposal; he boasted that all belonged to him. Thus, when disposed to be liberal, he took from others and bestowed upon his favourites; should any sufferer complain, there were no lawyer's costs, but the "shoe," or death. His power depended upon a perfect system of espionage, by which he obtained a knowledge of all that passed throughout his kingdom; that being divided into numerous small districts, each governed by a chief, who was responsible for the acts committed within his jurisdiction, the government was wonderfully simplified. Should a complaint be made against a governor, he was summoned before the king; if guilty, death, or the "shoe!" To be suspected of rebellion, was to die. A bodyguard of about 500 men, who were allowed to pillage the country at discretion, secured the power of the king, as with this organized force always at hand he could pounce upon the suspected and extinguish them at once: thus the tyrant held his sway over a population so timid that they yielded tamely to his oppression. Having now allied himself to the Turks, he had conceived the most ambitious views of conquering Uganda, and of restoring the ancient kingdom of Kitwara; but the total absence of physical courage will utterly frustrate such plans for extension, and Kamrasi the Cruel will never be known as Kamrasi the Conqueror.

Chapter XVI

KAMRASI'S ADIEU

It was the middle of November – not the wretched month that chills even the recollection of Old England, but the last of the ten months of rain that causes the wonderful vegetation of the fertile soil in Equatorial Africa. The Turks were ready to return to Shooa, and I longed for the change from this brutal country to the still wilder but less bloody tribe of Madi, to the north.

The quantity of ivory in camp was so large that we required 700 porters to carry both tusks and provisions, etc. for the five days' march through uninhabited country. Kamrasi came to see us before we parted; he had provided the requisite porters. We were to start on the following day; he arrived with the Blissett rifle that had been given him by Speke. He told me that he was sorry we were going, and he was much distressed that he had burst his rifle – he had hammered a large bullet in the endeavour to fit the bore; and the lump of lead having stuck in the middle, he had fired his rifle and split the barrel, which being of remarkably good metal had simply opened. He told me that it did not matter so very much after all, as he had neither powder nor ball (this was false, as Ibrahim had just given him a quantity), therefore his rifle would have been useless if sound; but he added, "You are now going home, where you can obtain all you require, therefore you will want for nothing; give me, before you leave, the little double-barrelled rifle that YOU PROMISED me, and a supply of ammunition!" To the last moment he was determined to persevere in his demand, and, if possible, to obtain my handy little Fletcher 24 rifle, that had been demanded and refused ever since my residence in his country. I was equally persistent in my refusal, telling him that there were many dangers on the road, and I could not travel unarmed.

On the following morning our people crossed the river: this was a tedious operation, as our party consisted of about 700 porters and eighty armed men: Ibrahim had arranged to leave thirty men with Kamrasi to protect him from the M'was until he should return in the following season, when he promised to bring him a great variety of presents. By 4 p.m. the whole party had crossed the river with ivory and baggage. We now brought up the rear, and descended some fine crags of granite to the water's edge; there were several large canoes in attendance, one of which we occupied, and, landing on the opposite shore, we climbed up the steep ascent and looked back upon Unyoro, in which we had passed ten months of wretchedness. It had poured with rain on the preceding day, and the natives had constructed a rough camp of grass huts.

On the break of day on the 17th November we started. It would be tedious to describe the journey, as, although by a different route, it was through the same country that we had traversed on our arrival from Shooa. After the first day's march we quitted the forest and entered upon the great prairies. I was astonished to find after several days' journey a great difference in the dryness of the climate. In Unyoro we had left the grass an intense green, the rain having been frequent: here it was nearly dry, and in many places it had been burnt by the native hunting parties. From some elevated points in the route I could distinctly make out the outline of the mountains running from the Albert Lake to the north, on the west bank of the Nile; these would hardly have been observed by a person who was ignorant of their existence, as the grass was so high that I had to ascend a white ant-hill to look for them; they were about sixty miles distant, and my men, who knew them well, pointed them out to their companions.

The entire party, including women and children, amounted to about 1,000 people. Although they had abundance of flour, there was no meat, and the grass being high there was no chance of game. On the fourth day only I saw a herd of about twenty tetel (hartebeest) in an open space that had been recently burnt. We were both riding upon oxen that I had purchased of Ibrahim, and we were about a mile ahead of the flag in the hope of getting a shot; dismounting from my animal, I stalked the game down a ravine, but upon reaching the point that I had resolved upon for the shot, I found the herd had moved their position to about 250 paces from me. They were all looking at me, as they had been disturbed by the oxen and the boy Saat in the distance. Dinner depended on the shot. There was a leafless bush singed by the recent fire; upon a branch of this I took a rest, but just as I was going to fire they moved off – a clean miss! Whizz went the bullet over them, but so close to the ears of one that it shook its head as though stung by a wasp, and capered round and round; the others stood perfectly still, gazing at the oxen in the distance. Crack went the left-hand barrel of the little Fletcher 24, and down went a tetel like a lump of lead, before the satisfactory sound of the bullet returned from the distance. Off went the herd, leaving a fine beast kicking on the ground. It was shot through the spine, and some of the native porters, having witnessed the sport from a great distance, threw down their loads and came racing towards the meat like a pack of wolves scenting blood. In a few minutes the prize was divided, while a good portion was carried by Saat for our own use; the tetel, weighing about 500 lbs., vanished among the crowd in a few minutes.

On the fifth day's march from the Victoria Nile we arrived at Shooa; the change was delightful after the wet and dense vegetation of Unyoro: the country was dry, and the grass low and of fine quality. We took possession of our camp, that had already been prepared for us in a large courtyard well cemented with cow-dung and clay, and fenced with a strong row of palisades. A large tree grew in the centre. Several hits were erected for interpreters and servants, and a tolerably commodious hut, the roof overgrown with pumpkins, was arranged for our mansion.

That evening the native women crowded to our camp to welcome my wife home, and to dance in honour of our return; for which exhibition they expected a present of a cow.

Much to my satisfaction, I found that my first-rate riding ox that had been lamed during the previous year by falling into a pitfall, and had been returned to Shooa, was perfectly recovered; thus I had a good mount for my journey to Gondokoro.

Some months were passed at Shooa, during which I occupied my time by rambling about the neighbourhood, ascending the mountain, making duplicates of my maps, and gathering information, all of which was simply a corroboration of what I had heard before, excepting from the East. The Turks had discovered a new country called Lira, about thirty miles from Shooa; the natives were reported as extremely friendly, and their country as wonderfully fertile and rich in ivory. Many of the people were located in the Turks' camp; they were the same type as the Madi, but wore their hair in a different form: it was woven into a thick felt, which covered the shoulders, and extended as low upon the back as the shoulderblade.

They were not particular about wearing false hair, but were happy to receive subscriptions from any source; in case of death the hair of the deceased was immediately cut off and shared among his friends to be added to their felt. When in full dress (the men being naked) this mass of felt was plastered thickly with a bluish clay, so as to form an even surface; this was most elaborately worked with the point of a thorn, so as to resemble the cuttings of a file: white pipe-clay was then arranged in patterns on the surface, while an ornament made of either an antelope's or giraffe's sinew was stuck in the extremity and turned up for about a foot in length. This when dry was as stiff as horn, and the tip was ornamented with a tuft of fur – the tip of a leopard's tail being highly prized.

I am not aware that any Lord Chancellor of England or any member of the English bar has ever penetrated to Central Africa, therefore the origin of the fashion and the similarity in the wigs is most extraordinary; a well-blacked barrister in full wig and nothing else would thoroughly impersonate a native of Lira. The tribe of Lira was governed by a chief; but he had no more real authority than any of the petty chiefs who ruled the various portions of the Madi country. Throughout the tribes excepting the kingdom of Unyoro, the chiefs had very little actual power, and so uncertain was their tenure of office that the rule seldom remained two generations in one family. On the death of the father, the numerous sons generally quarrelled for his property and for the right of succession, ending in open war, and in dividing the flocks and herds, each settling in a separate district and becoming a petty chief; thus there was no union throughout the country, and consequently great weakness. The people of Lira were fighting with their friends the Langgos – those of Shooa with the natives of Fatiko; nor were there two neighbouring tribes that were at peace. It was natural that such unprincipled parties as the Khartoum traders should turn this general discord to their own advantage; thus within the ten months that I had been absent from Shooa a great change had taken place in the neighbourhood. The rival parties of Koorshid and Debono, under their respective leaders, Ibrahim and Mahommed Wat-el-Mek, had leagued themselves with contending tribes, and the utter ruin of the country was the consequence. For many miles' circuit from Shooa, the blackened ruins of villages and deserted fields bore witness to the devastation committed; cattle that were formerly in thousands, had been driven off, and the beautiful district that had once been most fertile was reduced to a wilderness. By these wholesale acts of robbery and destruction the Turks had damaged their own interests, as the greater number of the natives had fled to other countries; thus it was most difficult to obtain porters to convey the ivory to Gondokoro. The people of the country had been so spoiled by the payment in cows instead of beads for the most trifling services, that they now refused to serve as porters to Gondokoro under a payment of four cows each; thus, as 1,000 men were required, 4,000 cows were necessary as payment. Accordingly *razzia* must be made.

Upon several expeditions, the Turks realized about 2,000 cows; the natives had become alert, and had driven off their herds to inaccessible mountains. Debono's people at their camp, about twenty-five miles distant, were even in a worse position than Ibrahim; they had so exasperated the natives by their brutal conduct, that tribes formerly hostile to each other now coalesced and combined to thwart the Turks by declining to act as porters; thus their supply of ivory could not be transported to Gondokoro. This led to extra violence on the part of the Turks, until at last the chief of Faloro (Werdella) declared open war, and suddenly driving off the Turks' cattle, he retired to the mountains, from whence he sent an impertinent message inviting Mahommed to try to rescue them.

This act of insolence united the rival trading parties against Werdella: those of Ibrahim and Mahommed agreed to join in an attack upon his village. They started with a force of about 300 armed men, and arriving at the foot of the mountains at about 4 a.m. they divided their force into two parties of 150 men each, and ascended the rocky hill upon two sides, intending to surprise the village on one side, while the natives and their herds would be intercepted in their flight upon the other.

The chief, Werdella, was well experienced in the affairs of the Turks, as he had been for two or three years engaged with them in many *razzia*s upon the adjoining tribes – he had learnt to shoot while acting as their ally, and having received as presents two mus- kets, and two brace of pistols from Debono's nephew Amabile, he thought it advisable to supply himself with ammunition; he had therefore employed his people to steal a box of 500 cart ridges and a parcel containing 10,000 percussion caps from Mahommed's camp. Werdella was a remarkably plucky fellow; and thus strength- ened by powder and ball, and knowing the character of the Turks, he resolved to fight.

Hardly had the Turks' party of 150 men advanced half way up the mountain path in their stealthy manner of attempting a surprise, when they were assailed by a shower of arrows, and the leader who carried the flag fell dead at the report of a musket fired from behind a rock. Startled at this unexpected attack, the Turks' party recoiled, leaving their flag upon the ground by the dead standard-bearer. Before they had time to recover from their first panic, another shot was fired from the same shelter at a distance of about thirty paces, and the brains of one of the Turks' party were splattered over his comrades, as the ball took the top of his head completely off. Three Bagara Arabs, first-rate elephant hunters, who were with the Turks, now rushed forward and saved the flag and a box of ammunition that the porter had thrown down in his flight. These Arabs, whose courage was of a different class to that of the traders' party, endeav- oured to rally the panic-stricken Turks, but just as they were feebly and irresolutely advancing, another shot rang from the same fatal rock, and a man who carried a box of cartridges fell dead. This was far too hot for the traders' people, who usually had it all their own way, being alone possessed of firearms. A disgraceful flight took place, but Werdella was again too much for them. On their arrival at the bottom of the hill, they ran round the base to join the other division of their party; this effected, they were consulting together as to retreat or advance, when close above their heads from an overhanging rock another shot was fired, and a man dropped, shot through the chest. The head of Werdella was distinctly seen grinning in triumph; the whole party fired at him! "He's down!" was shouted, as the head disappeared; a puff of smoke from the rock, and a shriek from one of the Turks at the sound of another musket shot from the same spot, settled the question; a man fell mortally wounded. Four men were shot dead, and one was brought home by the crestfallen party to die in two or three days; five shots had been fired, and five killed, by one native armed with two guns against 300 men. "Bravo, Werdella!" I exclaimed, as the beaten party returned to camp and Ibrahim described the fight. He deserved the Victoria Cross. This defeat completely cowed the cowardly Turks; nor would any persuasions on the part of Ibrahim induce them to make another *razzia* within the territory of the redoubted chief, Werdella.

During the absence of the traders' party upon various expeditions, about fifty men were left in their camp as headquarters. Nothing could exceed the brutality of the people; they had erected stills, and produced a powerful corn spirit from the native *merissa*; their entire time was passed in gambling, drinking, and fighting, both by night and day. The natives were ill-treated, their female slaves and children brutally ill-used, and the entire camp was a mere slice from the infernal regions. My portion of the camp being a secluded courtyard, we were fortunately independent.

On one occasion a *razzia* had been made; and although unsuccessful in cattle, it had been productive in slaves. Among the captives was a pretty young girl of about fifteen; she had been sold by auction in the camp, as usual, the day after the return from the *razzia*, and had fallen to the lot of one of the men. Some days after her capture, a native from the village that had been plundered confidently arrived at the camp with the intention of offering ivory for her ransom. Hardly had he entered the gateway, when the girl, who was sitting at the door of her owner's hut, caught sight of him, and springing to her feet, she ran as fast as her chained ankles would allow her, and threw herself in his arms, exclaiming, "My father!" It was her father, who had thus risked his life in the enemy's camp to ransom his child.

The men who were witnesses to this scene immediately rushed upon the unfortunate man, tore him from his daughter, and bound him tightly with cords.

While this was enacting, I happened to be in my hut; thus I was not an eye-witness. About an hour later, I called some of my men to assist me in cleaning some rifles. Hardly had we commenced, when three shots were fired within a hundred paces of my hut. My men exclaimed, "They have shot the *Abid* (native)!" "What native?" I inquired. They then related the story I have just described. Brutal as these bloodthirsty villains were, I could hardly believe in so cold-blooded a murder. I immediately sent my people and the boy Saat to verify it; they returned with the report that the wretched father was sitting on the ground, bound to a tree, dead; shot by three balls.

I must do Ibrahim the justice to explain that he was not in the camp; had he been present, this murder would not have been committed, as he scrupulously avoided any such acts in my vicinity. A few days later, a girl about sixteen, and her mother, who were slaves, were missing; they had escaped. The hue and cry was at once raised. Ibrahimawa, the "Sinbad" of Bornu, who had himself been a slave, was the most indefatigable slave-hunter. He and a party at once started upon the tracks of the fugitives. They did not return until the following day; but where was the runaway who could escape from so true a bloodhound? The young girl and her mother were led into camp tied together by the neck, and were immediately condemned to be hanged. I happened to be present, as, knowing the whole affair, I had been anxiously awaiting the result. I took this opportunity of explaining to the Turks that I would use any force to prevent such an act, and that I would report the names of all those to the Egyptian authorities who should commit any murder that I could prove; neither would I permit the two captives to be flogged – they were accordingly pardoned. (It will be observed that at this period of the expedition I had acquired an extraordinary influence over the people, that enabled me to exert an authority which saved the lives of many unfortunate creatures who would otherwise have been victims.)

There was among the slaves a woman who had been captured in the attack upon Fowooka. This woman I have already mentioned as having a very beautiful boy, who at the time of the capture was a little more than a year old.

So determined was her character, that she had run away five times with her child, but on every occasion she had been recap-

tured, after having suffered much by hunger and thirst in endeavouring to find her way back to Unyoro through the uninhabited
wilderness between Shooa and Karuma. On the last occasion of her
capture, the Turks had decided upon her being incorrigible, therefore she had received 144 blows with the *coorbatch* and had been
sold separately from her child to the party belonging to Mahommed
Wat-el-Mek. Little Abbai had always been a great pet of Mrs.
Baker's, and the unfortunate child being now motherless, he was
naturally adopted, and led a most happy life. Although much under
two years old, he was quite equal in precocity to a European child
of three; in form and strength he was a young Hercules, and,
although so young, he would frequently follow me out shooting for
two or three miles, and return home with a guinea-fowl hanging
over his shoulder, or his hands full of pigeons. Abbai became very
civilized; he was taught to make a Turkish *salaam* upon receiving a
present, and to wash his hands both before and after his meals. He
had the greatest objection to eat alone, and he generally invited
three or four friends of about his own age to dine with him; on such
occasions, a large wooden bowl, about twenty inches in diameter,
was filled with soup and porridge, around which steaming dish the
young party sat, happier in their slavery than kings in power.

There were two lovely girls of three and eight years of age that
belonged to Ibrahim; these were not black, but of the same dark
brown tint as Kamrasi and many of the Unyoro people. Their
mother was also there, and their history being most pitiable, they
were always allowed free access to our hut and the dinner bowl.
These two girls were the daughters of Owine, one of the great
chiefs who were allied with Fowooka against Kamrasi. After the
defeat of Fowooka, Owine and many of his people with their families quitted the country, and forming an alliance with Mahommed
Wat-el-Mek, they settled in the neighbourhood of his camp at Faloro, and built a village. For some time they were on the best terms,
but some cattle of the Turks being missed, suspicion fell upon the
new settlers. The men of Mahommed's party desired that they
might be expelled, and Mahommed, in a fit of drunken fury, at once
ordered them to be massacred. His men, eager for murder and plunder, immediately started upon their bloody errand, and surrounding
the unsuspecting colony, they fired the huts and killed every man,

including the chief, Owine; capturing the women and children as slaves. Ibrahim had received the mother and two girls as presents from Mahommed Wat-el-Mek. As the two rival companies had been forced to fraternize, owing to the now generally hostile attitude of the surrounding tribes, the leaders had become wonderfully polite, exchanging presents, getting drunk together upon raw spirits, and behaving in a brotherly manner – according to their ideas of fraternity.

There was a peculiar charm in the association with children in this land of hardened hearts and savage natures: there is a time in the life of the most savage animal when infancy is free from the fierce instincts of race; even the lion's whelp will fondle the hand that it would tear in riper years: thus, separated in this land of horrors from all civilization, and forced by hard necessity into the vicinity of all that was brutal and disgusting, it was an indescribable relief to be surrounded by those who were yet innocent, and who clung in their forsaken state to those who looked upon them with pity. We had now six little dependents, none of whom could ever belong to us, as they were all slaves, but who were well looked after by my wife; fed, amused, and kept clean. The boy Abbai was the greatest favourite, as, having neither father nor mother, he claimed the greatest care: he was well washed every morning, and then to his great delight smeared all over from head to toes with red ochre and grease, with a cock's feather stuck in his woolly pate. He was then a most charming pet savage, and his toilette completed, he invariably sat next to his mistress, drinking a gourd-shell of hot milk, while I smoked my early morning pipe beneath the tree. I made bows and arrows for my boys, and taught them to shoot at a mark, a large pumpkin being carved into a man's head to excite their aim. Thus the days were passed until the evening; at that time a large fire was lighted to create a blaze, drums were collected, and after dinner a grand dance was kept up by the children, until the young Abbai ended regularly by creeping under my wife's chair, and falling sound asleep: from this protected spot he was carried to his mat, wrapped up in a piece of old flannel (the best cloth we had), in which he slept till morning. Poor little Abbai! I often wonder what will be his fate, and whether in his dreams he recalls the few months of happiness that brightened his earliest days of slavery.

Although we were in good health in Shooa, many of the men were ill, suffering generally from headache; also from ulcerated legs; the latter was a peculiar disease, as the ulcer generally commenced upon the anklebone and extended to such a degree that the patient was rendered incapable of walking. The treatment for headache among all the savage tribes was a simple cauterization of the forehead in spots burnt with a hot iron close to the roots of the hair. The natives declared that the water was unwholesome from the small stream at the foot of the hill and that all those who drank from the well were in good health. I went down to examine the spring, which I found beautifully clear, while the appearance of the stream was quite sufficient to explain the opposite quality. As I was walking quietly along the bank, I saw a bright ray of light in the grass upon the opposite side; in another moment I perceived the head of a crocodile which was concealed in the grass, the brightness of the sun's reflection upon the eye having attracted my attention. A shot with the little 24 rifle struck just above the eye and killed it; it was a female, from which we extracted several large eggs, all with hard shells.

The shooting that I had while at Shooa was confined to antelopes; of these there was no variety excepting waterbuck and hartebeest. Whenever I shot an animal the Shooa natives would invariably cut its throat, and drink the hot blood as it gushed from the artery. In this neighbourhood there was a great scarcity of game the natives of Lira described their country as teeming with elephants and rhinoceros; a fine horn of the latter they brought with them to Shooa. There is only one variety of rhinoceros that I have met with in the portions of Africa that I have visited: this is the two-horned, a very exact sketch of which I made of the head of one that I cut off after I had shot it. This two-horned black rhinoceros is extremely vicious. I have remarked that they almost invariably charge any enemy that they smell, but do not see; they generally retreat if they observe the object before obtaining the wind.

In my rambles in search of game, I found two varieties of cotton growing indigenous to the country: one with a yellow blossom was so short in the staple as to be worthless, but the other (a red blossom) produced a fine quality that was detached with extreme ease from the seeds. A sample of this variety I brought to England, and deposited the seed at the Royal Botanical Gardens at Kew. A large quantity was reported to be grown at Lira, some of which was brought me by the chief; this was the inferior kind. I sketched the old chief of Lira, who when in full dress wore a curious ornament of cowrie shells upon his felt wig that gave him a most comical appearance, as he looked like the caricature of an English judge. The Turks had extended their excursions in their search for ivory, and they returned from an expedition sixty miles east of Shooa, bringing with them two donkeys that they had obtained from the natives. This was an interesting event, as for nearly two years I had heard from the natives of Latooka, and from those of Unyoro, that donkeys existed in a country to the east. These animals were the same in appearance as those of the Soudan; the natives never rode, but simply used them to transport wood from the forest to their villages; the people were reported as the same in language and appearance as the Lira tribe.

Chapter XVII

THE NATIVES IN MOURNING

The hour of deliverance from our long sojourn in Central Africa was at hand; it was the month of February, and the boats would be at Gondokoro. The Turks had packed their ivory; the large tusks were fastened to poles to be carried by two men, and the camp was a perfect mass of this valuable material. I counted 609 loads of upwards of 50 lbs. each; thirty-one loads were lying at an outstation: therefore the total results of the ivory campaign during the last twelve months were about 32,000 lbs., equal to about 9,630 lbs. when delivered in Egypt. This was a perfect fortune for Koorshid.

We were ready to start. My baggage was so unimportant that I was prepared to forsake everything, and to march straight for Gondokoro independently with my own men; but this the Turks assured me was impracticable, as the country was so hostile in advance that we must of necessity have some fighting on the road; the Bari tribe would dispute our right to pass through their territory.

The porters were all engaged to transport the ivory, but I observed that the greater number were in mourning for either lost friends or cattle, having ropes twisted round their necks and waists, as marks of sorrow.

About 800 men received payment of cattle in advance; the next day they had all absconded with their cows, having departed during the night. This was a planned affair to "spoil the Egyptians:" a combination had been entered into some months before by the Madi and Shooa tribes, to receive payment and to abscond, but to leave the Turks helpless to remove their stock of ivory. The people of Mahommed Wat-el-Mek were in a similar dilemma; not a tusk could be delivered at Gondokoro.

This was not my affair. The greater portion of Ibrahim's immense store of ivory had been given to him by Kamrasi; I had guaranteed him a hundred cantars (10,000 lbs.) should he quit Obbo and proceed to the unknown south; in addition to a large quantity that he had collected and delivered at Gondokoro in the past year, he had now more than three times that amount. Although Kamrasi had on many occasions offered the ivory to me, I had studiously avoided the acceptance of a single tusk, as I wished the Turks to believe that I would not mix myself up with trade in any form, and that my expedition had purely the one object that I had explained to Ibrahim when I first won him over on the road to Ellyria more than two years ago: the discovery of the Albert Lake. With a certain number of presents of first class forty-guinea rifles and guns, etc. etc., to Ibrahim, I declared my intention of starting for Gondokoro. My trifling articles of baggage were packed: a few of the Lira natives were to act as porters, as, although the ivory could not be transported, it was necessary for Ibrahim to send a strong party to Gondokoro to procure ammunition and the usual supplies forwarded annually from Khartoum; the Lira people who carried my luggage would act as return porters.

The day arrived for our departure; the oxen were saddled and we were ready to start. Crowds of people came to say goodbye, but, dispensing with the hand-kissing of the Turks who were to remain in camp, we prepared for our journey towards home. Far away although it was, every step would bring us nearer. Nevertheless there were ties even in this wild spot, where all was savage and unfeeling – ties that were painful to sever, and that caused a sincere regret to both of us when we saw our little flock of unfortunate slave children crying at the idea of separation. In this moral desert, where all humanized feelings were withered and parched like the sands of the Soudan, the guilelessness of the children had been welcomed like springs of water, as the only refreshing feature in a land of sin and darkness. "Where are you going?" cried poor little Abbai in the broken Arabic that we had taught him. "Take me with you, *Sitty* (lady)!" And he followed us down the path, as we regretfully left our proteges, with his fists tucked into his eyes, weeping from his heart, although for his own mother he had not shed a tear. We could not take him with us; he belonged to Ibrahim; and had I purchased the child to rescue him from his hard lot and to rear him as a civilized being, I might have been charged with slave dealing. With heavy hearts we saw him taken up in the arms of a woman and carried back to camp, to prevent him from following our party that had now started.

We had turned our backs fairly upon the south, and we now travelled for several days through most beautiful park-like lands, crossing twice the Un-y-Ame stream, that rises in the country between Shooa and Unyoro, and arriving at the point of junction of this river with the Nile, in latitude 3 degrees 32 minutes N. On the north bank of the Un-y-Ame, about three miles from the embouchure of that river where it flows into the Nile, the tamarind tree was shown me that forms the limit of Signor Miani's journey from Gondokoro, the extreme point reached by any traveller from the north until the date of my expedition. This tree bore the name of *Shedder-el-Sowar* (the traveller's tree), by which it was known to the traders' parties. Several of the men belonging to Ibrahim, also Mahommed Wat-el-Mek, the *vakeel* of Debono's people, had accompanied Signor Miani on his expedition to this spot. Loggo, the Bari interpreter, who had constantly acted for me during two years, happened to have been the interpreter of Signor Miani; he confessed to me how he had been compelled by his master's escort to deceive him, by pretending that a combined attack was to be made upon them by the natives.

Upon this excuse, Miani's men refused to proceed, and determined to turn back to Gondokoro; thus ended his expedition. I regarded the tree that marked the limit of his journey with much sympathy. I remembered how I had formerly contended with similar difficulties, and how heartbreaking it would have been to have returned, baffled by the misconduct of my own people, when the determination of my heart urged me forward to the south; thus I appreciated the disappointment that so enterprising a traveller must have felt in sorrowfully cutting his name upon the tree, and leaving it as a record of misfortune.

With a just tribute to the perseverance that had carried him farther than any European traveller had penetrated before him, we continued our route over a most beautiful park of verdant grass, diversified by splendid tamarind trees, the dark foliage of which afforded harbour for great numbers of the brilliant yellow-breasted pigeon. We shortly ascended a rocky mountain by a stony and difficult pass, and upon arrival at the summit, about 800 feet above the Nile, which lay in front at about two miles' distance, we halted to enjoy the magnificent view. "Hurrah for the old Nile!" I exclaimed, as I revelled in the scene before me: here it was, fresh from its great parent, the Albert Lake, in all the grandeur of Africa's mightiest river. From our elevated point we looked down upon a broad sheet of unbroken water, winding through marshy ground, flowing from W.S.W. The actual breadth of clear water, independent of the marsh and reedy banks, was about 400 yards, but, as usual in the deep and flat portions of the White Nile, the great extent of reeds growing in deep water rendered any estimate of the positive width extremely vague. We could discern the course of this great river for about twenty miles, and distinctly, trace the line of mountains on the west bank that we had seen at about sixty miles' distance when on the route from Karuma to Shooa; the commencement of this chain we had seen when at Magungo, forming the Koshi frontier of the Nile. The country opposite to the point on which we now stood was Koshi, which, forming the west bank of the Nile, extended the entire way to the Albert Lake. The country that we occupied was Madi, which extended as the east bank of the Nile to the angle of the Victoria Nile (or Somerset River) junction opposite Magungo. These two countries, Koshi and Madi, we had seen from Magungo when we had viewed the exit of the Nile from the lake, as though a tail-like continuation of the water, until lost in the distance of the interminable valley of high reeds. Having, from Magungo, in lat. 2 degrees 16 minutes, looked upon the course of the river far to the north, and from the high pass, our present point, in lat. 3 degrees 34 min. N., we now comprised an extensive view of the river to the south; the extremities of the limits of view from north and south would almost meet, and leave a mere trifle of a few miles not actually inspected.

Exactly opposite the summit of the pass from which we now scanned the country, rose the precipitous mountain known as Gebel Kookoo, which rose to a height of about 2,500 feet above the level of the Nile, and formed the prominent feature of a chain which bordered the west bank of the Nile with few breaks to the north, until within thirty miles of Gondokoro. The pass upon which we stood was the southern extremity of a range of high rocky hills that formed the east cliff of the Nile; thus the broad and noble stream that arrived from the Albert Lake in a sheet of unbroken water received the Un-y-Ame River, and then suddenly entered the pass between the two chains of hills, – Gebel Kookoo on the west, and the ridge that we now occupied upon the east. The mouth of the Un-y-Ame River was the limit of navigation from the Albert Lake. As far as the eye could reach to the southwest, the country was dead flat and marshy throughout the course of the river; this appearance proving the correctness of the information I had received from the natives of Unyoro, and from Kamrasi himself, that the Nile was navigable for some days' journey from the Albert Lake. Precisely the same information had been given to Speke, and the river level at this point showed by his thermometer so great a difference between that of Karuma, that he had concluded the fall of 1,000 feet must exist between the foot of Karuma Falls and the Albert Lake; this, as already described, I proved to be 1,275 feet.

It would be impossible to describe the calm enjoyment of the scene from this elevated pass, from which we confirmed the results of our own labours and of Speke's well-reflected suggestions. We were now on the track by which he and Gant had returned; but I believe they had rounded the foot of the hill that we had ascended; the two routes led to the same point, as our course brought us at right angles with the Nile that flowed beneath us. Descending the pass through a thorny jungle, we arrived at the river, and turning suddenly to the north, we followed its course for about a mile, and then bivouacked for the evening. The Nile, having entered the valley between Gebel Kookoo and the western range, was no longer the calm river that we had seen to the south: numerous rocky islands blocked its course, and mud-banks covered with papyrus rush so obstructed the stream that the river widened to about a mile – this width was composed of numerous channels, varying in breadth between the obstructing rock and island. Upon one of the rush-covered islands a herd of elephants was discovered, almost concealed by the height of the vegetation. As they approached the edge of the water and became exposed, I tried about twenty shots at them with the Fletcher rifle, sighted to 600 yards, but in no instance could I either touch or disturb them by the bullets; this will afford some idea of the width of the river, the island appearing to be in the middle of the stream.

A short distance below this spot, the Nile rapidly contracted, and at length became a roaring torrent, passing through a narrow gorge between perpendicular cliffs, with a tremendous current. In some places the great river was pent up between rocks, which confined it to a width of about 120 yards, through such channels the rush of water was terrific, but to a casual observer approaching from the north, the volume of the Nile would have been underrated, unless calculated by the velocity of the stream.

From this point we followed the bank of the Nile over a difficult route, down steep ravines and up precipitous crags, by a winding path along the foot of the range of syenite hills that hemmed in the river on the west bank. Several considerable waterfalls added to the grandeur of the pass, through which for many miles the angry Nile chafed and roared like a lion in its confined den.

At length we arrived at a steep descent, and dismounting from our oxen after a walk of about a quarter of a mile over rough stones, we reached the Asua River, about a quarter of a mile above its junction with the Nile. The bed was rocky; but although the Atabbi had subscribed its waters above the point where we now crossed, there was merely a trifling stream occupying about a quarter of the river's bed, with a current of about two and a half miles an hour. Crossing this on foot, the water in the deepest part reached to the middle of my thighs. The Asua river, as already described at the time that I crossed it on the route from Farajoke to Shooa, is a mountain torrent formidable during the rains; quickly flooding and quickly emptying from its rapid inclination, it is exhausted during the dry season.

The crossing of this river was a signal for extra precaution in the arrangement of our march: we had entered the territory of the ever-hostile Bari tribe; we had been already warned that we could not pass to Gondokoro without being attacked.

We slept on the road, about seven miles to the north of the Asua. On the following morning we started. The route led over a fine country parallel with the Nile, that still continued in a rock-bound channel on the west of the march. Throughout the route from the Un-y-Ame junction, the soil had been wretchedly poor, a mass of rock and decomposed granite forming a sand that quickly parched during the dry season. The level of the country being about 200 feet above the Nile, deep gullies cut the route at right angles, forming the natural drains to the river.

In these ravines grew dense thickets of bamboos. Having no native guide, but trusting solely to the traders' people, who had travelled frequently by this route, we lost the path, and shortly became entangled amongst the numerous ravines. At length we passed a village, around which were assembled a number of natives. Having regained the route, we observed the natives appearing in various directions, and as quickly disappearing only to gather in our front in increased numbers. Their movements exciting suspicion, in a country where every man was an enemy, our party closed together; we threw out an advance guard, – ten men on either flank, – the porters, ammunition, and effects in the centre; while about ten men brought up the rear. Before us lay two low rocky hills covered with trees, high grass, and brushwood, in which I distinctly observed the bright red forms of natives painted according to the custom of the Bari tribe.

We were evidently in for a fight. The path lay in a gorge between the low rocky hills in advance. My wife dismounted from her ox, and walked at the head of our party with me, Saat following behind with the gun that he usually carried, while the men drove several riding-oxen in the centre. Hardly had we entered the pass, when – whizz went an arrow over our heads. This was the signal for a repeated discharge. The natives ran among the rocks with the agility of monkeys, and showed a considerable amount of daring in standing within about eighty yards upon the ridge, and taking steady shots at us with their poisoned arrows. The flanking parties now opened fire, and what with the bad shooting of both the escort and the native archers, no one was wounded on either side for the first ten minutes. The rattle of musketry, and the wild appearance of the naked vermilion-coloured savages, as they leapt along the craggy ridge, twanging their bows at us with evil but ineffectual intent, was a charming picture of African life and manners. Fortunately the branches of numerous trees and intervening clumps of bamboo frustrated the good intentions of the arrows, as they glanced from their aim; and although some fell among our party, we were as yet unscathed. One of the enemy, who was most probably a chief, distinguished himself in particular, by advancing to within about fifty yards, and standing on a rock, he deliberately shot five or six arrows, all of which missed their mark; the men dodged them as they arrived in their uncertain flight: the speed of the arrows was so inferior, owing to the stiffness of the bows, that nothing was easier than to evade them. Any halt was unnecessary. We continued our march through the gorge, the men keeping up an unremitting fire until we entered upon a tract of high grass and forest; this being perfectly dry, it would have been easy to set it on fire, as the enemy were to leeward; but although the rustling in the grass betokened the presence of a great number of men, they were invisible. In a few minutes we emerged in a clearing, where corn had been planted; this was a favourable position for a decisive attack upon the natives, who now closed up. Throwing out skirmishers, with orders that they were to cover themselves behind the trunks of trees, the Baris were driven back. One was now shot through the body, and fell; but recovering, he ran with his comrades, and fell dead after a few yards.

What casualties had happened during the passage of the gorge I cannot say, but the enemy were now utterly discomfited. I had not fired a shot, as the whole affair was perfect child's play, and any one who could shoot would have settled the fortune of the day by half a dozen shots; but both the traders' people and my men were shooters, but not hitters. We now bivouacked on the field for the night.

During the march on the following day, the natives watched us at a distance, following in great numbers parallel with our route, but fearing to attack. The country was perfectly open, being a succession of fine downs of low grass, with few trees, where any attack against our guns would have been madness.

In the evening we arrived at two small deserted villages; these, like most in the Bari country, were circular, and surrounded by a live and impenetrable fence of euphorbia, having only one entrance. The traders' people camped in one, while I took up my quarters in the other. The sun had sunk, and the night being pitch dark, we had a glorious fire, around which we placed our *angareps* opposite the narrow entrance of the camp, about ten yards distant. I stationed Richarn as sentry outside the gateway, as he was the most dependable of my men, and I thought it extremely probable that we might be attacked during the night: three other sentries I placed on guard at various stations. Dinner being concluded, Mrs. Baker lay down on her *angarep* for the night. I drew the balls from a double No. 10 smooth bore, and loaded with cartridge containing each twenty large-mould shot (about a hundred to the pound); putting this under my pillow I went to sleep. Hardly had I begun to rest, when my men woke me, saying that the camp was surrounded by natives. Upon inquiry I found this to be correct; it was so dark that they could not be seen without stooping to the ground and looking along the surface. I ordered the sentries not to fire unless hostilities should commence on the side of the natives, and in no case to draw trigger without a challenge.

Returning to the *angarep* I lay down, and not wishing to sleep, I smoked my long Unyoro pipe. In about ten minutes, bang went a shot, quickly followed by another from the sentry at the entrance of the camp. Quietly rising from my bed, I found Richarn reloading at his post. "What is it, Richarn?" I asked. "They are shooting arrows into the camp, aiming at the fire, in hopes of hitting you who are sleeping there," said Richarn. "I watched one fellow," he continued, "as I heard the twang of his bow four times. At each shot I heard an arrow strike the ground between me and you, therefore I fired at him, and I think he is down. Do you see that black object lying on the ground?" I saw something a little blacker than the surrounding darkness, but it could not be distinguished. Leaving Richarn with orders not to move from his post, but to keep a good lookout until relieved by the next watch, I again went to sleep.

Before break of day, just as the grey dawn slightly improved the darkness, I visited the sentry; he was at his post, and reported that he thought the archer of the preceding night was dead, as he had heard a sound proceeding from the dark object on the ground after I had left. In a few minutes it was sufficiently light to distinguish the body of a roan lying about thirty paces from the camp entrance. Upon examination, he proved to be a Bari: his bow was in his hand, and two or three arrows were lying by his side; thirteen mould shot had struck him dead; one had cut through the bow. We now searched the camp for arrows, and as it became light we picked up four in various places, some within a few feet of our beds, and all horribly barbed and poisoned, that the deceased had shot into the camp gateway.

This was the last attack during our journey. We marched well, generally accomplishing fifteen miles of latitude daily from this point, as the road was good and well known to our guides. The country was generally poor, but beautifully diversified with large trees, the tamarind predominating. Passing through the small but thickly populated and friendly little province of Moir, in a few days we sighted the well-known mountain Belignan that we had formerly passed on its eastern side when we had started on our uncertain path from Gondokoro upwards of two years ago. The mountain of Belignan was now N.E. from our point of observation.

We had a splendid view of the Ellyria Mountain, and of the distant cone, Gebel el Assul (Honey Mountain) between Ellyria and Obbo. All these curiously shaped crags and peaks were well known to us, and we welcomed them as old friends after a long absence; they had been our companions in times of doubt and anxiety, when success in our undertaking appeared hopeless. At noon on the following day, as we were as usual marching parallel with the Nile, the river, having made a slight bend to the west, swept round, and approached within half a mile of our path; the small conical mountain, Regiaf, within twelve miles of Gondokoro, was on our left, rising from the west bank of the river. We felt almost at home again, and marching until sunset, we bivouacked within three miles of Gondokoro. That night we were full of speculations. Would a boat be waiting for us with supplies and letters? The morning anxiously looked forward to at length arrived. We started; the English flag had been mounted on a fine straight bamboo with a new lance head specially arranged for the arrival at Gondokoro. My men felt proud, as they would march in as conquerors; according to White Nile ideas such a journey could not have been accomplished with so small a party. Long before Ibrahim's men were ready to start, our oxen were saddled and we were off, longing to hasten into Gondokoro and to find a comfortable vessel with a few luxuries and the post from England. Never had the oxen travelled so fast as on that morning; the flag led the way, and the men in excellent spirits followed at double-quick pace. "I see the masts of the vessels!" exclaimed the boy Saat. "*El hambd el Illah* (Thank God)!" shouted the men. "Hurrah!" said I. "Three cheers for Old England and the sources of the Nile! Hurrah!" and my men joined me in the wild, and to their ears savage, English yell. "Now for a salute! Fire away all your powder, if you like, my lads, and let the people know that we're alive!" This was all that was required to complete the happiness of my people, and loading and firing as fast as possible, we approached near to Gondokoro. Presently we saw the Turkish flag emerge from Gondokoro at about a quarter of a mile distant, followed by a number of the traders' people, who waited to receive us. On our arrival, they immediately approached and fired salutes with ball cartridge, as usual advancing close to us and discharging their guns into the ground at our feet. One of my servants, Mahomet, was riding an ox, and an old friend of his in the crowd happening to recognise him, immediately advanced, and saluted him by firing his gun into the earth directly beneath the belly of the ox he was riding; the effect produced made the crowd and ourselves explode with laughter. The nervous ox, terrified at the sudden discharge between his legs, gave a tremendous kick, and continued madly kicking and plunging, until Mahomet was pitched over his head and lay sprawling on the ground; this scene terminated the expedition.

Dismounting from our tired oxen, our first inquiry was concerning boats and letters. What was the reply? Neither boats, letters, supplies, nor any intelligence of friends or the civilized world! We had long since been given up as dead by the inhabitants of Khartoum, and by all those who understood the difficulties and dangers of the country. We were told that some people had suggested that we might possibly have gone to Zanzibar, but the general opinion was that we had all been killed. At this cold and barren reply, I felt almost choked. We had looked forward to arriving at Gondokoro as to a home; we had expected that a boat would have been sent on the chance of finding us, as I had left money in the hands of an agent in Khartoum – but there was literally nothing to receive us, and we were helpless to return. We had worked for years in misery, such as I have but faintly described, to overcome the difficulties of this hitherto unconquerable exploration; we had succeeded – and what was the result? Not even a letter from home to welcome us if alive! As I sat beneath a tree and looked down upon the glorious Nile that flowed a few yards beneath my feet, I pondered upon the value of my toil. I had traced the river to its great Albert source, and as the mighty stream glided before me, the mystery that had ever shrouded its origin was dissolved. I no longer looked upon its waters with a feeling approaching to awe for I knew its home, and had visited its cradle. Had I overrated the importance of the discovery? And had I wasted some of the best years of my life to obtain a shadow? I recalled to recollection the practical question of Commoro, the chief of Latooka: "Suppose you get to the great lake, what will you do with it? What will be the good of it? If you find that the large river does flow from it, what then?"

Chapter XVIII

THE LATEST NEWS FROM KHARTOUM

The various trading parties were assembled in Gondokoro with a total of about three thousand slaves; but there was consternation depicted upon every countenance. Only three boats had arrived from Khartoum – one diahbiah and two noggurs – these belonged to Koorshid Aga. The resume of news from Khartoum was as follows:

"Orders had been received by the Egyptian authorities from the European governments to suppress the slave-trade. Four steamers had arrived at Khartoum from Cairo. Two of these vessels had ascended the White Nile, and had captured many slavers; their crews were imprisoned, and had been subjected to the bastinado and torture; the captured slaves had been appropriated by the Egyptian authorities.

"It would be impossible to deliver slaves to the Soudan this season, as an Egyptian regiment had been stationed in the Shillook country, and steamers were cruising to intercept the boats from the interior in their descent to Khartoum; thus the army of slaves then at Gondokoro would be utterly worthless.

"The plague was raging at Khartoum, and had killed 15,000 people; many of the boats' crews had died on their passage from Khartoum to Gondokoro of this disease, which had even broken out in the station where we then were: people died daily.

"The White Nile was dammed up by a freak of nature, and the crews of thirty vessels had been occupied five weeks in cutting a ditch through the obstruction, wide enough to admit the passage of boats."

Such was the intelligence received by the latest arrival from Khartoum. No boats having been sent for me, I engaged the diahbiah that had arrived for Koorshid's ivory; this would return empty, as no ivory could be delivered at Gondokoro. The prospect was pleasant, as many men had died of the plague on board our vessel during the voyage from Khartoum; thus we should be subject to a visitation of this fearful complaint as a wind-up to the difficulties we had passed through during our long exile in Central Africa. I ordered the vessel to be thoroughly scrubbed with boiling water and sand, after which it was fumigated with several pounds of tobacco, burnt within the cabin.

Three days were employed in ferrying the slaves across the river in the two noggurs, or barges, as they must be returned to their respective stations. I rejoiced at the total discomfiture of the traders, and, observing a cloud of smoke far distant to the north, I spread the alarm that a steamer was approaching from Khartoum! Such was the consternation of the traders' parties at the bare idea of such an occurrence that they prepared for immediate flight into the interior, as they expected to be captured by government troops sent from Khartoum to suppress the slave-trade. Profiting by this nervous state of affairs, I induced them to allow the boat to start immediately, and we concluded all our arrangements, contracting for the diahbiah at 4,000 piastres (40 pounds). The plague having broken out at Gondokoro, the victims among the natives were dragged to the edge of the cliff and thrown into the river; it is impossible to describe the horrible effluvium produced by the crowds of slaves that had been confined upon the limited area of the station. At length the happy moment arrived that we were to quit the miserable spot. The boat was ready to start – we were all on board, and Ibrahim and his people came to say good-bye. It is only justice to Ibrahim to say, that, although he had been my great enemy when at Gondokoro in 1863, he had always behaved well since peace was established at Ellyria; and, although by nature and profession a slave-hunter, like others of the White Nile, he had frequently yielded to my interference to save the lives of natives who would otherwise have been massacred without pity.

I had gained an extraordinary influence over all these ruffianly people. Everything that I had promised them had been more than performed; all that I had foretold had been curiously realized. They now acknowledged how often I had assured them that the slave-trade would be suppressed by the interference of European powers, and the present ruin of their trade was the result; they all believed that I was the cause, by having written from Gondokoro to the Consul-general of Egypt in 1863, when the traders had threatened to drive me back. Far from retaliating upon me, they were completely cowed. The report had been spread throughout Gondokoro by Ibrahim and his people that their wonderful success in ivory hunting was chiefly due to me; that their sick had been cured; that good luck had attended their party; that disaster had befallen all who had been against me; and that no one had suffered wrong at our hands. With the resignation of Mahommedans they yielded to their destiny, apparently without any ill feeling against us. Crowds lined the cliff and the high ground by the old ruins of the mission station to see us depart. We pushed off from shore into the powerful current; the English flag that had accompanied us all through our wanderings now fluttered proudly from the masthead unsullied by defeat, and amidst the rattle of musketry we glided rapidly down the river, and soon lost sight of Gondokoro.

What were our feelings at that moment? Overflowing with gratitude to a Divine Providence that had supported us in sickness, and guided us through all dangers. There had been moments of hopelessness and despair; days of misery, when the future had appeared dark and fatal; but we had been strengthened in our weakness, and led, when apparently lost, by an unseen hand. I felt no triumph, but with a feeling of calm contentment and satisfaction we floated down the Nile. My great joy was in the meeting that I contemplated with Speke in England, I had so thoroughly completed the task we had agreed upon.

Silently and easily we floated down the river; the oars keeping us in midstream. The endless marshes no longer looked so mournful as we glided rapidly past, and descended the current against which we had so arduously laboured on our ascent to Gondokoro. As we thus proceeded on our voyage through the monotonous marshes and vast herds of hippopotami that at this season thronged the river, I had ample leisure to write my letters for England, to be posted on arrival at Khartoum, and to look back upon the results of the last few years. The Nile, cleared of its mystery, resolves itself into comparative simplicity. The actual basin of the Nile is included between about the 22-degree and 39-degree East longitude, and from 3 degrees South to 13 degrees North latitude. The drainage of that vast area is monopolized by the Egyptian river. The Victoria and Albert Lakes, the two great equatorial reservoirs, are the recipients of all affluents south of the Equator; the Albert Lake being the grand reservoir in which are concentrated the entire waters from the south, in addition to tributaries from the Blue Mountains from the north of the Equator. The Albert N'Yanza is the great basin of the Nile: the distinction between that and the Victoria N'Yanza is, that the Victoria is a reservoir receiving the eastern affluents, and it becomes a starting point or the most elevated SOURCE at the point where the river issues from it at the Ripon Falls: the Albert is a reservoir not only receiving the western and southern affluents direct from the Blue Mountains, but it also receives the supply from the Victoria and from the entire equatorial Nile basin. The Nile as it issues from the Albert N'Yanza is the entire Nile; prior to its birth from the Albert Lake it is not the entire Nile. A glance at the map will at once exemplify the relative value of the two great lakes. The Victoria gathers all the waters on the eastern side and sheds them into the northern extremity of the Albert: while the latter, from its character and position, is the direct channel of the Nile that receives all waters that belong to the equatorial Nile basin. Thus the Victoria is the first SOURCE; but from the Albert the river issues at once as the great White Nile.

It is not my intention to claim a higher value for my discovery than is justly due, neither would I diminish in any way the lustre of the achievements of Speke and Grant; it has ever been my object to confirm and support their discoveries, and to add my voice to the chorus of praise that they have so justly merited. A great geographical fact has through our joint labours been most thoroughly established by the discovery of the sources of the Nile. I lay down upon the map exactly what I saw, and what I gathered from information afforded by the natives most carefully examined.

My exploration confirms all that was asserted by Speke and Grant: they traced the country from Zanzibar to the northern watershed of Africa, commencing at about 3 degrees South latitude, at the southern extremity of the Victoria N'Yanza. They subsequently determined the river at the Ripon Falls flowing from that lake to be the highest source of the Nile. They had a perfect right to arrive at this conclusion from the data then afforded. They traced the river for a considerable distance to Karuma Falls, in lat. 2 degrees 15 minutes N.; and they subsequently met the Nile in lat. 3 degrees 32 minutes N. They had heard that it flowed into the Luta N'Zige, and that it issued from it; thus they were correct in all their investigations, which my discoveries have confirmed. Their general description of the country was perfect, but not having visited the lake heard of as the Luta N'Zige, they could not possibly have been aware of the vast importance of that great reservoir in the Nile system. The task of exploring that extraordinary feature having been accomplished, the geographical question of the sources of the Nile is explained. Ptolemy had described the Nile sources as emanating from two great lakes that received the snows of the mountains of Ethiopia. There are many ancient maps existing upon which these lakes are marked as positive: although there is a wide error in the latitude, the fact remains, that two great lakes were reported to exist in Equatorial Africa fed by the torrents from lofty mountains, and that from these reservoirs two streams issued, the conjunction of which formed the Nile. The general principle was correct, although the detail was wrong. There can be little doubt that trade had been carried on between the Arabs from the Red Sea and the coast opposite Zanzibar in ancient times, and that the people engaged in such enterprise had penetrated so far into the interior as to have obtained a knowledge of the existence of the two reservoirs; thus may the geographical information originally have been brought into Egypt.

The rainfall to within 3 degrees north of the Equator extends over ten months, commencing in February and terminating in the end of November. The heaviest rains fall from April till the end of August; during the latter two months of this season the rivers are at their maximum: at other times the climate is about as uncertain as that of England; but the rain is of the heavy character usual in the tropics. Thus the rivers are constant throughout the year, and the Albert Lake continues at a high level, affording a steady volume of water to the Nile. On the map given to me by Captain Speke he has marked the Victoria Nile below the Ripon Falls as the Somerset River. As I have made a point of adhering to all native names as given by him upon that map, I also adhere to the name Somerset

River for that portion of the Nile between the Victoria and the Albert Lakes; this must be understood as Speke's Victoria Nile source; bearing the name of Somerset, no confusion will arise in speaking of the Nile, which would otherwise be ambiguous, as the same name would apply to two distinct rivers – the one emanating from the Victoria and flowing into the Albert; the other the entire river Nile as it leaves the Albert Lake. The White Nile, fed as described by the great reservoirs supplied by the rains of equatorial districts, receives the following tributaries:

From the East bank:
The Asua, important from 15th April till 15th November: dry after that date.
From West bank:
The Ye, third class; full from 15th April till 15th November.
From West bank:
Another small river, third class; full from 15th April till 15th November.
Ditto The Bahr el Gazal:
little or no water supplied by this river.
From East bank:
The Sobat, first class; full from June to December.

The Bahr Giraffe I omit, as it is admitted by the natives to be a branch of the White Nile that leaves the main river at the Aliab country and reunites in lat. 9 degrees 25 minutes between the Bahr el Gazal and the Sobat. The latter river (Sobat) is the most powerful affluent of the White Nile, and is probably fed by many tributaries from the Galla country about Kaffa, in addition to receiving the rivers from the Bari and Latooka countries. I consider that the Sobat must be supplied by considerable streams from totally distinct countries east and south, having a rainfall at different seasons, as it is bank-full at the end of December, when the southern rivers (the Asua, etc.) are extremely low. North from the Sobat, the White Nile has no other tributaries until it is joined by the Blue Nile at Khartoum, and by its last affluent the Atbara in lat. 17 degrees 37 minutes. These two great mountain streams flooding suddenly in the

Ethiopia

end of June, fed by the rains of Abyssinia, raise the volume of the Nile to an extent that causes the inundations of lower Egypt.

The basin of the Nile being thus understood, let us reflect upon the natural resources of the vast surface of fertile soil that is comprised in that portion of Central Africa. It is difficult to believe that so magnificent a soil and so enormous an extent of country is destined to remain for ever in savagedom, and yet it is hard to argue on the possibility of improvement in a portion of the world inhabited by savages whose happiness consists in idleness or warfare. The advantages are few, the drawbacks many. The immense distance from the seacoast would render impossible the transport of any merchandise unless of extreme value, as the expenses would be insupportable. The natural productions are nil, excepting ivory. The soil being fertile and the climate favourable to cultivation, all tropical produce would thrive; cotton, coffee, and the sugarcane are indigenous; but although both climate and soil are favourable, the conditions necessary to successful enterprise are wanting – the population is scanty, and the material of the very worst; the people vicious and idle. The climate, although favourable for agriculture, is adverse to the European constitution; thus colonization would be out of the question. What can be done with so hopeless a prospect? Where the climate is fatal to Europeans, from whence shall civilization be imported? The heart of Africa is so completely secluded from the world, and the means of communication are so difficult, that although fertile, its geographical position debars that vast extent of country from improvement: thus shut out from civilization it has become an area for unbridled atrocities, as exemplified in the acts of the ivory traders.

many changes taken place since 1856

Difficult and almost impossible is the task before the missionary. The Austrian mission has failed, and the stations have been forsaken; their pious labour was hopeless, and the devoted priests died upon their barren field. What curse lies so heavily upon Africa and bows her down beneath all other nations? It is the infernal traffic in slaves – a trade so hideous, that the heart of every slave and owner becomes deformed, and shrinks like a withered limb incapable of action. The natural love of offspring, shared with the human race by the most savage beast, ceases to warm the heart of the wretched slave. Why should the mother love her child, if it is born to become the property of her owner – to be sold as soon as it can exist without the mother's care? Why should the girl be modest, when she knows that she is the actual property, the slave, of every purchaser? Slavery murders the sacred feeling of love, that blessing that cheers the lot of the poorest man, that spell that binds him to his wife, and child, and home. Love cannot exist with slavery – the mind becomes brutalized to an extent that freezes all those tender feelings that Nature has implanted in the human heart to separate it from the beast; and the mind, despoiled of all noble instincts, descends to hopeless brutality. Thus is Africa accursed: nor can she be raised to any scale approaching to civilization until the slave trade shall be totally suppressed. The first step necessary to the improvement of the savage tribes of the White Nile is the annihilation of the slave trade. Until this be effected, no legitimate commerce can be established; neither is there an opening for missionary enterprise – the country is sealed and closed against all improvement.

Nothing would be easier than to suppress this infamous traffic, were the European powers in earnest. Egypt is in favour of slavery. I have never seen a government official who did not in argument uphold slavery as an institution absolutely necessary to Egypt, thus any demonstration made against the slave-trade by the government of that country will be simply a pro forma movement to blind the European powers. Their eyes thus closed, and the question shelved, the trade will resume its channel. Were the reports of European consuls supported by their respective governments, and were the consuls themselves empowered to seize vessels laden with slaves, and to liberate gangs of slaves when upon a land journey, that abominable traffic could not exist. The hands of the European consuls are tied, and jealousies interwoven with the Turkish question act as a bar to united action on the part of Europe; no Power cares to be the first to disturb the muddy pool. The Austrian consul at Khartoum, Herr Natterer, told me, in 1862, that he had vainly reported the atrocities of the slave trade to his government – no reply had been received to his report. Every European government knows that the slave trade is carried on to an immense extent in Upper Egypt, and that the Red Sea is the great slave lake by which these unfortunate creatures are transported to Arabia and to Suez –

but the jealousies concerning Egypt muzzle each European power. Should one move, the other would interfere to counteract undue influence in Egypt. Thus is immunity insured to the villanous actors in the trade. Who can prosecute a slave trader of the White Nile? What legal evidence can be produced from Central Africa to secure a conviction in an English court of law? The English consul (Mr. Petherick) arrested a Maltese, the nephew of Debono; the charge could not be legally supported. Thus are the consuls fettered, and their acts nullified by the impossibility of producing reliable evidence; the facts are patent; but who can prove them legally?

Stop the White Nile trade; prohibit the departure of any vessels from Khartoum for the south, and let the Egyptian government grant a concession to a company for the White Nile, subject to certain conditions, and to a special supervision. (There are already four steamers at Khartoum.) Establish a military post of 200 men at Gondokoro; an equal number below the Shillook tribe in 13 degrees latitude, and, with two steamers cruising on the river, not a slave could descend the White Nile.

Should the slave-trade be suppressed, there will be a good opening for the ivory trade; the conflicting trading parties being withdrawn, and the interest of the trade exhibited by a single company, the natives would no longer be able to barter ivory for cattle; thus they would be forced to accept other goods in exchange. The newly discovered Albert Lake opens the centre of Africa to navigation. Steamers ascend from Khartoum to Gondokoro in latitude 4 degrees 55'. Seven days' march south from that station the navigable portion of the Nile is reached, where vessels can ascend direct to the Albert Lake – thus an enormous extent of country is opened to navigation, and Manchester goods and various other articles would find a ready market in exchange for ivory, at a prodigious profit, as in those newly-discovered regions ivory has a merely nominal value. Beyond this commencement of honest trade, I cannot offer a suggestion, as no produce of the country except ivory could afford the expense of transport to Europe. If Africa is to be civilized, it must be effected by commerce, which, once established, will open the way for missionary labour; but all ideas of commerce, improvement, and the advancement of the African race

They hadn't discovered oil yet or its value
also mineral mining

that philanthropy could suggest must be discarded until the traffic in slaves shall have ceased to exist.

Should the slave trade be suppressed, a field would be opened, the extent of which I will not attempt to suggest, as the future would depend upon the good government of countries now devoted to savage anarchy and confusion.

Any government that would insure security would be the greatest blessing, as the perpetual hostilities among the various tribes prevent an extension of cultivation. The sower knows not who will reap, thus he limits his crop to his bare necessities.

The ethnology of Central Africa is completely beyond my depth. The natives not only are ignorant of writing, but they are without traditions – their thoughts are as entirely engrossed by their daily wants as those of animals; thus there is no clue to the distant past; history has no existence. This is much to be deplored, as peculiarities are specific in the type of several tribes both in physical appearance and in language. The Dinka, Bari, Latooka, Madi, and Unyoro or Kitwara, are distinct languages on the east of the Nile, comprising an extent of country from about 12 degrees north to the Equator.

The Makkarika have also a distinct language, and I was informed in Kamrasi's country, that the Malegga, on the west of the Albert Lake, speak a different tongue to that of Kitwara (or Unyoro) – this may possibly be the same as the Makkarika, of which I have had no experience by comparison. Accepting the fact of five distinct languages from the Equator to 12 degrees N. lat., it would appear by analogy that Central Africa is divided into numerous countries and tribes, distinct from each other in language and physical conformation, whose origin is perfectly obscure. Whether the man of Central Africa be pre-Adamite is impossible to determine; but the idea is suggested by the following data. The historical origin of man, or Adam, commences with a knowledge of God.

Throughout the history of the world from the creation of Adam, God is connected with mankind in every creed, whether worshipped as the universal sublime Spirit of omnipotence, or shaped by the forms of idolatry into representations of a deity. From the creation of Adam, mankind has acknowledged its inferiority, and must bow down and worship either the true God or a graven image;

or something that is in heaven or in earth. The world, as we accept that term, was always actuated by a natural religious instinct. Cut off from that world, lost in the mysterious distance that shrouded the origin of the Egyptian Nile, were races unknown, that had never reckoned in the great sum of history – races that we have brought to light, whose existence had been hidden from mankind, and that now appear before us like the fossil bones of antediluvian animals. Are they vestiges of what existed in a pre-Adamite creation?

The geological formation of Central Africa is primitive; showing an altitude above the sea level averaging nearly 4,000 feet. This elevated portion of the globe, built up in great part of granitic sandstone rocks, has never been submerged, nor does it appear to have undergone any changes, either volcanic or by the action of water. Time, working through countless ages with the slow but certain instrument of atmospheric influence, has rounded the surface and split into fragments the granite rocks, leaving a sandy base of disintegrated portions, while in other cases the mountains show as hard and undecayed a surface as though fresh from Nature's foundry. Central Africa never having been submerged, the animals and races must be as old, and may be older, than any upon the earth.

No geological change having occurred in ages long anterior to man, as shown by Sir R. I. Murchison theoretically so far back as the year 1852, when Central Africa was utterly unknown, it is natural to suppose that the races that exist upon that surface should be unaltered from their origin. That origin may date from a period so distant, that it preceded the Adamite creation. Historic man believes in a Divinity; the tribes of Central Africa know no God. Are they of our Adamite race? The equatorial portion of Africa at the Nile sources has an average altitude above the sea-level of about 4,000 feet; this elevated plateau forms the base of a range of mountains, that I imagine extends, like the vertebrae of an animal, from east to west, shedding a drainage to the north and south. Should this hypothesis be correct, the southern watershed would fill the Tanganika lake: while farther to the west another lake, supplied by the southern drainage, may form the head of the river Congo. On the north a similar system may drain into the Niger and Lake Tchad: thus the Victoria and the Albert Lakes, being the two great reservoirs or sources of the Nile, may be the first of a system of

African equatorial lakes fed by the northern and southern drainage of the mountain range, and supplying all the principal rivers of Africa from the great equatorial rainfall. The fact of the centre of Africa at the Nile sources being about 4,000 feet above the ocean, independently of high mountains rising from that level, suggests that the drainage of the Equator from the central and elevated portion must find its way to the lower level and reach the sea. Wherever high mountain ranges exist, there must also be depressions; those situated in an equatorial rainfall must receive the drainage from the high lands and become lakes, the overflow of which must form the sources of rivers, precisely as exemplified in the sources of the Nile from the Victoria and the Albert Lakes.

The fact that Sir Roderick Murchison, as a geologist, laid down a theory of the existence of a chain of lakes upon an elevated plateau in Central Africa, which theory has been now in great measure confirmed by actual inspection, induces me to quote an extract from his address at the anniversary meeting of the Royal Geographical Society, 23d May, 1864. In that address, he expressed opinions upon the geological structure and the races of Central Africa, which preceded those that I formed when at the Albert Lake. It is with intense interest that I have read the following extract since my return to England:

"In former addresses, I suggested that the interior mass and central portions of Africa constituting a great plateau occupied by lakes and marshes from which the waters escaped by cracks or depressions in the subtending older rocks, had been in that condition during an enormously long period. I have recently been enabled, through the apposite discovery of Dr. Kirk, the companion of Livingstone, not only to fortify my conjecture of 1852, but greatly to extend the inferences concerning the long period of time during which the central parts of Africa have remained in their present condition, save their degradation by ordinary atmospheric agencies. My view, as given to this Society in 1852, was mainly founded on the original and admirable geological researches of Mr. Bain in the colony of the Cape of Good Hope. It was, that, inasmuch as in the secondary or mesozoic age of geologists, the northern interior of that country was occupied by great lakes and marshes, as proved by the fossil reptile discovered by Bain, and named Dicynodon by Owen, such it has remained for countless ages, even up to the present day. The succeeding journeys into the interior, of Livingstone, Thornton and Kirk, Burton and Speke, and Speke and Grant, have all tended to strengthen me in the belief that Southern Africa has not undergone any of those great submarine depressions which have so largely affected Europe, Asia, and America, during the secondary, tertiary, and quasi modern periods.

"The discovery of Dr. Kirk has confirmed my conclusion. On the banks of an affluent of the Zambesi, that gentleman collected certain bones, apparently carried down in watery drifts from inland positions, which remains have been so fossilized as to have all the appearance of antiquity which fossils of a tertiary or older age usually present. One of these is a portion of the vertebral column and sacrum of a buffalo, undistinguishable from that of the Cape buffalo; another is a fragment of a crocodile, and another of a water-tortoise, both undistinguishable from the forms of those animals now living. Together with these, Dr. Kirk found numerous bones of antelopes and other animals, which, though in a fossil condition, all belonged, as he assured me, to species now living in South Africa.

"On the other hand, none of our explorers, including Mr. Bain, who has diligently worked as a geologist, have detected in the interior any limestones containing marine fossil remains, which would have proved that South Africa had, like other regions, been depressed into oceanic conditions, and re-elevated. On the contrary, in addition to old granitic and other igneous rocks, all explorers find only either innumerable undulations of sandstones, schistose, and quartzose rocks, or such tufaceous and ferruginous deposits as would naturally occur in countries long occupied by lakes and exuberant jungles, separated from each other by sandy hills, scarcely any other calcareous rocks being found except tufas formed by the deposition of landsprings. It is true that there are marine tertiary formations on the coasts (around the Cape Colony, near the mouth of the Zambesi opposite Mozambique, and again on the coasts of Mombas opposite Zanzibar), and that these have been raised up into low-coast ranges, followed by rocks of igneous origin. But in penetrating into the true interior, the traveller takes a final leave of all such formations; and in advancing to the heart of the continent, he traverses a vast region which, to all appearance, has ever been under terrestrial and lacustrine conditions only. Judging, indeed, from all the evidences as yet collected, the interior of South Africa has remained in that condition since the period of the secondary rocks of geologists! Yet, whilst none of our countrymen found any evidences of old marine remains, Captain Speke brought from one of the ridges which lay between the coast and the lake Victoria N'Yanza a fossil shell, which, though larger in size, is undistinguishable from the Achatina perdix now flourishing in South Africa. Again, whilst Bain found fossil plants in his reptiliferous strata north of the Cape, and Livingstone and Thornton discovered coal in sandstone, with fossil plants, like those of our old coal of Europe and America, – yet both these mesozoic and palaeozoic remains are terrestrial, and are not associated with marine limestones, indicative of those oscillations of the land which are so common in other countries.

"It is further to be observed, that the surface of this vast interior is entirely exempt from the coarse superficial drift that encumbers so many countries, as derived from lofty mountain-chains from which either glaciers or great torrential streams have descended. In this respect, it is also equally unlike those plains of Germany, Poland, and Northern Russia, which were sea-bottoms when floating icebergs melted and dropped the loads of stone which they were transporting from Scandinavia and Lapland.

"In truth, therefore, the inner portion of Southern Africa is, in this respect, as far as I know, geologically unique in the long conservation of ancient terrestrial conditions. This inference is further supported by the concomitant absence, throughout the larger portion of all this vast area, i.e. south of the Equator, of any of those volcanic rocks which are so often associated with oscillations of the terra firma (although Kilimandjaro is to a great extent igneous and volcanic, there is nothing to prove it has been in activity during the historic era).

"With the exception of the true volcanic hills of the Cameroons recently described by Burton, on the west coast, a little to the north of the Equator, and which possibly may advance southwards towards the Gaboon country, nothing is known of the presence of any similar foci of sub-aerial eruption all round the coasts of Africa south of the Equator. If the elements for the production of them had existed, the coastline is precisely that on which we should expect to find such volcanic vents, if we judge by the analogy of all volcanic regions where the habitual igneous eruptions are not distant from the sea, or from great internal masses of water. The absence, then, both on the coasts and in the interior, of any eruptive rocks which can have been thrown up under the atmosphere since the period when the tertiary rocks began to be accumulated, is in concurrence with all the physical data as yet got together. These demonstrate that, although the geologist finds here none of those characters of lithological structure and curiously diversified organic remains which enable him to fix the epochs of succession in the crust of the earth in other quarters of the globe, the interior of South Africa is unquestionably a grand type of a region which has preserved its ancient terrestrial conditions during a very long period, unaffected by any changes except those which are dependent on atmospheric and meteoric influences.

"If, then, the lower animals and plants of this vast country have gone on unchanged for a very long period, may we infer that its human inhabitants are of like antiquity? If so, the Negro may claim as old a lineage as the Caucasian or Mongolian races. In the absence of any decisive fact, I forbear, at present, to speculate on this point; but as, amid the fossil specimens procured by Livingstone and Kirk, there are fragments of pottery made by human hands, we must wait until some zealous explorer of Southern Africa shall distinctly bring forward proofs that the manufactured articles are of the same age as the fossil bones. In other words, we still require from Africa the same proofs of the existence of links which bind together the sciences of geology and archaeology which have recently been developed in Europe. Now, if the unquestioned works of man should be found to be coeval with the remains of fossilized existing animals in southern Africa, the travelled geographer, who has convinced himself of the ancient condition of its surface, must admit, however unwillingly, that although the black man is of such very remote antiquity, he has been very stationary in civilization and in attaining the arts of life, if he be compared with the Caucasian, the Mongolian, the Red Indian of America, or even with the aborigines of Polynesia. (The most remarkable proof of the inferiority of the Negro, when compared with the Asiatic, is, that whilst the latter has domesticated the elephant for ages, and rendered it highly useful to man, the Negro has only slaughtered the animal to obtain food or ivory.)"

CHAPTER XIX

THE BLACK ANTELOPE

We continued our voyage down the Nile, at times scudding along with a fair wind and stream, when a straight portion of the river allowed our men respite from the oars. This was the termination of the dry season, in this latitude 7 degrees (end of March); thus, although the river was nearly level with the banks, the marshes were tolerably firm, and in the dryer portions the reeds had been burnt off by the natives. In one of these cleared places we descried a vast herd of antelopes, numbering several thousands. The males were black, and carried fine horns, while the females were reddish-brown and without horns. Never having shot this species, I landed from the boat, which I ordered to wait in a sheltered nook, while, accompanied by the boy Saat and Richarn, I took the little Fletcher 24 rifle and commenced a stalk.

The antelopes did not evince their usual shyness, and with a tolerable amount of patience I succeeded in getting within about 120 paces of two splendid black bucks that were separated from the herd; a patch of half-burnt reeds afforded a good covering point. The left-hand buck was in a good position for a shoulder shot, standing with his flank exposed, but with his head turned towards me. At the crack of the rifle he sprang upon his hind legs, – gave two or three convulsive bounds, and fell. His companion went off at full speed, and the left-hand barrel unfortunately broke his hind leg, as the half-burnt reeds hindered a correct aim. Reloading, while my men bled the dead buck, I fired a long shot at the dense mass of antelopes who were now in full retreat at about 600 yards' distance crowded together in thousands. I heard, or fancied I heard, the ball strike some object, and as the herd passed on, a reddish object remained behind that we could hardly distinguish, but on nearer approach I found a doe lying dead – she had been by chance struck by the ball through the neck at this great distance. The game being at full speed in retreat, my sport would have been over had we not at that moment heard shouts and yells exactly ahead of the vast herd of antelopes. At once they halted, and we perceived a number of natives, armed with spears and bows, who had intercepted the herd in their retreat, and who now turned them by their shouts exactly towards us. The herd came on at full speed; but seeing us, they slightly altered their line, and rushed along, thundering over the ground almost in single file, thus occupying a continuous line of about half a mile in length. Running towards them at right angles for about a quarter of a mile, I at length arrived at a white ant-hill about ten feet high; behind this I took my stand within about seventy yards of the string of antelopes that were filing by at full gallop. I waited for a buck with fine horns. Several passed, but I observed better heads in their rear; they came bounding along. "Crack!" went the rifle; and a fine buck pitched upon his head. Again the little Fletcher spoke, and down went another within ten yards of the first. "A spare gun, Richarn!" and Oswell's Purdey was slipped into my hand. "Only one barrel is loaded," said Richarn. I saw a splendid buck coming along with a doe by his side; she protected him from the shot as they came on at right angles with the gun; but knowing that the ball would go through her and reach him on the other side, I fired at her shoulder, – she fell dead to the shot, but he went off scatheless. I now found that Richarn had loaded the gun with twenty mould shot instead of ball; these were confined in a cartridge, and had killed her on the spot.

I had thus bagged five antelopes; and, cutting off the heads of the bucks, we left the bodies for the natives, who were anxiously watching us from a distance, but afraid to approach. The antelope first shot that was nearer to the boat, we dragged on board, with the assistance of ten or twelve men. The buck was rather larger than an average donkey; colour, black, with a white patch across the withers; a white crown to the head; white round the eyes; chest black, but belly white; the horns about two feet four inches long, and bending gracefully backwards.

A few days after this incident we arrived at the junction of the Bahr el Gazal, and turning sharp to the east, we looked forward to arriving at the extraordinary obstruction that since our passage in 1863 had dammed the White Nile.

There was considerable danger in the descent of the river upon nearing this peculiar dam, as the stream plunged below it by a subterranean channel with a rush like a cataract. A large diahbiah laden with ivory had been carried beneath the dam on her descent from Gondokoro in the previous year, and had never been seen afterwards. I ordered the *reis* to have the anchor in readiness, and two powerful hawsers; should we arrive in the evening, he was to secure the vessel to the bank, and not to attempt the passage through the canal until the following morning. We anchored about half a mile above the dam.

This part of the Nile is boundless marsh, portions of which were at this season terra firma. The river ran from west to east; the south bank was actual ground covered with mimosas, but to the north and west the flat marsh covered with high weeds was interminable.

At daybreak we manned the oars and floated down the rapid stream. In a few minutes we heard the rush of water, and we saw the dam stretching across the river before us. The marsh being firm, our men immediately jumped out on the left bank and manned the hawsers – one fastened from the stern, the other from the bow; this arrangement prevented the boat from turning broadside on to the dam, by which accident the shipwrecked diahbiah had been lost. As we approached the dam, I perceived the canal or ditch that had been cut by the crews of the vessels that had ascended the river; it was about ten feet wide, and would barely allow the passage of our diahbiah. This canal was already choked with masses of floating vegetation and natural rafts of reeds and mud that the river carried with it, the accumulation of which had originally formed the dam.

Having secured the vessel by carrying out an anchor astern and burying it on the marsh, while a rope fastened from the bow to the high reeds kept her stern to the stream, all hands jumped into the canal and commenced dragging out the entangled masses of weeds, reeds, ambatch wood, grass, and mud that had choked the entrance. Half a day was thus passed, at the expiration of which time we towed our vessel safely into the ditch, where she lay out of danger. It was necessary to discharge all cargo from the boat, in order to reduce her draught of water. This tedious operation completed, and many bushels of corn being piled upon mats spread upon the reeds beaten flat, we endeavoured to push her along the canal. Although the obstruction was annoying it was a most interesting object.

The river had suddenly disappeared: there was apparently an end to the White Nile. The dam was about three-quarters of a mile wide; it was perfectly firm, and was already overgrown with high reeds and grass, thus forming a continuation of the surrounding country. Many of the traders' people had died of the plague at this spot during the delay of some weeks in cutting the canal; the graves of these dead were upon the dam. The bottom of the canal that had been cut through the dam was perfectly firm, composed of sand, mud, and interwoven decaying vegetation. The river arrived with great force at the abrupt edge of the obstruction, bringing with it all kinds of trash and large floating islands. None of these objects hitched against the edge, but the instant they struck they dived under and disappeared. It was in this manner that the vessel had been lost – having missed the narrow entrance to the canal, she had struck the dam stem on; the force of the current immediately turned her broadside against the obstruction; the floating islands and masses of vegetation brought down by the river were heaped against her, and heeling over on her side she was sucked bodily under and carried beneath the dam; her crew had time to save themselves by leaping upon the firm barrier that had wrecked their ship. The boatmen told me that dead hippopotami had been found on the other side that had been carried under the dam and drowned.

Two days' hard work from morning till night brought us through the canal, and we once more found ourselves on the open Nile on the other side of the dam. The river was in that spot perfectly clean; not a vestige of floating vegetation could be seen upon its waters; in its subterranean passage it had passed through a natural sieve, leaving all foreign matter behind to add to the bulk of the already stupendous work.

All before us was clear and plain sailing. For some days two or three of our men had been complaining of severe headache, giddiness, and violent pains in the spine and between the shoulders. I had been anxious when at Gondokoro concerning the vessel, as many persons had died on board of the plague during the voyage from Khartoum. The men assured me that the most fatal symptom was violent bleeding from the nose; in such cases no one had been known to recover. One of the boatmen, who had been ailing for some days, suddenly went to the side of the vessel and hung his head over the river; his nose was bleeding!

Another of my men, Yaseen, was ill; his uncle, my *vakeel*, came to me with a report that "his nose was bleeding violently!" Several other men fell ill: they lay helplessly about the deck in low muttering delirium, their eyes as yellow as orange-peel. In two or three days the vessel was so horribly offensive as to be unbearable – the plague had broken out! We floated past the river Sobat junction; the wind was fair from the south, thus fortunately we in the stern were to windward of the crew. Yaseen died; he was one who had bled at the nose. We stopped to bury him. The funeral hastily arranged, we again set sail. Mahommed died; he had bled at the nose. Another burial. Once more we set sail and hurried down the Nile. Several men were ill, but the dreaded symptom had not appeared. I had given each man a strong dose of calomel at the commencement of the disease; I could do nothing more, as my medicines were exhausted. All night we could hear the sick, muttering and raving in delirium, but from years of association with disagreeables we had no fear of the infection. One morning the boy Saat came to me with his head bound up, and complained of severe pain in the back and limbs, with all the usual symptoms of plague: in the afternoon I saw him leaning over the ship's side; his nose was bleeding violently! At night he was delirious. On the following morning he was raving, and on the vessel stopping to collect firewood he threw himself into the river to cool the burning fever that consumed him. His eyes were suffused with blood, which, blended with a yellow as deep as the yolk of egg, gave a horrible appearance to his face, that was already so drawn and changed as to be hardly recognised. Poor Saat! The faithful boy that we had adopted, and who had formed so bright an exception to the dark character of his race, was now a victim to this horrible disease. He was a fine strong lad of nearly fifteen, and he now lay helplessly on his mat, and cast wistful glances at the face of his mistress as she gave him a cup of cold water mixed with a few lumps of sugar that we had obtained from the traders at Gondokoro.

We arrived at Fashoder, in the Shillook country, where the Egyptian government had formed a camp of a thousand men to take possession of the country. We were well received and hospitably entertained by Osman Bey, to whom our thanks are due for the first civilized reception after years of savagedom. At Fashoder we procured lentils, rice, and dates, which were to us great luxuries, and would be a blessing to the plague-smitten boy, as we could now make some soup. Goats we had purchased in the Shir country for molotes (iron hoes) that we had received in exchange for corn at Gondokoro from Koorshid's agent who was responsible for the supply I had left in depot. We left Fashoder, and continued our voyage towards Khartoum.

Saat grew worse and worse: nothing would relieve the unfortunate boy from the burning torture of that frightful disease. He never slept, but night and day he muttered in delirium, breaking the monotony of his malady by occasionally howling like a wild animal. Richarn won my heart by his careful nursing of the boy, who had been his companion through years of hardship. We arrived at the village of Wat Shely, only three days from Khartoum. Saat was dying. The night passed, and I expected that all would be over before sunrise; but as morning dawned a change had taken place, – the burning fever had left him, and although raised blotches had broken out upon his chest and various parts of his body, he appeared much better. We now gave him stimulants; a teaspoonful of araki that we had bought at Fashoder was administered every ten minutes on a lump of sugar. This he crunched in his mouth, while he gazed at my wife with an expression of affection, but he could not speak. I had him well washed and dressed in clean clothes that had been kept most carefully during the voyage, to be worn on our entree to Khartoum. He was laid down to sleep upon a clean mat, and my wife gave him a lump of sugar to moisten his mouth and relieve his thickly furred tongue. His pulse was very weak, and his skin cold. "Poor Saat," said my wife, "his life hangs upon a thread. We must nurse him most carefully; should he have a relapse, nothing will save him." An hour passed, and he slept. Karka, the fat, good-natured slave woman, quietly went to his side: gently taking him by the ankles and knees, she stretched his legs into a straight position, and laid his arms parallel with his sides. She then covered his face with a cloth, one of the few rags that we still possessed. "Does he sleep still?" we asked. The tears ran down the cheeks of the savage but good-hearted Karka, as she sobbed, "He is dead!"

We stopped the boat. It was a sandy shore; the banks were high, and a clump of mimosas grew above high water mark. It was there that we dug his grave. My men worked silently and sadly, for all loved Saat: he had been so good and true, that even their hard hearts had learnt to respect his honesty. We laid him in his grave on the desert shore, beneath the grove of trees. Again the sail was set, and, filled by the breeze, it carried us away from the dreary spot where we had sorrowfully left all that was good and faithful. It was a happy end – most merciful, as he had been taken from a land of iniquity in all the purity of a child converted from Paganism to Christianity. He had lived and died in our service a good Christian. Our voyage was nearly over, and we looked forward to home and friends, but we had still fatigues before us: poor Saat had reached his home and rest. Two faithful followers we had buried, – Johann Schmidt at the commencement of the voyage, and Saat at its termination.

A few miles from this spot, a head wind delayed us for several days. Losing patience, I engaged camels from the Arabs; and riding the whole day, we reached Khartoum about half an hour after sunset on the 5th of May, 1865.

On the following morning we were welcomed by the entire European population of Khartoum, to whom are due my warmest thanks for many kind attentions. We were kindly offered a house by Monsieur Lombrosio, the manager of the Khartoum branch of the Oriental and Egyptian Trading Company.

I now heard the distressing news of the death of my poor friend Speke. I could not realize the truth of this melancholy report until I read the details of his fatal accident in the appendix of a French translation of his work. It was but a sad consolation that I could confirm his discoveries, and bear witness to the tenacity and perseverance with which he had led his party through the untrodden path of Africa to the first Nile source. This being the close of the expedition, I wish it to be distinctly understood how thoroughly I support the credit of Speke and Grant for their discovery of the first and most elevated source of the Nile in the great Victoria N'Yanza.

Although I call the river between the two lakes the Somerset, as it was named by Speke upon the map he gave to me, I must repeat that it is positively the Victoria Nile, and the name Somerset is only used to distinguish it, in my description, from the entire Nile that issues from the Albert N'Yanza.

Whether the volume of water added by the latter lake be greater than that supplied by the Victoria, the fact remains unaltered: the Victoria is the highest and first-discovered source; the Albert is the second source, but the entire reservoir of the Nile waters. I use the term "source" as applying to each reservoir as a head or main starting-point of the river. I am quite aware that it is a debated point among geographers, whether a lake can be called a source, as it owes its origin to one or many rivers; but, as the innumerable torrents of the mountainous regions of Central Africa pour into these great reservoirs, it would be impossible to give preference to any individual stream. Such a theory would become a source of great confusion, and the Nile sources might remain forever undecided; a thousand future travellers might return, each with his particular source in his portfolio, some stream of insignificant magnitude being pushed forward as the true origin of the Nile.

I found few letters awaiting me at Khartoum: all the European population of the place had long ago given us up for lost. It was my wish to start without delay direct for England, but there were extraordinary difficulties in this wretched country of the Soudan. A drought of two years had created a famine throughout the land, attended by a cattle and camel plague, that had destroyed so many camels that all commerce was stagnated. No merchandise could be transported from Khartoum; thus no purchases could be made by the traders in the interior: the country, always wretched, was ruined. The plague, or a malignant typhus, had run riot in Khartoum: out of 4,000 black troops, only a remnant below 400 remained alive!

This frightful malady, that had visited our boat, had revelled in the filth and crowded alleys of the Soudan capital.

The Blue Nile was so low that even the noggurs drawing three feet of water could not descend the river. Thus, the camels being dead, and the river impassable, no corn could be brought from Sennaar and Watmedene: there was a famine in Khartoum – neither fodder for animals, nor food for man. Being unable to procure either camels or boats, I was compelled to wait at Khartoum until the Nile should rise sufficiently to enable us to pass the cataracts between that town and Berber. (The want of water in the Blue Nile, as here described, exemplifies the theory that Lower Egypt owes its existence during the greater portion of the year entirely to the volume of the White Nile.)

We remained two months at Khartoum. During this time we were subjected to intense heat and constant dust storms, attended with a general plague of boils. Verily, the plagues of Egypt remain to this day in the Soudan. On the 26th June, we had the most extraordinary dust storm that had ever been seen by the inhabitants. I was sitting in the courtyard of my agent's house at about 4:30 p.m.: there was no wind, and the sun was as bright as usual in this cloudless sky, when suddenly a gloom was cast over all, – a dull yellow glare pervaded the atmosphere. Knowing that this effect portended a dust storm, and that the present calm would be followed by a hurricane of wind, I rose to go home, intending to secure the shutters. Hardly had I risen, when I saw approaching, from the S.W. apparently, a solid range of immense brown mountains, high in air. So rapid was the passage of this extraordinary phenomenon, that in a few minutes we were in actual pitchy darkness. At first there was no wind, and the peculiar calm gave an oppressive character to the event. We were in "a darkness that might be felt." Suddenly the wind arrived, but not with the violence that I had expected. There were two persons with me, Michael Latfalla, my agent, and Monsieur Lombrosio. So intense was the darkness that we tried to distinguish our hands placed close before our eyes; not even an outline could be seen. This lasted for upwards of twenty minutes: it then rapidly passed away, and the sun shone as before; but we had felt the darkness that Moses had inflicted upon the Egyptians.

The Egyptian government had, it appeared, been pressed by some of the European Powers to take measures for the suppression of the slave-trade: a steamer had accordingly been ordered to capture all vessels laden with this in famous cargo. Two vessels had been seized and brought to Khartoum, containing 850 human beings – packed together like anchovies, the living and the dying festering together, and the dead lying beneath them. European eye-witnesses assured me that the disembarking of this frightful cargo could not be adequately described. The slaves were in a state of starvation, having had nothing to eat for several days. They were landed in Khartoum; the dead and many of the dying were tied by the ankles, and dragged along the ground by donkeys through the streets. The most malignant typhus, or plague, had been engendered among this mass of filth and misery, thus closely packed together. Upon landing, the women were divided by the Egyptian authorities among the soldiers. These creatures brought the plague to Khartoum, which, like a curse visited upon this country of slavery and abomination, spread like a fire throughout the town, and consumed the regiments that had received this horrible legacy from the dying cargo of slaves. Among others captured by the authorities on a charge of slavetrading was an Austrian subject, who was then in the custody of the consul. A French gentleman, Monsieur Garnier, had been sent to Khartoum by the French Consulate of Alexandria on a special inquiry into the slave trade; he was devoting himself to the subject with much energy.

While at Khartoum I happened to find Mahommed Her, the *3vakeel* of Chenooda's party who had instigated men to mutiny at Latooka, and had taken my deserters into his employ. I had promised to make an example of this fellow; I therefore had him arrested, and brought before the Divan. With extreme effrontery, he denied having had anything to do with the affair, adding to his denial all knowledge of the total destruction of his party and of my mutineers by the Latookas. Having a crowd of witnesses in my own men, and others that I had found in Khartoum who had belonged to Koorshid's party at that time, his barefaced lie was exposed, and he was convicted. I determined that he should be punished, as an example that would insure respect to any future English traveller in those regions. My men, and all those with whom I had been connected, had been accustomed to rely most implicitly upon all that I had promised, and the punishment of this man had been an expressed determination.

I went to the Divan and demanded that he should be flogged. Omer Bey was then Governor of the Soudan, in the place of Moosa Pasha deceased. He sat upon the divan, in the large hall of justice by the river. Motioning me to take a seat by his side, and handing me his pipe, he called the officer in waiting, and gave the necessary orders. In a few minutes the prisoner was led into the hall, attended by eight soldiers. One man carried a strong pole about seven feet long, in the centre of which was a double chain, riveted through in a loop. The prisoner was immediately thrown down with his face to the ground, while two men stretched out his arms and sat upon them; his feet were then placed within the loop of the chain, and the pole being twisted round until firmly secured, it was raised from the ground sufficiently to expose the soles of the feet. Two men with powerful hippopotamus whips stood, one on either side. The prisoner thus secured, the order was given. The whips were most scientifically applied, rind after the first five dozen, the slave-hunting scoundrel howled most lustily for mercy. How often had he flogged unfortunate slave women to excess, and what murders had that wretch committed, who now howled for mercy! I begged Omer Bey to stop the punishment at 150 lashes, and to explain to him publicly in the divan, that he was thus punished for attempting to thwart the expedition of an English traveller, by instigating my escort to mutiny.

This affair over – all my accounts paid – and my men dismissed with their hands full of money, – I was ready to start for Egypt. The Nile rose sufficiently to enable the passage of the cataracts, and on the 30th June we took leave of all friends in Khartoum, and of my very kind agent, Michael Latfalla, well known as Hallil el Shami, who had most generously cashed all my bills on Cairo without charging a fraction of exchange. On the morning of 1st July, we sailed from Khartoum to Berber.

On approaching the fine basalt hills through which the river passes during its course from Khartoum, I was surprised to see the great Nile contracted to a trifling width of from eighty to a hundred and twenty yards. Walled by high cliffs of basalt upon either side, the vast volume of the Nile flows grandly through this romantic pass, the water boiling up in curling eddies, showing that rocky obstructions exist in its profound depths below.

Our voyage was very nearly terminated at the passage of the cataracts. Many skeletons of wrecked vessels lay upon the rocks in various places: as we were flying along in full sail before a heavy gale of wind, descending a cataract, we struck upon a sandbank – fortunately not upon a rock, or we should have gone to pieces like a glass bottle. The tremendous force of the stream, running at the rate of about ten or twelve miles per hour, immediately drove the vessel broadside upon the bank. About sixty yards below us was a ridge of rocks, upon which it appeared certain that we must be driven should we quit the bank upon which we were stranded. The *reis* and crew, as usual in such cases, lost their heads. I emptied a large waterproof portmanteau, and tied it together with ropes, so as to form a lifebuoy for my wife and Richarn, neither of whom could swim; the maps, journals, and observations, I packed in an iron box, which I fastened with a tow-line to the portmanteau. It appeared that we were to wind up the expedition with shipwreck, and thus lose my entire collection of hunting spoils. Having completed the preparations for escape, I took command of the vessel, and silenced the chattering crew.

My first order was to lay out an anchor up stream.

This was done: the water was shallow, and the great weight of the anchor, carried on the shoulders of two men, enabled them to resist the current, and to wade hip-deep about forty yards up the stream upon the sandbank.

Thus secured, I ordered the crew to haul upon the cable. The great force of the current bearing upon the broadside of the vessel, while her head was anchored up stream, bore her gradually round. All hands were now employed in clearing away the sand, and deepening a passage: loosen ing the sand with their hands and feet, the powerful rapids carried it away. For five hours we remained in this position, the boat cracking, and half filled with water however, we stopped the leak caused by the strain upon her timbers, and having, after much labour, cleared a channel in the narrow sandbank, the moment arrived to slip the cable, hoist the sail, and trust to the heavy gale of wind from the west to clear the rocks, that lay within a few yards of us to the north. "Let go!" And all being prepared, the sail was loosened, and filling in the strong gale with a loud report, the head of the vessel swung round with the force of wind and stream. Away we flew! For an instant we grated on some hard substance: we stood upon the deck, watching the rocks exactly before us, with the rapids roaring loudly around our boat as she rushed upon what looked like certain destruction. Another moment, and we passed within a few inches of the rocks within the boiling surf. Hurrah! We are all right! We swept by the danger, and flew along the rapids, hurrying towards Old England.

We arrived at Berber, the spot from which we had started upwards of four years ago for our Atbara expedition. Here we were most hospitably received by Monsieur and Madame Laffargue, a French gentleman and his charming wife, who had for many years been residents in the Soudan. It is with feelings of gratitude that I express my thanks to all Frenchmen that I have met in those wild countries, for courtesies and attention, that were appreciated by me like unexpected flowers in a desert. I can only hope that Frenchmen may, when in need, receive the same kindness from my country-men, when travelling in lands far distant from LA BELLE FRANCE.

I determined upon the Red Sea route to Egypt, instead of pass-ing the horrible Korosko desert during the hot month of August. After some delay I procured camels, and started east for Souakim, from whence I hoped to procure a steamer to Suez.

This route from Berber is not the usual caravan road: the coun-try was in rather a disturbed state, owing to the mutiny of all the black troops in the Egyptian service in the Taka province; and the Hadendowa Arabs, who are at no time the best of their race, were very excited. The first eight days' journey are devoid of water, except at two stations, the route being desert. Our party consisted of my wife, Richarn, Achmet, and Zeneb; the latter was a six-foot girl of the Dinka tribe, with whom Richarn had fallen in love and mar-ried during our sojourn at Khartoum.

Zeneb was a good girl, rather pretty, as strong as a giraffe, and a good cook; a very valuable acquisition for Richarn. Her husband, who had been my faithful follower, was now a rich man, being the owner of thirty napoleons, the balance of his wages. Achmet was an Egyptian servant, whom I had recently engaged in Khartoum. I had also offered a Swiss missionary the protection of our party.

One day, during the heat of noon, after a long march in the burning sun through a treeless desert, we descried a solitary tree in the distance, to which we hurried as to a friend. Upon arrival, we found its shade occupied by a number of Hadendowa Arabs. Dismounting from our camels, we requested them to move and to give place for our party – as a tree upon the desert is like a well of water, to be shared by every traveller. Far from giving the desired place, they most insolently refused to allow us to share the tree. Upon Richarn attempting to take possession, he was rudely pushed on one side, and an Arab drew his knife. Achmet had a *coorbatch* (hippopotamus whip) in his hand that he had used on his camel; the act of raising this to threaten the Arab who had drawn his knife was the signal for hostilities. Out flashed the broadswords from their sheaths, and the headman of the party aimed a well-intended cut at my head. Parrying the cut with my sun umbrella, I returned with a quick thrust directly in the mouth, the point of the peaceful weapon penetrating to his throat with such force that he fell upon his back. Almost at the same moment I had to parry another cut from one of the crowd that smashed my umbrella completely, and left me with my remaining weapons, a stout Turkish pipe-stick about four feet long, and my fist. Parrying with the stick, thrusting in return at the face, and hitting sharp with the left hand, I managed to keep three or four of the party on and off upon their backs, receiving a slight cut with a sword upon my left arm in countering a blow which just grazed me as I knocked down the owner, and disarmed him. My wife picked up the sword, as I had no time to stoop, and she stood well at bay with her newly acquired weapon that a disarmed Arab wished to wrest from her, but dared not close with the naked blade. I had had the fight all my own way, as, being beneath the tree (the boughs of which were very near the ground), the Arabs, who do not understand the use of the point, were unable to use their swords, as their intended cuts were intercepted by the branches. Vigorous thrusting and straight hitting cleared the tree, and the party were scattered right and left, followed up by Richarn and Achmet, armed with double-barrelled rifles. I was determined to disarm the whole party, if possible. One of the Arabs, armed with a lance, rushed up to attack Richarn from behind; but Zeneb was of the warlike Dinka tribe, and having armed herself with the hard wood handle of the axe, she went into the row like Joan of Arc, and hastening to the rescue of Richarn, she gave the Arab such a whack upon the head that she knocked him down on the spot, and seizing his lance she disarmed him. Thus armed, she rushed into the thickest of the fray.

"Bravo, Zeneb!" I could not help shouting. Seizing a thick. stick that had been dropped by one of the Arabs, I called Richarn and our little party together, and attacking the few Arabs who still offered resistance, they were immediately knocked down and disarmed. The leader of the party, who had been the first to draw his sword and had received a mouthful of umbrella, had not moved from the spot where he fell, but amused himself with coughing and spitting. I now ordered him to be bound, and threatened to tie him to my camel's tail and lead him a prisoner to the Governor of Souakim, unless he called all those of his party who had run away. They were now standing at a distance in the desert, and I insisted upon the delivery of their weapons. Being thoroughly beaten and cowed, he conferred with those whom we had taken prisoners, and the affair ended by all the arms being delivered up. We counted six swords, eleven lances, and a heap of knives, the number of which I forget.

I ordered the entire party to stand in a line; and I gave them their choice, whether the ringleaders would receive a flogging from me, or whether I should tie them to the tails of camels and lead them to the Turkish Governor of Souakim? They immediately chose the former; and, calling them from the rank, I ordered them to lie down on the ground to receive punishment.

They submitted like dogs; Richarn and Achmet stood over them with their whips, ready for the word. At this moment an old white-headed Arab of my caravan came to me: kneeling down, he stroked my beard with his dirty hands, and implored pardon for the offenders. Thoroughly understanding the Arab character, I replied, "They are miserable sons of dogs, and their swords are like the feathers of a fowl; they deserve flogging, but when a white head asks for pardon, it should be granted. God is merciful, and we are all his children." Thus was the affair ended to the satisfaction of our side. I broke all the lances into fragments upon a rock, – ordered Zeneb to make a fire with the wood of the handles, to boil some coffee; and tying the swords into a bundle, we packed the lance-heads and knives in a basket, with the understanding that they should be delivered to their owners on our arrival at the last well, after which point there would be water on the route every day.

From that place, there would be no fear of our camels being stolen, and of our being deserted in the desert.

On arrival at the well a few days later, I delivered the weapons to their owners as promised, they having followed our party. Souakim is about 275 miles from the Nile at Berber. At Kokreb, about half-way, we entered the chain of mountains that extends from Suez parallel with the Red Sea to the south; many portions of this chain are four or five thousand feet above the sea-level. The mountains were exceedingly beautiful, their precipitous sides of barren rock exhibiting superb strata of red and grey granite, with vast masses of exquisite red and green porphyry. Many hills were of basalt, so black, that during an entire day's journey the face of the country appeared like a vast desert of coal, in broken hills and blocks strewed over the surface of the ground. Kokreb was a lovely oasis beneath the high mountains, with a forest of low mimosas in full leaf, and a stream running from the mountains, the produce of a recent storm. Throughout this country there are no rivers that should be noticed on a map, as the torrents are merely the effects of violent storms, which, falling upon the mountains several times during the rainy season from June to the end of August tear their boisterous way along their stony course and dry up in a few hours, becoming exhausted in the sand of the deserts. For some days our course lay along a deep ravine between stupendous cliffs; this was the bed of a torrent, that, after heavy storms, flowed through the mountains, inclining to the east; in this were pools of most beautifully clear water. In many places the nooks among the cliffs were fringed with lovely green trees. It was extraordinary to observe the activity of the camels in climbing the most difficult passes, and in picking their way among the rocks and stones that obstructed the route. In many places camels might be seen grazing upon the green mimosa bushes, that growing among the rocks high upon the mountains had tempted the animals into places that I should not have believed they could have reached.

After a journey of twenty-four days from the Nile at Berber, we emerged from the mountain-pass, and from the elevated embouchure we obtained a sudden and most welcome view of the Red Sea. We now quickly descended: the heat increased every hour; and after a long day's march, we slept within a few miles of Souakim. On the following morning we entered the town.

Souakim is a considerable town; the houses are all built of coral. The principal dwellings, and the custom house and government offices are situated on an island in the harbour. We were received with much attention by the governor, Moomtazze Bey, who very kindly offered us a house. The heat was frightful, the thermometer 115 degrees F and in some houses 120 degrees F.

There is no doubt that Souakim should be the port for all exports and imports for the Soudan provinces. Were a line of steamers established from Suez, to call regularly at Souakim, at a moderate freight, it would become a most prosperous town, as the geographical position marks it as the nucleus for all trade with the interior. At present there is no regularity: the only steamers that touch at Souakim are those belonging to the Abdul Azziz Company, who trade between Suez and Jedda. Although advertised for distinct periods, they only visit Souakim when they think proper, and their rates are most exorbitant.

There was no steamer upon our arrival. After waiting in intense heat for about a fortnight, the Egyptian thirty-two gun steam frigate, Ibralaimeya, arrived with a regiment of Egyptian troops, under Giaffer Pasha, to quell the mutiny of the black troops at Kassala, twenty days' march in the interior. The General Giaffer Pasha, and Mustapha Bey the captain of the frigate, gave us an entertainment on board in English style, in honour of the completion of the Nile discovery. Giaffer Pasha most kindly placed the frigate at our disposal to convey us to Suez, and both he and Mustapha Bey endeavoured in every way to accommodate us. For their extreme courtesy I take this opportunity of making my acknowledgment.

Orders for sailing had been received, but suddenly a steamer was signalled as arriving: this was a transport, with troops. As she was to return immediately to Suez, I preferred the dirty transport rather than incur a further delay. We started from Souakim, and after five days' voyage we arrived at Suez. Landing from the steamer, I once more found myself in an English hotel. The spacious inner court was arranged as an open conservatory; in this was a bar for refreshments, and Allsopp's Pale Ale on draught, with an ice accompaniment. What an Elysium! The beds had sheets and pillowcases, neither of which had I possessed for years.

The hotel was thronged with passengers to India, with rosy, blooming English ladies, and crowds of my own countrymen. I felt inclined to talk to everybody. Never was I so in love with my own countrymen and women; but they (I mean the ladies) all had large balls of hair at the backs of their heads! What an extraordinary change! I called Richarn, my pet savage from the heart of Africa, to admire them. "Now, Richarn, look at them!" I said. "What do you think of the English ladies? Eh, Richarn? Are they not lovely?"

"*Wah Illahi!*" exclaimed the astonished Richarn, "they are beautiful! What hair! They are not like the negro savages, who work other people's hair into their own heads; theirs is all real – all their own – how beautiful!"

"Yes, Richarn," I replied, "all their own!" This was my first introduction to the chignon.

We arrived at Cairo, and I established Richarn and his wife in a comfortable situation, as private servants to Mr. Zech, the master of Sheppard's Hotel. The character I gave him was one that I trust has done him service: he had shown an extraordinary amount of moral courage in totally reforming from his original habit of drinking. I left my old servant with a heart too full to say good-bye; a warm squeeze of his rough but honest black hand, and the whistle of the train sounded – we were off!

I had left Richarn, and none remained of my people. The past appeared like a dream-the rushing sound of the train renewed ideas of civilization. Had I really come from the Nile Sources? It was no dream. A witness sat before me; a face still young, but bronzed like an Arab by years of exposure to a burning sun; haggard and worn with toil and sickness, and shaded with cares, happily now past; the devoted companion of my pilgrimage, to whom I owed success and life – my wife.

I had received letters from England, that had been waiting at the British Consulate; the first I opened informed me, that the Royal Geographical Society had awarded me the Victoria Gold Medal, at a time when they were unaware whether I was alive or dead, and when the success of my expedition was unknown. This appreciation of my exertions was the warmest welcome that I could have received on my first entrance into civilization after so many years of savagedom: it rendered the completion of the Nile Sources doubly grateful, as I had fulfilled the expectations that the Geographical Society had so generously expressed by the presentation of their medal before my task was done.

APPENDIX

COMPUTATION OF MR. BAKER'S OBSERVATIONS. HEIGHTS OF STATIONS ABOVE THE MEAN LEVEL OF THE SEA DETERMINED BY BOILING-WATER OBSERVATIONS BY S. W. BAKER, Esq. COMPUTED BY E. DUNKIN, Esq. OF GREENWICH OBSERVATORY.

	Feet
Tarrangolle	247
Obbo	3,480
Shoggo	3,770
Asua River	2619
Shooa	3,619
Rionga's Island	3,685
Karuma, below falls	3,737
Karuma, south of falls	,796
South of Karuma, at river level	3,794
M'Rooli, river level, junction of Kafoor	3,796
West of M'Rooli, on road to Albert Lake	4,291
Land above lake, east cliff	4,117
Albert N'Yanza, lake level	2,448
Shooa Moru, island of Patooan	2,918
Gondokoro	1,636

The above heights will be found to differ considerably from those given by Mr. Baker in his letter written from Khartoum in May, 1865, and published in the *Times* newspaper in June. This arises from Mr. Baker having corrected his observations, whilst in the interior of Africa, from what have since proved erroneous data: the above are the correct computations of the same observations.

REMARKS ON THE THERMOMETER B. W. USED BY MR. S. W. BAKER IN DETERMINING HEIGHTS.
By Staff Commander C. George, Curator of Maps, Royal Geographical Society.

This thermometer was one of the three supplied by the Royal Geographical Society to Consul Petherick, in 1861, and was made by Mr. Casella.

At Gondokoro, in March, 1862, it was lent to Mr. Baker, who made all his observations with it, and brought it back safe: it has, therefore, been in use about 4 and 3/4 years.

On November 9th, 1865, Mr. Baker returned it to the Royal Geographical Society, and it was immediately taken to Mr. Casella, who tested its accuracy by trying its boiling point, in nearly the same manner as Mr. Baker had made his observations. The result by two independent observers was that the boiling-point had increased in its reading by 0 degree point 75 in 4 and 3/4 years, or 0 degree point 172 yearly.

On November 23d the thermometer was again tested by Mr. Baker at the Kew Observatory. The observation was made under the same conditions as those near the Albert N'Yanza, as nearly as it was possible to make it. (By immersion in boiling water.) The result gave the thermometer 0 degree point 80 too much at the boiling point.

The readings of the thermometer have, therefore, been too much; and by reducing the readings, it elevates all positions at which observations were made.

Table No. 1 – In this table the error obtained at Kew Observatory has been treated like that of a chronometer, the error being assumed increasing and regular.

Table No. 2 is to correct the height, computed by Mr. Dunkin, using the quantity taken from Table No. 1.

Table No. 1

Month	1861	1862	1863	1864	1865
January	--	0'143	0'314	0'487	0'659
February	--	'157	'328	'501	'673
March	'00	'172	'344	'516	'688
April	'014	'186	'358	'530	'702
May	'028	'200	'372	'544	'716
June	'043	'214	'387	'559	'730
July	'057	'228	'401	'573	'744
August	'071	'243	'415	'587	'758
September	'086	'257	'430	'602	'772
October	'100	'271	'444	'616	'786
November	'114	'285	'458	'630	0'800
December	0'129	0'300	0'473	0'645	--

Table No. 2

At the elevation of 3,500 feet, 1 degree equals about 520 feet, from which the following:

Degrees	Feet	Degrees	Feet	Degree	Feet
1'0	520	'7	364	'3	156
'9	468	'6	312	'25	130
'8	416	'5	260	'2	104
'75	390	'4	208	'1	52